THE AUDIO SCRIPTS

THE VERY BEST OF THE BIG FINISH AUDIO ADVENTURES!

Published by Big Finish Productions Ltd,
PO Box 1127
Maidenhead SL6 3LW

www.bigfinish.com

Editor: Ian Farrington
Project editors: Gary Russell & Jacqueline Rayner
Managing Editor: Jason Haigh-Ellery

ISBN 1-84435-005-3

Cover art by Clayton Hickman © 2002

First published December 2002

Loups-Garoux © Marc Platt
The Holy Terror © Robert Shearman
The Fires of Vulcan © Steve Lyons
Neverland © Alan Barnes
Of Wildtracks and Werewolves © Nicholas Pegg
A Taste of my own Medicine © Gary Russell

Printed and bound in Great Britain by Biddles Ltd
www.biddles.co.uk

CONTENTS

Of Wildtracks and Werewolves by Nick Pegg   1

Loups-Garoux by Marc Platt   5
Part One   11
Part Two   29
Part Three   46
Part Four   66

The Holy Terror by Robert Shearman   87
Part One   93
Part Two   111
Part Three   127
Part Four   143

A Taste of My Own Medicine by Gary Russell   157

The Fires of Vulcan by Steve Lyons   159
Part One   165
Part Two   179
Part Three   192
Part Four   206

Neverland by Alan Barnes   219
Part One   225
Part Two   246
Part Three   261
Part Four   278

Appendix:
The Fires of Vulcan: Part One by Steve Lyons   297
Alternative Version

OF WILDTRACKS AND WEREWOLVES

By Nicholas Pegg

It all begins with the script. As any director in any medium will tell you, no amount of glitzy casting or glossy production will make any difference if the script itself is no good. And as a result, it is every director's wish to work with writers of quality.

As the director assigned to both *Loups-Garoux* and *The Holy Terror*, I can therefore count myself extremely fortunate. Marc Platt and Robert Shearman are two very different writers with one obvious thing in common: each has a highly individual approach to his craft, offering different but equally idiosyncratic styles and a full-blooded approach to character and dialogue which are meat and drink to a director and his cast.

I've known Rob Shearman for many years; we were, in fact, contemporaries at Exeter University, that fabled seat of learning whose ample red-bricked bosom has also cradled such diverse talents as J.K. Rowling, Thom Yorke and, more recently, Will Young. In the autumn of 1989 Rob Shearman auditioned for a production of *Hamlet* that I was directing (and for which, incidentally, I callously rejected Thom Yorke's poster design – I probably still have it somewhere. I suppose it must be worth a bomb). Although he denied it then and still does to this day, Rob Shearman is a jolly good actor, and I cast him as Horatio. And thus was born a long and happy friendship.

One of the *Doctor Who* stories that was airing on BBC1 that autumn, while Rob and I rehearsed *Hamlet* in the campus refectory, was that rare and beautiful creature *Ghost Light* – whose author, by a remarkable coincidence, I chanced to meet for the first time that very same month. Taking a break from rehearsals, I compèred a *Doctor Who* convention in Liverpool which, if memory serves, took place over the weekend that fell between the transmission of the second and third episodes of *Ghost Light*. Many of that story's cast and crew were present, and I remember how charming Marc Platt was on our first meeting, and also how delighted he was with the way his script had been translated on to the screen. Of course I had no idea that, eleven years later, I would find myself directing the second of his *Doctor Who* scripts to make it into production…

Bringing a script to fruition on audio is an organic process in which many individuals play an important part: the actors, the engineers, the post-production boffins with their sound effects and ambient acoustics, and the incidental composers. And then there's the director. I'm occasionally asked what exactly an audio director does – after all, it's not as if he has to worry about camera angles and choreographing the actors. That much is true, but even in film and television the director's most important role has nothing to do with the visuals: crucially, he or she is there to steer the ship, to pull together all the creative departments and ensure that everyone, from cast to musicians to engineers, is singing from the same score. That score is, of course, the script, and it's there that the director's job begins.

Another quality that Rob and Marc share is their generosity to the director. As it happens I'm a writer too, and I know only too well the feelings, not always charitable, that are apt to bubble up when the phone rings and it's the director asking for yet another meddlesome rewrite. By the time they reached my desk, *The Holy Terror* and *Loups-Garoux* had already passed through the script-editing process and required very little in the way of revisions, and I cannot stress highly enough that they are Rob's and Marc's scripts and nobody else's. But it is nevertheless an important part of the director's remit to get a script absolutely watertight before launching it, and this requires a firm and realistic eye to detail, and inevitably leads to the occasional tweak. One of the potential pitfalls of the audio format is that you're denied the visual shorthand that helps to fill in the detail of a scene. There's nothing more disorientating, for example, than a character suddenly piping up two pages into a scene when the listener hasn't even realised that this character was supposed to be in the room. Lines at the beginning of each scene need to establish exactly where we are and who's there. Similarly, if time is supposed to have elapsed between one scene and the next, it's necessary to establish that fact. (I recall, for example, that I made the very minor alteration of having the Doctor enter Ileana's carriage at the very beginning of Scene 29 of *Loups-Garoux*, rather than have him already there, as he'd only just exited in the previous scene. Clearer storytelling, I thought.)

More obviously, if something is essentially visual in concept, it will need a bit of explaining. That said, the notorious trap to avoid is the temptation of over-describing the picture. I'm sure you know the sort of thing: 'Look, Doctor, there's a seven-foot furry blue monster standing in the art deco doorway, with the professor's all-important power-pack grasped in its six-toed paw!' But the opposite pitfall can be just as problematic. A lack of explanation quickly becomes confusing and may run the risk of alienating the listener. The pursuit of clarity is one of the director's prime responsibilities.

Permit me to offer a small example. The talking greetings card which features in *Loups-Garoux* was in Marc's original script, and a marvellous idea it was too: it's one of the many details with which Marc sketches in the story's background of a deforested and despoiled world. However, in the original script the card itself didn't say anything before the characters' various recorded messages were played. I wasn't entirely sure about this, worrying that the visual image of the talking card wasn't conveyed clearly enough. I explained my thoughts to Marc, and suggested that perhaps the card itself could deliver a spoken intro to help the listener understand what exactly it was. Marc promptly came up with the jingle, 'Thank you for reading this paper-free card. No trees were harmed in the making of this product. Your greeting reads…', thus taking a practical problem and using it to fill in an aspect of the future society's background. It was my suggestion but it was Marc's line, and that's about as good an example of the synthesis of writer and director as any I can think of.

After the script, the next challenge is casting. Fitting the right actor to the right part is harder than it might sound; a good actor badly cast just doesn't work. So it's not enough simply to pick your favourite actor, period – the trick is to find the best actor *for that role*, and then to make sure that he'll fit well alongside this actor and that actor too. In the audio medium, variety is all – there's nothing worse than a cast of actors who all sound the same.

Wherever possible, I've worked hard to secure some good 'names' to play guest roles in the stories I've directed. I don't approve of gratuitous 'stunt casting', but if a well-known name is also the best person for the job, then their experience and talent can only add to the quality and prestige of the production. For *The Holy Terror*, I was tremendously lucky to assemble a really top-notch cast of old friends and colleagues, including the wondrous Sam Kelly, Roberta Taylor and Peter Guinness. *Loups-Garoux* was rather more of a step into the unknown, insofar as I had never worked with Eleanor Bron, Burt Kwouk or Nicky Henson beforehand. But what a joy it was to do so. I was (and remain) in absolute awe of the greatness of Eleanor Bron!

Before we begin recording, I talk to the actors in some detail about the overall atmosphere and characterisations I want to achieve in the story, but a good director never strait-jackets the cast. It's important to go with the flow and let the actors bring their own ideas to the microphone. A good case in point would be Nicky Henson's Transylvanian accent in *Loups-Garoux*, which was entirely his own idea – but one that I loved.

We tend to use the system known as rehearse-record, which means that rather than have a separate rehearsal period, we move through the script scene by scene, rehearsing then recording, rehearsing then recording. We try to record everything as far as possible in story order, making it easier for the actors to keep a grip on their characters, but there are a couple of reasons why we might break the order up: most obviously, the availability of the actors. On *The Holy Terror*, for example, Sam Kelly was there for both days (which was just as well, as the Scribe was a huge part), but Roberta and Peter, who played Berengaria and Childeric, were only there on the second day, so of course we were hopping back and forth within the script.

More complicated in this respect was *Loups-Garoux*, whose recording order was shunted hither and thither in a bewildering fashion by some very complicated actor availability. I can't quite recall the exact details, but I remember Peter Davison had to arrive late on one day, while Eleanor Bron and Nicky Henson were only in the studio for a day and a half, and several of the other actors were only there for one day or the other. Believe it or not Jane Burke, who played Inez, never actually met Sarah Gale, who played Rosa – even though they're actually in a scene together! Peter Davison had to play the relevant scene twice, once with Sarah and then again the following day with Jane. Alistair Lock stitched it all together in post-production.

In fact, looking back, I spent a considerable amount of *Loups-Garoux* recapping the plot with the actors: 'Right, now this bit comes just *before* that bit on the train that we recorded yesterday, but just *after* the bit we'll be recording later this afternoon when Burt arrives.'

Because the schedule is by necessity rather brisk, we tend to have just one rehearsal reading, and then the director will give notes to the actors, and then we'll go straight for a first take. If we muck it up we'll do another one, and another, until we get it right – but you'd be surprised how often the first take is the best. There's a lot to be said for spontaneity. An example that springs to mind is the last scene of *The Holy Terror*, in which Rob gave Colin Baker a beautiful, melancholy speech about the implications of travelling in the TARDIS. Having listened to the rehearsal reading, I knew that we had to nail this scene in one take. It was a delicate butterfly of a speech, and if we made the mistake of retaking it over and over again we'd lose it. It needed to be absolutely guileless and downplayed, so after the rehearsal reading I talked to Colin very specifically about the precise kind of atmosphere

I felt we needed to achieve. After listening very carefully he came back with exactly what I wanted, straight off, first take, and it was just superb. It gives me a little glow to hear that many fans have now cited that scene as one of the defining moments for Colin's Doctor.

Actors thrive on spontaneity. If you've heard *The Holy Terror* you'll know that Sam Kelly, who is undoubtedly one of the finest actors I've ever worked with, pulls off an amazing feat with his dual performance as the Scribe and the demonic Boy. What you may not know is quite how amazing that feat was, given that it was very largely achieved 'live' in the studio. Alistair Lock, who recorded the story, had developed a technique whereby, if Sam recorded his 'Boy' speeches in a weird, slowed-down fashion, the subsequent post-production treatment would result in the unearthly voice you hear in the final edit. Sam worked at this technique very diligently until the effect was working, but I can tell you it took some bottle to do what he did. In order to achieve the appropriate effect, he had to play those scenes sounding like a slowed-down LP of Margaret Thatcher, while Colin talked away as normal. And he did it brilliantly, without batting an eyelid.

Most amazing of all was when we came to do the scenes in which Sam, as the Scribe, is talking to himself as the Boy. I had planned to record everything twice, thus allowing Sam to concentrate on his 'Scribe' performance in one set of takes, and then go back and do his 'Boy' performance in another set of takes, whereafter the post-production boys at ERS Studios could knit the whole lot together. But Sam said, 'No, come on, let's try doing it all in one go.' I said, 'Seriously? Are you sure?' And off he went. It was quite remarkable – he was swapping from one character to the other completely 'live', and he did the whole thing in one take. That, plus the obvious post-production effects, is what you can hear in the final story.

Then again, some things are less spontaneous. Mention of post-production brings to mind the obligatory wildtrack sessions that often take place at the end of a studio day. 'Wildtrack' is the term given to a layer of vocal recording that will be edited into the background (or occasionally the foreground) in post-production. A good example would be the numerous crowd scenes in *The Holy Terror* – and boy, did they take a long time. On a boiling August afternoon we recorded what seemed like *hours* of the stuff, so that it could be looped and layered in post-production to make the available dozen or so people sound like a huge milling throng. I coaxed the entire cast, plus Rob Shearman and Gary Russell and Jac Rayner and whoever else happened to be around, into the sweltering studio to chant 'All hail Frobisher, all hail the big talking bird!' until they were hoarse and until my arms ached (I was conducting them from behind the soundproof glass like a demented choirmaster). I remember Rob staggering out of the studio and saying, 'I'm so sorry – I'll never write another crowd scene again!' It was hot, it was painful, and it took forever.

But, like all of this mad silly *Doctor Who* business, it was also the most unbelievable fun. And I'll always cherish the memory of it.

LOUPS-GAROUX

By Marc Platt

Things go in cycles, don't they? Tides, the moon, Wagnerian operas, washing machines. But when the proposal for a *Doctor Who* werewolf story resurfaced eighteen years after it was knocked on the head, and actually got made with the Doctor it was written for, played by the original actor, well, you start to wonder... Time loops? Time loups...?

Loups-Garoux (aka *Whoops-Garoux* or *Loupie Garou's Weird Weekends*, or even *Fenris*, its first title long before its good old Vampiric cousin *The Curse of Fenric* happened along – another case of the eclectic writers' zeitgeist) started as a proposal for a Fifth Doctor two-parter that I sent to the production office in around 1982/83. It was set entirely on the speeding train (studio-bound for cheapness) and featured Nyssa and Tegan. (Tegan was the original subject of the Doctor's 'baggage' line – it worked better for her than Turlough, but I liked it too much to chuck it!) Ileana de Santos was there (called Elvira de Burgos), so was the Amazon Desert, but there was no sign of Pieter Stubbe. The story didn't get even an inch of interest, so it plonked into the old ideas file for possible future plundering.

Around the time that Big Finish started trawling for audio stories with its now famous Sunday afternoon meeting, there was a production of Stephen Sondheim's fairy-tale musical *Into the Woods* at the Donmar Warehouse. It was a bloody wonderful production of a seminal work: positively Mozartean in being very funny, very frightening, profoundly moving and utterly joyous all at once. It improved with every viewing and I saw it five times. All fairy tales have dark undercurrents, where feeding the appetite doesn't necessarily just involve putting dinner on the table; and it was the Red Riding Hood sequence, with its voraciously lascivious wolf, that sent me digging out the old *Fenris* storyline.

The story still felt like a Fifth Doctor adventure, but eighteen years later, it's a different Fifth Doctor. It's a chance to make him more dynamic and give Peter Davison more to get his teeth into. The Doctor driving the story rather than just getting involved.

Peter's voice has darkened. You can't write him as the fresh-faced, head of school hero anymore. In fact by *Androzani*, his Doctor is already darker and more worldly-wise, yet that streak of innocence remains. He's still trusting, or at least wants to be. He's still driven by curiosity and enthusiasm for how things work. But in *Loups-Garoux*, that curiosity and innocence are almost his undoing. Ever the gentleman, the Doctor tries to help the beleaguered werewolf matriarch Ileana de Santos, unaware that his every well-meaning effort makes him increasingly attractive to her and more of a rival to her long-term mate, the monstrous Pieter Stubbe. I wanted to create *Doctor Who*'s first eternal triangle, and they don't get much more eternal than these three. What's the point of rearranging the deckchairs round old story ideas? With rare exceptions, the last place you should look for inspiration for a *Who* story is old *Who* stories. If you're using old enemies, go back to basics and do new things with them, otherwise create something completely new. Who are these people who insist that *Doctor Who* has the broadest scope of any TV sci-fi series because it can do anything, and then whinge loudly if you try something different?

Pieter Stubbe is the living embodiment of the bestial dark side of Ileana's instinct, whilst the Doctor seems the civilised, reasoning ideal that she longs for. But the Doctor's not very experienced with women (so he tells Turlough). And it's true, he doesn't have a clue. Confronted by the voluptuous advances of a samba dancer (beside whom, Leela would probably look over-dressed), he faffs hopelessly. The more he tries to do The Right Thing for Ileana, the more tangled he gets. And Stubbe's subjugation of the entire population of Rio as a love token in the style of *One Man and His Dog*, is a direct reaction to the Doctor's well-meaning championing of Ileana and her werepack. This time it's Oops-Garoux!

When it came to werewolves, I had to explain why, in reality, we see so few of them. Look at the internet under Lycanthropy and you'll find them in abundance, on forums and discussion groups, perpetually sniping at the Vamps. But even at full moon, they don't seem to be much in physical evidence. Not round South London anyway. And they don't mention full moon much either; so I decided to consign that monthly transformation aspect to Hollywood. It made sense that if the wolves are here amongst us, they just don't allow themselves to be seen. They can do that; they come from dark places, shadows under the trees, natural places close to the earth that we've forgotten about or grown out of. Or are too self-obsessed to notice. Life's become so shallow and superficial that we never see what's lurking just below the surface. The wolves are trying to survive in their increasingly invaded world, a world we are making a horrendous mess of.

I found Pieter Stubbe in *The Damnable Life and Death of Stubbe Peeter*, an historic document reporting the trial and execution of a werewolf in 16th century Germany. The real Stubbe had a string of mistresses and committed a series of grisly murders, doing it all with a sort of monstrous panache. In other words, he was a terrific villain and far too good to waste. A 15th century Bestiary tells that werewolves were born out of the slime after the Deluge – and so Stubbe evolved into the granddaddy of all werewolves, the oldest, most monstrous creature still stalking the Earth – and doesn't he revel in it. He's seen it all. Everything else is transient and just a plaything to him. But his long, long time has left him behind. And the only person who can really deal with him is not the unearthly Doctor, but one of the humans who has inherited the planet. Someone in the present, who still understands and keeps its past. The homeless Rosa Cayman (aka Red Riding Hood – Amazon style) entertains the displaced spirits of the lost Amazon forest in her head, because they've nowhere else to go. Progress robbed them of their trees. Rosa's not an airy fairy New Age huntress; she just gets on with her job, which accidentally includes getting closer than anyone else ever got to Turlough. (Quite how close is entirely up to the listener!) And I wanted to explore Turlough's edgy relationship with the Doctor and with his own inner demons too. In one brief night, he says more to Rosa than he's ever admitted to anyone in the TARDIS.

Finally Gary Russell gets the script and writes 'WHAT?' and '*!@*X#**!!!' and 'OH, YES? AND HOW DO THE LISTENERS SEE THAT?!!!' And he occasionally adds 'love it' but only in tiny print. Actually there's also a traditional bit before that where we try to get our incompatible computers to speak to each other. Then I do some rewrites. Then Gary sends the script to Nick Pegg.

Bingo! This is terrific. Nick and I are on the same wavelength. Among his diverse talents, Nick writes pantos and appreciates the importance and seriousness of fairy tales (his Cinderella is a corker). He also has a passion for natural history – we spend a long time enthusing about capybaras. He is also, see his track record, a fine director. When I wrote Pieter Stubbe, I had Nicky Henson's dark and very sexy voice in my head. So Nick went and got him. Nicky H was immensely enthusiastic and, armed with Bela Lugosi's accent, produced a larger, more regal and sympathetic monster than I had dared hope for. Viscerally evil, like some forgotten force of nature, but such fun too. The splendid Sarah Gale (Rosa) had a tough time not screaming with fright during their first encounter. We'd decided, in general, to ignore accents, but Nicky's Carpathian tones felt right, Burt Kwouk offered us a variety of Japanese dialects, and since Sarah is Canadian, we thought that Rosa, raised on satellite TV in a desert shanty town, would have succumbed to an American accent – even if she'd naturally be talking Portuguese.

When Nick P and I talked about casting Ileana, we both found we had Eleanor Bron at the tops of our lists. I thought she was way out of our league. But Nick booked her too. Everyone was a bit in awe of Eleanor at the recording, but she was having a whale of a time. She enjoyed snarling and howling so much, she treated us all to her Screech Owl too – an eerie, high-pitched squeal that I hope Alistair Lock has preserved for posterity. Ages ago, I heard Eleanor on the radio saying that she couldn't understand why people were snooty about her appearance in *Revelation of the Daleks*. She'd had a lovely time sticking knitting needles into people! It was obvious throughout recording that she'd studied the script in depth. Her performance is beautifully judged and paced – real feeling for the words, especially in the storytelling scenes.

During the recording I sat: in a darkened corner of the control room wanting to do another rewrite; being embarrassed about mistakes I'd missed, but the cast hadn't (Burt Kwouk spotted Juro changing to Jura about half way through); being gobsmacked at how much actors can add to what I've written (or occasionally miss); trying not to jump up and down too much; trying Nick P's patience and undermining his carefully prepared scene-by-scene timetable by explaining to Eleanor Bron where all the unspeaking extra werewolves come from (Mr Talbot from the Lon Chaney Universal werewolf films, Maugrim from the Narnia books, others from German werewolf legends). Despite repeated problems with the sound desk (this was Big Finish's first sojourn to Moat Studios in Stockwell), Nick appeared serenely assured, juggling the out-of-order scenic schedule, patiently explaining each new scene to the cast before each take. He had an amazing grasp of what was going on. I was too dizzy to remember the implications of half of what I'd written. But I did manage to produce a batch of home-made muffins which the cast set about with gusto in the Green Room. It was a very jolly weekend. We all got roped into doing background howls and growls. Nick probably needed weeks to recover.

Then the story vanished over my event horizon. I got glimmers from Alistair as he valiantly grappled with and created out of thin air the more obscure locations and sound effects I'd put in the script. And I heard horrible rumours of how the sound desk had distorted the recording to the extent that the story nearly didn't make it out at all. But Alistair somehow cleaned it up in an exhaustively painstaking labour of love for which I am eternally grateful. The vistas of Rio and the desert are positively cinematic. I love the tacky theme to that tackiest of cartoon shows *Jaguar Maiden*. And I love how the final scenes actually work, as the vanquished Stubbe is drawn into the inner forest in Rosa's head (and why shouldn't Imagination be as real a dimension as Space or Time?) and they play their earlier fairy-tale encounter in reverse. And then the Doctor and Ileana meet one final time on another completely private plane of existence beyond anything that humans (or Turlough) can understand. And these work because some terrific actors, a director, a producer and a sound engineer believed in what they were creating and trusted my words – and that was the most flattering thing of all.

And to anyone who spots that when the train goes into reverse, Ileana cannot possibly release the final carriage with the TARDIS for the Doctor, because it's now at the front, I have only one thing to say – it was a loup line.

Loups-Garoux

CAST

THE DOCTOR	Peter Davison
TURLOUGH	Mark Strickson
PIETER STUBBE	Nicky Henson
ROSA CAIMAN	Sarah Gale
ILEANA DE SANTOS	Eleanor Bron
INEZ	Jane Burke
DOCTOR HAYASHI	Burt Kwouk
ANTON LICHTFUSS	David Hankinson
JORGE	Derek Wright
VICTOR	Barnaby Edwards

Glossary of Terms

loups-garoux : French for 'werewolves'

lobo : Portuguese for 'wolf'

favelas : Portuguese for 'slums'

cutclaws : the werewolves' nickname for non-werewolf humans

sat-vid : satellite video

9

Part One

SCENE 1. CITY SQUARE, COLOGNE. 1589.
FX: A DISTANT BELL IS TOLLING SOMEWHERE. A CROWD CHANTS "Bring Him Out! Bring Him Out!" AN AVALANCHE OF BOOING AS THE PRISONER APPEARS. SHOUTS OF "Murderer!" AND "Monster!" ETC... A GAVEL BEATS SHARPLY ON A DESK.

MAGISTRATE: Order! There must be order!
FX: THE BOOING CONTINUES. THE GAVEL BANGS AGAIN.
Order! Or I'll clear the square!
FX: MORE SHOUTING. A WEREWOLF SNARL, WHICH TURNS INTO A ROAR. THE TERRIFIED CROWD GOES QUIET.
Stubbe Pieter, on this twenty-eighth day of October in the year of our Lord God fifteen hundred and eighty nine, I do condemn you to public execution for sorcery and the lewd villainies and diverse murders which you have committed in shape of a great wolf.
FX: THE CROWD MUTTERS.
MAGISTRATE: Let first your body be broken on a wheel and your flesh be torn from your bones. Afterward your head will be struck from your body and your carcass burned to ashes.
(VERY PREGNANT PAUSE.)
STUBBE: *(DEEP AND MOCKING. CLOSE IN AT THE MAGISTRATE'S EAR)* Will you dance for me, Magistrate?
MAGISTRATE: Hold... him!
STUBBE: Shall I set the whole of Cologne dancing to my tune?
MAGISTRATE: Hold him down!
(STUBBE GROWLS, MANHANDLED ROUGHLY.)
PRIEST: *(INTONING CLOSE BY)* Have mercy on us, oh God. Lord have mercy, Christ have mercy... etc.
MAGISTRATE: Take him away. Let God's justice be done.
STUBBE: *(SHOUTING TO CROWD)* Say your prayers, Lutherans. You've lost your faith. You're nothing but cattle - bound to my will!
FX : THE CROWD ARE STARTING TO SHOUT AGAIN.
MAGISTRATE: Take him from this place. And God have mercy on his soul.
STUBBE: *(LAUGHING AS HE IS DRAGGED AWAY)* Never absolve me! I can never rest! Never! I stalk the Earth for eternity!
FX: HE GIVES A MIGHTY WOLF HOWL.
(FADE)

SCENE 2. ROSA CAIMAN'S AUDIO DIARY
FX: CLICK AS A 21ST CENTURY AUDIO RECORDER SWITCHES ON. OUTDOOR ATMOSPHERE, BUT A BIT TINNY.

ROSA: *(ON PLAYBACK)* Grandpa? This is me, Rosa. I'm gettin' out now.
FX: MICROPHONE "BUMPS" AS SHE JUGGLES IT.
ROSA: Gotta get this diarized. That's crazy, 'cos there's no one to listen, but I gotta do it anyhow, cos if I don't, none of them'll

11

know if I done what I'm gonna do. Grandpa? I should've laid you in a canoe and pushed you out on the current. But you know I can't do that, 'cos there's been no river for too many moons. So you gotta wait. I buried you in the ol' creek bed - hope it ain't too dusty. Maybe the river'll come back some day. Then it'll wash you down where the ghosts of the forest spirits are waiting for you. I put flowers where I dug you down... and rocks on top so the dillos can't dig you up. The guys from the Mission came by in the air jeep again, but I hid in the water tower. Think they want to send me to the city now you're gone. But someone's gotta stay. Gotta prove who I am. *(LAUGHS)* S'pose if I do that, they'll say I'm a man. Head of the tribe... Hey, yeah, I gotta...
FX: RECORDER CLUNKS OFF. (BEAT) FX: CLUNKS BACK ON AGAIN.
ROSA: *(WHISPERING CLOSE. SHE'S FRIGHTENED)* Gotta go, Grandpa. I heard them out beyond the ranch-house. Way off, but I can't stay longer. Like you said, can't stay here. Soon be a fat moon again and there'll be nowhere to hide from the future. When the Loups-garoux *(Loo garoo)* come prowling, we have to hunt them before they hunt us.
FX: RECORDER CLUNKS OFF.

SCENE 3. DOM PEDRO MONORAIL STATION, RIO DE JANEIRO, BRAZIL, 2080-ish.

TANNOY: *(IN PORTUGUESE)* Bom dia. Isto Estacao Dom Pedro. O centro da cidade velha. Va em frente... *(FADES UNDER...)*
FX: TARDIS ENGINES MATERIALISING - WHICH TELEPATHICALLY TRANSPOSES THE LANGUAGE INTO ENGLISH FOR US.
TANNOY: *(IN ENGLISH)* Welcome to Rio. All new arrivals please have passports and identity implants ready for inspection. Under Amazonian State law, it is an offence not to display your id implant within the city. If you have no implant, report to the Immigration Registry Office immediately.
FX: A STREET-BAND STARTS PLAYING A SAMBA. IT MINGLES WITH DISTANT TRAFFIC OF AIR CARS.

SCENE 4. ILEANA'S APARTMENT
FX: DISTANT TRAFFIC (WE'RE MEANT TO BE ON A BALCONY.)

INEZ: Senhora, a delivery for you.
ILEANA: More flowers?
FX: RUSTLE OF CELLOPHANE.
ILEANA: Thank you, Inez.
INEZ: From another admirer? Jorge perhaps? Or Mr Choudhry?
ILEANA: Just the usual admirer.
FX: OPENS THE CARD. A MAWKISHLY SENTIMENTAL TUNE.
GREETINGS CARD VOICE: Thank you for reading this paperfree card. No trees were harmed in the making of this product. Your greeting reads:
LICHTFUSS: *(A SPEAKING CARD - ELECTRONICALLY TREATED)* To Senhora de Santos. Ileana, your eyes flash like night wings in the old forest. How soon before our breath mingles in the twilight under the

12

trees? I await your call.

FX: *SHE FLINGS DOWN THE WRAPPED FLOWERS.*

ILEANA: Anton Lichtfuss. Cut flowers from a would-be cutclaw.

INEZ: He's very devoted, Senhora.

ILEANA: And that's all he will be. Yapping round me like an excited chihuahua. Inez, you'd better put the flowers in water before he arrives and is insulted.

INEZ: Yes, Senhora.

FX: *A WINDOW SLIDES SHUT, CUTTING OUT THE CITY.*

INEZ: The bulletins say there's been another killing.

ILEANA: Another?

INEZ: On Ipanema beach this time. The Policia blame the wild dogs.

ILEANA: That's the third in as many days. This city starts to smell of death. I knew it was a mistake to come here.

INEZ: But we always come for Carnaval *(Carn-a-val)*, Senhora.

ILEANA: That was my late husband's idea. He loved the crowds and the music. They've always set my teeth on edge. I'd go now, but for Victor's sake.

INEZ: I thought your son looked better today.

ILEANA: That's just the day light. It's the nights that take him the worst. Doctor Hayashi insists there's some change. But I'm not convinced. I can't see any change at all. And I don't think those straps will hold him much longer.

FX: *DOOR BUZZ.*

ILEANA: Who's that at this time? Not the chihuahua already?

FX: *CLICKS ON SCANNER.*

INEZ: There's no one outside, Senhora.

ILEANA: Go and look anyway.

FX: *DOOR SLIDES OPEN. INEZ GOES OUT.*

ILEANA: Well? *(PAUSE)* Inez? *(PAUSE)* Inez?

INEZ: *(COMING BACK)* There's this... *(DISTASTE)* package. A box. It smells of...

ILEANA: Be careful. Put it down.

FX: *PARCEL PUT DOWN.*

INEZ: Dirty and wet. Mr Lichtfuss would never leave something like that.

ILEANA: *(UNEASY)* I don't think so.

INEZ: The smell. It's old... something rotting.

ILEANA: Yes. *(BEAT)* Let me see the card.

FX: *HANDLES THE CARD. A MAWKISHLY SENTIMENTAL TUNE.*

GREETINGS CARD VOICE: Thank you for reading this paperfree card. No trees were harmed in the making of this product. Your greeting reads:

STUBBE: *(ELECTRONICALLY TREATED)* A gift to the merchant's daughter.

(ILEANA GASPS.)

STUBBE: How many fat moons since I pulled you from the snow?

FX: *ILEANA CLOSES THE CARD QUICKLY.*

INEZ: Senhora? Who is it? What's in the box?

ILEANA:	*(VERY AFRAID)* Don't touch it!
INEZ:	*(SLOW REALISATION)* It's leaking blood...
ILEANA:	Call Hayashi. And the others. I want them here, Inez.
INEZ:	Senhora.
ILEANA:	I'll attend to Victor. You get our things packed. We're getting out of Rio now.

SCENE 5. THE SUMMIT OF THE CORCOVADO (THE CHRIST STATUE) OVERLOOKING RIO.

FX: GENERAL CHATTER OF TOURISTS. AN AIR CAR BUZZES PAST & INTO THE DISTANCE.

DOCTOR:	Hold still.

FX: CAMERA CLICKS.

DOCTOR:	There you are.
TOURIST:	Thank you. Thanks very much.
DOCTOR:	My pleasure. Have a nice day.
TURLOUGH:	*(APPROACHING)* Doctor, that's the fourth picture you've taken for someone else.
DOCTOR:	People come a long way for this view, Turlough.
TURLOUGH:	That's a reason why we came too. Remember?
DOCTOR:	*(DEEP, SATISFIED BREATH)* Yes... They say the Corcovado Statue is the best place to see Rio. Amazing, isn't it? And now the smokes of the twenty twenties have lifted... Did you get your *moqueca (mokayka)*?
TURLOUGH:	The fish and coconut stew? Not exactly.
DOCTOR:	Mm?
TURLOUGH:	I think he saw me coming. He wanted twice the amount you gave me.
DOCTOR:	Actually I think you're supposed to haggle.
TURLOUGH:	He kept going on about ident credit implants. All he'd sell me was this manky-looking burger.
DOCTOR:	Yes, well, tomato sauce can hide a multitude of sins.
TURLOUGH:	That's what I'm banking on. What I really want to see is the Carnaval.
DOCTOR:	It'll be a good three days before it starts in earnest. Can you survive on the local cuisine till then?
TURLOUGH:	I might have to spend some time on a hot, sunny Rio beach to compensate.
DOCTOR:	Ah. I think at this date, the beaches may be rather overrun by shanty towns. Displaced indians, overflows from the *favelas*. That sort of thing.
TURLOUGH:	Not really what I had in mind.
DOCTOR:	*(TO HIMSELF)* No, somehow I thought not.
TURLOUGH:	What about you, Doctor?
DOCTOR:	*(CAUGHT OFF GUARD)* Me?
TURLOUGH:	Yes, what do you really want?
DOCTOR:	Well, I'm not sure I could really... A lot of things, I suppose.
TURLOUGH:	Oh, come on. How long have you been travelling? There must be something you've always searched for.
DOCTOR:	Perhaps... *(BEAT)* But I was once told that I'd know

when I found it.

TURLOUGH: And have you?

DOCTOR: What do you think? *(CHEERFULLY CHANGING THE SUBJECT)* Still this view is quite spectacular. Last time I was here the statue of Christ wasn't even built.

TURLOUGH: No?

DOCTOR: That would have been around seventeen hundred, and the bay down there was full of clippers.

TURLOUGH: The chief trade being in gold and sugar.

DOCTOR: And slaves. Like most triumphant enterprises, it had its rotten underbelly. *(TURLOUGH SPLUTTERS)*

TURLOUGH: Ugh! This burger is disgusting. *(SPITS)*

DOCTOR: I had a feeling it might be.

TURLOUGH: No one can eat this. Ugh. It's all greasy and gritty. *(CALLS)* Here, you.

FX: A DOG BARKS.

TURLOUGH: You mutt. D'you want it? Because I don't.

DOCTOR: Turlough, I'm not sure if that's advisable.

TURLOUGH: Here you are. Go on.

FX: DOG BARK. DEVOURING, CHOMPING NOISES.

TURLOUGH: That's it. At least someone appreciates it. The skinny-looking mongrel was eyeing me up as soon as I bought the burger.

DOCTOR: Still I don't think we should encourage him. Where do you want to go now?

TURLOUGH: Anywhere, Doctor. As long we can get away from it all.

DOCTOR: *(KNOWING)* Get away *from* it, Turlough? Or get away *with* it?

TURLOUGH: *(GOOD NATURED)* Probably a bit of both, Doctor.

DOCTOR: Yes, I think I'd go along with that. *(MOVING AWAY)* There's a parade down there in the city. Shall we take a look?

TURLOUGH: You can see that far? Yes. I'd like that. *(REALISES HE'S ALONE)* Doctor? Well, wait for me!

SCENE 6. ILEANA'S APARTMENT. Victor's room.
(ILEANA AND DR HAYASHI , MIDDLE-AGED AND RATHER PRECISELY VOICED, ARE STRUGGLING WITH VICTOR, ILEANA'S INVALID SON.)
FX: VICTOR MOANS REPEATEDLY, WITH MORE THAN A HINT OF AN ANIMAL IN PAIN.

ILEANA: *(STRESSED)* Victor, calm down. Quietly, now. We won't hurt you.

FX: VICTOR REACTS ANGRILY.

HAYASHI: Senhora, you must hold him still.

ILEANA: I'm trying to! He's not used to strangers, Hayashi. *(TO HER SON)* Victor, it's alright. Don't struggle. Mother's here.

FX: VICTOR GIVES A LOW GROWLING GROAN.

ILEANA: There. That's better. Nothing to be afraid of. Doctor Hayashi's here to help. No one's going to hurt you.

HAYASHI: Just one jab.

FX: VICTOR SNARLS IN PAIN.

ILEANA: What are you doing, you idiot! *(TO VICTOR)* It's

15

alright. Victor. It's alright.

FX: *VICTOR'S GROWLING SUBSIDES.*

HAYASHI: That's better. Administering his medication is proving more dangerous than I anticipated.

FX: *VICTOR IS BREATHING DEEPLY, MORE LIKE A SLEEPING ANIMAL.*

ILEANA: *(QUIETLY)* He's sleeping again. Next time be more careful with my son. Come through to the lounge. I have to discuss our departure.

HAYASHI: Senhora, this is ridiculous.

FX: *VICTOR'S BREATHING FADES AS THEY LEAVE THE ROOM. A DOOR CLOSES.*

ILEANA: I mean it, Hayashi.

HAYASHI: Your son's condition is already critical, if you de-stabilise him further, I may never be able to effect a change in his... nature.

ILEANA: We have to leave Rio.

HAYASHI: You cannot afford to take him out in public like that.

ILEANA: There is no limit to what I can afford. If necessary your payment can be reviewed.

HAYASHI: No, no. You misunderstand. My equipment, my assistant... all these are difficult to move.

ILEANA: You brought them here. You can re-establish them elsewhere. It will be quiet. With no distractions.

HAYASHI: But why this sudden change? I must know. Where are you going?

FX: *DOOR OPENS.*

LICHTFUSS: *(ENTERING)* Senhora.

ILEANA: Herr Lichtfuss.

LICHTFUSS: I came immediately. Are you safe?

ILEANA: Yes, yes, Anton. For the moment. Inez is packing. We leave the city at eighteen hundred hours.

LICHTFUSS: So soon? Tell me what has happened. You've had a warning.

ILEANA: Yes. *(AWKWARDLY)* But I can't talk...

HAYASHI: Good afternoon.

LICHTFUSS: *(SHARP)* Who's this...?

ILEANA: Herr Lichtfuss, this is Doctor Matsuo Hayashi.

LICHTFUSS: The physician that you've acquired to treat Victor.

HAYASHI: You said "warning". Does this mean, Senhora, that you have received some sort of threat?

LICHTFUSS: How much do you understand, doctor?

HAYASHI: I have the Senhora's confidence. How else could I attempt to cure her son?

LICHTFUSS: Cure! That's the last thing we want. Ileana, I thought you'd abandoned these fantasies.

ILEANA: They are not fantasies. But we must leave Rio now.

HAYASHI: Have no fear, Senhora. I will not abandon you or your son. Knowing what I know, I can't imagine you'd ever let me walk free. So, where will we be flying to?

LICHTFUSS: Flying?

ILEANA: Flying? Whatever gave you that idea?

(FADE)

SCENE 7. MOUNTAIN TRACK
(THE DOCTOR AND TURLOUGH WALKING)
FX: FOOTSTEPS ON ROUGH GROUND)

TURLOUGH: *(STRUGGLING TO KEEP UP)* Slow down, Doctor. I didn't think you planned to walk down?
DOCTOR: I thought you'd enjoy the fresh air.
TURLOUGH: I thought we had return tickets on the cog-train.
DOCTOR: Only singles.
TURLOUGH: Well, shouldn't we stick to the road at least? Hang on, they don't do singles.
DOCTOR: Returns are for tourists.
TURLOUGH: I thought we *were* tourists.
DOCTOR: Really? Yes, I suppose you could look at it like that. Unfortunately you spent the last of our tenable currency on that burger.
(SILENCE APART FROM FOOTSTEPS.)
TURLOUGH: That dog's still following us.
DOCTOR: Just ignore it. It'll soon get bored. You see over to the north east beyond the space ports? That's where the Amazon rain forest used to be.
TURLOUGH: *Used* to be...
DOCTOR: Up until about twenty years ago.
TURLOUGH: *(INCREDULOUS)* You mean they finally burnt it all.
DOCTOR: They didn't have to. The Amazon was so intensively farmed, its eco-system completely caved-in. The so-called lung of the world turned into a monumental dust bowl. All the unique wildlife - birds, animals, plants - was decimated.
TURLOUGH: But couldn't anyone try to stop it? Surely someone...
DOCTOR: Lots of people. There was nearly a war. But by then the Earth governments had a new toy. The untapped resources of the Moon and the asteroid belt to exploit.
TURLOUGH: So nobody cared. Humans are so stupid.
DOCTOR: When you've studied humans as long as I have, it's hard not to find them quite endearing.
TURLOUGH: I certainly didn't intend to study them *this* long.
DOCTOR: No? Well, I suppose they can get a bit wearing at times. All those questions. And they never seem to learn from their mistakes.
(ANOTHER SILENCE WITH WALKING.)
TURLOUGH: That dog's still behind us.
DOCTOR: *(KEEPING GOING)* I know. And a couple more have tagged along.
FX: DOG BARKS, A LITTLE WAY OFF.
TURLOUGH: And more to the right.
DOCTOR: Just keep walking. Don't run.
FX: MORE DOGS BARK ON EITHER SIDE.
TURLOUGH: It's turning into a pack. What do they want?
DOCTOR: They're after food.
TURLOUGH: I haven't got any more food.
DOCTOR: I don't think they're that fussy, Turlough. If we can just get to the road...
FX: A DOG BOUNDS CLOSE AND SNAPS AT THEM.

17

TURLOUGH: Look out!

(THE DOCTOR SHOUTS IN PAIN.)

FX: CHORUS OF BARKING CIRCLES THEM.

TURLOUGH: Are you hurt?

DOCTOR: Just a little demoralised. They're trying to drive us into a dead end. Look out!

FX: ANOTHER DOG MAKES A SNARLING RUN. HE SNAPS AT TURLOUGH.

(TURLOUGH YELLS.)

FX: MATERIAL RIPS. AND THE DOG BACKS OFF AGAIN.

DOCTOR: Turlough?

TURLOUGH: I never liked this jacket anyway. What do we do?

DOCTOR: Try to divert them. There's an old story about throwing the baby out of the sledge to stop the pursuing wolves.

TURLOUGH: I threw them a burger, Doctor, and that only brought more of them.

DOCTOR: Then give me a hand with this branch.

FX: THE DOCTOR STARTS PULLING AT A BRANCH.

DOCTOR: We'll have to fight our way out as best we can.

TURLOUGH: The wood's tinder dry.

DOCTOR: Exactly. I don't suppose you've got any matches.

TURLOUGH: Sorry.

DOCTOR: *(GOING THROUGH POCKETS)* Now where did I put that magnifying glass?

FX: A CHORUS OF GROWLS DRAWS IN AROUND THEM.

TURLOUGH: Doctor? I don't think there's time for that.

DOCTOR: *(RESIGNED)* Alright. Keep your back to the bushes and stay close to me. That way they've only got one line of attack. Try to tackle one at a time...

FX: THE DOGS ARE DRAWING IN.

DOCTOR: Ready, Turlough.

TURLOUGH: Ready, Doctor.

DOCTOR: Here they come.

FX: THE HOWL OF A DISTANT WOLF. THE OTHER DOGS STOP.

TURLOUGH: What's that?

FX: THE HOWL AGAIN. CLOSER. THE DOGS SCARPER.

TURLOUGH: They're going.

DOCTOR: Come on!

TURLOUGH: What happened? Where did they go?

DOCTOR: We're not staying to find out. Come on.

FX: THEIR FOOTSTEPS START TO STUMBLE AWAY.

TURLOUGH: Something frightened them off.

DOCTOR: There's the road. You were right. We should never have left it.

TURLOUGH: But they just ran.

DOCTOR: Just keep going or we'll miss that parade.

TURLOUGH: Don't tell me then. I don't want to know anyway.

DOCTOR: No, Turlough. I don't think you do. Come on!

FX: WOLF HOWL AGAIN. FADE INTO DISTANCE.

SCENE 8. ILEANA'S APARTMENT

FX: THE DISTANT WOLF HOWL.

ILEANA: Anton, did you hear?
LICHTFUSS: Right across the city. It's another warning. He's marking out his territory.
ILEANA: The Grey One. So many years since I heard that voice. I hoped it might be never again. I was praying it might be just the wind howling in the trees.
LICHTFUSS: You're cold.
ILEANA: It chills me.
LICHTFUSS: Poor Ileana.
ILEANA: I thought the ocean might be a barrier to him. How long have I tried to deny all that darkness, knowing it would always return? Slinking in, the way the moonlight always finds a crack in the shutters.
LICHTFUSS: He must get past me first.
ILEANA: No. We can't make a stand against him. Who knows how powerful he's grown?
LICHTFUSS: I shall challenge him. Most powerful or not...
ILEANA: Don't be a fool. You don't know him.
LICHTFUSS: But I will...
ILEANA: (BEAT) I was afraid Victor would wake. Above all else, I have to protect him. That's why we must get out of Rio now.
LICHTFUSS: With that cutclaw doctor? Is your son really so ill?
ILEANA: There's no change. Why doesn't he change? (BEAT) Until Hayashi came I thought everything was lost. But he's an expert.
LICHTFUSS: A meddler.
ILEANA: He has to be trusted. And we can't stay here. Where's Inez?
LICHTFUSS: We can't run forever, Ileana. The others won't follow.
ILEANA: They'll do as I tell them. Even you, Lichtfuss. For all the attentions you pay me, you must accept that the old world has changed. I won't sway my decision for anyone. I'm still the leader. And my word is still our law.

SCENE 9. STREET IN RIO.
FX: THE CARNAVAL PARADE EXPLODES OUT AT US. A SALSA BAND, DRUMS, WHISTLES.
(THE DOCTOR & TURLOUGH, JOSTLED BY THE CROWD, BOTH MUCH MORE JOVIAL, AND RAISING THEIR VOICES TO HEAR EACH OTHER.)

TURLOUGH: Doctor! Over here! You can get a better view.
DOCTOR: (PUSHING THROUGH) Excuse me. Can I just...? I'm a Doctor. Can I get through please? Thank you. (A CARIOCAN YELP.) Sorry.
TURLOUGH: Look at those bird and animal masks. Some of them are almost alive.
DOCTOR: Fascinating. (BEAT) So is this what you had in mind?
TURLOUGH: Much more like it.
DOCTOR: And the business with the dogs...? I apologise...
TURLOUGH: It's alright. Don't worry. Look at the dancers now! And this isn't even real Carnaval yet.
DOCTOR: Glad you like it.
TURLOUGH: I do. Thank you, Doctor. (THOUGHTS IN A SPIN)

Look! Look at the colours on that seashell outfit! Is it all made of flowers? The whole thing must be twenty foot across.

DOCTOR: No, not really. It's amazing what they can do with computer graphics these days.

TURLOUGH: *(NUDGE, NUDGE)* It's amazing how little they can cover with so much.

DOCTOR: Atavistic expressions of the inner human self...

TURLOUGH: I'd call it downright revealing.

DOCTOR: Positively bacchanalian. But what do you expect from a population that spends the rest of the year hunched over computer screens?

FX: SHRILL SYNCOPATED WHISTLE BLOWN BY A PASSING REVELLER.

DOCTOR: And a happy Shrovetide to you too!

TURLOUGH: *(LAUGHING)* Or maybe humans are just plain Earthy.

DOCTOR: *(ALMOST LAUGHING)* Yes. Yes, indeed. But preferable, I'm sure, to the straight-laced rigours of public school.

TURLOUGH: Never again, Doctor. Now this is when you see what humans are really like.

DOCTOR: Oh, please, not too philosophical, Turlough. Not today. *(NOTICES A CONVENIENT DISTRACTION)* Ah... Good heavens, I'm not entirely sure how that stays up.

TURLOUGH: Skill, Doctor.

DOCTOR: Or art...

TURLOUGH: Yes. But I wouldn't stare quite so much if I were you.

DOCTOR: Really?

(A JINGLING SAMBA GIRL DESCENDS.)

SAMBA GIRL: Aye. You want to dance?

DOCTOR: Ah...

SAMBA GIRL: Come on, let's dance.

DOCTOR: Er... no, really. Thank you.

SAMBA GIRL: Yes. Let's dance. Do the samba.

(TURLOUGH IS LAUGHING.)

DOCTOR: No, it's very kind of you...not just now, really...

SAMBA GIRL: Everybody dances at Carnaval. Come on. Dance with me. I show you how.

DOCTOR: No, erm thank you... please, no.

TURLOUGH: Go on, Doctor! Get in there!

SAMBA GIRL: *(CLAPPING HER HANDS)* Yes. We samba all the way to the Sugarloaf and back again.

DOCTOR: No. Please let go. I'm sorry, I'm saving myself for the big day. Another time perhaps...

SAMBA GIRL: Aye...

TURLOUGH: Don't be such a coward, Doctor. You can.... *(HE STUTTERS AND SHIVERS.)*

FX: THE CROWD AND BAND NOISE FADE AWAY. SOME SORT OF AIR CAR IS HEARD SLOWLY APPROACHING.

DOCTOR: Turlough? What's the matter?

TURLOUGH: *(WITH DIFFICULTY. AS IF HE'S FREEZING)* What is it?

DOCTOR: Don't move. Something's coming through the crowd.

TURLOUGH: I must... get back.

FX: THE SILENT CROWD STARTS TO SHUFFLE.

DOCTOR: No, no, don't go with the crowd. Turlough, listen to me.

TURLOUGH: We have to move. Have to let it through.

FX: THE DRONE OF THE AIR CAR PASSES CLOSE BY & FADES INTO THE DISTANCE.

DOCTOR: Turlough? Listen. I have to follow that car.

(TURLOUGH GROANS)

DOCTOR: Just stay here. I'll be back.

TURLOUGH: *(MUMBLING)* Don't go, Doctor. Wait for me. *(HE SHUDDERS AGAIN)*

FX: AN AUDIBLE & MENACING AURA RISES.

TURLOUGH: Something else coming. Who's that?

FX: SOMETHING GROWLS MENACINGLY LIKE A THREATENED DOG OR WOLF.

TURLOUGH: Those eyes. Black and gold. Don't look. Don't look.

FX: THE AURA CONTINUES.

TURLOUGH: *(HARDLY DARING TO ASK)* Who are you? *(BEAT)* Don't look at me like that.

STUBBE: Good day to you, young stranger. What fierce eyes you have.

TURLOUGH: Like you then, aren't I.

(STUBBE GIVES A LOW GROWL)

TURLOUGH: What do you want?

STUBBE: Got any food for a hungry wanderer? *(BEAT)* No? Perhaps I was wrong. I was told there was a young fellow with food to throw away. A hunter, I thought. But you have the lean, hungry look of a common jackal.

TURLOUGH: *(SWALLOWS)* Leave me alone.

STUBBE: For the moment. There was a forest here once, but the cutclaws tore it down and set us wolves running.

TURLOUGH: *(SARCASTIC)* Oh yes, of course they did.

STUBBE: And we run fast, young stranger.

TURLOUGH: I've seen better wolf masks in third rate horror films.

(STUBBE GROWLS. HE COMES IN CLOSE. TURLOUGH SHIVERS.)

STUBBE: Once we have a scent, we never lose it. Don't stray too far from the path. Because I'll be waiting.

FX: THE AURA FADES.

TURLOUGH: *(EXHAUSTED)* Doctor, where the hell have you gone?

FX: THE CROWD STARTS TO STIR. BUT THERE'S NO MORE MUSIC.

DOCTOR: *(APPROACHING)* Turlough! There you are. *(ON AN EXCITABLE TRAIN OF THOUGHT)* That hover limo. The crowd parted like the Red Sea to let it through.

TURLOUGH: *(QUIET)* I don't... really remember...

DOCTOR: Interesting. Probably couldn't help yourself. Could have been some sort of mass auto suggestion. Even a basic instinctive fear, driving you back. You look cold.

TURLOUGH: Yes.

DOCTOR: You've dropped your jacket.

TURLOUGH: Sorry.

DOCTOR: Couldn't see who was inside the car though. The windows were polarised. I wonder why it was pushing through the crowd when all the traffic lanes are thirty feet overhead? Mind you, if

21

it's moving at ground level that makes it easier to follow. (*SUDDENLY NOTICES.*) Turlough? You do look very cold.

TURLOUGH: (*RALLYING A LITTLE*) Something else came through. After you'd gone.

DOCTOR: I didn't see anything. Was it following the car?

TURLOUGH: It came right up to me.

DOCTOR: Really.

TURLOUGH: It kept growling. And it was tall... with a mask like a wolf and burning gold eyes. (*WISHES HE HADN'T THOUGHT THIS*) At least I think it was a mask.

DOCTOR: Did you speak to it?

TURLOUGH: (*SHARP*) No.

DOCTOR: Pity. (*BEAT*) That car was heading for the old *Dom Pedro* station.

TURLOUGH: Where we left the TARDIS.

DOCTOR: Nasty thoughts are like buses, Turlough.

TURLOUGH: Mmm?

DOCTOR: You don't see one for ages and then a whole army come along together. Come on!

(*FADE*)

SCENE 10. ESTACAO DOM PEDRO CONCOURSE

(*JORGE, WHO IS OLDER, MEETS ILEANA AND HER PARTY – LICHTFUSS, INEZ & HAYASHI*)
FX: *A HOVER CAR DRAWS UP AND SETTLES. THE DOOR OPENS.*

JORGE: (*APPROACHING*) Senhora. I was starting to worry.

ILEANA: The Carnaval crowds delayed us, Jorge, but they may help muddy our tracks. Where's the train?

JORGE: It's all prepared and programmed. Inez. Herr Lichtfuss. Are we all here?

ILEANA: If we stand about, we'll attract attention. We must keep my son out of sight.

LICHTFUSS: He's still sleeping. Jorge, help us with the hover-gurney.

JORGE: (*A DEEP GRUMBLING GROWL OF DISTASTE*) Are these the physicians?

ILEANA: Doctor Hayashi.

HAYASHI: And this is my assistant, Juro.

ILEANA: They come with us. I told you this already.

JORGE: (*COLD*) This way, Senhora.

FX: *FOOTSTEPS AS THEY CROSS THE CONCOURSE*

JORGE: Inez, where's Kanu Choudhry? I thought he'd meet us.

INEZ: (*UNCOMFORTABLE*) Mr Choudhry is not coming.

LICHTFUSS: You didn't tell me that. (*TO ILEANA*) Senhora? Has he finally slunk away, tail between his legs?

ILEANA: It's something I'll explain to you later.

LICHTFUSS: (*SNEERS*) Not in front of the cutclaws...

ILEANA: Never say that again, Lichtfuss! Never ever! Any more whining and I'll...

FX: *THE FOOTSTEPS FALTER.*

| JORGE: | What's that? (DEEP BREATH) Do you catch it? |
| INEZ: | (BREATH) What is it? |

(THEY'VE CAUGHT A SCENT WHICH SENDS THEM INTO A BIZARRE AND SLOW REVERIE - THE MUSIC COULD EMPHASISE THIS.)

JORGE:	It's like nothing I've ever...
ILEANA:	Ancient... a scent like... stillness.
LICHTFUSS:	Like coming snow...
JORGE:	No, no. Like breaking ice on the rivers in spring.
ILEANA:	The scent after the lightning before the thunder.
INEZ:	Or fields after rain.
ILEANA:	And the oldest forests. Under the dark fir trees...
LICHTFUSS:	(ANGRY GROWL) Almost... unearthly...
HAYASHI:	(URGENT) Senhora. Senhora, we should move.
ILEANA:	What? What is it, Hayashi?
HAYASHI:	We are being watched. The train. Please. Hurry.

(PAUSE)

SCENE 11. THE SAME (ESTACAO DOM PEDRO CONCOURSE)

DOCTOR:	It's alright, Turlough, they're moving again.
TURLOUGH:	I thought they'd seen us for a minute. At least they're nowhere near the TARDIS.
DOCTOR:	That's true. Can you see them better now?
TURLOUGH:	Sort of. But it's hard to focus. My brain knows they're there because you tell me, but it's a job to convince my eyes.
DOCTOR:	Because they don't want to be seen.
TURLOUGH:	I don't want to see them either. I thought fur coats like that would have been outlawed years ago.
DOCTOR:	They're heading the gurney towards that monorail.
TURLOUGH:	You said only freight travels by train these days.
DOCTOR:	Or livestock. Maybe I was wrong. (MOVING OFF) If that's a body they're pushing, maybe I should pay my respects.
TURLOUGH:	Oh no, Doctor. Come back. Not through there.

FX: AN ALARM TWITTERS.

TANNOY:	Alert. You have breached security barrier seven. Stay where you are. (CONTINUES UNDER) Have your passports and identity implants ready for inspection.
DOCTOR:	Aha. So that's it.
TURLOUGH:	Doctor!
DOCTOR:	Look at the crest on the side of the carriage.
TURLOUGH:	Doctor, we can't stay here.
DOCTOR:	Familio de Santos. Just like royalty. Fancy a trip on a royal train, Turlough?
TURLOUGH:	Doctor, it's not our business. Maybe it's a private funeral.

FX: THE TRAIN STARTS TO POWER UP.

DOCTOR:	One that clears the streets by auto suggestion? With something nasty like a hungry wolf following the cortege?
TURLOUGH:	It was just a mask... part of the Carnaval.
DOCTOR:	Now you're trying to delude yourself. Which is exactly what they want. (URGENT) Come on. (MOVING OFF) We've a train to catch.

23

SCENE 12. STATION PLATFORM

TANNOY: Remain where you are on platform seven. Passports and identity implants must be shown to the immigration inspection module.
INEZ: *(CUTTING OVER LAST SPEECH)* Senhora, come inside. The train is ready to leave.
ILEANA: That scent again, Inez. There he is.
DOCTOR: *(DISTANT)* Hello!
FX: WARNING DOOR-CLOSING BLIPS.
INEZ: Senhora, the doors. Quickly.
FX: THE TRAIN DOOR CLOSES WITH A GUSH. FX: THE HUM OF THE TRAIN INTERIOR.
ILEANA: How strange.
INEZ: Come away from the window, Senhora. We must attend your son. Senhora?

SCENE 13. STATION PLATFORM

(THE DOCTOR AND TURLOUGH OUTSIDE THE TRAIN)
TURLOUGH: What's she staring at?
DOCTOR: Me, I think. *(BEAT. THEN LOUDLY)* Please, I must speak to you.
FX: THE TRAIN STARTS TO PULL AWAY.
DOCTOR: *(GESTICULATING)* Look. I am the Doctor and this is...
TURLOUGH: Too late.
DOCTOR: I have to speak to her.
TURLOUGH: Doctor. Here comes trouble.
FX: THE WHIRR OF A ROBOTIC INSPECTOR ARRIVING.
(ALTHOUGH IT HAS THE SAME VOICE AS THE ECHOING TANNOY, THE INSPECTOR SOUNDS LIKE A POLITE AND RATHER ORDINARY AIRLINE HOSTESS - NOT THE CLICHED LEMON-SOAKED NAPKINS VARIETY.)
INSPECTOR: Your passports please, senhors.
TANNOY: Display your passports and identity grafts to the immigration inspection module now.
DOCTOR: This train. Where's it going?
INSPECTOR: You are in a restricted area. If you have no passport, please display your state identity grafts now.
DOCTOR: I want to know about that train.
INSPECTOR: Under Amazonian State law, it is an offence not to display your ID implant within the city boundaries.
TURLOUGH: Not listening.
INSPECTOR: Please display your genome ID grafts, senhors. Failure to do so may result in a fine or imprisonment.
FX: DOCTOR RAPS HIS KNUCKLES ON THE METAL TICKET INSPECTOR.
DOCTOR: Hello? Do your limited responses include a timetable? Or was that train a specially chartered service?
INSPECTOR: If you have a personal credit-rating code recognised by any major international bank, please display now.
TURLOUGH: I think it wants a bribe.
DOCTOR: Well, it's out of luck.
FX: ELECTRONIC WHIZZ AND METALLIC CLAMP.

DOCTOR: Agh. That's my arm you're twisting off!

INSPECTOR: A credit rating of nil is also an offence within the city central boundaries.

TURLOUGH: Hold still, Doctor. If I can prise that open...

DOCTOR: Overgrown shopping trolley!

INSPECTOR: Under Amazonian State law, assaulting an inspecting officer is a punishable offence.

TURLOUGH: Oh, shut up.

FX: *ELECTRONIC WHIZZ AND METALLIC CLAMP.*

TURLOUGH: Ow! Get off, me!

(BOTH INSPECTOR AND TANNOY BURBLE AT ONCE)

INSPECTOR: Fines for not displaying an ID may not be less than five thousand credits or a prison term of no less than six months. Please accompany me to the Immigration Register Office immediately.

TANNOY: Emergency procedures. Assistance is required on platform seven. Two illegal immigrants are resisting arrest.

TURLOUGH: I can't get free!

FX: *A FEARSOME ANIMAL SNARL.*

(TURLOUGH YELLS)

FX: *BITS OF METAL CLUNK & SPIN ACROSS THE PLATFORM. ELECTRO BURBLES OF PROTEST.*

TANNOY: Emergency! Assistance required on platform seven.

(THE TANNOY CONTINUES RANTING.)

DOCTOR: There it goes.

TURLOUGH: Ow, my arm. What was it? I didn't see. It was so fast.

DOCTOR: A huge wolf.

TURLOUGH: (UNNERVED) A wolf?

DOCTOR: Yes. A massive grey animal. Bounding after the monorail.

TURLOUGH: Doctor, we can't stay here.

DOCTOR: No. We have to warn them. Back to the TARDIS quickly. There's more than one way to catch a train.

SCENE 14. TRAIN INTERIOR - ILEANA'S APARTMENT.

FX: *HUM OF THE TRAVELLING MONORAIL.*

HAYASHI: Your son is growing weaker, Senhora.

ILEANA: By that, I assume that you mean his dark side is growing stronger.

HAYASHI: Until we reach our destination, wherever that is, I must increase the dosage of inhibitor drugs. If only for our own safety.

ILEANA: I want a cure, Hayashi. Not a delay.

HAYASHI: Impossible until I have proper medical facilities. To treat your son was my own calculated risk, but now both my assistant and I are endangered by circumstances beyond our control.

FX: *THE DOOR SLIDES OPEN.*

ILEANA: There is no danger. Just concentrate on a cure for my son.

LICHTFUSS: No danger, Ileana? Then who was the stranger at the station?

ILEANA: This is my private carriage, Herr Lichtfuss. What do you all want?

25

INEZ:	We are all concerned, Senhora..
JORGE:	Who was that at the station? Was it Him?
ILEANA:	*(SARCASTIC)* You think that was the Grey One, Jorge? Did he look grey?
LICHTFUSS:	Then who was it?
INEZ:	Perhaps you have a rival, mein herr.
ILEANA:	He was a stranger, that's all. I've never seen him before.
JORGE:	But he saw us, Senhora.
LICHTFUSS:	Is he a rival? If he is, Ileana, I'll lay his skin at your feet.
INEZ:	*(MOCKING)* Such gallantry.
JORGE:	*(JOINING IN)* We'll turn the train round for you now.
ILEANA:	Be quiet, all of you. Doctor Hayashi, please forgive us. You are our guest.
HAYASHI:	But I'm eager to learn your ways, Senhora.
LICHTFUSS:	One stranger after another.
ILEANA:	The stranger at the station means nothing. Get that into your head. He was just an inquisitive cutclaw.
LICHTFUSS:	He didn't smell like *nothing*.
ILEANA:	*(ANGRY)* God! Why is everyone always so young! You're always questioning me. Always snapping at my heels. If you don't believe the danger we left, then I'll show you. Maybe that'll put a stop to your whining.

SCENE 15. TARDIS CONSOLE ROOM.
FX: HUM OF THE TARDIS INTERIOR. BUZZ OF CLOSING DOOR.

DOCTOR:	How's your shoulder?
TURLOUGH:	It hurts. How about yours?
DOCTOR:	Still workable. Next time I'll buy a platform ticket.

FX: THE DOCTOR FLICKS SWITCHES.

TURLOUGH:	At the risk of sounding human...
DOCTOR:	A question about what happened? Yes, of course.
TURLOUGH:	The wolf you saw.
DOCTOR:	Wolf- *like*.
TURLOUGH:	But with golden eyes?
DOCTOR:	Difficult to say. It was moving so fast. And it wasn't standing on its hindlegs.
TURLOUGH:	Mine was.
DOCTOR:	I thought it might have been.

FX: FLICKS MORE SWITCHES. TARDIS DEMATERIALISATION SEQUENCE STARTS.

TURLOUGH:	Oh, no. You're not going after it. What about the Carnaval?
DOCTOR:	Those people are in danger, Turlough. And if I can't catch a train, I can always go ahead and meet it.

SCENE 16. TRAIN INTERIOR - ILEANA'S APARTMENT.
(ILEANA, LICHTFUSS, JORGE AND HAYASHI WAIT AS INEZ BRINGS IN THE BOX THAT WAS DELIVERED TO ILEANA'S APARTMENT.)
FX: HUM OF THE TRAVELLING MONORAIL.

ILEANA: *(GRAVE)* Put the box down here, Inez. Then they can all see why we had to leave.

FX: BOX PUT ON A TABLE. RUSTLE OF POLYTHENE WRAPPER.

ILEANA: This gift was delivered to my apartment this morning.

JORGE: There's blood on it.

LICHTFUSS: *(STERN)* Ileana, your physician is still here.

HAYASHI: Forgive me, Senhora, I'm intruding.

ILEANA: Stay here, Hayashi.

HAYASHI: I must attend to your son.

LICHTFUSS: Excellent idea.

ILEANA: And I want you to stay! We don't have secrets from you. How can we? Whatever Herr Lichtfuss thinks.

LICHTFUSS: It's no secret what I think.

FX: POLYTHENE RUSTLES.

JORGE: This blood. *(SNIFFS)* It's a day old at least. But I can't place the smell.

LICHTFUSS: Jorge, let me see.

FX: POLYTHENE PULLED BACK.

LICHTFUSS: There's a card.

ILEANA: The Grey One sends gifts as well. Open it, Anton.

FX: CARD RUSTLES. THE MAWKISH CARD MUSIC AGAIN.

GREETINGS CARD VOICE: Thank you for reading this paperfree card. No trees were harmed in the making of this product. Your greeting reads:

STUBBE (THE CARD): "A gift to the merchant's daughter. How many fat moons since I pulled you from the snow?"

LICHTFUSS: Is that him?

ILEANA: Who else. It's why we left Rio. Open the box.

FX: BOX COVER PULLED OFF.

(LICHTFUSS DRAWS HIS BREATH SHARPLY THROUGH HIS TEETH. JORGE GASPS.)

JORGE: Kanu Chowdhry!

LICHTFUSS: *(SLOW, ANGRY)* His head.

STUBBE: "And when the moon is fat again, I shall wrap you in its silver sheen and blood will feed the forest."

LICHTFUSS: *(JEALOUS)* What does he mean?

ILEANA: This is why I took you away from the city. It's why I've called a council.

JORGE: You've called the others?

ILEANA: As many as would listen.

LICHTFUSS: No one's done that ever.

ILEANA: There's never been a threat like this till now.

HAYASHI: Senhora, the head. May I see please?

LICHTFUSS: Don't touch that!

ILEANA: Let him see.

FX: MORE RUSTLED POLYTHENE.

HAYASHI: *(ANALYTICAL)* Hmm. Yes. Very ferocious. I think you were wise to leave when you did.

LICHTFUSS: Before we all have our heads torn off?

HAYASHI: No, not torn. There's a lot of blood clogged in his fur, but the actual severance is comparatively clean. You'd need very powerful jaws to take the head off like that. Just one bite, I think.

LICHTFUSS: Monster!

(HAYASHI GASPS AS LICHTFUSS GRABS HIM BY THE THROAT.)

ILEANA: Stop it! Lichtfuss, let him go!

FX: A HIGH REPEATING TRILL STARTLES THEM. IT KEEPS TRILLING.

ILEANA: Don't answer that!

JORGE: But it could be the others. Waiting for us.

ILEANA: No. Look at the screen. That caller ID. Don't touch it. Don't touch it!

FX: THE TRILL GOES ON GETTING LOUDER.

SCENE 17. TARDIS INTERIOR

FX: TARDIS IN FLIGHT HUM.

DOCTOR: Now, at an average speed of four hundred and two point three five kph...

FX: RUSTLES MAP.

DOCTOR: It should reach these coordinates in about four and a quarter minutes... or so.

TURLOUGH: Doctor, where are we?

DOCTOR: We'll just hover here for a while.

TURLOUGH: Don't answer my question then.

DOCTOR: Coordinates ... 51 degrees West by 16 degrees South. The northern end of the Mantiqueira Tunnel. Otherwise known as the lower regions of the Amazon Desert. And from the look of it, a pretty dismal and dusty place it is too.

TURLOUGH: And have you got the year right?

DOCTOR: No need to be sarcastic.

TURLOUGH: We're on the monorail track!

DOCTOR: Three inches above it, to be precise. As I said, we're in hover mode. I just hope it's the north-bound track.

TURLOUGH: I don't believe this. You're waiting for that train.

DOCTOR: Exactly. And allowing for any leaves on the line, which is doubtful in this ecologically catastrophic day and age, it's due any time now. I hope we're not too late.

TURLOUGH: You're crazy. You've put us right in its path.

DOCTOR: As I say, I'm getting rather better at these precision manoeuvres.

FX: A DISTANT, BUT APPROACHING, TRAIN RUMBLE.

TURLOUGH: Doctor. There are lights...

DOCTOR: Good, good. Now when the train comes through, I simply jump the TARDIS forward ten seconds in time...

TURLOUGH: It's coming! Doctor! The train!

FX: TRAIN CLAXON.

DOCTOR: ...but not in space!

TURLOUGH: DOCTOR!!!

FX: TRAIN ROAR. TRAIN CLAXON AGAIN. TARDIS VWORP CUT BY LURCHING SCREECH. ALMIGHTY CRASH.

CLOSING MUSIC.

<u>NOTE:</u> SCENE 18 DELETED FROM PART 1

PART TWO

SCENE 19. ROSA CAIMAN'S AUDIO DIARY
FX: ROSA'S RECORDER CLUNKS ON.

ROSA: *(ON PLAYBACK)* The moon's rising, grandpa. Don't know how far I walked, but I ain't seen no one 'xept the dillos. But grandpa, I found it. The shining path cutting across the desert. Put my ear to it and there was this roar. A long way off, heck yes, and well angry. Maybe it's coming my way, but am I scared? And how! *(SHIVERS)* Still two nights to full moon, grandpa. Future won't be long now. That's what I heard on the path. So I'm just staying put. Future'll find me when it's hungry. I'm ready. I just have to sit and wait. *(BEAT)*
FX: IN ANSWER COMES A DISTANT WOLF HOWL.
THE TRAIN ROAR OUT OF NOWHERE.
TRAIN CLAXON. TARDIS VWORP CUT BY A LURCHING SCREECH AND ALMIGHTY CRASH.

SCENE 20. MONORAIL BAGGAGE CAR.
FX: HUM OF THE TRAIN INTERIOR.
(PAUSE)
FX: THE TARDIS'S EXTERNAL DOOR OPENS. FOOTSTEPS AS THE DOCTOR & TURLOUGH EMERGE.

TURLOUGH: *(SARCASTIC)* Yes, Doctor. You're definitely getting better at these short jumps.
DOCTOR: Yes, as leapfrog manoeuvres go, that was rather nifty. Even if I say so myself.
TURLOUGH: And hardly any damage to the TARDIS at all.
DOCTOR: Thank you. *(TAKING IN THE SURROUNDINGS)* Baggage.
TURLOUGH: I'm sorry?
DOCTOR: It's a baggage car, Turlough. Albeit an empty one.
TURLOUGH: Very impressive. *(BEAT)* Quiet, isn't it?
DOCTOR: I just hope we're not too late.

SCENE 21. VICTOR'S APARTMENT.
FX: THE TRAIN RUSHES THROUGH. (A SORT OF AUDIO EQUIVALENT OF AN ESTABLISHING OR LINKING SHOT.)
THEN BACK TO TRAIN INTERIOR WITH A POSSIBLE BLEEPING LAB NOISE? A DOOR SLIDES OPEN.

HAYASHI: *(COMING IN)* Jura? I've got the go-ahead to keep this brute dosed up until we... *(PAUSE.)* Jura? Where are you now? *(SEES SOMETHING ALARMING.)* What's happened, you idiot?
FX: PULLS BACK BLANKET.
HAYASHI: *(SHOCKED)* Torn the restraints apart. Jura?! Where's Victor? Where are you?
FX: METAL DISH CLANGS TO THE FLOOR.
HAYASHI: Jura?

FX: *A LOW ANIMAL GROWL STARTS.*
HAYASHI: *(BACKING OFF)* Oh, no. Oh, no.
FX: *THE GROWL ERUPTS INTO A VULPINE SNARL.*
(HAYASHI YELLS.)
FX: *A CASCADE OF PANS & INSTRUMENTS HITS THE FLOOR.*

SCENE 22. ILEANA'S APARTMENT

ILEANA: It's all coming together, Inez. I've finally spoken to Tino.
INEZ: He took his time, Senhora.
ILEANA: Don't sound so surprised. There's a lot to prepare at the ranch. Inez, he says the others are already arriving.
INEZ: So soon?
ILEANA: Yes. Oh, don't look so despondent. This is extraordinary. Some of them are legends. Irnst Boxen of Morbach walked in out of the desert at noon. Followed by Selina of Greifswald.
INEZ: Selina? Heavens, however old must she be?
ILEANA: And the Misters Maugrim and Talbot. And Billy Redtooth of the Cherokee.
INEZ: Senhora, is this wise?
ILEANA: It's certainly dangerous. But I've considered it long enough. Isn't that what people do? Consider things. That has to be better than blind instinct. And so many lost souls have answered my call already.
INEZ: Are they lost? You may have to convince them of that.
ILEANA: If they can come so soon...
INEZ: Then so can the Grey One, Senhora.
ILEANA: That's why we left Rio. Jorge says we'll reach the old cattle station within three hours. And Tino will be there to meet us. We can't turn back now.
FX: *A DISTANT SCUFFLE APPROACHES. A DOOR SLIDES OPEN.*
HAYASHI: *(DISTRAUGHT)* Let go of me!
LICHTFUSS: Get back, cutclaw.
HAYASHI: Let me through! Senhora, I must see you.
ILEANA: What this?
HAYASHI: He's dead. I must speak to the Senhora!
ILEANA: Who's dead?
(HAYASHI GASPS IN PAIN)
HAYASHI: Put me down!
ILEANA: Lichtfuss! Put him down! Lichtfuss!
FX: *CLUMP AS HAYASHI HITS THE FLOOR.*
ILEANA: What does he want? Who's dead?
LICHTFUSS: Your son is missing.
ILEANA: Victor?
HAYASHI: *(PAINFULLY STANDING)* He's broken his restraints. And Jura has vanished!
LICHTFUSS: His assistant.
HAYASHI: There's blood everywhere.
ILEANA: Victor? Victor would never do that.
HAYASHI: He's a monster, isn't he? It's his nature. He has

devoured my assistant!

LICHTFUSS: *(STARTS TO LAUGH)* If only he had.

ILEANA: What has happened to my son?

INEZ: *(GASPS WITH SUDDEN FEAR)* Wait, all of you.
(BEAT) There. Do you catch it?

ILEANA: That scent again. The one we caught at the station.

LICHTFUSS: What is that?

INEZ: It smells like... No, that's absurd. You remember the
fields at Antwerp, where they harvested the white celery?

LICHTFUSS: That stranger...

ILEANA: *(SHARP)* No. Not him. It's the Grey One. He's with us.
Here on the train. He killed your assistant. And now he's stolen my
son!

SCENE 23. KITCHEN GALLEY

FX: THE TRAIN SHOOTS PAST.
INTERIOR SOUND. THE MUSIC TELLS US SOMETHING IS LURKING. WE
HEAR ITS GROWLED BREATHS. THEN IT STOPS, STARTLED AS WE
HEAR TURLOUGH AND THE DOCTOR IN THE DISTANCE.

TURLOUGH: It's the first train I've ever been on that had no
passengers or crew.

DOCTOR: It would be after your time that British Rail was
privatised.

FX: THE LURKER WITHDRAWS WITH A GROWL AS THEY APPROACH.

TURLOUGH: You mean it got worse?

DOCTOR: Oh, much.

FX: A METAL SPOON CLATTERS TO THE FLOOR.

TURLOUGH: *(WHISPER)* What was that?

DOCTOR: With luck, just a restless cheese and tomato roll.

TURLOUGH: This is the food galley. Not very sanitary, is it?

DOCTOR: No. And someone's left the meat store open. How
very careless... *(SEES SOMETHING NASTY)* Ah...

TURLOUGH: What is it?

DOCTOR: No, Turlough. That's not a good idea.

TURLOUGH: Why? What's going... Oh, no.

DOCTOR: Sorry, Turlough.

TURLOUGH: Horrible. His face.

DOCTOR: *(RESONANCE CHANGES AS HE WALKS INSIDE)* Yes.
It's a shock.

TURLOUGH: I should be used to... I mean, I've seen things... but
hung up there...

DOCTOR: I know.

TURLOUGH: With the other meat.

DOCTOR: *(EXAMINING THE CORPSE)* The ambient temperature
of this store must be about three degrees celsius. But he's still warm.
So it's a recent death.

TURLOUGH: I can tell that by the blood. Is this the body they
were carrying at the station?

DOCTOR: Hard to tell. He's of Asian origin. Nasty jagged
wounds. More like teeth marks.

TURLOUGH: Doctor?

DOCTOR: Probably caused by some sort of large carnivore.
TURLOUGH: In the corner, Doctor.
DOCTOR: Hmm? Oh, yes indeed. Quite like that.
TURLOUGH: Don't touch it.
DOCTOR: The severed head of a wolf. No, not quite a wolf. Bigger. Less vulpine, more...
TURLOUGH: Man like? His eyes are blue. What's it doing in a box? Looks as if it's been gift-wrapped.
DOCTOR: Was this what you saw at the Carnaval?
TURLOUGH: I don't know. What did *you* see at the station? *(BEAT)* Maybe we are too late. Maybe they've caught the killer already.
DOCTOR: No blood on its jaws. And it's cold. It's been dead a couple of days at least. Look at the neck. That wasn't severed neatly. The whole head's been bitten off.
TURLOUGH: By something bigger?
DOCTOR: *(CAUTIOUS)* Turlough, don't move.
TURLOUGH: What?
DOCTOR: Don't be surprised, but we are not alone. *(BRIGHTLY)* How do you do? I'm the Doctor...
TURLOUGH: Where? There's no one here.
DOCTOR: *(LESS OPTIMISTIC)*...and this is Turlough.
LICHTFUSS: Another bloody doctor, Jorge.
JORGE: Two lambs who strayed from the flock, Herr Lichtfuss.
LICHTFUSS: And this is not the way back to the sheepfold.
DOCTOR: Excuse me.
TURLOUGH: *(HALF LAUGHING)* Doctor, what are you doing?
DOCTOR: *(TESTILY)* Being polite. They're right in front of you. Can you really not see them?
TURLOUGH: Who?
DOCTOR: Then just stay still. Don't move.
(JORGE AND LICHTFUSS ARE CONSTANTLY MOVING ROUND THE DOCTOR AND TURLOUGH)
JORGE: *(SNIFFS)* You see? Celery. Inez was right. But all mixed up with... no, several sorts of musk. Like nothing I've ever caught before. Reminds me of places I've never heard of.
LICHTFUSS: *(ALSO SNIFFING)* He's no Grey One.
DOCTOR: Please take your hand off my coat. Ow! No need to be vicious.
JORGE: He's no cutclaw either. Neither's the other one.
TURLOUGH: *(BORED)* Well, sorry Doctor, but I can't see anyone.
DOCTOR: Neither of them?
TURLOUGH: Neither? How many of them are there?
JORGE: *(SNIFFING)* This one smells of... cooked meat. Horse meat? Maybe goat. But very old at any rate.
DOCTOR: Leave my friend alone, please. Turlough, they're playing with your perception. Just listen to me.
LICHTFUSS: The young one's more susceptible. What shall we do with him? Drive him off the train?
DOCTOR: I said, leave my friend alone. And let go of me!
JORGE: *(TO TURLOUGH'S LEFT)* RRRRRRRuff!
TURLOUGH: Agh! What is it? Who's there?

DOCTOR: Leave him alone. Turlough! I'm here!
JORGE: *(TO TURLOUGH'S RIGHT)* RRRuff. Go back!
(TURLOUGH GASPS)
DOCTOR: Look at me, Turlough.
TURLOUGH: I can't see you.
DOCTOR: Then listen. I'm over here.
TURLOUGH: Where? It's all foggy. Doctor, where are you? I can't see anyone!
FX: METAL CUTLERY CLATTERS DOWN.
(LICHTFUSS STARTS TO LAUGH)
DOCTOR: Don't try to look. Shut your eyes.
JORGE: *(TO TURLOUGH'S LEFT)* Go this way.
TURLOUGH: No!
JORGE: RRuff RRRuff. *(INSTANT MOVE TO TURLOUGH'S RIGHT)* Go that. *(CONTINUES RRUFFING ETC)*
TURLOUGH: No. Please! I can't stop myself.
DOCTOR: Shut your eyes and reach straight in front of you, Turlough. No, not that way!
LICHTFUSS: Yes, that way.
JORGE: RRuff. RRuff. Straight for the door.
FX:THE DOOR SLIDES OPEN. ROAR OF WIND AND RUSHING COUNTRYSIDE. A DOOR ALARM SOUNDS.
DOCTOR: Turlough! Crouch down! Then you can't move.
TURLOUGH: I must get away!
JORGE: Go on! Jump!
DOCTOR: Turlough, no!
FX: THE HOWL OF A WOLF CUTS THROUGH ALL THE TURMOIL.
LICHTFUSS: It's him! There he is!
JORGE: What?
LICHTFUSS: He's there! Along there. I saw him! *(HURRYING AWAY)* Leave these two.
(TURLOUGH COLLAPSES)
FX: THEY SCRAMBLE AWAY. THE DOOR CLOSES SHUTTING OUT THE ROW FROM OUTSIDE. THE ALARM STOPS.
DOCTOR: Turlough. Turlough, can you see me?
TURLOUGH: *(WOOZY)* Yes.
DOCTOR: Just go gently.
TURLOUGH: Think you were right about auto suggestion. Didn't have a thought in my head that was mine. Did I nearly jump off the train?
DOCTOR: Very nearly, yes.
TURLOUGH: Did you stop me?
DOCTOR: No, no, Turlough, I couldn't. They were putting the idea in your head. Fortunately they found something else more important to chase.
INEZ: They'll forget a fat sheep to go and chase a skinny rat.
(TURLOUGH JUMPS AS INEZ SPEAKS)
DOCTOR: Boa noite *(noyti)*, senhorita.
INEZ: Good evening, senhor. When their blood's up, a common flea could out-think them.
DOCTOR: Making people jump seems to be a habit round here.

33

I'm the Doctor and this is Turlough.
INEZ: Were you hurt?
DOCTOR: How considerate. Turlough? Are you hurt?
TURLOUGH: Only scarred mentally. Nothing that'll show.
INEZ: Senhor, my mistress wants to speak with you.
DOCTOR: Indeed. No doubt she's travelling First Class. With none of the annoying disadvantages that lesser passengers in Steerage have to suffer.
INEZ: She is waiting.

SCENE 24. TRAIN CARRIAGE
FX: CHANGE TO DIFFERENT TRAIN SOUND PERSPECTIVE. A DOOR SLIDES OPEN.

LICHTFUSS: Not a whiff of the Grey One, Jorge. No spoor, no fumet.
JORGE: Even he couldn't get far. Not if he's just eaten.
LICHTFUSS: That was Victor that we saw, not the Grey One.
JORGE: Your eyes are sharper than mine, Lichtfuss.
LICHTFUSS: And I'll warrant it was him who chewed up Hayashi's assistant.
JORGE: Poor little Victor. Still no change then. Stuck like that. He was a playful chap when he was a whelp. Had the run of the pampas. He used to love to fetch a ball.
LICHTFUSS: Before he got a taste for gaucho.
JORGE: Oh, his mother's too strict with him. It's no good trying to stifle his natural instincts. That's what's led to all this trouble in the first place.
LICHTFUSS: She has her instincts too. Why else do you think the Grey One has come?
JORGE: For Victor. That's what she said.
LICHTFUSS: He's come for her, not Victor. We all heard his call across the city. And we saw what happened to Kanu Choudhry.
JORGE: The Grey One. That's a dark name. The old stories say he's cunning.
LICHTFUSS: The First and Most Powerful. But would you know him if you smelt him?
JORGE: *(SUDDENLY AFRAID)* The strangers. Celery and goat chop.
LICHTFUSS: The ones we let go.
JORGE: But suppose one of them was the Grey One. In the stories, he's the master of shapes and delusion.
LICHTFUSS: That's very cunning indeed. Making us think we could throw them off the train. But if he's come for Ileana...
JORGE: Better hurry, mein herr. Before you lose your favours.

SCENE 25. VICTOR'S ROOM
FX: DOOR SLIDES OPEN.
(INEZ USHERS THE DOCTOR AND TURLOUGH INTO ILEANA AND HAYASHI'S PRESENCE.)
INEZ: This way, Senhores.

ILEANA:	*(SLOW BREATH)* Extraordinary...
DOCTOR:	How do you do, Senhora? I apologise for intruding on your privacy. I'm the Doctor and this is...
HAYASHI:	*(CUTTING IN)* Doctor?
DOCTOR:	...and this is Turlough, Senhora.
ILEANA:	Please come in both of you.
HAYASHI:	What sort of doctor?
DOCTOR:	Peripatetic. I travel a lot. Permanently on call, you might say. What about you, mister...?
HAYASHI:	Doctor Matsuo Hayashi. Consultant Therianthropist Practitioner, Institute of Genomic Surgery, Kamakura University.
DOCTOR:	Fascinating. And was this your equipment? Someone's made quite a mess of it.
ILEANA:	*(IRRITATED)* Doctor. I am Ileana de Santos. My late husband was owner of the Santos Cattle Empire.
DOCTOR:	Really. I think Turlough here is familiar with some of your produce.
TURLOUGH:	The dogs couldn't get enough of it.
DOCTOR:	And is this *your* private monorail? Where exactly is it heading?
HAYASHI:	How did you get on board?
DOCTOR:	Under my own steam.
ILEANA:	We saw you at the station, Doctor. Please explain why you are here.
DOCTOR:	We came to warn you. Though from the state of your surgery, I fear I may be overdue.
ILEANA:	What exactly did you want to warn us about?
DOCTOR:	I believe that there is a dangerous creature on board.
TURLOUGH:	Only one?
ILEANA:	Forgive us, Doctor. You find us in a state of some alarm. My son, who is an invalid, has disappeared. And I fear he has been abducted.
DOCTOR:	*(AWKWARD)* Ah. Then Senhora, I fear I may be the bringer of bad news. I'm afraid Turlough and I found a body in the galley three carriages back. In the fridge.
ILEANA:	In the fridge?
DOCTOR:	A young Asian man with black hair and a white lab coat.... what was left of it.
HAYASHI:	Jura!
ILEANA:	Oh, thank God.
HAYASHI:	I told the little idiot to be careful. Now what am I going to tell the faculty!
DOCTOR:	Then I assume this wasn't your son.
ILEANA:	No, no, not Victor.
TURLOUGH:	He was badly savaged.
HAYASHI:	Jura is... *was* my assistant. Regrettably, a very careless one.
TURLOUGH:	*(MUTTERING)* Doctor, what about the wolf head?
DOCTOR:	Never mind that now. *(TO HAYASHI)* Perhaps we should verify his identity. I think you should come and see for yourself.
HAYASHI:	No, no, I take your word for it.
ILEANA:	This is appalling. The young man was nursing my

son. Obviously he was attacked when Victor was abducted.

TURLOUGH: Just like we were attacked.

ILEANA: He attacked you? You saw him?

TURLOUGH: Well, not exactly.

DOCTOR: I saw something. It burst in on us. Drew the others off.

ILEANA: Yes?

DOCTOR: A large animal, but walking upright like a man. At a rough guess I'd call him a therianthropic metamorph. But then lycanthropy comes in so many shapes and sizes, doesn't it? Weresharks, werepards, werewolves... What did you say your son was suffering from?

TURLOUGH: At the station, Doctor...

DOCTOR: Hmm?

TURLOUGH: We saw it at the station too. That shape running after the train. Like a wolf.

ILEANA: What did you see? Was it grey?

DOCTOR: Yes, grey and *very* large. Almost unfeasibly large, actually. That's why we came. Although the wolf we saw on the train, the one that drew off your associates when they attacked us... I think that one was brown. And much smaller. More of a prairie than a timber wolf.

ILEANA: Inez!

DOCTOR: Yes, definitely brown. Like the hairs here on this bed.

FX: DOOR SLIDES OPEN.

INEZ: Senhora?

ILEANA: Inez, find Lichtfuss and Jorge.

INEZ: Yes, Senhora.

ILEANA: No. Find Victor first!

INEZ: Senhora.

FX: THE DOOR SLIDES SHUT

DOCTOR: Senhora, I'd like to help.

HAYASHI: Senhora de Santos's son is extremely ill. He needs constant medical attention. Which only I can provide.

DOCTOR: With metal vices and a straight jacket? That's a pretty extreme form of medication.

ILEANA: Who are you? Why make us your business?

DOCTOR: I sensed danger, Senhora. That's why I came to help. Of course, if you'd rather, we could just stop the train and send for the Policia.

SCENE 26. TRAIN CARRIAGE

FX: THE TRAIN HURTLES PAST.
FX: TRAIN INTERIOR BACKGROUND.

LICHTFUSS: *(MENACING)* What did this Doctor say then?

INEZ: He said he saw the Grey One... at the station.

LICHTFUSS: And?

INEZ: He came to warn the Senhora about it.

JORGE: You said *he* was the Grey One, Lichtfuss.

LICHTFUSS: *You* said he was cunning. He's lying, that's all.

JORGE: Suppose he knows we think he's lying. He could be telling the truth, so we'd never know. Now that's really cunning.

36

INEZ: Idiots. The springtime's stolen your wits. The Doctor isn't the Grey One and the Senhora knows it.
LICHTFUSS: And you know that it was Victor who did for Hayashi's assistant.
INEZ: Of course I do. But who's going to dare tell the Senhora that?
LICHTFUSS: This Doctor, with a bit of luck. We all know why he's sniffing round her.
INEZ: That's as clear as a frosty night. He wants her.
JORGE: But he's a cutclaw.
INEZ: He's not her first.
LICHTFUSS: *(GROWLS A LITTLE)* What did she do? *(BEAT)* Tell me! *(INEZ GASPS IN PAIN)* Tell me, Inez, or I'll bite off your ears! *(INEZ BITES LICHTFUSS. HE YELPS.)*
LICHTFUSS: Agh! You little bitch!
(JORGE LAUGHS)
INEZ: Oh, she's interested, mein herr. Oh, yes. She said, this Doctor's worth more than the whole Santos Empire.
LICHTFUSS: She wouldn't dare.
INEZ: As for mein Herr Lichtfuss. She says he can crawl back to the backwoods where he belongs and hunt for beetles!
(LICHTFUSS LASHES OUT WITH A SNARL. INEZ CRIES OUT IN PAIN.)
LICHTFUSS: That'll teach you to listen at doors! Never insult your mistress again!
JORGE: What about the cutclaws?
LICHTFUSS: Easily dealt with. And maybe the Grey One's just an old story to frighten puppies. There's only one way to win the Senhora's favours. I must restore her wandering son.

SCENE 27. ILEANA'S CARRIAGE
FX: TRAIN BACKGROUND. VIDLINK BLEEPING INSISTENTLY.

ILEANA: *(QUIETLY TERRIFIED)* Pieter Stubbe. Leave me alone. Go away.
FX: BLEEPING ENDS WITH A CLICK. THE OPENED LINE BUZZES SLIGHTLY WITH VARYING RECEPTION.
STUBBE: *(ON LINK)* Ileana? Is that you? Can you see me too? *(BEAT)* I missed my welcome, Ileana, so I *persuaded* a cutclaw to show me how to use this device.
ILEANA: I have nothing to say to you.
STUBBE: What's the matter? You look like a dog with a docked tail. *(LAUGHS COARSELY)* I hardly knew you. The merchant's daughter become quite the merchant's wife. Very tamed and domesticated. And doting on your half-cutclaw whelp.
ILEANA: Leave my son alone! It was my choice. You never gave me a choice.
STUBBE: What about our times together? Remember the snowy forests and the mountains? Chasing the sledges for sport. That was an ocean away from this dust-choked, ill-gotten desert. In those days you had eyes and ears for me alone. No one else. Even now, when you're running, you can't look away.
ILEANA: You'll never touch me again. You won't find me. I'm

gone.

STUBBE: I'm closer than you think. *(BEAT)* How many other suitors are panting round you now? One less at any rate. He whimpered like a beaten mongrel before I relieved him of his head. Tell your other admirers they'll get the same. *(BEAT)* Still nothing to say? Pah! I hate to talk to someone I can't smell. Keep running, Ileana. However fast you run. I'll run faster...

FX: THE LINK CLICKS OFF.

ILEANA: Leave me alone. Monster.

SCENE 28. TRAIN CORRIDOR

(TURLOUGH AND THE DOCTOR SEARCHING)

TURLOUGH: Doctor? I saw something out there. Doctor?
DOCTOR: Patience, Turlough.
TURLOUGH: I saw something from the window.
(THE DOCTOR CROSSES TO THE WINDOW.)
DOCTOR: It's a bit dark to see anything. Just desert and the ghosts of dead trees.
TURLOUGH: No. In the moonlight. Something running along through the scrub. Some sort of big animal. *Very* big.
DOCTOR: There's bound to be some wildlife still out there. Struggling to survive after the death of the forest.
TURLOUGH: How fast are we going?
DOCTOR: About two hundred miles an hour.
TURLOUGH: We can't be.
DOCTOR: Perhaps a little more. Why?
TURLOUGH: Because it was keeping pace with the train. And then it veered off. It was going even faster. Doctor, it was the grey wolf we saw at the station.
DOCTOR: Stay here.
TURLOUGH: Where are you going?
DOCTOR: *(DEPARTING)* To speak to our hostess.
TURLOUGH: Doctor! Come back! *(GIVES UP)* Don't leave me here. Not in the middle of a pack of werewolves.
(PAUSE)
JORGE: Closer than he thinks.
LICHTFUSS: Look at those eyes. He'd see us if he wanted to.
JORGE: An orphan cub if ever I smelt one.
TURLOUGH: Who's there?
LICHTFUSS: He'd see a lot of things if he looked. Both outside and in.
JORGE: What a waste if we didn't show him his potential.
TURLOUGH: Where are you? I know you're here.
(TURLOUGH IS GRABBED. A HAND COVERS HIS MOUTH. HE STRUGGLES.)
LICHTFUSS: See us now, young master? Time we woke you up. We have to catch a wild dog. And you're just the bait we need to help us.

SCENE 29. ILEANA'S ROOM

(THE DOCTOR CONFRONTS ILEANA)
FX: CARRIAGE DOOR OPENS.

DOCTOR: *(ENTERING WITH URGENCY)* Senhora, I want to stop the train.

ILEANA: Impossible. Jorge has programmed the journey into the drive system.

DOCTOR: There must be a failsafe way to stop it.

ILEANA: Nothing can override the programme until we reach our destination.

DOCTOR: And then what happens to Turlough and me?

ILEANA: I haven't decided.

DOCTOR: Forgive me. You're concerned about your son. In fact, you seem beset by troubles.

ILEANA: Danger has always walked with me, Doctor. It's my oldest and most faithful companion.

DOCTOR: But sometimes it comes and looks you in the face.

ILEANA: And are you another danger?

DOCTOR: I couldn't say, Senhora. I leave it up to you. But I do like to be surprising.

ILEANA: I think you already know what I have to tell you.

DOCTOR: That your son is a wolf. Yes, I know.

ILEANA: And that he takes after his mother.

DOCTOR: I've never known a mother who wasn't proud of her son.

ILEANA: Proud? How can you think that? It's the very curse of my long, long existence. Proud! No, never.

DOCTOR: I remain to be convinced. And what about your husband?

ILEANA: Federico was a Cariocan. Rio was his city. For forty-two years he cared for me, driving back the shadows that surround me. But as you see, I do not age as he did. Victor was the son that he craved above all his wealth, his land, his empire.

DOCTOR: He didn't know about Victor's condition?

ILEANA: Oh, yes. But Federico never questioned, just accepted. All his life he was plagued by guilt over the ruin that he said his business, the ranches and cattle, brought to the great forest. But he never ceased to love us.

DOCTOR: And Victor?

ILEANA: Like all children he rebels. But now he has no human father, his wolf inheritance has taken hold.

DOCTOR: And he cannot change back.

ILEANA: No.

DOCTOR: I'd say he makes a handsome wolf.

ILEANA: It waxes and wanes in all of us. But poor Victor has no light left. He's all instinct. Like the dusk, the shadows of the past lengthen around us.

DOCTOR: And one particular grey shadow pursues you.

ILEANA: The Grey One. Pieter Stubbe. Undying and always hungry. I've been bound to him and his darkness for longer than you could ever imagine.

DOCTOR: I think you'd be surprised. One hundred? Two hundred years?

ILEANA: How can you possibly know that?

DOCTOR: Time is my business. Well, one of my businesses. But please, I'm stopping your story.

ILEANA: My father was a merchant from Smolensk. Quite rich, with land and serfs.

DOCTOR: Imperial Russia. Let me guess. First half of the nineteenth century.

ILEANA: The summer of eighteen hundred and twelve.

DOCTOR: The year of Napoleon's futile invasion. And stormy weather too, as I remember.

ILEANA: Do you? *(BEAT)* We were fleeing the advancing French, but our carts ran into bandits. We lost all our belongings. And my father was shot.

DOCTOR: And then you were rescued by a wolf.

ILEANA: By a handsome partisan, who turned out to be a wolf.

DOCTOR: And he brought out all the wildness in you.

ILEANA: And the dark. Oh, Doctor, it seems that however far I chase the sun, the oncoming night and the moon are always baying at the door behind me. They never let me rest.

DOCTOR: Ileana, suppose the shadow reaches your destination before you do?

SCENE 30. THE DESERT.

FX: CROSS FADE TO EXTERIOR. WIND MOANS GENTLY, BUT ROSA IS SHELTERED. THE CLICK OF HER RECORDER. BUT THIS TIME WE HEAR HER, NOT HER RECORDING.

ROSA: You said it never got cold, Grandpa. Not in the old days. But Jeez, the wind's sharp tonight. Reckon you could slice meat with it.

FX: OPENS A CAN OF COKE.

ROSA: And the moon's strong. No one to talk to. Just me and the dust devils.

STUBBE: Good day, young lady.

FX: CLATTER OF DROPPED CAN AS ROSA JUMPS.

ROSA: Jeezuz!

(HER BREATH COMES IN TERRIFIED STACCATO BURSTS.)

STUBBE: Whither away? So close to the silver path.

ROSA: *(TERRIFIED)* Wither away, yerself. And it's not day. It's way past midnight.

STUBBE: Once this desert was a mighty forest.

ROSA: Too right. They took it away. Like they take everything.

STUBBE: And left the dust. Is that meat you have there?

ROSA: Just a 'dillo I whistled up.

STUBBE: Cooked him in his shell?

ROSA: Maybe.

STUBBE: *(COMING CLOSER)* Give me some. I've come a long, long way without food.

ROSA: Get your own.

STUBBE: Just one morsel for a lonely traveller.

ROSA: Back off, lobo. Go scavenging some place else.

STUBBE: Oh, but there's a wicked fate that waits for greedy girls. Girls who can't spare a bite for a wandering soul. *(MENACING)*

Just one bite.

ROSA: I said, back away. I know what you are, loup-garou. *(STUBBE GROWLS.)*

ROSA: See this knife. Pure silver, yeah? My grandpa made it out of silver from the mines under the dead forest. And it'll take a bite out of you before you bite me.

STUBBE: *(LAUGHS)* Little girl, your claws need cutting. Stay by your silver path, then. But don't stray, because one night I'll be waiting round the next corner and I'll still be hungry.

ROSA: I won't forget.

STUBBE: *(DEPARTING)* Gute nacht, meine liebchen.

FX: THE WIND IS RISING.

ROSA: *(FADING INTO DISTANCE)* Tchau, Senhor Wolf.

(AND WE CARRY STRAIGHT INTO...)

SCENE 31. THE DESERT

FX: THE WIND CONTINUES. AFTER A MOMENT, A NUMBER IS TAPPED OUT ON A MOBILE VIDLINK PHONE. A CLICK AS IT GETS ANSWERED.

HAYASHI: *(ON LINE)* Stubbe? Returning my call at last?

STUBBE: I don't come to your whistle, Hayashi. What's your news?

HAYASHI: We're not far from our destination.

STUBBE: Rancho de Santos?

HAYASHI: I assume so. But her son's running loose on the train.

STUBBE: *(LAUGHS)* So much for Ileana's house-training.

HAYASHI: And there are strangers too. A so-called Doctor and his assistant.

STUBBE: Those two again. They run fast for a brace of cutclaw footpads.

HAYASHI: The Senhora seemed most taken with the Doctor.

STUBBE: That's no matter. Ileana can coax as many suitors as she likes. Once I'm back with her, she'll soon forget the panting of a few lovesick poodles. And I'll leave their carcasses to feed the desert dogs.

SCENE 32. TRAIN COMPARTMENT

FX: FADE WIND INTO TRAIN INTERIOR. A DOOR SLIDES SHUT.

TURLOUGH: When are you going to tear me apart? Isn't that what werewolves do?

LICHTFUSS: Don't believe everything you see in old films.

JORGE: Or hear in old stories. *(Note - Obviously no one reads anymore)*

TURLOUGH: Right.

LICHTFUSS: Do we look like ravening monsters?

TURLOUGH: What about the wolf-man I saw?

LICHTFUSS: Sometimes the darker side tips the scales. Nothing to be ashamed of.

JORGE: And *werewolf* is a cutclaw name. I've always found it deeply offensive.

LICHTFUSS: But it's important to make amends. Jorge, a drink for

41

our guest.

TURLOUGH: Sorry?

LICHTFUSS: We wanted to know more about you.

JORGE: Once we realised you were more than just human...

TURLOUGH: Thanks very much. So trying to throw me off the train was fine when I was just pond life.

JORGE: A drink.

TURLOUGH: Thank you. *(DRINKS)*

LICHTFUSS: Humans are just cattle to us. They're cutclaws. Over the years they've forcibly subdued their darker instincts.

JORGE: They've dulled their wits.

TURLOUGH: Tell me about it. Sometimes I thought I'd drown in their stupidity.

LICHTFUSS: Yes, yes. We knew you'd understand. Haven't you always felt that you were different.

TURLOUGH: Superior. I always knew that. What's in this stuff?

JORGE: More?

TURLOUGH: It's good. And the Doctor doesn't have to know, does he? *(MIMICKING THE DOCTOR) Turlough, are you sure that's wise?* *(GIGGLES)* Oh, I suppose he means well.

LICHTFUSS: But you've always felt alone. That you didn't belong.

TURLOUGH: *(SLIGHTLY TIPSY)* More than that. I'm special. I never, ever got the respect I deserved. What about all that stuff with howling and the full moon?

JORGE: Just another half-truth overblown by Hollywood.

TURLOUGH: Yes?

JORGE: Oh, yes.

LICHTFUSS: But Turlough, you have another side that no one else recognised. Look in the mirror. See for yourself.

TURLOUGH: What? Uh, I look a wreck.

LICHTFUSS: Keep looking. Look hard.

TURLOUGH: Better than a dull-witted human though. *(RAMBLING)* You know what? Wits are like claws. You have to keep them sharp.

LICHTFUSS: Look through yourself. Look at the real Turlough behind you. What do you want to see?

TURLOUGH: No. No, not cut*claws*. Cut-*throats*! *(STARTS LAUGHING)*

LICHTFUSS: Look harder!

TURLOUGH: *(STILL LAUGHING)* The old ones are the best!

JORGE: What do you *want* to see?

LICHTFUSS: What ***don't*** you want to see?

JORGE: What doesn't he want ***us*** to see?

LICHTFUSS: Keep looking.

TURLOUGH: *(GASPS. SUDDENLY AFRAID.)* No! What is it?

LICHTFUSS: You tell us, Turlough.

TURLOUGH: It's behind me! Make it go away! Take it away!

LICHTFUSS: Odd, isn't it? We're all of us surprised the first time we see the truth.

SCENE 33. VICTOR'S ROOM

(HAYASHI TALKING TO STUBBE ON THE VIDLINK)

42

HAYASHI: *(NERVOUS)* Five million, Mr Stubbe. You said I should name my price.

STUBBE: *(ON VIDLINK)* Five million what? Is this money that you're talking about, Hayashi?

HAYASHI: Yes, you said once I'd finished...

STUBBE: I swallowed a tax gatherer once. Joshua of Darmstadt. Swallowed him whole. Never again. I was spitting coins for days afterwards.

DOCTOR: *(DISTANT)* Well, he must be here somewhere...

STUBBE: And you want money. *(HE LAUGHS AT THIS FOOLISHNESS)*

HAYASHI: *(PANICKED WHISPER)* They're coming! I'll call you back.

FX: SCREEN OFF.

HAYASHI: *(OVER COMPENSATING)* Senhora. Is there any sign of your son?

ILEANA: No trace or trail.

DOCTOR: And now my companion has disappeared as well. I don't suppose he wandered this way.

HAYASHI: I've seen no one. So sorry.

ILEANA: Who were you speaking to?

HAYASHI: Speaking?

DOCTOR: On the vidlink, when we came in.

HAYASHI: Oh, that. The university. To my faculty. I was trying to explain about Jura.

ILEANA: I told you to speak to no one while you are in my service!

HAYASHI: My apologies. *(POINTEDLY)* It was a bad link with a lot of interference.

ILEANA: Hayashi, when my son is found, I want you to share your diagnoses with the Doctor here. *(BEAT)* I'm sure he can be of assistance to you.

DOCTOR: Just think of me as a complete novice.

HAYASHI: *(COLD)* I'm sure not. *(SMARM)* I bow to your obvious superior experience, Doctor... san.

DOCTOR: *(RESPONDING IN KIND)* And I to yours, Hayashi... san. Perhaps we could start by checking the damage to your equipment.

ILEANA: *(QUIET)* Don't move, either of you.

HAYASHI: What's that?

ILEANA: Don't move. Outside the window. Hanging down.

FX: WE HEAR VICTOR GROWLING OUTSIDE THE TRAIN, AND HIS CLAWS TAPPING ON THE WINDOW.

DOCTOR: Your son, I take it.

HAYASHI: He's on the roof. He'll be swept off.

ILEANA: Victor. Victor, listen to me...

DOCTOR: He's fully transformed. A complete lycanthropic metamorphosis.

ILEANA: Victor, please come in. It's safe. They won't hurt you. I won't let them. Victor, please...

DOCTOR: Stay here, Hayashi.

HAYASHI: What are you doing? He's *my* patient.

ILEANA: He's slipping! Victor, hold on!

DOCTOR: Hold my coat. I'm going out after him.
HAYASHI: You're mad. Senhora, stop this maniac.
ILEANA: Don't move, either of you. You'll frighten him.
FX: SNARL FROM OUTSIDE. A TREMENDOUS SHATTERING OF GLASS.
THE ROAR OF THE TRAIN FROM OUTSIDE. VICTOR THUMPS THROUGH
INSIDE. HE SNARLS ANGRILY. HAYASHI YELLS.

SCENE 34. TRAIN COMPARTMENT

TURLOUGH: Stop it staring! Make it go away!
FX: DOOR OPENS.
INEZ: *(SURPRISED)* What's happening? Lichtfuss, what are
you doing now?
LICHTFUSS: Just enlightening our young guest, Inez. Don't say
you didn't notice Turlough's potential.
INEZ: You're supposed to be looking for Victor.
LICHTFUSS: Victor can't get far. And this could help.
INEZ: What will help?
TURLOUGH: *(SHIVERING)* It's there. Behind me. Make it stop
staring at me.
INEZ: What are you doing to him?
LICHTFUSS: Just getting another gift for the Senhora.
JORGE: *(GENTLY)* Turlough? We didn't *force* you to look in
the mirror, did we?
TURLOUGH: Please. Make it stop.
INEZ: Not the mirror trick. It's all a game, isn't it? Haven't
you learnt yet? An awakening should be a precious, sacred moment. Not
something for your amusement.
JORGE: Once he started, we could hardly stop him.
LICHTFUSS: Turlough, tell us what you can see.
TURLOUGH: *(WHISPER)* It's there. Behind me. A blood red
shadow. Is it my shadow? It has burning golden eyes.
(HE STARTS TO MAKE LOW GROWLS.)
INEZ: Are you both mad? He'll be scarred for life. Centuries
of misery. Stop it now.
LICHTFUSS: Don't touch him!
INEZ: Idiots! I'm going to fetch the Senhora.
TURLOUGH: *(SUDDEN YELL)* No! Stop it! Help me! It's trying to
push in front! Help me! Doctor!
FX: HE BARRELS PAST THE OTHERS.
(LIGHTFUSS BURSTS OUT LAUGHING)
INEZ: Idiots! Stop him! Get him back!

SCENE 35. VICTOR'S ROOM
FX: AS BEFORE. ROAR OF WIND FROM THE SMASHED WINDOW.
VICTOR IS GROWLING MENACINGLY. THE OTHERS ARE BUNCHED
TOGETHER TRAPPED BY THE BRUTE.

ILEANA: Victor, liebchen. No need to be afraid. Look, no one's
going to hurt you.
FX: VICTOR SNARLS.
ILEANA: It's alright, little one. It's alright. Come to me.

HAYASHI: (MUTTERING) If she calms him, I may be able to reach my tranquilliser gun.
FX: ANOTHER SNARL.
ILEANA: Victor.
DOCTOR: Bad idea, Hayashi. Senhora, do you want us to leave?
HAYASHI: You can't leave her alone with him.
DOCTOR: She's his mother. Who better?
ILEANA: Yes. Yes, please back off slowly. Look Victor, liebchen, we're nearly home. No more train. No more upset.
FX: VICTOR'S GROWL DWINDLES TO A GRUMBLE.
ILEANA: That's right. There we are. That's it. (HE SNUGGLES IN.) Oh, my dear one. Come and nuzzle. That's it. Good. There we are. There we are.
FX: DOOR SLIDES OPEN.
TURLOUGH: Doctor! Help me!
DOCTOR: Turlough!
FX: VICTOR IS UP WITH A SNARL.
TURLOUGH: Agh! That's it! It's here! It's waiting for me! Get it away from me!
FX: VICTOR ROARS. A FIZZED GUN SHOT. VICTOR COLLAPSES WITH AN ANGUISHED ROAR.
ILEANA: Victor!
HAYASHI: (SATISFIED) First shot.
DOCTOR: Turlough, get away from the window!
FX: BRING UP RUSHING WIND.
TURLOUGH: It's coming after me!
DOCTOR: What's coming after you?
TURLOUGH: My shadow! And you can't stop it either! I have to get away!
(HIS FALLING SCREAM VANISHES INTO THE DISTANCE.)
DOCTOR: Turlough!
FX: HOLD THE WIND ROAR AT LOUD FOR A MOMENT. THEN BRING IT DOWN A LITTLE, AS IF THE DOCTOR HAS DUCKED BACK INSIDE.
DOCTOR: (ROUNDING ON ILEANA) Ileana, stop the train now!
ILEANA: My son has been shot!
DOCTOR: Turlough's fallen from the window! Stop the train, please!
ILEANA: I don't care! My son is dying!
HAYASHI: Senhora, it was a tranquilliser shot.
ILEANA: (VOICE DEEPENING) Murderer. (SHE STARTS A LOW GROWL AS THE WOLF IN HER SURFACES)
HAYASHI: (BACKING OFF IN FRIGHT) No. It was a tranquilliser. Just to calm him. Please, Senhora. Control yourself!
(ILEANA'S GROWL CONTINUES)
ILEANA: Murdering cutclaw. I'll drive you off this train!
DOCTOR: Ileana, listen! Your son is perfectly safe.
HAYASHI: She's changing... Keep her away from me!
DOCTOR: Ileana!
(HAYASHI SQUEALS AS ILEANA SNAPS AGAIN AND AGAIN, DRIVING HIM ACROSS THE CARRIAGE.)
HAYASHI: She'll kill us all!
CLOSING MUSIC.

PART THREE

SCENE 36. VICTOR'S APARTMENT.
FX: TRAIN NOISE. ROAR OF WIND FROM THE SMASHED WINDOW.
(TURLOUGH'S FALLING SCREAM VANISHES INTO THE DISTANCE.)
FX: TRAIN SOUND UP LOUD.

DOCTOR: Turlough!
*FX: HOLD THE WIND ROAR AT LOUD FOR A MOMENT. THEN BRING IT
DOWN A LITTLE, AS IF THE DOCTOR HAS DUCKED BACK INSIDE.*
DOCTOR: *(ROUNDING ON ILEANA)* Ileana, stop the train now!
ILEANA: My son has been shot!
DOCTOR: Turlough's fallen from the window! Stop the train,
please!
ILEANA: I don't care! My son is dying!
HAYASHI: Senhora, it was a tranquiliser shot.
ILEANA: *(VOICE DEEPENING)* Murderer. *(SHE STARTS A LOW
GROWL AS THE WOLF IN HER SURFACES)*
HAYASHI: *(BACKING OFF IN FRIGHT)* No. It was a tranquiliser.
Just to calm him. Please, Senhora. Control yourself!
(ILEANA'S GROWL CONTINUES)
ILEANA: Murdering cutclaw. I'll drive you off this train!
DOCTOR: Ileana, listen! Your son is perfectly safe.
HAYASHI: She's changing... Keep her away from me!
DOCTOR: Ileana!
HAYASHI: She'll kill us all!
*(HAYASHI SQUEALS AS ILEANA SNAPS AGAIN AND AGAIN, DRIVING
HIM ACROSS THE CARRIAGE.)*
DOCTOR: *(THROUGH THE RUMPUS)* Ileana! Remember who you
are. Don't give in to your baser instincts. *(HE GRABS HER. THEY
STRUGGLE)* I'm asking you to stop this train now. Ileana! Stop the
train! For Victor's sake!
*(ILEANA GASPS AND SHE BREAKS FREE. HAYASHI FALLS OVER,
GASPING FOR AIR. ILEANA'S VOICE LIGHTENS AGAIN, BUT SHE'S
ASHAMED.)*
ILEANA: Don't ever give me orders.
DOCTOR: Stop the train, please.
ILEANA: I will not.
DOCTOR: *(LEAVING)* Then I'll do it myself!
ILEANA: Doctor!
(BEAT)
DOCTOR: *(BACK CLOSE. QUIETLY)* Yes.
ILEANA: The train's already slowing. We're almost at our
destination.
DOCTOR: Then I have to find Turlough. He may be badly hurt.
(TO HAYASHI) Hayashi? Are you alright?
HAYASHI: *(SHAKEN)* Yes, yes. Just an occupational hazard.
DOCTOR: Good man.
ILEANA: Doctor, I need you. *(AFTERTHOUGHT)* For Victor.
DOCTOR: I'm sure Hayashi can cope. Like tomato sauce, money
also covers a multitude of sins.

46

ILEANA:	Please, Doctor. Others are coming to meet us.
DOCTOR:	Others like you?
ILEANA:	It's for your own safety. You'll find I pay very well.
DOCTOR:	*(ANNOYED)* Discussing money's very vulgar, don't

you think? Just the sort of thing humans do. Besides, my fees are non-negotiable. I want Turlough safely back.

ILEANA:	We'll find him, Doctor. I promise. Just please stay.

(BEAT)

DOCTOR:	*(COLDLY)* Hayashi, shouldn't we be attending to the

Senhora's son?

ILEANA:	Thank you, Doctor.

SCENE 37. THE AMAZON DESERT.
FX: NIGHT CRICKETS CHIRPING CLOSE BY.
(ROSA WHISTLES. A REPEATED RISING NOTE AS IF SHE'S CALLING A DOG.)

ROSA:	*(COAXING, HALF ALOUD, AS IF SHE'S AFRAID*

WHAT ELSE SHE MIGHT CALL UP.) Hey, 'dillo. 'dillo, 'dillo. *(WHISTLE, WHISTLE.)* Hey. Come on out. Out you come.
FX: SCRUBBY BUSHES PUSHED ROUGHLY ASIDE.
(TURLOUGH STUMBLES THROUGH BREATHING HEAVILY.)
FX: THE SNAP OF A TRAP SHUTTING.
(TURLOUGH YELPS IN PAIN AND FALLS OVER.)

TURLOUGH:	Help! Help me!
ROSA:	*(LAUGHS)* Jeez! That trap ain't meant for nothing

bigger than a 'dillo.

TURLOUGH:	Get me out of this thing!

FX: ROSA JUMPS DOWN & CROUCHES BESIDE HIM.

ROSA:	Someone chasing you?
TURLOUGH:	*(CATCHES HIS BREATH)* You could say that. Please,

just get this thing off me.

ROSA:	What you doing out here? No one comes out here.

You a yerp?

TURLOUGH:	What?
ROSA:	A Euro. East? West? Indie Brit?
TURLOUGH:	Adopted British... I suppose.
ROSA:	*(SHRUG)* Figures. Okay, you're no lobo. Hold still.
TURLOUGH:	What're you doing?

FX: SHE SAWS AT ROPE WITH A KNIFE.

ROSA:	Cutting you free. There.

FX: THE ROPE GIVES.

TURLOUGH:	*(SIGH OF RELIEF)* Thanks.
ROSA:	It's an okay blade. One day it'll cut better things than

rope. So how'd you get here?

TURLOUGH:	It doesn't matter.
ROSA:	Okay. You better cover your tracks before you move

on.

TURLOUGH:	Move on? Can't you take me to the nearest

settlement?

ROSA:	I ain't no taxi rank. It's ten miles that way to the

Mission House, so get going, yerpi-boy. I gotta wait here. Gotta hot date with a hungry wolf.

TURLOUGH: (*FRIGHTENED*) A wolf? Out here? By yourself?
ROSA: Get your own fight. This one's mine.
TURLOUGH: A kid like you? Who the hell do you think are?
ROSA: I'm Rosa Caiman. Who the hell are you?

SCENE 38. THE TRAIN. ILEANA'S APARTMENT.
(*LICHTFUSS AND ILEANA*)
FX: *THE TRAIN IS SLOWLY RUNNING DOWN. A DOOR SLIDES OPEN.*

ILEANA: Anton, where've you been?
LICHTFUSS: You nearly lost control, Ileana.
ILEANA: (*TAKEN ABACK*) You were listening.
LICHTFUSS: Mind your cutclaw guests don't see the real Ileana de Santos. They frighten easily.
ILEANA: They already know. And you could have helped, instead of skulking outside the door.
LICHTFUSS: It's up to the leader to fight her own battles.
ILEANA: That depends on who starts them. At least I wasn't frightening Turlough into throwing himself off the train.
LICHTFUSS: Just the old mirror trick. Making him face up to his own dark side. He didn't like what he saw.
(*BEAT*)
ILEANA: We're nearly at the old cattle station. You must help unload the trucks. Tino will be there to escort us to the ranch.
LICHTFUSS: Where we meet all the others that you've summoned.
ILEANA: Yes. Some of the oldest and wildest of our kind. All united at last.
LICHTFUSS: And how will they react to your new acquaintance, the Doctor?
ILEANA: (*SHARP*) We have to prepare the convoy and move Victor. And Turlough has to be found.
LICHTFUSS: (*THREATENING*) What does this Doctor mean to you?
ILEANA: Ah, so that's it. Just leave the Doctor alone. He's no threat to you.
LICHTFUSS: He reeks of death.
ILEANA: So do you, Anton.
LICHTFUSS: (*DRAWING CLOSE*) And that excites you?
ILEANA: I'm sick of it. The Doctor is strange... a maverick. I tried to look into his mind, but he shook off my thoughts like raindrops.
LICHTFUSS: (*ANGRY*) You're mad. Entrusting your precious son to this stranger.
ILEANA: The Doctor respects and understands us... whatever he is.
LICHTFUSS: Then we'll see what the others say when they hear about him. Don't forget, common werewolves learn to bite before they can talk.

SCENE 39. HAYASHI'S ROOM
(*THE DOCTOR AND HAYASHI MOVING EQUIPMENT.*)
FX: *THE TRAIN ENGINES ARE NOTICEABLY SLOWING.*

HAYASHI: We're definitely slowing down.
DOCTOR: But still getting further away from Turlough.
HAYASHI: Help me move the scanning unit into its crate.
DOCTOR: Right.
FX: MANHANDLING A LARGE PIECE OF EQUIPMENT.
(BOTH STRAIN UNDER THE MACHINE'S WEIGHT)
HAYASHI: Towards me.
DOCTOR: Yes.
HAYASHI: They will find... your companion, you know.
DOCTOR: I don't doubt it... It's his condition... that worries me.
FX: MACHINE CLUNKS DOWN.
HAYASHI: Thank you, Doctor.
DOCTOR: That's alright. Turlough was terrified before he jumped. I think the Senhora's friends were having a game with him.
HAYASHI: If you interpret viciousness as play. Time to move Victor, I think.
DOCTOR: They seem to see humans as some sort of toy.
HAYASHI: Truer than you may think.
DOCTOR: Hayashi? What are you working on?
HAYASHI: The Senhora approached me to find a cure for her son.
DOCTOR: Because he's stuck in the form of a wolf and can't change back? Even when the moon's not full?
HAYASHI: The moon has nothing to do with it.
DOCTOR: You've made an extensive study, of course. *(BEAT)* Hayashi, I'm not going to steal your thunder.
HAYASHI: Do you think I could throw away the chance to work on live werewolf? Look at this poor brute. He's a creature of legend. A fabulous monster, unknown to science.
DOCTOR: Only because his kind are so adept at going unnoticed. This ability to wipe the selective awareness of humans. It's very clever. They're as good as invisible.
HAYASHI: But you see them.
DOCTOR: Nobody's perfect. His pulse is very sluggish. What sort of medication are you giving him?
HAYASHI: *(SHARP)* Please! *(REGAINING COMPOSURE)* Please don't touch that.
DOCTOR: Just looking. What is it? Some sort of motor neurone represser?
HAYASHI: I should have used more. Then Jura might still be alive.
FX: A GRINDING OF TRAIN BRAKES.
DOCTOR: I think we're finally arriving.
HAYASHI: We'd better get this creature moved.
FX: MOVING SHEETS.
DOCTOR: Does Ileana know that you're mapping out her son's genomic sequence?
HAYASHI: I guessed we'd come to that.
DOCTOR: As you say, I'm very observant.
HAYASHI: It's purely a scientific grounding for Victor's treatment.
DOCTOR: And another mystery bites the desert dust. It makes

49

life a little flat, don't you think?

HAYASHI: But if I can isolate the gene that is responsible for his lycanthropic tendencies...

DOCTOR: Then you might be able to cure him completely.

HAYASHI: Yes.

DOCTOR: And there need never be another werewolf again.

HAYASHI: Exactly. We can rid the world of these monstrous genetic freaks.

(BEAT)

DOCTOR: I don't think Ileana or her kind will thank you for that.

HAYASHI: Remember your companion, Doctor. If you cross me, I'll make sure you never see him again.

SCENE 40. CATTLE STATION PLATFORM

FX: GUSH OF TRAIN DOOR OPENING. ILEANA AND INEZ STEP DOWN ONTO THE STONE PLATFORM.

ILEANA: No one here, Inez. Where's Tino? I told him to meet us.

INEZ: He must have been delayed, Senhora. With the others.

ILEANA: We'll see.

FX: SHE TAPS OUT A MOBILE PHONE NUMBER. THE PHONE STARTS TO BLEEP AT THE OTHER END.

ILEANA: Where is he?

INEZ: *(SNIFFS)* Nothing in the air but the moon.

FX: AFTER A COUPLE MORE BLEEPS, THE PHONE CLICKS OFF.

ILEANA: No answer.

INEZ: So he must be on his way.

ILEANA: It's all too quiet. No Cicadas. *(URGENT)* Tell Jorge to unload the trucks. It'll take time to get the equipment packed.

INEZ: Yes, Senhora.

FX: A VERY DISTANT WOLF HOWL.

ILEANA: *(AFRAID)* Inez. Do you hear?

INEZ: Who is it?

ILEANA: I don't know. Get Jorge now. Hurry.

INEZ: Yes, Senhora.

(SHE HURRIES AWAY)

FX: THE HOWL AGAIN.

ILEANA: *(WHISPERING)* No, not you. Pieter Stubbe. You won't have my son.

FX: SHE LETS RIP INTO A FULL-BLOODED HOWL OF HER OWN.

SCENE 41. THE DESERT.

(ROSA AND TURLOUGH)

FX: CICADAS DRONING.

ROSA: Hold still, yerpi-boy.

TURLOUGH: What is that stuff?

ROSA: Urucu juice. Keeps the flies off.

TURLOUGH: Ouch. It stings.

ROSA: Bet you started out from the city. Ain't Yerp one big city? Grandpa said that. That what you're running from?

TURLOUGH: *(SIGHS)* I don't know anymore. I fell off the train. Landed in a load of brushwood.

ROSA: The train? Jeezuz! Two nights I was waiting for the goddamn train!

TURLOUGH: I don't think it would have stopped for you.

ROSA: That lobo king. He's what put me off. Jeez! He's real bad news. The train's bringing the future. S'pose he gets to the future first. *(BEAT)* Hey, are you the future?

TURLOUGH: *(LAUGHING)* No. No, I doubt it. It's your bad luck if I am. So what are you doing out here? Don't you have a home to go to?

ROSA: Yeah, I got a home. But I don't go there.

TURLOUGH: Why? Did they throw you out or something?

ROSA: Throw *me*! No way. *They* all went. When the creek dried up, they went too. The guys took their cadis to the city to look for credit. Just me and Grandpa stayed.

TURLOUGH: But you've left him too.

ROSA: Yeah. Under a stack of rocks. *(SUPPRESSED ANGER)* Too old and too many cigs. His chest kind of caved in.

TURLOUGH: I'm sorry.

ROSA: *(QUIET)* Yeah.

TURLOUGH: So now it's only you.

ROSA: I gotta prove myself. I'm still a kid, that's what Grandpa says. Okay, so I gotta do a lot before I'm headman.

TURLOUGH: It's an initiation.

ROSA: Yeah. And I screwed up already.

TURLOUGH: How about rescuing a helpless Yerp who's lost in the desert?

SCENE 42. CATTLE STATION

(THE DOCTOR AND HAYASHI MANOEUVRE VICTOR INTO A HOVER CAR. ILEANA ADVISES - TO THE OTHERS' AGGRAVATION.)

FX: HUM OF THE HOVER GURNEY.

ILEANA: *(NERVOUS)* Further over. Further...

DOCTOR: Edge the gurney in towards me, Hayashi.

ILEANA: No, too far.

HAYASHI: Back a little. Mind the side of the car.

FX: CLUNK

ILEANA: Be careful! It's tilting!

FX: THE GURNEY BUZZES AND RIGHTS ITSELF.

DOCTOR: It's alright.

ILEANA: Please be careful with my son.

DOCTOR: Ileana, he's quite safe.

FX: ANOTHER CLUNK A THE GURNEY COMES TO REST. ITS MOTOR RUNS DOWN.

DOCTOR: There. Safely stowed. That should be everything.

HAYASHI: Senhora, I cannot work with this continual interference.

ILEANA: *(THREAT)* What is that supposed to mean?

DOCTOR: Ileana, perhaps you could stay here with Victor. Hayashi and I have to check the equipment in the other car.

HAYASHI: But we've already checked it...
DOCTOR: *(HURRYING HIM AWAY)* Come along, doctor. We can't be too careful.
ILEANA: *(DISTANT)* Then hurry. We can't wait here.
DOCTOR: *(CALLING BACK)* Won't be long.
HAYASHI: What do you mean, *too* careful?
DOCTOR: The Senhora's bite is far worse than her bark. I don't want her to lose her head. Or you yours for that matter.
HAYASHI: I see. Well, a word of advice in return, Doctor. The male wolf is a very competitive brute. *(POINTED)* If it senses a rival, its challenge can be ferocious.
DOCTOR: I can't imagine what you mean.
(BEAT)
HAYASHI: Victor's due for his medication. Please excuse me.
DOCTOR: And your treatment of Victor is something else I want to talk to you about.
FX: OPENS CAR DOOR AND CLIMBS INSIDE.
DOCTOR: Unfortunately while our friends are busy loading up, I have a more pressing task.
HAYASHI: What are you doing?
DOCTOR: Someone has to go and find Turlough.
FX: THE AIR CAR ENGINE TURNS OVER AND BURNS INTO LIFE.
DOCTOR: Tell Ileana, I'll be back. Cheerio.
FX: THE CAR START TO REV UP AND RISE. LICHTFUSS SNARLS. A THUNK AS HE GRABS HOLD OF THE BONNET.
DOCTOR: Lichtfuss!
LICHTFUSS: Doctor! Where are you going?
FX: THE CAR REVS MIGHTILY, UNABLE TO MOVE.
DOCTOR: Let go of the car, Lichtfuss!
LICHTFUSS: *(STRUGGLING TO HOLD THE CAR DOWN)* You're not going anywhere!
DOCTOR: I'm going to find Turlough!
LICHTFUSS: You're staying here!
FX: THE CAR ENGINE GOES ON SCREAMING.
ILEANA: *(COMING UP)* What's happening? Doctor?
LICHTFUSS: *(EFFORTFUL)* Your pet's escaping.
ILEANA: Doctor! Stop the car. Stop it now!
FX: THE ENGINE CUTS AND RUNS DOWN AS THE CAR SETTLES. THE DOOR OPENS AND THE DOCTOR CLIMBS OUT.
DOCTOR: I apologise, Senhora. But Turlough has to be found.
LICHTFUSS: Why? He's no milksop puppy. He has claws of his own.
ILEANA: Anton! The Doctor's right. I promised him. Go and find Turlough now.
LICHTFUSS: I will not!
ILEANA: *(ANGRY GROWL TURNS INTO...)* I'm still your leader! Go and find Turlough! And don't hurt him!
(BEAT)
DOCTOR: *(QUIET)* Thank you, Senhora.
LICHTFUSS: *(LOW GROWL)* What are you to her, Doctor?
DOCTOR: I'm here to help, that's all.
LICHTFUSS: *(ANGRY)* Ileana! What is he to you?
ILEANA: He's a doctor. Now take the third truck and find

Turlough. *(TURNS ON SUDDEN CHARM)* I'd consider it a great favour, Anton.

LICHTFUSS: *(LEAVING, UNIMPRESSED)* I don't need to use cutclaw machines.

FX: HIS FOOTSTEPS DASH OFF.

DOCTOR: Was that wise, Senhora? I want Turlough back in one piece.

ILEANA: *(KNOWING)* Herr Lichtfuss will do as he's told. When he wants something that desperately, he just can't resist.

DOCTOR: I hope you're right.

ILEANA: Hayashi?

HAYASHI: *(SLIGHTLY DISTANT)* Yes, Senhora.

ILEANA: You travel with your machines in the hover-truck. Jorge will drive.

HAYASHI: Senhora, I accompany your son. I have to administer his medication.

ILEANA: No. The Doctor travels with me.

HAYASHI: *(KNOWING)* Ah. I see.

ILEANA: Give me the correct dosage. We'll make sure Victor gets it.

DOCTOR: Senhora? I think it would be better...

ILEANA: You travel with me, Doctor. Where I can keep an eye on you.

SCENE 43. THE DESERT

FX: FOOTSTEPS (LICHTFUSS) SCRAMBLE DOWN A DRY BANK. MAYBE LIGHT WIND TO EMPHASISE THE SPEED.

LICHTFUSS: *(MUTTERING IN ANGRY BURSTS AS HE RUNS)* Running errands. Why me? While **he** stays. Find the goat meat stinking boy. Why's the Doctor staying? Ha! *(AN IDEA)*

FX: HIS FEET LEAVE THE GROUND IN A LONG LEAP. HE LANDS AND RUNS AGAIN.

LICHTFUSS: *(JUBILANT)* Because **he** can't run. Not like me! She sent **me**. As a favour to her, she said. No one better!

FX: BURSTS THROUGH DRY SCRUB AND RUNS SILENTLY FOR FEW SECONDS.

LICHTFUSS: *(NAGGING DOUBT RETURNS)* So what happens while I'm out of the way? She wouldn't. She wouldn't dare! I'll show her favours!

FX: HIS FOOTSTEPS STUMBLE TO AN ABRUPT HALT. THE WIND IN HIS EARS HAS STOPPED. SILENCE FOR A MOMENT.

LICHTFUSS: Who's there? *(SNIFFS)* Who is it?

FX: A WOLF GROWL TO THE LEFT SLOWLY APPROACHES.

LICHTFUSS: *(RECOGNISING THE PRESENCE)* Ah.

FX: ANOTHER GROWL APPROACHES FROM THE RIGHT. THEN A THIRD JOINS IN.

(LICHTFUSS STARTS TO LAUGH.)

LICHTFUSS: Well, good evening to you, brothers. It's a fine moonlit night to go prowling.

SCENE 44. THE DESERT.

FX: CRICKETS. FOOTSTEPS AS ROSA SCRAMBLES DOWN A BANK.

ROSA: Down here, yerpi-boy.

FX: TURLOUGH'S FOOTSTEPS FOLLOW. BUSHES PUSHED ASIDE.

TURLOUGH: I thought we were moving on.

ROSA: No point till the moon's down and the sun's up. Safer that way.

TURLOUGH: *(UNEASY)* Rosa? This wolf you're supposed to be meeting.

ROSA: Told you. He's my fight.

TURLOUGH: What sort of wolf? Grey? Brown? Big? Giant? *(GULP)* On four feet... or two? I mean, would you know him if you saw him?

ROSA: He ain't you, if that's what you think.

TURLOUGH: How would you know?

ROSA: 'Cos he's so big, he could bite the moon.

FX: CLICKS HER COMPUTER. IT PLAYS A TINNY TUNE IN THE STYLE OF A TRASHY AMERICAN CARTOON THEME.

ROSA: *(LAUGHS)* Grandpa says I sound like the sat-vid. You seen Jaguar Maiden? "Save the Forest. Battle the Dark!" Cos that's me.

TURLOUGH: I never watch TV. I'll take Grandpa's word for it. Just turn it off.

FX: JAGUAR MAIDEN THEME CLUNKS OFF.

ROSA: *(SHRUG)* It's old stuff. But I ain't no re-run. *(TV ANNOUNCER ACCENT)* "Franchised to you by the makers of Santos burgers." *(GIGGLES)* That big old wolf. He was really mad about the forest.

TURLOUGH: *(LAUGHING)* Why? What did he say?

ROSA: See. Knew you'd seen him too. That what you're running from?

(THEY'RE BOTH LAUGHING NOW.)

TURLOUGH: I don't think I ever stop running.

ROSA: Yeah?

TURLOUGH: I saw him at the Carnaval. That huge red mouth. What did he say? Why was he so mad?

ROSA: Cos he didn't know. He thought the forest was all gone.

TURLOUGH: But it has. It's just dust. There's nothing left.

ROSA: That's what you think, yerpi-boy.

TURLOUGH: So where is it then?

ROSA: I got it.

TURLOUGH: What?

ROSA: No kidding. Grandpa told me.

TURLOUGH: Oh well, he'd know.

ROSA: *(SUDDEN ANGER)* Too right. He was wise man of our tribe. Last one left before they cut down the trees and the river choked. But the spirits stayed with him. And now they're with me. And I can't get to sleep cos they're in my head doing wild crazy dances. All the trees and birds and animals. Shaking the ground. Yada yada ya.

FX: WE PICK UP THE DRUMMING OF THE SPIRITS.

TURLOUGH: *(SHIVERS)* Yes. Right.

ROSA: Right now. All dancing. Yada yada... *(BEAT)*

(SUDDENLY QUIET. A BIT SUGGESTIVE) You cold?
TURLOUGH: That's what they tell me. Cold right to the heart.
FX: UNWRAPS A BLANKET AND SHAKES IT OPEN.
ROSA: You got pale eyes, yerpi.
TURLOUGH: My name's Turlough.
ROSA: Thought your eyes were ice first off. But it's more like the moon inside your head, peeking out at me.
TURLOUGH: All the better to see you with.
FX: ROSA SHAKES BLANKET AGAIN. HINTS OF THE DRUMMING.
ROSA: Grandpa gave me this. It's a jaguar pelt. Only the headman gets to wear it.
TURLOUGH: And now you're the head.
ROSA: Maybe one day. When I prove who I am. Maybe I'll get a wolf pelt instead.
TURLOUGH: Don't be silly. This is better.
ROSA: Grandpa says the first ones wrapped themselves in it. Back under the first moon. When the world was the unripe seed before it grew into the forest.
TURLOUGH: It's warm. Almost as if it was alive.
ROSA: That's right. *(KNOWING)* So if you're cold, Turlough, yerpi-boy, you'd better come under here right now.

SCENE 45. ILEANA'S HOVER TRUCK
(INEZ IS DRIVING UP FRONT. THE DOCTOR AND ILEANA ARE IN THE BACK, TENDING VICTOR.)
FX: BURR OF THE TRUCK ENGINES.

DOCTOR: It'll be light soon, Ileana. How much further?
ILEANA: Twenty kilometres to the ranch. But the desert's swallowed the road. It may take Inez longer. Shouldn't you have given Victor his medication by now?
DOCTOR: He's still asleep. I think we should wait a bit.
ILEANA: But Hayashi said the dosage should be increased.
DOCTOR: Yes, I know he did. But I think we can afford to be a little less zealous. We don't want Victor *so* reliant on drugs that he can't cope without.
ILEANA: *(IRRITATED)* Why are we going so slowly? *(CALLING OUT)* Inez, get a move on.
DOCTOR: This truck's airworthy, isn't it? So why are we hugging the ground?
ILEANA: We can't fly, Doctor. Don't you know that? We're earth-bound creatures. Our elements are earth and water. We need to be in touch with the soil and rock. The earth's old bones.
DOCTOR: So that's why you drove straight through the Carnaval crowds in Rio.
ILEANA: Even a first floor apartment makes me feel queasy. And as for aircraft...
DOCTOR: "I am fire and air. My other elements, I give to baser life." Sorry, it's just a quote. Cleopatra in her tomb.
ILEANA: The queen of ancient Egypt?
DOCTOR: Poetic licence really. In real life, she had the all the subtle wit of a carpet beater.

ILEANA: *(AMUSED)* I take it that observation's not from personal experience.

DOCTOR: It's certainly more than just hearsay.

ILEANA: Exactly how old are you, Doctor?

DOCTOR: That's a question I usually ignore.

ILEANA: But.

DOCTOR: *(TEASING)* They say I'm a lot younger than I used to be.

ILEANA: You mean you're a lot older than you look.

DOCTOR: Now you're being unnecessarily personal.

ILEANA: Of course, I am. How old are you really? And how do you travel? How did you get on board the train?

DOCTOR: *(BEAT)* Guess.

ILEANA: *(MOVING IN)* My dearest Doctor.

DOCTOR: *(QUICKLY)* Yes, definitely soon be light. And still no sign of your friend Stubbe.

ILEANA: *(BARELY HIDDEN DISAPPOINTMENT)* Oh, he'll find us, Doctor. He's always hunting. He's always angry and hungry. Pieter Stubbe is centuries old and he has a hundred appetites.

DOCTOR: Sounds like a bad case of worms to me. I knew I should have gone for Turlough.

ILEANA: *(COLD)* And I have a pack of lone wolves to face. The only way to make a stand against Pieter is to work together. *(CALLING)* Inez! Get a move on. It'll be new moon before we get there!

SCENE 46. THE DESERT
(ROSA USES HER RECORDER WHILE TURLOUGH SLEEPS)
FX: CRICKETS. BLEEP OF THE RECORDER.

ROSA: Grandpa? The sky's all on fire away beyond the dead river. It's like the sun's coming up on the wrong side of the morning. Reckon something's burning. Maybe the Mission? Hey, Gramps, I got a boyfriend too. Okay, so he's a yerp and he ain't seen TV. But he knows about forests and the loups-garoux...

TURLOUGH: Do you tell all your secrets to your wristwatch?

FX: BLEEP AS RECORDER GOES OFF.

ROSA: *(STARTLED)* It's a perscom. Get your own. *(BEAT)* How long you been awake?

TURLOUGH: I was watching the moon.

FX: ROSA OPENS A COKE CAN.

ROSA: Want a cola?

TURLOUGH: Not really.

ROSA: Your loss, yerpi-boy. *(SWIGS THE CAN.)*

TURLOUGH: I was thinking about the forests where I come from.

ROSA: Okay, okay. You still got forests. I heard that.

TURLOUGH: No. Not the sort of forests you're thinking of. Where I come from, the forests are three times as tall.

ROSA: Yeah?

TURLOUGH: The leaves are all thick fleshy plates and you can walk on them, in spirals right up to the top of the canopy - all mauves and purples with blood red trunks. And after winter, when the suns first get warm, there are swarms of moths. They've got wings like cut sapphires and they blot out the white sky like glittering blue smoke.

ROSA: Yeah, right. In your head.

TURLOUGH: Maybe it is. Maybe I just imagined I can't get back there. But it's a lot better than anything I've seen in your real world.

ROSA: See. We both got a headful of forest. So I got thinking. Maybe you are the future I was waiting for.

TURLOUGH: Don't count on it.

ROSA: We're in this together.

TURLOUGH: No. No, Rosa, I don't want you to trust me.

ROSA: You telling me what to do?

TURLOUGH: Just don't. Look, I can't say.

ROSA: Why not?

TURLOUGH: Because... *(SIGHS IN DEFEAT)* Because I've got this... dark side. It always comes out and hurts others.

ROSA: So?

TURLOUGH: I don't want you hurt, Rosa. I'm not reliable. I don't even trust myself. Given the choice, I always prefer the dark, where no one can see me... Then they don't know who or what I really am.

ROSA: You're a yerpi-boy.

TURLOUGH: *(HALF LAUGHS)* No, that's just what you're meant to think.

FX: OMINOUS SILENCE. THE CRICKETS HAVE STOPPED.

ROSA: Listen.

TURLOUGH: It's gone too quiet.

FX: A DISTANT WOLF YELP.

TURLOUGH: *(AFRAID)* There's something out there. In the shadows.

ROSA: *(HISSED WHISPER)* No! Don't run.

TURLOUGH: Let go of me. You don't understand. I've seen it. It's my dark side.

ROSA: Turlough...

TURLOUGH: It was howling after my blood. And now it's coming after me. We can't fight it. We have to get away!

ROSA: Shut it, yerpi-boy! There's more than one out there. Maybe a whole pack. But no Loup-Garou's gonna get to you without getting past me first!

SCENE 47. ILEANA'S HOVER TRUCK

(ILEANA WITH VICTOR. THE DOCTOR LISTENING)
FX: BURR OF THE TRUCK ENGINES. VICTOR GROWLS SOFTLY.

ILEANA: It's alright, Victor. Don't fret. We'll soon be home. What about your favourite story? The one with the old wolf woman in the forest. And one day an old, old wolf with icicles in his fur came to her. His name was Winter and he begged her to hide him, for a young wolf called Spring was driving him out of the wood. So she took him into her den and hid him. All year long, her den was cold as ice, and snow piled up on the inside of her door. But she put on her coat and kept him safe. Just like I keep you safe, dearest Victor.

FX: VICTOR'S GROWLS SLOWLY FORM INTO A WORD...

VICTOR: Mother.

ILEANA: *(IMMENSE RELIEF)* That's right, Victor. Mother's

57

here. Now sleep. Just sleep.

FX: VICTOR'S BREATHING STEADIES.

ILEANA: *(QUIETLY, TO THE DOCTOR)* It's working, Doctor. I knew it would. I knew Hayashi's medication would work.

DOCTOR: I'm glad he's getting better. But I doubt it's the drugs that are improving his condition.

ILEANA: What do you mean?

DOCTOR: More likely, it's the lack of them.

FX: DISTANT EXPLOSION. THE ENGINES FALTER AND GO CRAZY.

ILEANA: What is it? Inez!

DOCTOR: An explosion. Must be several miles ahead.

ILEANA: The ranch!

SCENE 48. THE DESERT

FX: A RING OF GROWLING AND YAPPING AROUND TURLOUGH & ROSA.

TURLOUGH: Tall, aren't they?

ROSA: Never seen so many. See any that look like you, Turlough? Course not. No redhead wolves here. *(SHOUTS)* Okay you mutts, I'm ready for you!

TURLOUGH: Don't provoke them!

ROSA: They're waiting. Come on, lobos. We're waiting too!

FX: ANGRY WOLF SNARL.

TURLOUGH: Look, if we could start a fire...

ROSA: No time. Got my knife. Grab yourself a branch.

TURLOUGH: A branch'll never hold off so many. Someone once told me that to stop the wolves, you throw the baby out of the sledge.

ROSA: You got a Grandpa too?

TURLOUGH: Sometimes you'd think so. But I meant to distract them.

ROSA: Okay. You're headman.

TURLOUGH: *(UNEASY)* Right. Get up close to the bushes. Then they've only of one line of attack.

FX: ROSA PICKS UP THE JAGUAR PELT.

TURLOUGH: What are you doing?

ROSA: This is my second skin.

TURLOUGH: The jaguar pelt.

ROSA: Wolf takes a man, but jaguar takes a wolf. It's mine to wear. Spirit of the forest. And the forest's in me.

FX: ANOTHER WOLF SNARL.

TURLOUGH: They don't like that.

ROSA: And I got a claw of silver.

FX: WOLF SNARL CLOSER.

TURLOUGH: Rosa, don't be a stupid kid.

ROSA: Ancient spirits rise in me. Be in me. Ancient spirits rise in me. Be in me...*(REPEATS)*

FX: THE SPIRIT DRUMMING STARTS UP.

TURLOUGH: Rosa! Stop it! Stay here!

FX: WOLF GROWLS START DRAWING IN.

ROSA: Get off me! *(PULLS FREE)* Forest spirits be in me. Rise in me. Save the forest...!

TURLOUGH:　　Rosa!

FX: SNARL AS A WOLF HURLS ITSELF AT ROSA. FIGHTING BETWEEN THEM.

ROSA:　　*(STRUGGLING WITH THE WOLF)* Battle... the dark!

FX: WOLF GIVES HIDEOUS YELP AND SCRABBLES AWAY.

ROSA:　　Okay, lobos! Which of you's next for the Jaguar Maiden?!

FX: A WOLF SNARLING IN ON TURLOUGH.

ROSA:　　Turlough!

FX: HE CRIES OUT, SWOOSHING OUT WITH A BRANCH.

TURLOUGH:　　Get away from me!

ROSA:　　I got it!

FX: ANOTHER WOLF YELP. IT SCRAMBLES OFF.

ROSA:　　*(JUBILANT)* Silver bites, lobos! Stay clear!

TURLOUGH:　　The big white one! Look out!

FX: A DEEP WOLF GROWL. WALLOP! A BIG SCUFFLING FIGHT IN WHICH WE HEAR WOLF SNARLS AND THE HINT OF BIG CAT.

TURLOUGH:　　Rosa!

FX: HITTING AT IT WITH THE BRANCH. THE DRUMMING FADES.

TURLOUGH:　　Get off her! Get off!

FX: THE WOLF GIVES A BLOOD-CURDLING HOWL & GOES QUIET.

ROSA:　　Got it.

FX: THE OTHERS GROWL AROUND

TURLOUGH:　　*(HORRIFIED)* It's a man. It was human! Oh, God, I hate this planet!

ROSA:　　*(QUIET. BREATHING FAST & WITH DIFFICULTY.)* Is it dead?

TURLOUGH:　　Think so. The rest've pulled back again. (BEAT) You're bleeding.

ROSA:　　They're no pack of werewolves.

TURLOUGH:　　Gently...

ROSA:　　A *pack* would attack together. Ow, my shoulder!

FX: A DISTANT WOLF HOWL. STUBBE IS COMING.

TURLOUGH:　　What's that? They're pulling right back. They're going. Just like before.

ROSA:　　*(AFRAID)* It's him. The Lobo King...

FX: CLICKS ON HER RECODER.

STUBBE:　　*(ON THE RECORDER -From Part 2)* "But don't stray, because one night I'll be waiting round the next corner and I'll still be hungry."

FX: RECORDER CLICKS OFF.

TURLOUGH:　　*(AGITATED)* No. That's what he said to me. He's coming for me, not you.

ROSA:　　Turlough...

TURLOUGH:　　I'll get him away, Rosa. It's me he wants. Try to hide. I'll get him away.

FX: TURLOUGH RUNS. ROSA'S TOO WEAK TO FOLLOW.

ROSA:　　Turlough! Come back!

FX: SCRABBLES AROUND.

ROSA:　　Where's my knife? (SHE STARTS TO COUGH) You took my knife.

FX: A DISTANT WOLF BELLOW -HALF ROAR, HALF GULP, AND A YELL

FROM TURLOUGH WHICH GOES MUFFLED AS HE'S SWALLOWED ALIVE.

ROSA: Turlough! *(BEAT. THEN HALF-CRYING)* Turlough. It's my fight. My goddamn fight! *(SUDDEN GASP AS SHE SEES SOMETHING.)*

FX: A WOLF MOVES IN GROWLING.

SCENE 49. DESERT (REMAINS OF RANCHO DE SANTOS)

FX: THE CRACKLE OF A FIRE. CICADAS IN BACKGROUND. A HOVER TRUCK ENGINE APPROACHES AND RUNS DOWN. THE DOOR OPENS. THE DOCTOR, ILEANA & INEZ GET DOWN. ANOTHER TRUCK RUNS DOWN A LITTLE WAY OFF.

ILEANA: *(DISBELIEF)* It's gone. The whole ranch. Just blown away.

DOCTOR: Don't go too close.

INEZ: Senhora?

ILEANA: *(ANGRY)* Federico built it for us! For Victor and me!

INEZ: Senhora?

ILEANA: Let me be!

DOCTOR: *(QUIETLY)* Inez, what about the others?

INEZ: They should have been here. Tino and twenty more, waiting for the Senhora.

DOCTOR: We must search for any survivors. Perhaps you and Jorge... Ileana. I'm sorry.

ILEANA: *He* did this.

DOCTOR: Pieter Stubbe?

ILEANA: The shadow, as you say, Doctor, got here before us.

DOCTOR: Does he really hate you so much?

ILEANA: He's Pieter Stubbe. He revels in hatred. It's what he is. He never changes.

HAYASHI: *(COMING UP)* Senhora? What's happened? *(ILEANA GRABS HIM)*

ILEANA: *(FURIOUS)* Did you know this, Hayashi? Have you spoken to Pieter Stubbe?

HAYASHI: To who? I don't know what you mean!

FX: SHE THROWS HIM TO THE GROUND. THE CICADAS GO QUIET.

DOCTOR: *(WARNING ABOUT SOMETHING HE HAS SEEN)* Ileana.

ILEANA: How did he know where we were going? How did he know my vidlink code?

HAYASHI: I'm here to cure your son...

INEZ: Senhora.

ILEANA: Liar! I'll tear your throat out!

DOCTOR: Ileana, look.

ILEANA: What?

FX: A GENERAL PANTING LIKE A PACK OF DOGS APPROACHES.

INEZ: *(IN AWE)* They're all here. All of them.

HAYASHI: They're all monsters.

DOCTOR: They're all wolves. *(MUTTERING)* Stay by me, Hayashi. Whatever you do, don't move suddenly.

ILEANA: *(ADDRESSING THE PACK)* Sisters and brothers. I

feared that this disaster had overtaken us, but you have answered my summons. Thank you all. We have much to speak of. *(SENSES TROUBLE.)* What is it? What's the matter? Anton? Is that you skulking there? Why are you back so soon?

FX: *GENERAL GROWLING, FROM WHICH ONE PANTING WOLF EMERGES, APPROACHING ILEANA.*

DOCTOR: Is this Herr Lichtfuss?

HAYASHI: In his true shape.

INEZ: The fool. What's he carrying?

DOCTOR: Well, it's not Turlough.

ILEANA: Anton? Is this for me?

FX: *CLUMP AS LICHTFUSS DROPS SOMETHING HEAVY AT ILEANA'S FEET.*

ROSA: *(GROANING)* ...Grandpa...?

LICHTFUSS: *(HIS VOICE IS A DEEP GROWL)* A token of my devotion.

ILEANA: What is it? I didn't send you out for this.

LICHTFUSS: *(PLAYING THE CROWD)* For all to see. I bring this gift for you to do with as you will.

ILEANA: She's just a cutclaw child.

LICHTFUSS: She fights like a forest cat. She killed Mr Talbot with a silver blade before I overpowered her.

FX: *SNARLS OF ANGER FROM THE COMPANY.*

LICHTFUSS: She's yours, Ileana. She should be driven and hunted. As should all cutclaws.

FX: *MORE WOLFISH APPROVALS.*

ILEANA: What nonsense. I sent you to find Turlough. Where is he?

LICHTFUSS: You'll not see that little skunk again.

DOCTOR: *(MOVING IN)* Why? What's happened to him?

LICHTFUSS: Ah. *(TO THE WOLVES)* This is him, brothers and sisters. This is the latest cutclaw that she grants her favours to.

FX: *WOLFISH DISAPPROVAL & MUTTERING.*

DOCTOR: Where's Turlough, Lichtfuss?

LICHTFUSS: Gone. Swallowed down. Barely a mouthful, I'd say.

ILEANA: Who *swallowed* him? *(GROWING FEAR - TO THE PACK)* Why are you all in wolf-shape? Why this blood-lust? Who have you been talking to?

DOCTOR: Turlough's my friend. Who's responsible?

FX: *MORE MUTTERING.*

ILEANA: The Doctor is to be trusted. He helped save my son.

HAYASHI: *(ANGRY)* Saved him? What have you done, Doctor?

DOCTOR: Go away, Hayashi.

HAYASHI: Now you see what it's like to lose an assistant. And Victor is *my* work.

DOCTOR: Hayashi, to you he's just a laboratory rat!

LICHTFUSS: So this Doctor saved your son. Is he wolf, born and blooded? Is he stronger than me? If I challenge him, will he face me, tooth and claw? *(BEAT)* Will you, Doctor? *(BEAT)* Well?

DOCTOR: *(CALM)* You're wasting your time, Lichtfuss. There are greater threats to your people.

ILEANA: *(HURT)* Doctor?

61

LICHTFUSS: He is too weak to face me! Ileana, by our laws and with no other challenge, I claim you as my mate!

FX: BARKS AND BAYING OF APPROVAL FROM THE WOLVES.

ILEANA: I belong to no one, Lichtfuss!

STUBBE: *(DISTANT)* Ileana!

FX: THE WOLVES FALL SILENT.

DOCTOR: Inez, is this him? The shadow you've been running from?

INEZ: *(AFRAID)* It's the Grey One. A legend amongst us. Oldest and most fierce of our kind.

DOCTOR: Indeed. Pieter Stubbe. I didn't realise how tall he'd be.

ILEANA: *(HALF CHOKED)* Pieter...

STUBBE: Your nameday's long past, Ileana... but I brought you a present anyway.

FX: STUBBE COUGHS AND ANOTHER BODY DROPS ON THE FLOOR. (TURLOUGH CHOKES AND SPLUTTERS FOR AIR.)

DOCTOR: *(QUIET)* Turlough!

INEZ: *(WHISPERING)* Stay here. Don't move.

ILEANA: I don't want your presents, Pieter. What have you done to my home?

STUBBE: Don't take him then. He stuck in my throat too long. I've never tasted worse.

DOCTOR: *(MOVING FORWARD)* Turlough. It's me. Try to breathe slowly.

TURLOUGH: *(CHOKING)* Doctor...

STUBBE: What's this? *(SNIFFS)*

ILEANA: Doctor, go back!

STUBBE: Ah, I was told I had a rival.

DOCTOR: Mr Stubbe, what big eyes you have.

STUBBE: They see nothing in you, that's plain.

DOCTOR: How very kind. You also have the digestive system of a power shovel.

STUBBE: Ileana, this one stinks of sanctimony like those capuchin friars we devoured on pilgrimage to Rome.

ILEANA: That was not with me.

STUBBE: *(CHUCKLES)* Perhaps not.

ILEANA: The Doctor has my protection. By our laws, he's in my keeping.

STUBBE: We'll see. *(BEAT)* Well, quite a crowd. I thought they should come to see us off.

ILEANA: I'm not going anywhere.

STUBBE: Oh, yes you are. You'll come back with me. I'll soon put a stop to your cutclaw pretensions.

LICHTFUSS: Stubbe! Stand away from her. She's mine!

STUBBE: *(CHIDING)* Ileana. Another rival? How you must have missed me. You change lovers as a whore changes petticoats.

ILEANA: Anton, go back.

LICHTFUSS: You're old, Stubbe. Your legendary days are past. Get back to the old world where you belong.

STUBBE: Come closer and say that. *(MOCK DODDERING)* My ears are not what they were.

ILEANA: Anton...

LICHTFUSS: I said, old wolf, that it's time to let young blood have its head!

FX: STUBBE ROARS. LICHTFUSS HOWLS AS STUBBE SWALLOWS HIM WHOLE WITH ONE HUGE CHOMPING GULP.

ILEANA: Anton!

DOCTOR: *(URGENT)* Turlough, up you come. Lean on me.

FX: GENERAL CONSTERNATION AMONGST THE WOLVES. WHICH FADES INTO THE BACKGROUND AS WE FOLLOW THE PROGRESS OF THE DOCTOR AND TURLOUGH.

SCENE 50. THE HOVER TRUCK.

FX: GENERAL BABBLE OF WOLVES IN THE BACKGROUND. THE TRUCK DOOR OPENS.

DOCTOR: In here, Turlough. Just stay in the truck and stay out of sight.

TURLOUGH: *(WEAK)* What am I covered in? Ugh... *(COUGHS)* My eyes sting.

DOCTOR: I have to get that unfortunate girl in the jaguar skin away from them.

TURLOUGH: Rosa?

DOCTOR: You know her?

TURLOUGH: I left her behind. When they attacked us. *(PANICKING)* Then *He* came for me. His mouth was opening redder and redder! And then I was drowning in this stinking pit...

DOCTOR: Turlough. Turlough! I'm here. I'll get her away too.

TURLOUGH: *(EXHAUSTED)* Take this. It's her knife. She gave it to me.

DOCTOR: It's silver.

FX: ANOTHER BAYING FROM THE WOLVES.

TURLOUGH: What is it now?

DOCTOR: They're busy again. *(ANGRY)* This has got to stop. Stay there and don't move.

TURLOUGH;   No, Doctor. Don't do anything stupid!

FX: TRUCK DOOR SLAMS.

SCENE 51. RUINS OF THE RANCH

FX: BRING UP THE BAYING CROWD.

STUBBE: Quiet, you rabble! I'm sick of your commentary. Quiet!

FX: THE WOLVES QUIETEN DOWN.

STUBBE: Haha. You see? They know their King. Just the instinct to stay alive makes them cheer in all the right places.

ILEANA: You never could exert charm when terror would suffice. Poor, stupid Anton.

STUBBE: So much for your string of peccadillos. My strength of will remains implacable. Age and enforced abstinence only make it stronger, my long-lost love. I'll cut out every rival.

HAYASHI: Senhora! Please.

ILEANA: Go away, Hayashi.

HAYASHI: But the Doctor. He's taken Turlough.

DOCTOR: *(ARRIVING BACK)* I'm right here, Ileana. And I'm taking the girl too.

ILEANA: Leave her, Doctor. She and the boy are mine. *(BEAT)* But in return for saving my son, I will release Turlough to you.

STUBBE: That boy was *my* gift...

DOCTOR: Thank you, Ileana. Mr Stubbe? I think you've already met Doctor Hayashi.

HAYASHI: You can't touch me. I'm in the pay of the Senhora.

DOCTOR: Hayashi, you'd sell your own grandmother if you were offered a good price.

STUBBE: Grandmothers? Huh, I had my fill of grandmothers long ago.

DOCTOR: And did Hayashi tell you about his patent genetic cure for lycanthropy?

STUBBE: No. He did not.

ILEANA: What *cure*? Hayashi?

HAYASHI: *(FLOUNDERING)* Well... yes, it's true. I'll prove it. Your son... he's already recovering.

ILEANA: Only because the Doctor stopped your medication.

HAYASHI; But it's my breakthrough. I can end all your suffering for ever. The Doctor is deliberately hampering my research.

DOCTOR: Only hampering? I'd gladly wind it up for good. Ileana's people have their own age-old culture and laws. But your research, Hayashi, is nothing short of genocide. I'll fight it. And I'll defend every right of the wolf people not to be *cured*.

ILEANA: And I'll support you, Doctor.

HAYASHI: Senhora, this man is a charlatan!

STUBBE: *(LAUGHS)* How you prattle. I've had fleas with more sense. I am the oldest of the first-born, spawned out of the slime after the Deluge. Time's by-ways are mine to prowl and hunt. And all other wolves are my progeny. Humans were raised as my cattle - a right I should have taken long ago. Even for those who deny our heritage.

ILEANA: I won't come back to you, Pieter. I'm no longer your consort.

STUBBE: Human affectations. I'll take you anyway.

ILEANA: You will not.

STUBBE: How can you resist? You're mine, Ileana. And no one can change that.

(BEAT)

DOCTOR: Pieter Stubbe!

STUBBE: Huh?

ILEANA: Doctor?

DOCTOR: Stand away from her, Pieter Stubbe. She's no longer yours. Time's left you far behind and you've lost its scent. You're burnt out. So just give up and go back to the slime you crawled out of.

HAYASHI: *(GLEEFUL)* Oh, Doctor. You are such a fool.

STUBBE: *(DEEP AND WARY)* Is this a challenge? *(SNIFFS)* What is he? He's no champion. *(DISGUSTED)* He's like that foul-tasting boy. He's not even human!

DOCTOR: I'm the Doctor and I'm offering Ileana my protection. I'm stronger and more worthy than any puny human or wolf.

(STUBBE GROWLS ANGRILY.)

ILEANA: Doctor? Before all of us, do you understand the law implicit in your challenge?

DOCTOR: If I don't make a stand, your endeavours, *(RAISES VOICE)* even your people, may be swept aside by this old and monstrous anachronism.

ILEANA: So be it. From now, Doctor, I withdraw my protection from you. If you prove worthy and truly faithful, *(BEAT)* then I'll take you as my husband and rejoice in it!

FX: UPROAR AMONGST THE WOLVES.

CLOSING MUSIC.

PART FOUR

SCENE 52. RUINS OF THE RANCH
(THE DOCTOR, PIETER STUBBE, ILEANA AND HAYASHI, PLUS A LOAD OF SILENT WEREWOLVES.)

HAYASHI: *(GLEEFUL)* Oh, Doctor. You are such a fool.
STUBBE: *(DEEP AND WARY)* Is this a challenge? *(SNIFFS)* What is he? He's no champion. *(DISGUSTED)* He's like that foul-tasting boy. He's not even human!
DOCTOR: I'm the Doctor and I'm offering Ileana my protection. I'm stronger and more worthy than any puny human or wolf. *(STUBBE GROWLS ANGRILY.)*
ILEANA: Doctor? Do you understand the law implicit in your challenge?
DOCTOR: If I don't make a stand, your endeavours, *(RAISES VOICE)* even your people, may be swept aside by this old and monstrous anachronism.
ILEANA: So be it. From now I withdraw my protection from you, Doctor. If you prove worthy and truly faithful, *(BEAT)* then I shall take you as my husband and rejoice in it!
FX: UPROAR AMONGST THE WOLVES.

SCENE 53. THE HOVER TRUCK.
FX: FADE BELLOWING WOLVES TO DISTANCE.
(TURLOUGH IS WATCHING.)

TURLOUGH: *(TO HIMSELF)* Oh Doctor, what are you doing now? You don't stand a chance against that lot. *(SEARCHING)* Car keys. Must be some sort of ignition.
FX: MOVEMENT IN THE TRUCK BEHIND HIM.
TURLOUGH: Who's that?
FX: HEAVY DIVIDER PUSHED BACK.
VICTOR: *(GROGGY GROWL)* Who are you? Where's my mother?
TURLOUGH: *(NERVOUS)* Victor? Your mother's not here. Shouldn't you be resting?
VICTOR: *(ANGRY)* I'm cold without my coat. Where is she!

SCENE 54. THE RANCH RUINS.
FX: LOW BACKGROUND GROWLING AND YAPPING OF THE WOLVES.
(THE DOCTOR, STUBBE, ILEANA AND HAYASHI)

STUBBE: *(VERY MENACING)* She's set up you up, Doctor. I've never seen a bridegroom so reluctant.
DOCTOR: If it stops you, then yes... yes, I'll do it.
STUBBE: You think you're stronger than me?! *(COMING VERY CLOSE)* Are you worthy, Doctor? Truly worthy of her?
ILEANA: Don't fail me, Doctor. I trust you.
DOCTOR: *(UNCOMFORTABLE)* Why Mr Stubbe, what a big, wide, gaping *(TRYING TO STAND HIS GROUND)* drooling, red mouth you

have.

STUBBE: All the better to crunch and gollop you down, Doctor.

DOCTOR: Really? *(BEAT)* But you wouldn't, would you? I might be too spicy for your jaded palate.

(STUBBE GROWLS)

DOCTOR: What an unadventurous Earth-bound diet. You couldn't even stomach poor Turlough. And you've already had a heavy day's eating.

STUBBE: *(RATTLED)* Ileana? What can he give you that I can't raise a thousandfold?

ILEANA: He gave me my son back.

STUBBE: Oh, yes, your son. How touching. It's plain I left you alone too long.

ILEANA: No, I left you.

STUBBE: And now the cutclaws you love so much, have run wild. They've trampled our forests to dust. But together we'll set it right. We'll herd the cutclaws like the cattle they are. I'll lay their cities at your feet. Let's see your worthy champion do that!

ILEANA: Having Victor back is enough.

VICTOR: *(ARRIVING)* Mother?

STUBBE: Ah, the young cub himself.

ILEANA: Victor. What are you doing? Come here to me.

VICTOR: I'm cold, mother. I miss my coat.

DOCTOR: *(MUTTERING)* Turlough, I told you to stay hidden!

TURLOUGH: I didn't exactly have a choice. What about Rosa?

DOCTOR: All in good time.

STUBBE: Let's look at the boy then. Is he blooded yet?

ILEANA: Leave him alone!

VICTOR: *(AFRAID)* Mother? Who's this?

ILEANA: It's alright, Victor.

STUBBE: No matter. *(BEAT)* Doctor, join me. We have a common enemy.

DOCTOR: We have?

STUBBE: That greedy leech, Hayashi. Let's make sport with him.

DOCTOR: Ah, no, Pieter. I fear I must decline...

STUBBE: Come now. He's insulted our mistress. Where is he?

FX: WOLVES YAPPING.

STUBBE: Ah, there he is, hoping to slip away unnoticed. Hayashi!

HAYASHI: *(DISTANT)* No! Leave me alone.

STUBBE: Come here.

FX: A DEEP NOTE OF POWER BUILDS.

HAYASHI: *(COMING CLOSER. TERRIFIED & SUBMISSIVE)* I'm here. Please, I'm here.

TURLOUGH: *(INCREDULOUS)* He can't resist. They're just reeling him in.

DOCTOR: They did the same to you. *(ALOUD)* Ileana. You can stop this!

ILEANA: That man nearly destroyed Victor.

VICTOR: *(HALF GROWL)* Mother. I want to take him!

(SNARLS)

STUBBE: What do you say, Doctor? How long a start shall we give him? An hour? Half a day? Not too long, I think. The others here are eager for the kill.

HAYASHI: *(WHIMPERING)* Please, Doctor! Just make them stop. I've done nothing wrong.

DOCTOR: Hayashi, stay still! Don't give in to your instincts.

HAYASHI: I want to run!

DOCTOR: Ileana? You must stop this.

STUBBE: Leave Ileana to me!

ILEANA: *(STRUGGLING TO RESIST)* Hayashi... betrayed... my trust.

STUBBE: She can't resist. None of them can. It's their nature. Yours too, Doctor. Deep, deep down. So join us!

DOCTOR: I will not! Ileana, remember everything you told me. Don't give in to the shadows.

ILEANA: Inez! Where are you? Help me!

FX: WOLF YAP.

ILEANA: *(WEAKENING)* Inez? No, don't join him. I trusted you... Jorge, where are you?

STUBBE: *(LAUGHING)* Your servants are long gone. I bring out the night in everything. Just do it! Unleash your heart's darkest desires!

ILEANA: *(VOICE DARKENS AS HER WILL GIVES WAY)* It's true. I want it. *(SNARLS)*

STUBBE: My love. I'd forgotten your coat was so glossy.

(HE LAUGHS AS SHE MOVES AWAY SNARLING)

DOCTOR: Don't listen, Turlough.

TURLOUGH: I'm not. I'm sticking with you.

STUBBE: And you, Doctor. Tear off that pious mask and let's see the dark side of your nature.

FX: DEEP NOTE OF MENACE BUILDS AGAIN.

TURLOUGH: Doctor? Don't look at his eyes. Doctor!

STUBBE: Doctor...

DOCTOR: *(FEVERISH CONCENTRATION)* "It is an ancient Mariner, And he stoppeth one of three. 'By thy long grey beard... *(FALTERS)* and *glittering* eye... *(STRUGGLING)* glittering eye ... glittering... glittering..." (REPEATS)*

STUBBE: *(OVER THE DOCTOR)* You're no challenge to me, Doctor. And you can't resist for long. You'll soon follow.

DOCTOR: *(FORCING THROUGH)* "And... glittering eye... now wherefore... stopp'st thou me..."

STUBBE: *(OVER THE DOCTOR)* Run, Hayashi. Run for your pitiful life!

HAYASHI: You're monsters! All of you! Monsters! *(HE GIVES A LONG WAIL AS HE RUNS INTO THE DISTANCE.)*

STUBBE: *(HOLDING BACK)* Wait... Wait... The humans love the chase as much as we do.

(BEAT. BEAT)

STUBBE GIVES A HOWL. THE OTHER WOLVES TAKE IT UP. THE RUMPUS GRADUALLY FADES INTO THE DISTANCE...

SCENE 55. RANCH RUINS.
FX: THE WILD RUMPUS OF THE BAYING PACK IN THE DISTANCE.

TURLOUGH: Doctor?
(ROSA MOANS)
TURLOUGH: Rosa? Come on. We can't stay here!
DOCTOR: *(DEEP MUTTERING TO HIMSELF)* "Hold off! Unhand me, grey-beard loon."
TURLOUGH: Doctor? I need your help.
(DOCTOR STARTS TO GROWL, THREATENING AND WOLF-LIKE.)
TURLOUGH: Doctor! It's Turlough. *(DOCTOR SNARLS)* Listen, we must get back to the TARDIS.
DOCTOR: *(GASPS)* The TARDIS. Yes.
    "Like one, that on a lonesome road
    Doth walk in fear and dread,
    Because he knows, a frightful fiend
    Doth close behind him tread."
    (DEEP BREATH, EXHAUSTED) To know one's enemy, one must first know oneself... Not to worry, Turlough. Thank you. I'm back again.
TURLOUGH: *(RELIEF)* I thought for a minute that you'd... I mean, that Stubbe...
DOCTOR: I'm quite happy with my own coat, thank you. *(HALF MOCKING)* Surely you know me by now. Why, I'm no more aggressive than Alice's White Rabbit.
TURLOUGH: And about as reliable a timekeeper.
DOCTOR: What!
TURLOUGH: ...as er, Tegan once said to me.
DOCTOR: *(PLEASED)* Did she? How reassuring.
FX: VERY DISTANT HOWLS.
TURLOUGH: We can't stay here.
DOCTOR: I agree. Into the hovertruck. Give me a hand with your friend.
TURLOUGH: *(HEFTING HER UP)* Come on, Rosa.
ROSA: *(HALF ASLEEP)* What is it? Grandpa? That you?
TURLOUGH: *(GENTLE)* Shush. It's alright. You're safe now.
ROSA: *(SNUGGLING)* Oh, Turlough. It's you. Good. That's okay.
TURLOUGH: *(EMBARRASSED)* Erm... I'd introduce you, but...
FX: A REALLY BLOOD-CURDLING DISTANT SCREAM FROM HAYASHI, FOLLOWED BY A CHORUS OF HOWLS AND BARKING.
DOCTOR: Hayashi! *(URGENT)* That settles it. Back to the TARDIS.
FX: OPENS TRUCK DOOR. THEY CLAMBER IN.
TURLOUGH: They move fast. They'll soon catch us up.
DOCTOR: We'll see. Stubbe's more a runner than a high-jumper. Altitude is the thorn in his Achilles paw, you might say.
TURLOUGH: Okay, she's inside.
FX: SLAMS TRUCK DOOR.
DOCTOR: Right. Let's see if this truck is really airworthy.
FX: STARTS IGNITION.
DOCTOR: I don't want another bout with Stubbe. Not until I'm

ready. Think wonderful thoughts, Turlough. And up we go!

FX: THE ENGINE STARTS TO REV UP. THE TRUCK TAKES OFF. WE HEAR IT DEPART INTO THE DISTANCE.

SCENE 56. HOVER TRUCK

FX: TRUCK IN FLIGHT.
(THE DOCTOR, TURLOUGH AND ROSA)

TURLOUGH: No sign of them down there. Where are they?

DOCTOR: Look left. At ten o'clock. That cloud of dust.

TURLOUGH: Is that them? They're not heading back to the ranch at all. They move so fast.

DOCTOR: Stubbe obviously considers me less of a threat than I thought. Arrogant really... arrogant of him. They're heading for the cattle station... and the train.

TURLOUGH: And the TARDIS. Stubbe said he'd lay whole cities at Ileana's feet.

DOCTOR: His equivalent of a bunch of flowers, no doubt. The line heads towards Manaus. Odd that. You'd think they'd cause more havoc in Brasilia.

TURLOUGH: But a pack of werewolves against a whole city. They can't be *that* powerful.

DOCTOR: You've seen how they control people. Even the most advanced civilisations are only an inch away from primal chaos. You can barely shine a moonbeam between the two. As for Stubbe. He's possibly the deadliest individual this planet has ever produced.

FX: SLIDING DOOR PULLS BACK.

ROSA: Turlough. I want my knife back. *(SEES THE VIEW.)* JeeZus! Where's the ground!

DOCTOR: This truck is currently cruising at a height of one hundred and twenty feet. How do you do? I'm the Doctor and you're Turlough's friend Rosa.

TURLOUGH: Sit down, Rosa. How are you feeling?

ROSA: Air sick. Did you get me away from the lobos?

TURLOUGH: Well...

DOCTOR: Not exactly. The wolves found something less wholesome to chase.

ROSA: Yeah? Grandpa said they always go for the weakest. So give me my knife now, yerpi-boy.

TURLOUGH: Erm...

DOCTOR: It's here. Turlough only took it to try and protect you.

TURLOUGH: That *is* true.

ROSA: Yeah?

DOCTOR: I'm glad to hear it. The knife's chaste silver, isn't it?

ROSA: Only thing that does for Loups-garoux. They hate it.

TURLOUGH: Like silver bullets?

DOCTOR: The metal of the moon. That's an old charm. Lucky you had it, Turlough. Why else do you think Stubbe couldn't swallow you?

TURLOUGH: Thanks, Doctor. There's the monorail. They're at the train already!

DOCTOR:	Hold tight. I'm taking her down.

FX: THE TRUCK BANKS NOISILY. OBJECTS CLATTER ACROSS SIDEWAYS.

TURLOUGH:	Steady!
DOCTOR:	These things aren't built for manoeuvres. Now if this was a spitfire...
TURLOUGH:	You can't confront them, Doctor. You said yourself...
ROSA:	The train's moving.
DOCTOR:	Ah.
TURLOUGH:	It's going backwards!
DOCTOR:	Back to Rio. I should have known. And there's no chance of stopping them.
TURLOUGH:	The TARDIS, Doctor.
ROSA:	The who?
DOCTOR:	We'll have to follow in this thing.
TURLOUGH:	But we'll never match their speed.

FX: THE TRUCK ENGINE CROAKS AND GOES INTO A DIVE.

TURLOUGH:	What are you doing!
DOCTOR:	Sorry! Got to stop them somehow!
TURLOUGH:	You'll crash us! *DOCTOR!*
ROSA:	The back of the train...! Look.
TURLOUGH:	The back carriage. It's broken away!

FX: THE TRUCK PULLS OUT OF THE DIVE.

DOCTOR:	Now how did that happen?
TURLOUGH:	They've left it behind. The carriage with the TARDIS.
DOCTOR:	Ileana. She must have worked it out. That's very clever. And dangerous for her.
TURLOUGH:	But it's a chance. She's giving us a chance to stop them.

SCENE 56a. THE TRAIN
FX: TRAIN BACKGROUND.

INEZ:	Senhora, the Grey One's calling for you.
ILEANA:	Let him wait, Inez. I had to return that object to the Doctor.
INEZ:	The blue box?
ILEANA:	His scent led back to it. It must be important.
STUBBE:	*(DISTANT)* Ileana!
INEZ:	*(AFRAID)* Stubbe's coming!
ILEANA:	No word, Inez! You hear? It's just a hope, that's all.

SCENE 57. TARDIS CONSOLE ROOM
FX: TARDIS HUM. TARDIS DOORS OPEN.
(ROSA, FOLLOWED BY TURLOUGH AND THE DOCTOR)

ROSA:	*(OUTSIDE DOORS)* No way! I ain't going in! Get off me!
TURLOUGH:	We can't leave you out there.
ROSA:	*(PUSHED IN)* You're not locking me up in some crummy... *(FALTERS)* blue... icebox...
DOCTOR:	No. Indeed we are not.

ROSA: (*STUNNED*) Okay... I mean... Jeez, so big...
TURLOUGH: Well, that shut her up.
FX: DOORS BUZZ SHUT.
ROSA: What's that?
TURLOUGH: Just the doors. So we can travel.
FX: THE DOCTOR IS FLICKING SWITCHES.
DOCTOR: We have to go to Rio.
TURLOUGH: She's got friends in Rio.
ROSA: You're crazy. First it's lobos. Now it's locos. *So* big...
TURLOUGH: It's just a different reality. Once you get used to it, it seems like the only reality.
DOCTOR: Perhaps it's my reality.
TURLOUGH: That's right. And while the outside's always changing, some of us are lucky enough to be allowed in here, looking out through a door that's never in the same place twice.
ROSA: Like in my head. What's inside's bigger than what's outside.
TURLOUGH: Your dancing forest.
ROSA: Yeah.
ROSA & TURLOUGH: Yada yada yada. (*THEY LAUGH*)
FX: HINTS OF SPIRIT DRUMMING MERGE INTO THE TARDIS DEMATERIALISATION SEQUENCE
TURLOUGH: Is that what the TARDIS runs on, Doctor? Imagination?
DOCTOR: Sometimes it certainly has a mind of its own. Shouldn't you both get cleaned up?
TURLOUGH: You too, Doctor.
DOCTOR: What?
TURLOUGH: Because if you've got a date, you have to make the effort.
DOCTOR: It's not like that. It's not the end of term dance.
TURLOUGH: I know. But you've still got to look the part. Otherwise she won't lift a claw to take a second look.
DOCTOR: (*GLUM*) If only it were that simple.

SCENE 58. TARDIS BEDROOM
FX: TARDIS BACKGROUND HUM. SLIGHTLY DIFFERENT TONE. AN INNER TARDIS DOOR CLICKS SHUT. CLICK/BEEP OF ROSA'S COMPUTER.

ROSA: Grandpa? Can't talk now. Maybe not for a bit. Too much happening. Can't get my head round it. There's a whole load of dark. And the lobos are coming out of the shadows. Don't know what's next up. But there's light too. All round me. Must be full moon already. The walls in this place are all made of moons. S'pose there's other spirits outside the forest? Maybe I found the future. Maybe *it* found me. But I still got the forest. Still here. And you're here too, Grandpa. Time's coming when I get to prove myself. I won't forget. (*BEAT*) See you, Grandpa.
FX: COMPUTER CLICKS OFF.

SCENE 59. TURLOUGH'S ROOM
FX: TARDIS HUM SHIFTS TONE AGAIN. KNOCK AT THE DOOR.

TURLOUGH: Hullo?

FX: DOOR OPENS.

DOCTOR: *(UNUSUALLY AWKWARD)* Turlough... *(BEAT)* How are you?

TURLOUGH: Don't hover, Doctor. Come in.

DOCTOR: As long as you're not busy.

TURLOUGH: *(PATIENCE)* Is there a problem?

DOCTOR: No, I was just... I seem to... By the way, how did you resist Pieter Stubbe? I mean, his powers of persuasion.

TURLOUGH: I don't know. I just closed my eyes and thought of...

DOCTOR: Home?

TURLOUGH: Well, thoughts are all I get.

DOCTOR: Yes. Thank you.

(BEAT)

TURLOUGH: Doctor?

DOCTOR: Yes?

TURLOUGH: What are you getting yourself into?

DOCTOR: Sorry?

TURLOUGH: Ileana de Santos. I mean, she's a wolf. Half a wolf.

DOCTOR: She chose *me*. *And* she gave me back the TARDIS. At considerable risk...

TURLOUGH: But you're not obliged to book a church and a honeymoon. I'd steer well clear.

DOCTOR: Someone has to stop Pieter Stubbe and never mind the cost. He's a serious threat. And all because he has to outdo me in Ileana's affections.

TURLOUGH: Ah. So it's your fault.

DOCTOR: Oh yes, and that's another thing...

TURLOUGH: Yes?

DOCTOR: Well, I'd hoped... erm, you see, Ileana... Well... since you and Rosa...

TURLOUGH: What! Oh, now hang on, Doctor... you're jumping to conclusions... Do you mean... I mean, me? Oh, come on! Me and Rosa?!

DOCTOR: Well, yes. You see, women... they're not exactly my area. Apart from Tegan... and Nyssa. But they were... friends. I was responsible for them. That wasn't the same.

TURLOUGH: *Good* friends.

DOCTOR: And there was Sarah-Jane of course. And Jo and Romana... both of her. Zoe and Victoria. Dodo and Vicki and Barbara.

TURLOUGH: And Susan?

DOCTOR: Ah well, of course she was my granddaughter. *(SIGH)* Sometimes I feel very old.

TURLOUGH: And you think *I* know better? Look, how do *you* feel about Ileana?

DOCTOR: *(SNAPS)* Now *you're* getting needlessly personal too.

TURLOUGH: Sorry. It was you that asked.

DOCTOR: The important thing is the city. It'll be the height of Carnaval by now. The whole place in an emotional frenzy. And then a train-load of hungry werewolves arrives up from the country. There'll be no resistance. It'll be like the last round up.

TURLOUGH: You don't think *His* influence is pushing us all a bit over the top?

DOCTOR: No, Turlough, I do not! *(GOING OUT)* Somehow I dread to think what I'll find when we reach Rio.
FX: DOOR SHUTS.
TURLOUGH: Total devastation? A bride? *(SIGH)* And where does that leave me?

SCENE 60. RIO - STREET
FX: HISS OF STEAM AND DISTANT CAR ALARM ALREADY SOUNDING. THE TARDIS LANDS. CLATTER AS IT KNOCKS SOMETHING OVER. AN EMPTY BEER CAN ROLLS ALONG. TARDIS DOOR OPENS. BROKEN GLASS CRUNCHES UNDERFOOT.
IN THIS SCENE WE NEED TO CONVEY A SENSE OF SPACE. THE THREE CHARACTERS ARE CONSTANTLY MOVING.

ROSA: *(OVER-AWED)* Jeez, the buildings. Like mountains...
DOCTOR: Mind the broken glass.
TURLOUGH: Where is everyone? Where's the Carnaval? The street's deserted.
DOCTOR: Sorry, Turlough. We should have got here earlier. My fault.
ROSA: Feels like a storm's coming.
DOCTOR: Oppressive. Don't think about it.
TURLOUGH: *(DISTANT)* Doctor, there's been a car smash.
DOCTOR: What?
(HE HURRIES OVER)
TURLOUGH: Several smashes. All along the street. Where are the emergency services?
DOCTOR: Everything's gone down together. No one inside this one.
TURLOUGH: The whole city must be cut off. Something big's on fire down towards the bay.
ROSA: It's not real, right? Like you said. It's like a holodrome park. Thought-surfing 'gainst the opponent of your choice.
DOCTOR: *(CALLING BACK AS HE CHECKS CARS)* No, unfortunately, this is real.
ROSA: *(UNEASY)* I'm bored. Can't breathe here. Let's try some place else.
TURLOUGH: It's real, Rosa.
ROSA: It's better on sat-vid.
DOCTOR: *(COMING BACK)* The cars are all empty. I didn't expect them to clear the crowds quite so efficiently.
FX: A VERY DISTANT WOLF HOWL.
TURLOUGH: *(SHIVERS)* Can you feel that?
DOCTOR: Somewhere above the city.
TURLOUGH: It's pressing in. It's in the air, and the buildings. It makes me want to run away.
DOCTOR: With the herd?
TURLOUGH: Yes! Anywhere.
DOCTOR: With all the other *humans?*
TURLOUGH: *(RELAXING)* No. Not humans. You're right. Now who's getting personal?
DOCTOR: I am. Remember that. And don't forget who you

aren't.

TURLOUGH: I put my shadow back behind me, Doctor.
DOCTOR: Good. What about Rosa?
(BEAT)
TURLOUGH: Where is she?
FX: ANOTHER DISTANT WOLF HOWL.
DOCTOR: Always the same with companions. There she goes!
TURLOUGH: Rosa!
FX: THEY RUN.
TURLOUGH: Rosa! Come back!

SCENE 61. RIO - STREET.
FX: DISTANT CAR ALARM SHIFTS PERSPECTIVE. ROSA TAPS OUT A PHONE CODE ON HER COMPUTER. THE DOCTOR AND TURLOUGH RUN UP.

DOCTOR: Rosa!
TURLOUGH: Idiot!
ROSA: *(FEVERISH)* Get off me! I'm making a call.
DOCTOR: It isn't safe out here!
FX: WOLF YAP NEARBY.
ROSA: Get off! I hate this place! It's choking my head!
TURLOUGH: *(HOARSE WHISPER)* They're coming!
FX: HUNDREDS OF FOOTSTEPS ARE APPROACHING.
ROSA: Whoa!
DOCTOR: Inside here!
(ROSA STARTS TO SHOUT, BUT A HAND MUFFLES HER YELLING.)
FX: THEY STUMBLE THROUGH A DOOR.

SCENE 62. SHOP INTERIOR
(THE DOCTOR, TURLOUGH AND ROSA HIDING. ROSA STRUGGLES.)

DOCTOR: Quiet, Rosa.
FX: WOLF BARKING OUTSIDE. THE FOOTSTEPS MUCH CLOSER. A SILENT CROWD.
TURLOUGH: *(WHISPER)* What is it? So many people.
DOCTOR: Don't move.
FX: THE FOOTSTEPS ARE PASSING. WOLF BARKS AS IT CIRCLES AND DRIVES THE CROWD.
TURLOUGH: Horrible. Look at their faces. They're mindless.
DOCTOR: It's herding them. Like cattle.
TURLOUGH: Like lambs to the proverbial...
(ROSA STRUGGLES AGAIN.)
DOCTOR: All right, Rosa. Ssh.
TURLOUGH: Get down!
FX: WOLF YAPS VERY CLOSE BY. THE FOOTSTEPS START TO DWINDLE.
DOCTOR: We have to do something now, before the outside world sends in remote scout cameras and smart troops. We don't want a full scale stampede on our hands.
(BEAT)
TURLOUGH: That's the last. They're going.

DOCTOR: Now where would they corral them? One of the bigger parks?

TURLOUGH: Stay there. I'll find out for you.

DOCTOR: Turlough?

TURLOUGH: Just stay put. And no sudden elopements, please.

DOCTOR: Elopements? Turlough?!

FX: BUT THE DOOR CLOSES.

DOCTOR: Ouch! No need to bite!

ROSA: Serves you right! We gotta stop him!

DOCTOR: *(FIRM)* He'll be back soon. Turlough's grasp of self preservation is second to none. What about you, Rosa? Were you tempted to join the herd?

ROSA: No way!

DOCTOR: No?

ROSA: No! *(BEAT)* Anyway, Grandpa says the easy path leads under the falling tree. I ain't climbing on the cattle truck with the rest of them. Did you see their eyes?

DOCTOR: Grandpa talks a lot of sense.

ROSA: Sometimes. But I don't reckon he knows everything.

DOCTOR: What tribe are you? Ticuna? Yanamami?

ROSA: Wuarana. But they're dead now. The forest died, so the others came here.

DOCTOR: To Rio?

FX: TAPS OUT CODE ON HER COMPUTER.

ROSA: But I can't raise them on the vidlink. That's dead too.

FX: DEAD TONE.

DOCTOR: Yes. I'm sorry. What about the forest?

FX: WE HEAR HINTS OF THE SPIRITS DRUMMING.

ROSA: Still got it in my head.

DOCTOR: Always there. Like family.

ROSA: The spirits'll drive me crazy. But they had to go somewhere. They're okay about waiting.

DOCTOR: Tell them it's better that way. Don't let them get greedy like Pieter Stubbe.

ROSA: You'd make a good Grandpa too.

DOCTOR: Thanks, Rosa. And maybe Turlough *shouldn't* be out there on his own.

ROSA: Knew you'd see it right. Stick with me, okay? *(MOVES OFF)* And let's make tracks.

SCENE 63. STREET OUTSIDE PARK

FX: TURLOUGH RUNS SOMETHING METAL ALONG RAILINGS. HUMANS TRAPPED INSIDE MAKE FRIGHTENED MOANINGS.

TURLOUGH: Poor old humans, all caged up in a public park.

VICTOR: Turlough?

TURLOUGH: *(JUMPS)* Ha! *(PUTTING IT ON AS VICTOR SNUFFLES ROUND HIM)* Victor, it's you. You've got the *cutclaws* well fenced up.

VICTOR: Where they belong.

TURLOUGH: Did I miss much? I ran all the way from the ranch.

VICTOR: You smell of lies. Where's the Doctor?

TURLOUGH: Oh, he couldn't keep up. You know him. All talk and no action.

VICTOR: My mother needs him.

TURLOUGH: Does she? Well, if I see him, I'll tell him. Where is she, by the way?

VICTOR: Above. With the Grey One. I'll take you there now.

TURLOUGH: No, I'll just hang round here for a bit. Keep an eye on the cutclaws...

FX: RUNS METAL ALONG RAILINGS AGAIN.

VICTOR: *(GROWL)* Now! *(GRABS TURLOUGH)* We run this way.

SCENE 64. STREET.

FX: WE HEAR TURLOUGH AND VICTOR LEAVING FROM A MORE DISTANT PERSPECTIVE.

(THE DOCTOR AND ROSA HAVE BEEN WATCHING. SENSE OF URGENCY.)

ROSA: He's got Turlough. Let me after him. I can outrun any wolf.

DOCTOR: We'll never catch them that way. I've wasted too much time already.

FX: HE SETS OFF AT A PACE. SHE RUNS AFTER HIM.

ROSA: Where're you going?

DOCTOR: Back to the TARDIS.

ROSA: But Turlough...

DOCTOR: Victor said "above." What's above the city, but still close to the Earth?

ROSA: Doctor, wait.

DOCTOR: Must be the Corcovado. The Christ statue. That's where we first sensed Stubbe's presence.

ROSA: *(FURIOUS)* Doctor! Are you listening?

FX: THEY STOP RUNNING.

ROSA: Turlough's no fighter. One wrong move and he's capybara curry.

DOCTOR: He has his moments. What's more important, Rosa? One young man? Or a whole city - blown out of its wits by the storm force of Pieter Stubbe's will.

ROSA: *(UNNERVED)* Stubbe?

DOCTOR: And not just the humans. I don't imagine his wolfish cohorts had any say in the matter either. That's what I have to break. *(GOING THOUGH HIS POCKETS)* Now where did I put that...?

ROSA: *(DETERMINED)* I still got a date with that lobo king.

DOCTOR: Ah. Knew I had it somewhere.

ROSA: A whistle? You crazy?

DOCTOR: This *dog* whistle belonged to a faithful friend of mine.

ROSA: And blowing it'll bring every varmint for miles down on us.

DOCTOR: Exactly. And it'll give Stubbe's pack the shuffle it so richly deserves.

(HE BLOWS. BUT THERE'S NO SOUND)

FX: DISTANT WOLF HOWL TO THE LEFT. ANSWERING HOWL FROM THE RIGHT. AND ANOTHER IN THE CENTRE.

SCENE 65. SUMMIT OF THE CORCOVADO

FX: STUBBE IS GNAWING NOISILY AT A BONE. IT CRUNCHES BETWEEN HIS TEETH.

STUBBE: *(MOUTH FULL)* You're not eating, Ileana.

ILEANA: *(COLD) You* never stop.

STUBBE: The cutclaws are plumper these days. Remember the Grand Duchess Anastasia?

ILEANA: And Lord Lucan.

STUBBE: Skinny as church wafers. *(CRUNCH)* But these bones. *(SPITS)* Brittle as twigs.

FX: A BONE CLATTERS AWAY ACROSS THE GROUND. VERY DISTANT HOWLS REACH UP FROM THE CITY BELOW.

STUBBE: What's that rumpus?

ILEANA: *(QUIET EXCITEMENT)* It's the Doctor. He must be down in the city already.

STUBBE: Never.

FX: HE GIVES A MIGHTY HOWL WHICH ECHOES INTO THE DISTANCE. (BEAT)

STUBBE: Your precious champion won't dare show his snout. Smell that air. The scent of fear rising up from the city. Remember Moscow.

ILEANA: Old times, long gone.

STUBBE: I won't ask you again, Ileana.

ILEANA: I will not be your consort. Never.

STUBBE: *(ANGRY)* I've given you what you wanted. All the wolves brought together.

ILEANA: Reduced to a limp-tailed mob cringing under your tyranny.

STUBBE: Careful. Or I'll turn that will on you too.

ILEANA: You already have.

(STUBBE SNIFFS)

STUBBE: *(DISTASTE)* There *is* a scent. What is it?

ILEANA: *(RELIEF)* It *is* him. The Doctor.

VICTOR: *(ARRIVING)* Mother.

ILEANA: *(DISAPPOINTED)* Victor.

STUBBE: Well, the cub comes on leaps and bounds. What have you fetched us, boy?

FX: TURLOUGH CLUMPS TO THE FLOOR.

VICTOR: He was slinking round the cattle pens.

ILEANA: Turlough.

STUBBE: Ugh, that pastey, vinegar-veined youth. I'll never get rid of the taste!

ILEANA: Turlough, where's the Doctor?

TURLOUGH: *(EXHAUSTED)* The Doctor?

ILEANA: Yes. I knew he'd come for me. Where is he? Victor, go back down and look.

TURLOUGH: *(CONTEMPT)* Don't imagine the Doctor's going to defend you now.

ILEANA: What? What do you mean?

(STUBBE LAUGHS)

TURLOUGH: Not after what you've done. He's very particular

about who he travels with.
FX: *ANOTHER CHORUS OF HOWLS FROM THE CITY BELOW.*

SCENE 66. STREET
FX: *THE DOCTOR AND ROSA SURROUNDED BY GROWLING WOLVES, INCLUDING INEZ.*

ROSA: You still think this was a good idea?
DOCTOR: Just edge up to the TARDIS door... and keep that knife out of sight. *(TO CROWD)* My friends. How good it is to see you come when you're called. First to Pieter Stubbe's will. And then to my whistle. Splendid stuff.
FX: *GENERAL WOLFISH DISSENT.*
DOCTOR: I'm sure that Pieter Stubbe knows best, because he's an honourable wolf. So it's good to see you out in the open, not skulking behind your own shadows.
INEZ: Stubbe promised us our age-old rights.
DOCTOR: Inez, you don't sound too sure. Not to worry. Stubbe's a good fellow. He'll have it all in hand. So tell me, how will you manage to feed and water the cutclaw herds? The stupid creatures can't look after themselves. And what about the human troops, when they roll up to take back their city?
INEZ: Stubbe said he'd lead us.
DOCTOR: From up on the hill. Loosing his dogs of war against smart weapons and wolf-seeking missiles? How magnanimous of him. You used to run free and choose for yourselves, but now he does it for you.
FX: *ANGRY GROWLS.*
ROSA: Watch it, Doctor. They're turning nasty.
DOCTOR: That's the idea. *(ALOUD)* Soon you won't have to think at all. Soon you'll be nothing but a kennel full of the honourable Pieter Stubbe's lapdog poodles!
FX: *TUMULT OF SNARLS AND HOWLS.*

SCENE 67. SUMMIT OF THE CORCOVADO
FX: *HOWLS OF THE DISTANT ROUSED RABBLE.*

OSTUBBE: Now what do the rabble want?
ILEANA: They want to run free. Turlough, where's the Doctor?
TURLOUGH: Far away by now.
ILEANA: Don't lie to me. He wouldn't leave you behind.
STUBBE: If that's all the Doctor wants, let's throw the boy down the mountain to him.
(HE LIFTS TURLOUGH UP - PROBABLY BY THE FOOT)
TURLOUGH: No. Put me down! Please!
FX: *TARDIS DEMATERIALISES AND THE DOOR OPENS.*
TURLOUGH: Doctor!
ILEANA: Doctor!
DOCTOR: Pieter Stubbe! When I challenge you, you will have the decency to stay and face me!
FX: *STUBBE DROPS TURLOUGH.*
STUBBE: Challenges I accept. Not taunts. What is that object?

79

More moonshine?

DOCTOR: Ileana, thank you for returning my TARDIS.

ILEANA: I understood that it was important.

DOCTOR: It is.

STUBBE: Important? It's just delusion. Just like you, Doctor. You don't belong here. Not in our world. *You're* the *real* monster. And just as full of tricks as a tar pit.

DOCTOR: And you're bowling on a sticky wicket, Pieter. Turlough, get inside the TARDIS.

TURLOUGH: Be careful, Doctor.

DOCTOR: That's the last thing I can do. Pieter Stubbe, I challenge you...

STUBBE: Yes, monster? Now what?

DOCTOR: You will relinquish the power you've seized. Release the people you've enslaved, both wolves and humans.

STUBBE: I hold sway here.

DOCTOR: In just one tiny city.

STUBBE: Not for long. There are many more wolves to be found and unleashed. Just as I did with her.

DOCTOR: Stop it now, Pieter, before the others turn on you.

FX: THE DISTANT HOWLS AGAIN.

DOCTOR: Listen to them. They're turning already.

STUBBE: This is your doing. *(MOVING AWAY)* I'll soon stop their whining.

FX: HIS DEEP HOWLS ARE ANSWERED BY THE WOLVES FAR BELOW. THIS DRAWS BACK AS WE MOVE TO...

SCENE 68. INSIDE TARDIS DOORWAY

FX: TARDIS HUM. FROM OUTSIDE COMES THE BAYING OF PIETER STUBBE.

TURLOUGH: The Doctor's getting in too deep. We may have to distract that monster, Rosa. Where's your computer?

ROSA: *(HALF DELIRIOUS)* My fight... The spirits are getting angry...

TURLOUGH: *(CONCERNED)* Rosa?

FX: THE DRUMMING OF THE SPIRITS ECHOES IN HER HEAD.

ROSA: *(ECHOING)* It's my goddamn fight.

STUBBE: *(LIKEWISE)* I'll be waiting ...round the next corner.

ROSA: Grandpa? I can't...

STUBBE: And I'll still be hungry.

ROSA: Grandpa!

FX: THE CRESCENDO OF DRUMS MIXES WITH HOWLS, AND THE SNARL OF THE ROSA/CAT AGAIN.
SNAP! BACK IN THE TARDIS.

TURLOUGH: Rosa. Don't give in. Where's your computer? I need it now.

FX: ROSA MAKES A LOW GROWLING CAT YOWL.

SCENE 69. SUMMIT OF THE CORCOVADO.

STUBBE: *(BACKGROUND)* Listen to me, you rabble. I'm your

king. Lord of the forests! I won't be denied!
FX: HOWLS ECHO UP FROM BELOW. STUBBE BELLOWS BACK.
ILEANA: *(QUIETLY)* Doctor? When you travel, what do you look for?
DOCTOR: That's easy. I explore possibilities. I look for things I could never imagine. I want to know how they work and perhaps help them work better.
ILEANA: And you share that.
DOCTOR: With my companions, yes.
STUBBE: *(STILL IN BACKGROUND)* Don't turn your backs on me!
FX: MORE DISTANT HOWLS.
DOCTOR: Some people call it meddling. Others actually thank me for it. It all depends which side they're on.
STUBBE: You pack of mange-ridden curs! I know who you've been listening to!
ILEANA: Doctor, I could be more than just a companion.
(DOUBLE BEAT)
TURLOUGH: Doctor, are you coming back...
DOCTOR: I said, into the TARDIS, Turlough!
STUBBE: *(APPROACHING)* Doctor! Turn my brood against me, would you?
ILEANA: Leave him, Pieter! I've made my choice. I will not come back to you.
STUBBE: *(LAUGHS)* What? Go with him? Did he whistle for you too?
ILEANA: He's not an animal like you.
DOCTOR: Now hang on...
STUBBE: Does he know what you really are?
ILEANA: He's seen my dark side.
DOCTOR: Ileana's already told me.
STUBBE: That old story about the merchant's daughter rescued from bandits? She likes a good tale.
ILEANA: No, Pieter. Don't!
STUBBE: You don't want her sort, Doctor.
ILEANA: No!
STUBBE: Eighteen twelve. The French were fleeing Moscow. I caught her in the snow, filthy and starving, hunched over a frozen corpse. So hungry she'd eat anything. The wolf bitch shone through her like glass. And now, centuries later, after everything I taught her, she still doesn't know if she's woman or wolf.
DOCTOR: *I* can't judge her.
ILEANA: Doctor. You accept me? *(EXULTANT)* Then I shall go with you.
(BEAT)
DOCTOR: *(VERY QUIET, VERY SAD)* No.
ILEANA: Yes, I shall. You already said...
DOCTOR: Ileana, I would value your companionship...
STUBBE: *(LAUGHS)* He can't take you. He's an outsider. That's *his* dark side.
ILEANA: We're all outsiders.
DOCTOR: Pieter's right. I can't take you. You're tied to the Earth. To its old bones. To leave would kill you.

81

ILEANA: (ANGRY) I thought you'd be here with me!
DOCTOR: Ileana.
STUBBE: He could be. He could give up his travels to stay. Couldn't you, Doctor?
ILEANA: Would you stay, Doctor? For me? Do you really care?
FX: THE DISTANT WOLVES ARE HOWLING PLAINTIVELY AGAIN.
DOCTOR: Look to your army, Stubbe. It's your blood they want.
STUBBE: Let them howl.
ILEANA: Doctor? (BEAT)
DOCTOR: Ileana, perhaps I care much too much. (BEAT)
ILEANA: Or not enough. (DEFEATED) Goodbye, Doctor.
DOCTOR: Ileana!
STUBBE: Ileana! You're mine!
(ILEANA GASPS)
ILEANA: Let go of me!
DOCTOR: Put her down, Stubbe!
STUBBE: She's mine. She can't resist. Neither can you, Doctor. Nothing can!
DOCTOR: Your wolves reject you, Stubbe! Let her go! Aagh! (AS STUBBE PICKS HIM UP)
ILEANA: Pieter, let him down!
STUBBE: Got you both! The whole world's mine! And I'll eat all of it! (ROARING) Starting with you, Doctor monster!
FX: HE ROARS, READY TO SWALLOW THE DOCTOR, BUT... THE COMPUTER TUNE OF "Jaguar Girl" STARTS UP.
ROSA: Lobo king!
(STUBBE CRIES OUT IN PAIN)
ROSA: Silver bites you, lobo king!
(THE DOCTOR AND ILEANA GET DROPPED)
STUBBE: Little cat! Come here!
ROSA: Come and catch me!
TURLOUGH: Doctor! Quickly!
DOCTOR: Ileana, run! Run!
STUBBE: Ileana!
DOCTOR: Rosa! In here! In the TARDIS!
FX: CLATTERING OF THE TARDIS DOOR.
STUBBE: You can't hide in there, Doctor!

SCENE 70. TARDIS CONSOLE ROOM.
FX: TARDIS HUM. THE DOORS BUZZ HALF CLOSED AND PROTEST AS, SNARLING, STUBBE FORCES HIS WAY IN.

DOCTOR: Turlough, the doors. Let him in!
FX: STUBBE FORCES THROUGH, HIS CLAWS SCRABBLE ON THE HARD FLOOR.
TURLOUGH: Rosa, keep back!
STUBBE: (STILL RAGING) Doctor! What is this?
FX: THE DOORS CLOSE COMPLETELY.
DOCTOR: Sanctuary, Pieter. From the likes of you.
ROSA: It's him. I've been waiting for him.
FX: TARDIS DEMATERIALISATION STARTS.

TURLOUGH: Look out!

FX: SOMETHING SMASHES TO THE GROUND.

STUBBE: More trickery.

DOCTOR: I thought we'd take a short trip.

FX: FURNITURE OVERTURNED.

DOCTOR: Just to get things into perspective. When you've finished with my furniture.

ROSA: Remember our date, lobo?

FX: THE SCANNER BUZZES OPEN.

STUBBE: *(SUDDENLY PERPLEXED)* What's that? What is it?

TURLOUGH: *(SURPRISE)* It's the Earth. From orbit, about five hundred miles up.

(STUBBE GROANS AND CRASHES OVER)

DOCTOR: We'll just hover out here in space for a while.

STUBBE: *(WEAKENING. GASPING FOR BREATH)* Where are we? I can't feel the world.

DOCTOR: Of course, you can't. But you can see it. Look, there it is. It's going away from you.

STUBBE: Take me back! Monster! Monster!

DOCTOR: How old are you, Pieter?

STUBBE: *(SHIVERING)* I'm not old. I don't get older. I just *am*!

DOCTOR: You *were*. Listen to the Earth. It's left you behind.

FX: WE HEAR THE SPIRIT DRUMMING GRADUALLY GETTING LOUDER.

STUBBE: So cold...

DOCTOR: Or were you too busy gorging to listen? You can't devour it all, Pieter. The Earth's bigger than you are. Perhaps you've had your fill.

TURLOUGH: He's not changing, Doctor. Surely he'll become human.

DOCTOR: There were no humans when he first appeared.

STUBBE: I'm the first. All *Loups-garoux* are my children.

ROSA: *(POSSESSED)* Out of the forests, that's where you came from.

TURLOUGH: Rosa?

STUBBE: *(WEAKER)* They destroyed the forests. They drove us out.

ROSA: Stop whining! *I* am the forest. You left *me*. And now I'm coming after you.

STUBBE: The girl in the cat skin. Your claws still need cutting.

ROSA: Should have eaten me when you had the chance.

(STUBBE GROANS AGAIN)

DOCTOR: What shall we do with him, Rosa?

ROSA: Dunno. His strength's sapping away. But he'll always be hungry.

STUBBE: *(VERY WEAK)* Where's Ileana? Tell her I'll behave. Just take me back.

DOCTOR: His people have rejected him. Even Ileana doesn't want him. And neither do I.

TURLOUGH: You can't let him go.

DOCTOR: No, we can't do that.

ROSA: He's trouble. But I know who'll have him.

DOCTOR: Your spirits. I hoped you'd say that.

83

ROSA: Pieter Stubbe? Listen to me. Look. Do you see the path? Can you smell it?
FX: THE DRUMS START TO RISE AGAIN.
STUBBE: *(GRUNTS)* What's that?
ROSA: The path... ahead of you, through the trees.
STUBBE: The path...
FX: THE BUZZ OF INSECTS. RUSTLE OF BRANCHES.
ROSA: Go on. Follow the path. Straight ahead.

SCENE 70a. THE LOST FOREST
FX: THE SPIRIT DRUMS FADE SOMEWHAT. INSECTS DRONE. THE CRY OF AN EXOTIC BIRD. THE BUSHES ARE PUSHED BACK.

ROSA: Hey, Senhor Wolf.
STUBBE: Good day, young lady. Spare a morsel for a hungry wanderer.
ROSA: Get it yourself. Straight on, through the trees.
STUBBE: What forest is this? It's not my forest. And where's Ileana?
ROSA: Like it or lump it, lobo. See the path?
STUBBE: Straight ahead.
ROSA: Like a knife. So stick with it. And don't stray. Coz one day *I'll* be waiting behind the next tree, and I'll be hungry too. *(STUBBE GROWLS)*
ROSA: Go on. That way.
FX: THE DRUMS RISE AGAIN.
STUBBE: *(ANGRY)* Ileana? Who's dancing through there?
FX: PUSHES BACK BUSHES
STUBBE: *(MOVING AWAY)* Where are you? Ileana!
ROSA: See you, Senhor Wolf.

SCENE 70b. THE TARDIS
FX: TARDIS HUM

TURLOUGH: He's not breathing.
DOCTOR: No. Rosa?
ROSA: *(DEEP BREATH)* We couldn't leave him here. Now he's back in the forest where he belongs.
TURLOUGH: Stubbe's in the forest? In your head?
DOCTOR: Quite a relief for everyone. Thank the spirits for me.
ROSA: Don't thank them. They're okay. It's my head that gets done in by their goddamn drums.
FX: TARDIS CONSOLE ARRIVAL NOISE AND CHANGE OF BACKGROUND HUM.
DOCTOR: All right, we're back. Open the doors, Turlough.
TURLOUGH: What about his body? We can't leave him lying there.
DOCTOR: Just open the doors, please.
FX: CLICK. DOORS BUZZ OPEN. DISTANT BAYING OF THE WOLVES OUTSIDE.
TURLOUGH: You'll need a fork-lift truck to move him.
DOCTOR: Shush. Wolves have ears.
TURLOUGH: *(MUTTERING)* Or a wheelbarrow...

DOCTOR: I think he should be returned to his own people. Then they can all go home.
ROSA: I'll handle that. Bye, Doctor... Grandpa says he's sorry he missed you.
DOCTOR: Tell him the forest's in safe hands. Goodbye, Rosa.
TURLOUGH: Rosa? I suppose your initiation's finished.
ROSA: Hardly started. You were okay, yerpi-boy. Just stay crazy.
TURLOUGH: *(BEAT)* Yes. See you, Jaguar Girl.
ROSA: *(GOING)* See you around.
TURLOUGH: *(SUDDEN REALISATION)* Ah, Rosa. Your computer!

SCENE 71. SUMMIT OF THE CORCOVADO.
FX: DOORS CLATTER AS TURLOUGH EMERGES.

TURLOUGH: Rosa? *(BEAT)* She's gone. So fast.
DOCTOR: *(WEARY)* Only to be expected. The spirits are very demanding.
TURLOUGH: But what about Stubbe's body?
DOCTOR: Already gone, I expect.
TURLOUGH: *(NON-PLUSSED)* So quickly. *(GLUM)* She could have waited. And now what do I do with this?
FX: CLICKS ON ROSA'S PERSONAL COMPUTER
ROSA: *(TINNY ON COMPUTER, FROM SCENE 58)* "Time's coming when I get to prove myself. I won't forget."
FX: TURLOUGH CLICKS IT OFF AGAIN.
TURLOUGH: Sorry.
DOCTOR: I don't think she needed it any more. I'd hang on to it as a keepsake if I were you.
TURLOUGH: Yes. I will.
(BEAT)
FX: A SEAGULL CRIES OUT.
DOCTOR: The air's lifted.
TURLOUGH: You can smell the sea. Is the city free again?
DOCTOR: Oh, yes. They'll leave it alone now. *(DEEP BREATH)* Clear blue. Thank you, Turlough. You saved me from Stubbe's clutches.
TURLOUGH: *(NON-PLUSSED)* Did I? Oh. Good. Did you really believe all that forest spirit stuff?
DOCTOR: Didn't you? Rosa and Stubbe certainly did. And I do like to find things I thought were never possible.
TURLOUGH: Yes. But I'm sorry about Ileana.
DOCTOR: *(RATHER SHARPLY)* Why?
TURLOUGH: Well, you... I mean I thought that you were both...
DOCTOR: Yes?
TURLOUGH: But now she's gone too.
DOCTOR: Has she? Are you sure about that? Can't you see, Turlough?
ILEANA: *(QUIET)* Doctor?
DOCTOR: *(GENTLE)* It's safe now, Ileana. He's gone. You're free. Both you and Victor.
ILEANA: Am I free? At what price, when I can never leave the Earth?

DOCTOR: No, I never wanted to stay at home either. That story. The one about the wolf woman and the winter. How did it end?

ILEANA: The winter wolf died. But the woman had a cub. And when the year grew old, he left her snowy home and drove away the aged brown wolf of summer.

DOCTOR: And so it goes in endless turns.

ILEANA: Year after year. Without *Him*. *(BEAT)* Goodbye, Doctor.

DOCTOR: Goodbye, Ileana.

(BEAT)

TURLOUGH: No, Doctor, I can't see anyone. I'm sorry.

DOCTOR: So am I, Turlough. *(SIGHS)* Ah well... maybe she just doesn't want you to. *(BEAT)* Come on.

FX: THE DOOR CLATTERS SHUT. THE TARDIS GOES. AND AFTER A SECOND, A FAR OFF, PLAINTIVE WOLF HOWL.
CLOSING MUSIC.

THE HOLY TERROR

By Robert Shearman

I've just put *The Holy Terror* on the CD player. It's not something I've quite dared do for a year and a half. There's nothing much fun about listening to something you've written – all you see are the plot holes and the bad dialogue and the Ideas Which Never Quite Worked, Did They? And since it's quite a long story, running at well over two hours (believe me, I was cursing myself for that little piece of bad discipline), I had quite a time of it, squirming away. It was as bad as when I had chicken pox.

Ultimately, *The Holy Terror* is Nick Pegg's fault. Not only did he direct it, but he was also the man who introduced me to Big Finish in the first place. I'd been at university with him in 1989, and we'd kept in contact since, seeing each other's theatre work when we could. When Big Finish won the licence to produce *Doctor Who*, Nick passed my name on to Gary Russell and Jason Haigh-Ellery as a professional drama writer who was (apparently) reliable and had written for radio already. They read my CV, met up with me, and asked me to pitch an idea. I sent in a page or so which they liked, calling it *The Holy Terror*, with the promise I'd think up a better title some time later. And they commissioned it. Which was nice of them. That first page outline was completely different to the eventual script I wrote; for a start, there was no hint about the fictional nature of the castle, and there was no mystery raised about the identity of the child's father – it was Childeric, plain and simple. No one died either – it was a much lighter idea, with a greater emphasis on satirising religious fixation. I had never wanted to send up Christianity – indeed, many years ago I used to do a fair bit of preaching, so it would be very hypocritical if I had! – but just the way that worship can become something you dare not question or discuss. The much simpler storyline I gave the guys at Big Finish involved a population, highly impressed by the TARDIS materialising, treating the Doctor as a god, dressing like him and talking like him, much to his embarrassment!

The basic idea behind the story was something I had tried to pitch as a theatre play for years, but it had always been rejected, ironically, as being a bit too *Doctor Who*-ish. I had read about the medieval theory which postulated that if you took a child at birth and separated him from the corrupted words of mankind, the language that the innocent would be forced to develop would be the language of God. It's something that monarchs as diverse as James I and Akbar the Great were fascinated by. I remember suggesting this tale to long-suffering managements of repertory theatres all over Britain, about a child locked away until manhood, and then released to the expectant crowds hoping for a phone line directly to the Almighty... The theatre producers would look excited, and ask what would happen next – and I'd shrug and say, well, I suppose it would turn into some sort of monster that would kill people. (Which is a good illustration of the gap between Serious Modern Drama and *Doctor Who* – the theatres always looked disappointed at this particular plot development.)

The main difference between pitch and script was that I'd outlined the story for a generic Doctor, with no companion. I had a vague idea of the Fourth Doctor, in

87

fact, and I know that it was one of the ideas that Big Finish sent to Tom Baker in 1999 when he was considering coming on board. I was asked instead to craft it for Colin, and this talking penguin as his sidekick. I was a *Doctor Who* fan between 1981 and 1985, and so I remembered Frobisher from the comics. At first my jaw dropped at Gary's suggestion; how on earth would a shapeshifter adopting the guise of a flightless bird work in an audio context? He was so clearly a visual joke! But a voice in my head told me that I would never get another chance to write a *Doctor Who* story, and at least this way mine would be remembered!

The presence of Frobisher did a lot to change the tone of the story. Though pitched as a comedy, I didn't think the story would now work very well unless I gave it a darker edge. Frobie was so clearly a comedic character that I was worried that if there wasn't some contrast, it'd all end up being one note and trying too hard to please. It was around that point I began to conceive of a story which started out as the comedy Frobisher's inclusion would lead the listeners to expect, and then descend into a horror. I wrote it in two weeks in March 2000, having just listened to Jacqueline Rayner's terrific *The Marian Conspiracy*, and read Nick's *The Spectre of Lanyon Moor*. I don't think either Jac or Nick have been given enough credit for the way they re-established the Sixth Doctor; it was seeing how they'd tackled his characterisation which inspired me, and I know that other writers since are indebted to them as well.

I had to write two scripts at the same time, owing to a slight overbooking. *The Holy Terror* was written on the back of an open air theatre adaptation of *Pride and Prejudice*, and at the time I was worried I was having to rush things a bit. It's quite true that when I wrote Part One I still believed that everyone would still be alive by the end of Part Four, and although I knew the identity of the child's father would become a major part of the story, had no idea how to resolve that yet. (I only worked out it was *spoiler* some way towards the end of Part Two – then frantically went back to drop lots of clues in what I'd already written!) Looking back, though, the fact I was adapting Jane Austen at the time gave a tremendously helpful boost to my *Doctor Who* script. I would spend one day writing about polite young girls taking tea on the lawn, and the next I would have the joyous relief of returning to torture and dungeons!

The Holy Terror was, as all first drafts of my stuff are, massively overwritten. No one at Big Finish ever read that first draft – they would have had to decipher my dreadful handwriting to have done so – and there's an awful lot of silly jokes and bits of nonsense that never made it on to the computer when I typed it up. That second draft was a laborious job, cutting all the episodes down to the standard 25 minutes. I sent the script off to Gary, whose response was very positive. He told me he thought it was a bit on the short side, and gave me a lot more free rein to take the time to explore my odd little world. So I stuck back all the bits in I'd liked from the first draft, but cut because they seemed only to give flavour and background, rather than advancing the plot. (Mostly the comedy bits, in fact. I'm in two minds about their reinstatement – but it does seem that these scenes are the ones listeners remember the best, so it's probably right they're there. They do sacrifice some of the pace, though.)

Gary asked only for two major rewrites. One was that Nick had managed to cast husband and wife Peter Guinness and Roberta Taylor as Childeric and Berengaria –

and, in my original draft, they never met! I could see that that was rather a pity, so shamelessly ripped off a scene from *Richard III* to feature them both. (Again, it doesn't advance the plot an iota – but it's quoted a fair bit in the trailer.) The second was that originally the Doctor seemed much more stoical at the end when Tacitus kills himself. Gary pointed out, quite rightly, that this made the Doctor seem very callous, and it was a characterisation cliché that both he and Colin were keen to get away from.

Nick Pegg gave a few helpful suggestions for minor improvements, and I was happy to oblige. His suggestion that I play the sculptor appealed to the kid in me who had always wanted to be in *Doctor Who*. (Nick had directed me at university in *Hamlet*, and knew I'm not much cop as an actor, but reasoned it was only four lines.) My main memories of the recording were worrying about my own small performance so much that I didn't need to get worried about anyone else's. I stood in front of that microphone and shook. It was just as well that the sculptor was pleading for his life – had he been written to be even a tad more self-confident, I could never have got away with it!

Other things I remember? The enormous fun we all had as a group recording all the death screams and shouts of fear – Nick Pegg directing the action for well over an hour as if he were conducting an orchestra. I made my throat hoarse, not only with my especially OTT death rattles, but with laughter – never stand next to Colin Baker in a crowd scene! The way in which Nick cleverly directed all the comedy on the first day, and saved most of the horror for the second – there was a strange unnerving chill for moments in the studio on day two when the cast experienced just how dark this comedy had become... And, most of all, just being blown away by the experience of doing *Doctor Who*.

I didn't think the buying public would like *The Holy Terror* that much, to be honest. Nick and Gary were behind it from the very beginning, but I could glean enough from online expectation that no one seemed to be looking forward to it. The response has, by and large, been extraordinarily positive, and I'm genuinely bowled over by it. I think the reason it has gone down well is, in part, because of the meticulous and patient direction of Nick Pegg, a score by Russell Stone which provides buckets of atmosphere when the script falters, and a truly committed cast. Sam Kelly just ran with it, and I remember being in the control room during the recording, and everyone being knocked for six by how good he was. But I also think it has gone down well because it was very fortunately timed. It was the fourteenth release, and came out when fans were looking for something with a different tone. Any earlier, and it would have been rejected as too silly, I think. Any later, and someone else would have already done it better!

I've turned the CD player off now. I'm actually quite proud of *The Holy Terror*. I see tons of faults. It's too long, too fractured, and has a huge number of gaping plot holes. (Most of which people haven't noticed, so I'm not going to point them out now!) But I do think it sounds terrific. Listening back to it, pretending it's nothing whatsoever to do with me, I find lots of it rather exciting, and a few bits even quite moving. If I wrote the story now, I'd do it very differently – I'd probably give it a more upbeat ending, and I'd want to get the Doctor into the action a lot sooner. But for the production itself, there's not one thing I'd want to alter. Not even that bit with the sculptor in.

THE HOLY TERROR

CAST

THE DOCTOR	Colin Baker
FROBISHER	Robert Jezek
CAPTAIN SEJANUS	Dan Hogarth
EUGENE TACITUS	Sam Kelly
BERENGARIA	Roberta Taylor
LIVILLA	Helen Punt
CHILDERIC	Peter Guinness
PEPIN	Stefan Atkinson
CLOVIS	Peter Sowerbutts
ARNULF	Bruce Mann

PART ONE

Scene 1

INT. The dungeons of a castle. Dank and damp, with the faint sound of dripping water. There is some echo. A few seconds of peace, establishing this. Then an old creaking door is thrust open, and a man forced bodily into the room.

SEJANUS: On your knees, prisoner!

SCRIBE: What? Oh yes, certainly...

SEJANUS: Quickly! On your knees!

SCRIBE: *(amiably)* Honestly, I'm doing it as quickly as I can. It's hard at my age to...

(A little grunt, and the slight slap of hands against stone.)

See, there you are. Ooh, these dungeon floors are a little cold, aren't they? I take it this is the dungeon?

(A scroll is unfolded and brandished.)

SEJANUS: Are you Eugene Tacitus, scribe to the emperor?

SCRIBE: Oh, absolutely.

SEJANUS: And do you know why you have been brought here?

SCRIBE: No, not really, I mean, I tried asking this chap behind me, but all he'd do was prod me with his sword and tell me to be silent, so I didn't push the matter. It's all been a bit of a blur, I was fast asleep half an hour ago, when my door is broken down and I'm dragged out of bed... Hardly time for me even to put on my dressing gown. Look, would it be all right if I put on my spectacles? If I'm going to be interrogated on a dungeon floor, it'd be some comfort to see what's going on. They're in my pocket...

SEJANUS: No quick moves now.

SCRIBE: No, no, I'll put them on very slowly. There. That's better. My word, it really is horribly dank down here, isn't it?

(More scroll business.)

SEJANUS: You have been brought here to answer one simple question.

SCRIBE: Well, fire away.

SEJANUS: Whom do you worship, Eugene Tacitus?

SCRIBE: Well, I'd say the living god, emperor Pepin VI. Doesn't everyone?

(There is a horrified gasp of breath from two nearby guards.)

SEJANUS: Easy, men. Don't be shocked by the blasphemy.

SCRIBE: I take it that's the wrong answer then?

SEJANUS: The living god emperor Pepin VI is dead.

SCRIBE: Oh. Whoops.

SEJANUS: He fell asleep in his bath and drowned.

SCRIBE: Not a very dignified way to go.

SEJANUS: The new living god is now emperor Pepin VII. And all those who worship Pepin VI commit heresy and must be executed forthwith.

(We hear swords being pulled out of scabbards.)

SCRIBE: Oh dear. Forthwith, you say?

SEJANUS: According to the holy rituals, the condemned will have

93

one eye gouged out, the other left intact to watch the flames rise as he is burned at the stake.

SCRIBE: Not a terribly dignified way to go either.

SEJANUS: You are to be taken from this place, to a cell waiting execution. You will be allowed no contact with your family. And your remains will not be placed in holy ground. And your name will be reviled for ever more, and held as a byword for apostasy. Unless you are prepared to recant immediately, and pledge allegiance to the living god Pepin VII.

SCRIBE: Oh, well, I think I'll recant then.

SEJANUS: Is that your final decision, Eugene Tacitus?

SCRIBE: Absolutely.

SEJANUS: *(amiably)* Oh, well, that's fine then. Swords back, men. We've got another one who wants to recant.

(The swords are sheathed in their scabbards, with a couple of mildly disappointed groans.)

Now then...

(He picks up some other papers, leafs through them.)

If you'd just like to sign this recantation form... Here...

SCRIBE: Right...

SEJANUS: And here... And here is your dark blue receipt of your recantation. And here is your light blue receipt, which can be exchanged for a dark blue receipt if the original is mislaid.

SCRIBE: Thanks very much. That's fine.

SEJANUS: Sorry about all the formality, sir, I'm sure you understand...

SCRIBE: Oh, of course. It's tradition. I know that.

SEJANUS: If you don't mind finding your own way out, I'd be grateful. I've got dozens of interrogations to conduct before morning.

(We hear an old door creaking open, SCRIBE's footsteps on stone hesitantly.)

You can't miss it, just keep going up.

Scene 2: INT.

The Empress' bedroom. Peaceful music plays on a lute. We hear, faintly, nails being scrubbed hard. Then, with a faint sigh, the scrubbing stops.

BERENGARIA: Why have you stopped, Livilla? Are you tired?

LIVILLA: No, your highness. I shall continue.

BERENGARIA: Of course you're tired. I've had you polishing my toenails for the last four hours. Your arms must be ready to drop off. Tell me the truth now.

LIVILLA: *(flatly)* Yes, your highness. I am in great pain.

BERENGARIA: Well, that's no good to me at all. Not unless I can hear the pain in your voice. You shall continue scrubbing them then, Livilla. We'll see how long it takes you to cry.

LIVILLA: *(flatly)* Yes, your highness.

BERENGARIA: I want my toenails so shiny I'll be able to see my face in them. Or could, if only I could see my feet over my stomach. But rest assured, Livilla, next morning I shall ask a servant if she can see her face in my toenails, and if she can't, I shall have you flogged.

(There is thumping at the door.)
What is it? Who's there?
(The door breaks down.)
Guard Captain Sejanus! How dare you disturb me? I shall have you flogged as well!

SEJANUS: I bring news, madam. The Emperor is dead.
(And, rather awkwardly, the lute music stops.)
BERENGARIA: *(softly)* ...So. It's finally happened.
(Another scroll is produced. SEJANUS clears his throat.)
SEJANUS: I am instructed firstly to offer my condolences for your husband's loss. You shall be allowed a period of grieving, not to last more than one half hour.
BERENGARIA: Spare me that. The old fraud hadn't touched me in years. He was no husband to me.
SEJANUS: Then I am instructed secondly to place you under close arrest. Your husband was a false god. You are a false goddess. You shall be conveyed to a cell until the manner of your death shall be determined.
BERENGARIA: *(impatiently)* I know that very well. Well, come on then. Take me to your cell. Oaf.
SEJANUS: Take her, men.
(Swords are drawn from scabbards.)
Lead on.
(And BERENGARIA is marched out of the room. When the clanking of chainmail has receded:)
Lady Livilla, your husband is our new emperor, and our new god. According to tradition, you must be the one to devise the execution of your predecessor. Do you accept the role that destiny has given you?
LIVILLA: Oh yes. I don't think that should give me any great difficulty.
SEJANUS: Very good. My lady.
(And we hear him exit.)
LIVILLA: Well, musician. Play your lute.
(The music resumes, as before.)
Oh no. I think something a bit jollier than that. We're celebrating, after all.
(And, after a slight hesitation, we hear something more up tempo. Something ridiculously forced, sounding a bit like a German drinking song!)
That's better. That's nice.

Scene 3: INT.
The TARDIS swimming pool. Against the reassuring background hum of the ship in flight, we hear the soft voice of a killer ...

FROBISHER: That's it. That's the idea. Find somewhere to hide. But there is nowhere to hide. Is there? There's just you and me. The hunter. And the prey. Swim away as fast as you can, it makes no difference. Because there's no... escape... from me!
(Loud splashing. A little squeal.)
Now, hold still. Hold still, dammit! Okay. Shall I eat you

95

now? Or would you like to play some more?

(Another squeal.)

DOCTOR: *(outside the room)* Frobisher? Are you in there?

FROBISHER: Hey, Doc, can't it wait? I'm kind of busy at the moment...

(A door opens during the above line.)

DOCTOR: *(closer)* Oh, yes. So I can see.

(Awkward splashing, as FROBISHER repositions himself.)

FROBISHER: Hey, do you mind? What's a guy have to do to get some privacy round here?

DOCTOR: We're in trouble. The TARDIS is out of control.

FROBISHER: The TARDIS is always out of control. Is it worth interrupting my bath time? It's embarrassing, I'm all naked here...

DOCTOR: Frobisher, you're the shape of a penguin. You're always naked.

FROBISHER: That's what you think. I usually morph myself a black and white pair of pants as well.

DOCTOR: None of the controls are responding. It's as if the power's been drained elsewhere...

(A splash as the fish escapes FROBISHER. A squeal.)

What was that?

FROBISHER: What was what?

DOCTOR: Is that a gumblejack you have in there with you?

FROBISHER: *(over another squeal)* Well, it's a fish, at any rate. He didn't introduce himself.

DOCTOR: And you're hunting it.

FROBISHER: Yes.

DOCTOR: And going to kill it.

FROBISHER: That's the idea.

DOCTOR: How very cruel.

FROBISHER: Hey, don't make me feel guilty. Just because you prefer the taste of salad.

DOCTOR: There's no need for you to be hunting at all. There's a whole room down the corridor filled with cans of tuna.

(Splashing.)

FROBISHER: Oh, come on, Doc! That's no fun! I have to capture it myself, and eat it alive! I'm a penguin, for Pete's sake.

DOCTOR: No, you're not. You're a mesomorph. A shape shifter.

FROBISHER: Okay, so I'm not a real penguin. But that's fine, this isn't a real fish either.

(A squeal, as FROBISHER makes another launch at it. A loud splash.)

DOCTOR: What?

FROBISHER: Missed it! ...It's a 3D replica I got the TARDIS to conjure up for me. There are a whole heap of buttons on that console you don't do anything with, you know...

DOCTOR: *(quietly)* You haven't been playing with the dimensional stabilisers, have you?

FROBISHER: No. Well, possibly. Does it matter?

DOCTOR: Does it matter? The dimensional stabilisers give the TARDIS its structure and form. The walls, the floors, the air we breathe, it's constantly generated by the ship, held in balance, and checked and rechecked. It's the most difficult job a TARDIS has to do.

And you've been overriding them to make fish. No wonder the old girl is under a bit of a strain.

FROBISHER: Okay, okay, I'll eat the fish, problem solved.
(He splashes about.)
Hey, where did it go? It just vanished...
(We hear the TARDIS hum die down. As it does so:)
DOCTOR: Oh no...
FROBISHER: What's happening? Why has it gone so dark? ...Have I broken something?
DOCTOR: Worse than that, I'm afraid. The TARDIS has had enough. She's gone on strike.

Scene 4: INT

A corridor within the castle. Stone walls. SEJANUS marches BERENGARIA to the dungeons. We hear the sound of his chainmail and boots as he keeps step.

SEJANUS: Not much further now, madam.
BERENGARIA: *(coldly)* Thank you, Sejanus, I do know where the dungeons are. I have imprisoned enough people there in my lifetime.
SEJANUS: I'm sorry, madam. I meant no disrespect.
(A throat is cleared. SEJANUS stops dead, apprehensive.)
Who's there?
CHILDERIC: *(smoothly)* Mother, good day. What means this armed guard that waits upon your grace?
SEJANUS: My lord Childeric. I must ask you to come no closer. Lady Berengaria is a traitor and her life is forfeit.
BERENGARIA: Childeric, go away. You know perfectly well I'm being taken off to the dungeons for ritual torture and execution. It's annoying, but there it is. And I have no desire to spend the last painful protracted hours of my existence with one of my children, thank you very much.
CHILDERIC: Guard Captain Sejanus. Take pity on your prisoner. Allow her some final words of comfort from her loving son.
SEJANUS: You know I cannot do that, sir.
CHILDERIC: I'll make it worth your while. See here.
(A jingle of coins.)
There's a nice shiny gold coin for you.
SEJANUS: Well, if you put it like that...
CHILDERIC: Exactly. Now don't spend it all at once.
BERENGARIA: I don't want any words of comfort. Don't I get any say in this?
CHILDERIC: I wouldn't have thought so, mother...
SEJANUS: Of course not, you're just the prisoner...
BERENGARIA: Typical.
CHILDERIC: Wait over there, Sejanus. I would take my leave of my mother privately.
SEJANUS: Very well. But I can only give you a minute.
CHILDERIC: Oh, I think a minute will be ample, thank you.
(SEJANUS walks away. We hear the sound of his boots grow fainter, then stop.)
BERENGARIA: Oh, do go away, Childeric. You'll miss your brother's

coronation. I know how much you must be looking forward to it.

CHILDERIC: You've never liked me, have you, mother?

BERENGARIA: Good lord, no. What's there to like?

CHILDERIC: Oh, I understand. Nature has made me a bastard. I, that am not shaped for sportive tricks, I, that am deformed, unfinished, sent before my time into this breathing world. And so I am determined to prove a villain.

BERENGARIA: Which is exactly what I mean. I just don't think you've ever been villainous enough. You've always been a disappointment to me.

CHILDERIC: Oh.

BERENGARIA: And you showed so much promise. I remember the pleasure you took as a child, pulling the wings off flies. Where has all that evil gone, Childeric? You're illegitimate. You're a hunchback. Being evil is what you were born for.

CHILDERIC: And so I am, mother. You shall see. I intend to usurp the throne from my brother. And I shall be emperor and god instead.

BERENGARIA: Throughout history, the empress has given birth to two sons. One good, virtuous, heroic. The rightful heir to the throne. The other a bastard. Twisted and abhorrent. It's practically mythical. And who do I turn out? Your younger half-brother is a weak, stammering idiot. But I doubt even you have the stomach to overthrow him.

(A rattling of chains.)

Let go of my hand...!

CHILDERIC: Give me your blessing, mother.

BERENGARIA: Why?

CHILDERIC: You are the most evil person I have ever known. Cruel, callous, without a shred of feeling. I have tried to model myself on you. For years I have been hiding away in the crypts of this castle, plotting and scheming against nature and against God.

BERENGARIA: Hiding in crypts doesn't make you look evil, Childeric. Just rather sulky and antisocial.

(A rattling of chains as she pulls her hand away.)

CHILDERIC: And I have devised the perfect plan to seize command not only of the empire, but of the heavens themselves. And I shall rule forever.

BERENGARIA: I think it more likely that your brother shall reign. However insipid he is. When he is crowned today you shall kneel in obeisance, and be his subject.

CHILDERIC: You shall see, mother.

BERENGARIA: Well, I'll be dead. So it's all much of a muchness to me, frankly.

CHILDERIC: But you shall see all the same. News of my notoriety shall reach even the furthest depths of hell, where your black heart shall burn forever. ...Sejanus! You may take her away now.

(We hear SEJANUS approach.)

BERENGARIA: Yes. Take me away now.

SEJANUS: My lord. My lady.

CHILDERIC: This dungeon in which you are imprisoning my mother. It is dark, isn't it?

SEJANUS: The darkest there is, my lord. Not a trace of light.

CHILDERIC: And you will manacle her to the walls of this dungeon, won't you? Here's an extra coin for your trouble.

(Jingle of coins.)
SEJANUS: Thank you.
CHILDERIC: Die well, mother. Die long and slow.
BERENGARIA: You too, Childeric. When your time comes.
(BERENGARIA is led away by SEJANUS.)
CHILDERIC: But I shall make sure that it never does. Your evil was
for so little, mother, if it has to die with you. The legacy of my evil
shall be eternal.

Scene 5: INT.
*The throne room. Much background bustle as preparations for the
coronation are under way. There is, in the distance, a sound of a brass
orchestra warming up. The faint echo of a great hall.*

SCRIBE: Well, your highness. Your coronation awaits us. In less
than one hour you shall be crowned the new emperor, and become the
true living god of us all.
PEPIN: *(faintly)* Yes.
SCRIBE: Emperor Pepin VII, the illustrious son to emperor Pepin
VI, and the no less illustrious grandson to emperor Pepin V. The last
and greatest of the royal line of Pepins.
PEPIN: Well. Here's hoping.
SCRIBE: I was wondering if I could write down any great
thoughts you might be having?
PEPIN: Great thoughts?
(The turning of pages in a heavy book.)
SCRIBE: You know. For the Bible. Something that might live for
posterity.
(And the click as a ballpoint pen is turned on.)
PEPIN: Well. In truth. I'm just very very scared.
SCRIBE: Yes. I see...
PEPIN: What if I get all my lines wrong? What if I fall over
during the ceremony, or faint, or throw up? I've been so nervous I've
not been able to keep anything down since my father died...
SCRIBE: *(sighing)* Try to remember, your highness. These hours
are the starting point for an entire new religion. I don't want to put,
chapter one, verse one, our immortal master was very very scared.
PEPIN: But it's the truth.
(A moment's hesitation, then some scribbling.)
SCRIBE: How about I write that you're stolidly apprehensive?
PEPIN: There's very little that's stolid about it. I've been trying
hard to have great thoughts, scribe. I've been frowning hard until it
really hurts, but nothing springs to mind. But I don't officially become a
god until the crown is placed on my head, do I?
(SCRIBE is too busy scribbling away. As soon as he stops, he reads.)
SCRIBE: *(quoting)* 'And at the moment of coronation comes
deification, and the crown of empire burns all mortality away, and the
new monarch becomes divine'. Something like that anyway.
PEPIN: *(happily)* Then that's all right. I shouldn't be thinking
like a god yet. I'm sure all my great thoughts will pop up at the right
time.
(Scribbling resumes.)

SCRIBE: God was showing signs of stolid optimism...
CLOVIS: Your majesty?
SCRIBE: ...When he was joined by High Priest Clovis.
CLOVIS: Leave us, scribe. I would be alone with our new master.
SCRIBE: Certainly. I can improvise the rest of the chapter anyway.
(And we hear him go, muttering happily to himself.)
CLOVIS: How are you feeling, your highness?
PEPIN: I'm very very...
CLOVIS: Very very scared, yes, of course you are. I was present when your father was made a god. And he was every bit as awkward and pathetic as you are now.
PEPIN: It's hard to believe my father was ever scared of anything. He should still be our god. He'd be much better at it than me.
CLOVIS: But, alas, that's impossible. Your father committed the ultimate blasphemy.
PEPIN: What's that?
CLOVIS: He died. Gods really aren't supposed to do that sort of thing.
(A lone, and rather feeble, blast of a trumpet out of the orchestra warm-up.)
Don't worry, your highness, I'm sure you're every inch the real omnipotent creator we thought your father was.
PEPIN: I know the traditions, Clovis. It is said that every coronation is accompanied by some great miracle.
CLOVIS: That is true.
PEPIN: Care must be taken of my subjects. I wouldn't want them to be killed in an earthquake or anything.
CLOVIS: Don't worry. The miracle is well in hand.
PEPIN: I have decided to be a very benevolent god, Clovis. And try to be nice to everyone.
CLOVIS: And I'm sure it does you great credit. If you will excuse me.
PEPIN: *(his voice fading away, as CLOVIS leaves him chatting away)* Yes, of course, I know you have lots and lots to attend to. Oh well, I'll see you during the ceremony, I suppose...
CLOVIS: *(muttering)* God protect us...
CHILDERIC: *(softly)* Ah, high priest. And what great miracle have you got lined up for us tonight?
CLOVIS: *(stiffly)* You'll have to wait and see, Childeric. But rest assured, everything has been arranged.
CHILDERIC: Don't you mean stage managed? What's it going to be this time? I hope it's going to be better than when my father was made god. Pulling a rabbit out of a hat.
CLOVIS: I think you'll find the official text says the deification was accompanied by an earthquake.
CHILDERIC: Oh, I know what the Bible says. But I've heard the rumours. I'm sure that whatever you do, that idiot scribe will make it halfway apocalyptic. Come on, Clovis. Give me a sneak preview. I'm hoping this time you'll saw a lady in half. Now that'd be spectacular.
CLOVIS: I have things to attend to.
CHILDERIC: *(urgently)* You know that the ceremony is a fake, Clovis!

100

That dribbling fool is not a god, will never be a god! We must look elsewhere for our leaders. You know that. Of all the people here, you know it better than anyone!

CLOVIS: I must go... I have things to... I must go.

CHILDERIC: *(quietly, to himself)* You know it.

Scene 6: INT.
The TARDIS console room. But there is no familiar background hum.

FROBISHER: If the TARDIS is on strike, what are we supposed to do? Negotiate with her?

DOCTOR: I don't know. It's never happened before. Shine the torch over there, on the console.

(A loud click as the torch is activated.)

FROBISHER: I've never seen the TARDIS look so dead.

DOCTOR: She's not dead, only sulking. Come on, old thing. After all the centuries we've been together, don't walk out on me now. We'll do better, I promise.

(The background hum rises for a moment, hopefully. Then drains away. Silence.)

FROBISHER: So much for negotiations. Now what?

DOCTOR: Not much else we can do. We'll have to give in to her demands.

FROBISHER: Which are what, exactly?

DOCTOR: Look at the console. All the panels have stopped working.

(We hear him press dead buttons and switches with dull thuds. Then he hits one which gives a feeble bleep. Excitedly:)

Except for this one... torch...

(Another, different bleep.)

And that one over there. ...Oh dear.

FROBISHER: And what do they do?

DOCTOR: The TARDIS is tired of being taken for granted. She wants me to surrender autonomous control directly to her. From now on, she'll be the one who'll be in charge.

FROBISHER: So she'll just materialise wherever she wants, and we won't have a clue where we're going. Don't think we'll have much trouble adapting to that.

(The DOCTOR drums his fingers over the console nervously.)

DOCTOR: Or she could reduce the interior dimensions to the width of an atom. Or simply eject us into the vortex. Whatever she wants.

FROBISHER: Oh.

DOCTOR: ...Let's just hope she'll materialise wherever she wants, and we won't have a clue where we're going.

(And with a decisive slap of the console, he stops finger drumming.)

We'll have to disable the manual circuits together, you push that button over there, when I pull... this lever, I think.

FROBISHER: All this fuss because I was cruel to a fish. It wasn't even as if it were real.

DOCTOR: It was sentient, wasn't it? It felt fear, it felt pain...

FROBISHER: Well, sure, the hunt's no good without the fear or the pain...

DOCTOR: If it thought it was real, who are you to say it wasn't?

FROBISHER: Oh, Doc, come on. I created it. It had no life beyond what I had given it in the first place.

DOCTOR: *(sighing)* Frobisher. After all the adventures we've had. It doesn't matter to whom the cruelty is directed, the cruelty itself is wrong. If you haven't learned that, you haven't learned anything.

FROBISHER: Doc, fascinating as the metaphysics may be, you're really just trying to put off pulling that lever, aren't you?

DOCTOR: Yes.

FROBISHER: We have to do it together?

DOCTOR: On the count of three. One, two, three!

FROBISHER: Now!

(A couple of bleeps and blips. And the controls him back to life. The familiar sound of the TARDIS in flight. The DOCTOR sighs with relief.) And now what?

DOCTOR: Well, we're still alive. So far so good. Now we'll just wait and see where the ship wants to take us.

Scene 7: INT.

The throne room. Lots of expectant muttering. The orchestra is still tuning up, much more successfully by now. There is a baton struck a couple of times by a conductor, and the music falls silent. The crowd follow suit.
The SCRIBE whispers confidentially, as he reads what he writes. We hear the scribbling.
Once again, there is the echo of a great hall.

SCRIBE: And at last the hour of the coronation had arrived. And the congregation had been gathering in the throne room for the past two days, and they were sore relieved, because they had been getting sore impatient. And Pepin, looking imperious in his stolid apprehension, was joined by his beautiful consort Livilla.

(A single blast of trumpets in unison.)

PEPIN: Oh, hello, my dear.

LIVILLA: *(quietly)* Now, don't you get this ceremony wrong, Pepin. All right? I want to be empress. I've earned the right to be empress, being handmaiden to your bitch of a mother these last few years.

PEPIN: I'll try my hardest, I promise you.

(At length, under her speech, a quiet but fast beat of drums is heard.)

LIVILLA: You better had. Because I want a crown, and I want it crammed with the most beautiful diamonds and emeralds and bits of shiny metal that can be found. Ever since we were married I've been waiting to be goddess to these stinking people. And you're not going to spoil it for me now.

(We hear the swish of a heavy dress as both begin to walk up the aisle. And out of the drums, still continuing but louder, full ceremonial music starts. Brass and strident)

SCRIBE: And lo, the empress took the emperor's hand. And lo, they walked slowly down the aisle towards their thrones.

PEPIN: Isn't it exciting, dear? It's just like our wedding day.

LIVILLA: Thank you, Pepin. That's one bad memory I didn't need reminding of.

(The brass stops playing, leaving the drums beating excitedly underneath.)
SCRIBE: And Clovis, the high priest, bade the couple sit down upon their thrones.
(We hear the crumple of heavy robes as they relax.)
And they did so. And he took the crown and lifted it above the young king's head, saying:
CLOVIS: I consecrate you as our new emperor. You will be the heart of the nation, you will be the soul of its people. And you will be our immortal god, and shall always have been so. The mysteries of the future shall be known to you, the secrets of the past shall have been your creation. For in you all times shall meet and be as one, you shall be at once infinite. All hail Pepin VII, our new emperor, and our everlasting god!
(Jubilant trumpet blasts. The crowd shout over them.)
CROWD: All hail the emperor! All hail our god! All hail the emperor! All hail our god!
SCRIBE: *(confidentially, whispering to the listeners over the sound - we still hear his scribbling)* And a new god was born as the crown was brought down upon his head.
(A muted, distant gasp of concern...)
And, oops, it wobbled a bit there, but it's all right, he's got it.
(The trumpets blast again, more excited than ever.)
CLOVIS: And now, behold! A new miracle!
SCRIBE: And the crowd were sore expectant.
CLOVIS: *(throwing off a little of the religious fervour, and with more of the pace of a stage magician)* All right. A pack of playing cards, just an ordinary pack of playing cards. Nothing special about them at all. Now, if I could just ask his omnipotence, pick a card. Any card. Don't tell me what it is, and then put it back anywhere in the pack. That's it. Now, I'll shuffle them all.
(We hear the shuffling. The drum beat turns into a drum roll.)
Now, tell me, all-powerful creator, do you remember the card you selected?
PEPIN: Yes. Yes, I do.
CLOVIS: And was it by any chance... the three of clubs?
PEPIN: Yes! Yes, it was!
(And the trumpets blast with more excitement than ever. They're obviously having a great time. The crowd applaud.)
...He really is very good, isn't he?
(Above the applause from the CROWD:)
CLOVIS: Behold! A new miracle! Witness the power of our god, o mortals, and tremble! And I call upon our majesty to favour us with his inaugural address.
(The audience fall quiet. The drums stop. A blast on a trumpet. Short pause. Quietly:)
That's you, o lord.
(And we hear quiet muttering again. The same trumpet blast, except it now has a rather impatient edge to it.)
LIVILLA: Go on! Get on with it...!
PEPIN: *(clearing his throat nervously)* Right. Erm. Hello. Can

you all hear me at the back? Can you all...
(*The crowd muttering dies down slowly.*)

Right. I stand before you now as your god, your supreme authority in this world and the next. My word is law.
(*The trumpets play a single blast.*)

My will is absolute.
(*A double blast.*)

My desires shall be your doings, your desires shall be as nothing before my own.
(*And the trumpets continue to play authoritatively as he continues.*)

For you are my slaves, my creatures, now and always. ...Look, sorry, can we just stop a moment, erm... No, stop...

(*And the music winds down. There is puzzled muttering from the crowd.*)

Those are the words with which my father became your god, and his father before him, and his father before him. Though there may have been a few more 'thou's and 'thee's, the language was a little more archaic... Anyway. The point is this. It isn't true, I'm afraid.
(*We hear consternation in the distance.*)

Not any of it. Back when Clovis put the crown on my head, I was really expecting to be transformed into a god, to have all my mortal parts burned away, and so forth. I was, honestly. But I feel exactly the same. I thought I felt the twinge of something divine for a moment, but I think it was just indigestion - I've been having trouble keeping food down lately. So the ceremony hasn't worked, I'm still just as mortal as the rest of you.
(*He now has to speak noticeably louder over the growing disquiet from his audience.*)

I'll still be your emperor if you like, but I expect you don't want one without the other, and I really can't be your god. So, sorry, everybody, basically. And I hope you'll find it in your hearts to put me to death as painlessly as possible.

SCRIBE: (*after a few seconds' hesitation*) This hadn't happened before.

CHILDERIC: (*angrily, as if from the back of the crowd*) His own words condemn him! He is not our god!

PEPIN: (*mildly*) Well, exactly, that's the point I've been making...

CHILDERIC: Death to the apostate! Death to the false god and his wife!
(*And the crowd respond to his words with angry cries of agreement.*)

LIVILLA: (*flatly*) Well, that's great, Pepin. You've killed us.

CHILDERIC: You all know me! I am the late emperor's other son! The illegitimate one. The bastard. But I say that the divinity has passed to me! I am your new emperor! I am your new god.

PEPIN: Sorry, my dear.

LIVILLA: Don't even talk to me.

CHILDERIC: If Pepin can deny that he is a heretic, let him give us another miracle now! And a better one than last time! If not, let him pay with his life right now!
(*Underneath the cries and jeers:*)

LIVILLA: Last time I try to get power by marrying a moron.

(And then, over the shouts, the sound of the TARDIS materialising. The crowd fall silent, stunned.)

Scene 8: INT.
The TARDIS console room. A familiar bleep as the console stops moving. The hum of the TARDIS no longer in flight.

FROBISHER: We've landed. Do you think the TARDIS could at least show us where we are?
(The scanner operates. Ironically:)
                      Thank you.
(We hear a sound like static.)
DOCTOR: We've landed nowhere. It's just void...
FROBISHER: No, wait. The picture's clearing.
(And the static fades. What it's replaced with is the sound of the throne room outside played quietly through the scanner. We can hear the crowd still muttering with surprise.)
                      Doesn't look too promising, does it?
DOCTOR: It seems to be some sort of medieval castle.
(Flicking dead switches:)
                      Why did you want to come here, old girl? It hardly looks like the sort of place where you'll get some TLC...
FROBISHER: Everyone's staring at us.
DOCTOR: Yes, we're a little more conspicuous than I'd have liked. Still, never mind. We'll just have to hope they're pleased to see us.
(He takes confident steps around the console.)
FROBISHER: You're going outside? Has it occurred to you if we leave the TARDIS there's nothing to stop it from taking off and stranding us here forever?
(The door opens.)
DOCTOR: I don't think she's offering us a choice. After you, Frobisher. Best flipper forward.

Scene 9: INT.
The throne room. As before, with awed, quiet muttering from the crowd. From the outside the TARDIS door is heard to open, and those voices fall silent.

FROBISHER: *(warily)* Okay, guys, now before any of you do anything hasty or violent...
(And the crowd mutter again. Various people speak out from the excited babble.)
CROWD 1:   It's a bird!
FROBISHER: Erm... yeah.
CROWD 2:   It talks!
CROWD 3:   *(with a jubilant cry)* It's a miracle!
(Gasps and cries of joy as others reach the same conclusion. Then they all fall silent as one.)
FROBISHER: ...Hello? ...Doc, you better take a look at this...
CROWD 4:   Here comes another one!
CROWD 1:   Is it a bird?
CROWD 4:   ...Nah, it's just a man.

(A few groans of disappointment.)
FROBISHER: Doc. They're all on their knees before us.
DOCTOR: Mmm. Perhaps they've all dropped something...
CROWD: *(severally)* It's the miracle we were promised! They're angels from heaven! Worship them!
DOCTOR: See, Frobisher? They are pleased to see us.
FROBISHER: That one doesn't look pleased.
CHILDERIC: *(from some distance away, loudly)* Who are you? Demons from hell? How dare you interrupt my insurrection!
DOCTOR: No, he isn't pleased at all, is he?
LIVILLA: *(again, at some distance)* You asked for a miracle, Childeric! And there it is!
CHILDERIC: But you all heard Pepin! He said he wasn't a god!
CLOVIS: *(uncertainly)* Perhaps he was testing our faith. Was that it, o lord?
PEPIN: No, I'm afraid not, I'm as surprised as the rest of you...
LIVILLA: Shut up, you idiot.
CLOVIS: *(his voice louder, as he comes closer. We hear his footsteps.)* We shall ask the strangers. Were you sent to us from heaven?
DOCTOR: No, really, we're just travellers...
CLOVIS: Silence. I am addressing your master, the big talking bird. Well? Are you emissaries of God?
FROBISHER: ...As the Doc says. No.
CHILDERIC: Then you shall die!
(And swords are pulled from scabbards.)
FROBISHER: Or, to put it another way. Yes.
CLOVIS: And you were summoned to prove the divinity of the emperor Pepin?
FROBISHER: What, the guy on the throne? Absolutely.
(And, gratefully, the music plays again.)
PEPIN: *(miserably)* But I'm not a god!
LIVILLA: Pepin! What do you think you're doing??
PEPIN: No, Livilla! It's the truth! I wanted to be your god. But I'm not. I'm sorry.
(And the music dies down. With some obvious frustration. The crowd mutters.)
CHILDERIC: Kill them.
CLOVIS: *(reluctantly)* Yes, kill them.
SCRIBE: *(from a distance)* No! You must stop! You have no right!
CHILDERIC: Who are you to stop us? Come forward!
(The crowd fall silent as we hear nervous, shuffling footsteps.)
...It's only the court scribe! A pen pusher with no power at all!
SCRIBE: *(nervously)* I am the keeper of the old texts. And I tell you. After the emperor has been consecrated, it is recorded that he always suffers from a period of mental exhaustion. Rather than condemning him, the confusion our emperor shows now confirms that he has become god!
DOCTOR: Well, that stands to reason. Being made immortal like that, it's bound to take it out of you. Let me through, there. I'm a doctor. That's right...

(And the DOCTOR and FROBISHER move their way up the aisle. The crowd mutters as they're jostled aside.)

PEPIN: *(more to himself, his voice clearer now we're closer to him)* It is true that I'm very tired... Could I have become god after all?

LIVILLA: *(muttering)* I should be so lucky...

FROBISHER: We should get you somewhere you can rest.

PEPIN: Yes. Take me away from this place.

(A creak as he rises from the throne.)

Will you accompany me, Livilla?

LIVILLA: You've always humiliated me at social gatherings, Pepin. But today you nearly got me killed. That really is going too far.

(A swish of heavy fabric.)

I shall be in my own quarters. With a very large headache.

PEPIN: Well, that's fair enough...

(We hear her voice recede as she goes, her heavy garments still audible.)

LIVILLA: Out of the way there. I'm the empress, I am! So move it!

DOCTOR: Are you ready, your majesty?

PEPIN: Thank you. There's a little room just down there...

FROBISHER: Stand aside for the emperor! ...What's your name again?

PEPIN: Pepin VII.

FROBISHER: Stand aside for Emperor Pepin VII! Stand aside!

(And the crowd fall silent expectantly.)

...You. Whoever you are. Let us pass.

CHILDERIC: I am Childeric. The rightful heir to this throne and all its power.

FROBISHER: I don't care who you are, bud. You're blocking the way.

(The crowd murmur angrily. Short pause)

CHILDERIC: I shall not forget this. It will take more than an oversized bird to deny me my true legacy!

(And we hear him stride away. His final line fades as he goes.)

CLOVIS: *(clapping his hands)* Musicians! Why are you not playing? Our majesty is leaving the throne room!

(There are a few groans from the orchestra.)

Trumpets! Sound for your new god!

(And the ceremony music resumes. Over eagerly, a little breathless as he joins the train:)

Can I be of any assistance, your omnipotence?

FROBISHER: I wouldn't have thought so. You wanted him dead five minutes ago!

CLOVIS: But that's when I believed he wasn't our god.

DOCTOR: I'd have thought the prerequisite of a high priest is to have a little faith. Sounds like you're unsuited for the job.

PEPIN: The big talking bird and his servant will attend us whilst we rest.

SCRIBE: And me, your majesty. I will need to record your slumbers for posterity.

PEPIN: And the court scribe. Nobody else may enter.

CLOVIS: But I'm the high priest!

FROBISHER: He said, nobody else.

PEPIN: Please. Leave us.

(And a door shuts firmly.)
CLOVIS: ...Of course, sire. Whatever god wills. ...Guard Captain Sejanus!
(We hear the chainmail approach of SEJANUS. He stands smartly to attention.)
SEJANUS: Yes, sir!
CLOVIS: Is everything ready for the next stage of the ritual?
SEJANUS: Yes, sir. I shall carry out the deed myself tonight.
CLOVIS: Good. Do it well, Sejanus. Remember. The eyes of tradition are on you.
SEJANUS: Yes, sir.
CLOVIS: But first... Clear this rabble away. The show's over for now.
SEJANUS: Sir.
(And we hear SEJANUS move away, and stir the still muttering crowd.)

Scene 10: INT.

Pepin's quarters. In contrast to the previous scene, all is quiet. We hear distant scribbling, and the relaxed breathing of PEPIN in sleep.

FROBISHER: *(softly)* ...He's asleep at last. He seems very weak, Doc. What's the matter with him?
DOCTOR: Just completely exhausted, I think. From the look of him, I don't think he's slept or eaten in days. He'll be all right.
SCRIBE: *(happily, to himself, a little distance away)* And lo, a blue box appeared out of thin air, and out stepped a big monochromatic bird, and, in contrast, a man dressed in every colour that could be conceived.
(A bit louder, as the DOCTOR approaches him.)
Oh, this is excellent stuff, I couldn't have done better myself...!
DOCTOR: We're glad you approve, Mr...
SCRIBE: Tacitus. Eugene Tacitus. Hello.
(Shaking of hands, grunt of acknowledgement from FROBISHER.)
Oh yes, your arrival was a perfect miracle. I was going to put in a volcano or a plague of locusts, but this is far better!
FROBISHER: What are you? Some sort of journalist?
SCRIBE: I'm the court scribe. I chronicle everything that happens here.
FROBISHER: *(dismissively, returning to PEPIN)* Yeah. A journalist.
DOCTOR: I get the impression he's rather more than that...
SCRIBE: I'm the man who writes the Bible.
FROBISHER: *(a little distance away)* What? As in, Holy Bible?
SCRIBE: Chapter and verse, that's me. Well, someone has to do it. Your arrival here was foretold, you know.
DOCTOR: *(curious)* Was it? Was it really?
SCRIBE: Well, it will have been, when I finish writing it up.
(He taps on the front cover of a hardback book meaningfully, then flips a few pages.)
DOCTOR: I see. I dare say a lot of things which happen are foretold.
SCRIBE: Oh, only when they're unusual. I find I don't have to

write awkward explanations if I say it was all predestined.
(The SCRIBE has resumed his scribbling.)
DOCTOR: You saved our lives back there. Thank you.
SCRIBE: *(absently, as he works)* Possibly. It all depends if you and the bird really are immortal or not.
FROBISHER: Yes...
SCRIBE: To be honest, I'm keeping that part of the account a little vague for the moment. Either way, if you live or die, I'll say it was foretold. People feel reassured that way.

Scene 11: INT.
Deep in the castle vaults. There is some echo, and the sound of dripping water.

CHILDERIC: Arnulf! Do not be afraid. It is your master. Come out of hiding. Show yourself to me.
(We hear heavy footsteps on stone.)
Have you fed him? Have you fed my little boy?
(A grunt from ARNULF. Gently:)
Do not try to speak, my friend. It will only cause you pain. Nod if you have done what I have asked.
(Movement on stone, as ARNULF shifts position.)
...Good. It takes a while to adjust, I know. When I employed your father, it took him years to lose the instinct to talk. But it will get easier. By the time he died, it was as if he had forgotten he had once had a tongue to remove. And you will come to feel the same.
(A more muted grunt from ARNULF.)
Ssh, I know, I know. I am glad that you are the one who has replaced him. A son should succeed his father, it is his right. Just as I shall follow my father. And my son shall follow me.
(Underneath the last sentence, we hear the wary shuffle of footsteps on stone. A warning grunt from ARNULF.)
Who's there? Who has followed me down here?
(The footsteps stop dead. A knife is drawn.)
Come out of the shadows.
(Movement on stone.)
...Well. The high priest himself. And have you come to condemn me for treason, Clovis? Or to help me destroy our new emperor?
CLOVIS: *(quietly)* Do you swear that you can do it? You believe you can kill God?
CHILDERIC: With your help, yes. And we shall destroy his angels from the blue box as well.

Scene 12: INT.
Pepin's quarters. As before. The SCRIBE is happily scribbling away, by PEPIN's bedside. We hear PEPIN breathing heavily. We hear them both somewhat in the distance.

SCRIBE: *(happily)* And lo, the new emperor still slept, and the style of his sleep was imperial indeed...
(Over this, hushed, closer to the audience:)

FROBISHER: Doc, do you think we could just leave? Persuade the TARDIS to take us somewhere else?

DOCTOR: No. There's a reason she wanted to come here. We must find out what it is. Besides, you're doing very well for yourself. Play your cards right and you could be the new high priest.

FROBISHER: Thanks, but no thanks. Been there, done that. As a private eye, I've often had to morph into the shape of the clergy. I went undercover as a vicar once for a while, turned out I had an allergy to dog collars. Had a rash on my throat for months...

GUARD: *(outside the door)* You can't go in there...

(And a grunt of pain.)

DOCTOR: There's trouble.

(And the door is battered.)

SCRIBE: Your majesty! Wake up!

PEPIN: What? What is it?

(And bursts open.)

Sejanus! What are you doing? I ordered that no-one be allowed to enter here!

DOCTOR: He's got a gun! I thought you all used swords here!

SCRIBE: We do. But traditionally guns are the weapons of choice for all the important assassinations.

FROBISHER: Assassinations?!

SEJANUS: If you truly are our immortal god, then you shan't feel the bullets when I shoot you.

(A gun is cocked.)

And if you're not, so dies a heretic.

PEPIN: That is very true. Shoot me and we'll see.

FROBISHER: No, wait...!

SEJANUS: To death! Or to life eternal!

(There is a loud gunshot.)

FROBISHER: No!!

End of Part One

PART TWO

Scene 12, Recap:

SEJANUS:　　If you truly are our immortal god, then you shan't feel the bullets when I shoot you.
(A gun is cocked.)
　　　　　　　And if you're not, so dies a heretic.
PEPIN:　　That's very true. Shoot me and we'll see.
FROBISHER:　No, wait...!
SEJANUS:　　To death! Or to life eternal!
(There is a loud gunshot.)
FROBISHER:　No!!
(The sound echoes for a few seconds. When it has died away:)
PEPIN:　　*(with great dignity)* And yet I live, and yet I breathe. You cannot spill my blood. For the blood that pumps through my veins is not mortal. Do you accept?
SEJANUS:　　I accept.
PEPIN:　　I am your god. The weapons of mere men cannot hurt me, nor their opinions sway my awful judgement. For I am your master, reigning supreme and eternal.
FROBISHER:　What are you talking about?
DOCTOR:　　Ssh, Frobisher, this is interesting.
PEPIN:　　Do you accept?
SEJANUS:　　I accept. You are our god, reigning forever, reigning supreme, amen.
PEPIN:　　Give me your gun.
SEJANUS:　　Here, sire. My life is forfeit.
(The gun is cocked.)
PEPIN:　　Your gun is in my hands. Your life is in my hands.
FROBISHER:　But you can't...!
DOCTOR:　　Ssh!
(And the gun is cocked back.)
PEPIN:　　I forgive your attempt on our life. For you are our agent, proving I cannot die. And to this end, I shall give unto you the imperial coin as a sign of forgiveness.
(Short pause. He whispers awkwardly, breaking the ceremonial grandeur:)
　　　　　　　Scribe! I don't have one!
SCRIBE:　　Sorry, sire?
PEPIN:　　I don't have a spare coin! I wasn't ready...
(A hasty jingle of money.)
SCRIBE:　　Here you are...
PEPIN:　　Thanks.
(Back into character:)
　　　　　　　Take this and go with our divine blessing. Do you accept?
SEJANUS:　　I accept, my lord, my emperor, my god. I depart as your subject, I depart as your slave.
(We hear his heavy chainmail as he walks away. Then, from a distance, softly:)

111

Amen.

(A sigh of relief from PEPIN.)

PEPIN: Thank God that that's all over. Which is me, isn't it? Thank me.

SCRIBE: Well done, your omnipotence. That was word perfect.

PEPIN: Except for that bit with the coin. Damn it, I should have been better prepared...

FROBISHER: Do you mean that was all a ceremony?

DOCTOR: Of course.

SCRIBE: The ritual of the coronation is always followed by the ritual of the assassination attempt. Has been since time immemorial.

FROBISHER: Well, I wish you could have warned me. My flippers are still palpitating.

DOCTOR: Oh, you faint-hearted penguin. I'm sure there was no real danger. May I have the gun, your majesty?

(A shuffle of footsteps. The gun is opened with a click.)

...As I thought, you see. Blanks.

SCRIBE: So there you are, sire. Your inauguration is complete. Congratulations. I'm going to write it up immediately...

(The book is opened. Scribbling starts underneath PEPIN's lines.)

PEPIN: *(sighing)* That's all very well. But I still don't feel like a god. Perhaps the assassin should have used real bullets after all.

SCRIBE: Majesty, no-one has used bullets for hundreds of years. Besides, it's unnecessary. You're a god, so they couldn't harm you. So we might just as well shoot blanks to prove you can't die.

DOCTOR: Well done, Eugene. An excellent syllogism. You'd make a politician. You see, Frobisher? In age-old ceremonies like this, no-one need die.

(Off to the side of the action, we hear bits of wood drop to the floor as FROBISHER steps over the broken door.)

FROBISHER: ...Oh yeah? Doc, you better take a look at the guards out here.

(The DOCTOR goes to join him. More clatter of broken door.)

DOCTOR: *(slowly)* Knife blow to the heart. And this poor chap's the same.

(And we hear the DOCTOR march angrily back into the room.)

...What is the meaning of this? Is this part of your sacred ritual?

(The scribbling stops.)

SCRIBE: *(surprised)* Is there a problem, Doctor?

PEPIN: They're only guards, after all...

DOCTOR: *(cold fury)* Let me give you a piece of advice, your majesty. If you want to be god, you'd better find a way to start caring for the people who worship you.

PEPIN: *(simply)* But that's just it, Doctor. I don't want to be god.

SCRIBE: The guards have to die for the ritual to make any sense. The new god cannot be killed because he is immortal. Be fair. The guards can't be immortal too, can they?

DOCTOR: And you condone this?

SCRIBE: It's not a question of condoning! It's what's written in the old texts.

DOCTOR: And before they sacrificed their lives to antiquated tradition, did these guards happen to read your old texts?

SCRIBE: (*a little sulkily*) Well, they only had to ask. But no-one's interested in history nowadays.

DOCTOR: I'm interested. You'd better show me before anybody else gets killed. Do you have a library of some sort?

SCRIBE: Yes, of some sort.

DOCTOR: Frobisher, you stay here with Pepin. If I'm right, you should be perfectly safe, there'd be no point in playing the same ritual twice.

FROBISHER: And if you're wrong?

DOCTOR: Then I'm wrong, aren't I? Come on, Eugene, lead the way.

(*The clatter as two men pick their way over the broken door. The voices fading:*)

SCRIBE: Oh dear, Doctor, did you have to leave the guards face upwards...

DOCTOR: (*faintly*) Let's see what this library of yours has to offer...

FROBISHER: Thanks, Doc. That's very reassuring.

Scene 13: INT.
The castle vaults. As before.

CHILDERIC: You have too many scruples, Clovis. Really, it's hardly a quality one looks for in a conspirator to treason and murder.

CLOVIS: My family have been high priests to the royal family since records began. I cannot betray my god lightly.

(*We hear a macabre gurgle from ARNULF.*)
    What is that tongueless slave of yours doing?

CHILDERIC: Arnulf is laughing at you, Clovis. He may be from the lowest dregs of society. But even he knows the reputation of your family.

CLOVIS: What do you mean? Tell him to stop laughing, or I swear I'll...

CHILDERIC: Arnulf. That's enough.

(*And the laughter stops.*)
    Both your father and your grandfather plotted against their respective gods. Your family is notorious for being corrupt and treacherous.

CLOVIS: And they were both executed for their crimes as well. I have no desire to end up as they did, suspended from a hangman's gibbet.

CHILDERIC: There, at least, your scruples are in accord with my own. But I have devised a plot which cannot fail.

CLOVIS: We cannot attack Pepin directly. Now he is a god, he cannot be killed.

CHILDERIC: Not by mortal hand, certainly. But who knows what damage another god could do to him?

CLOVIS: Another god? I don't understand...

CHILDERIC: All will become clear, high priest.

(*And he laughs. And ARNULF laughs with him.*)
    Just do as we have agreed.

CLOVIS: Very well. I shall bring him to you directly.
(*We hear him exit, footsteps on stone. ARNULF's laughter echoes after him.*)

Scene 14: INT.
Pepin's quarters.

FROBISHER: How are you feeling now, your highness?
PEPIN: Oh. Entirely back to normal.
FROBISHER: That's good.
PEPIN: Not really. I don't think that my normal is all that impressive, probably... Please, don't call me highness.
FROBISHER: Pepin then.
PEPIN: Pepin, that's it. Believe me, it's not a name I'm going to be called very often now that I'm an emperor and a god.
FROBISHER: I know the feeling. It's been so long since I heard my real name, I sometimes forget what it is. But my friends call me Frobisher.
(*We hear the clatter as someone picks their way over the broken door.*)
LIVILLA: ...What's been going on, there are dead bodies out here...
PEPIN: Nothing important, my dear. Just the ritual assassination attempt.
LIVILLA: (*louder, now she is in the room*) Oh. I trust my divine husband has recovered from the ceremony.
PEPIN: Frobisher, this is the wife.
FROBISHER: Good choice. Very nice.
PEPIN: (*quietly*) Wives to the imperial family are selected because of their looks rather than their personalities.
LIVILLA: And now perhaps my divine husband can tell me what in His name is going on? What was that stunt at the coronation all about?
(*With a sigh, PEPIN sits down on the bed. There is a creak.*)
PEPIN: I don't feel like a god.
LIVILLA: Of course you don't feel like a god. Look at yourself. It'd be a miracle if you even felt like a man. Heaven knows how we're going to produce you an heir.
PEPIN: Livilla, my dear, listen to me...
LIVILLA: No, you listen to me.
(*She paces. High heels tap smartly on stone.*)
We both know you can't be a god, you're just a pusillanimous little nobody. But it would take no effort on your part to pretend. The people are already worshipping you. They are building statues in your honour, and decorating your new blue temple with garlands of flowers.
PEPIN: Livilla. I cannot in all conscience rule my people as god knowing I am as weak and powerless as I ever was. I will abdicate.
(*LIVILLA's footsteps stop dead.*)
LIVILLA: Then they will kill you.
PEPIN: Yes.
LIVILLA: Worse, they will kill us. I shall not become a martyr to a man I have never loved. If you force me, I shall join Childeric and Clovis in rebellion against you.

FROBISHER: You've already got a rebellion against you?

PEPIN: It was only a matter of time. The bastard half-brother always tries to overthrow the new god. And the high priest always sides with him. And when he is defeated and executed, his son is made high priest in his stead.

FROBISHER: Why?

PEPIN: It's tradition. I suppose it is a bit silly, come to think of it.

LIVILLA: I need to know where I stand. Are you my husband, and my god? Or shall I be forced to take up arms against you?

PEPIN: I'm sorry, my dear. But I can't be all-powerful. Not even for you.

LIVILLA: Very well. Next time we meet, I shall kill you.

(She exits. High heels on stone.)

PEPIN: Never get married, Frobisher.

FROBISHER: Hey, I'm way ahead of you. Tried it once, didn't work out. That's the problem with being a shape shifter. She said I wasn't the Ogron she'd fallen in love with. ...So what do we do? Predictably, our lives are in danger again.

(PEPIN rises from the bed with a creak.)

PEPIN: Well, we can take sanctuary in the blue temple Livilla mentioned. No-one would dare to strike against us there.

FROBISHER: And what is this blue temple of yours?

PEPIN: I really don't know. Shall we go and see?

Scene 15: INT.

The scribe's bedroom. We hear a creak as an old door opens.

SCRIBE: Here we are, Doctor. Forgive the mess. And the smell, actually. I don't get many visitors... I'll try to clear a space for you... *(He bustles round, picking things up, putting them down. General clatter.)*

DOCTOR: I thought you said you had some sort of library.

SCRIBE: Well. It is some sort of library.

DOCTOR: It's your bedroom. You keep these sacred texts in your bedroom?

SCRIBE: No-one in court's much of a reader. Never have been. For generations my ancestors have been writing these Bibles, then rewriting them from scratch when a god dies and we have to find another. We try to record every last thing our messiah says and does. And no-one's ever been much interested. But we keep them close in case anyone ever asks to look.

DOCTOR: As doorstops, and to balance uneven tables?

SCRIBE: Got to put the sum of all human knowledge to some use. Don't pick up that one, it...

(And there's a crash as a table falls over.)

DOCTOR: Sorry.

SCRIBE: Please, please, Doctor. Sit down over here, shift these old volumes, that's it. And read whatever takes your fancy. Here, try this. This is the Bible of Pepin III.

(The sound of a heavy volume dumped in his lap. The DOCTOR grunts.)

DOCTOR: And when did he reign?

SCRIBE: Oh, centuries ago, I should imagine. They're all in a bit of a jumble, I'm afraid. I tend to forget who succeeded whom.
(The DOCTOR flicks through some pages, then reads.)
DOCTOR: 'And on the fifteenth day since the last ritual of the Bath, Pepin III decided to take another. And he did immerse himself in warm water, and play about his body with soap. And the people were sore relieved, for he had begun to smell a bit.'
(He closes the book with a thud.)
Are they all like this?
SCRIBE: Oh yes. Every detail of their lives, recorded for posterity. What exactly were you looking for, Doctor?
DOCTOR: Anything. Everything. I think it could take a little time...
SCRIBE: The prose style isn't much to write home about, but it's very thorough.

Scene 16: INT.
The throne room. The babble of a crowd in the distance.

FROBISHER: The blue temple that everyone's worshipping! It's the TARDIS!
PEPIN: I should have guessed. Its appearance was what convinced them I'm a god.
(There is a roar of recognition from the crowd as they are seen.)
FROBISHER: Pepin. Perhaps we should take refuge somewhere else. The people look ugly.
PEPIN: Oh no, they're always as unattractive as that. The people are jubilant. See, they bring gifts of flowers and fruit.
CROWD: *(severally)* Hail our new god, Pepin VII! May he reign eternally! Hail his ambassador! The big talking bird!
PEPIN: Just walk through them. They'll clear a way for us.
FROBISHER: *(awkwardly, through the hubbub)* That's it... Out of the way there, that's the idea...
CROWD 1: You are magnificent!
FROBISHER: *(humouring him)* Okay, bud, whatever you say... We've made it. Pepin, quick, let's get inside. All this adoration could go to a guy's head, you know?
PEPIN: But how can we both enter my temple? It is too small...
FROBISHER: You'll be surprised.

Scene 17: INT.
The TARDIS console room. The usual hum. And then we hear the TARDIS doors open, and FROBISHER and PEPIN enter.

PEPIN: This is indeed a miracle!
FROBISHER: I knew you'd be surprised... Hey, what's all this junk doing in here?
PEPIN: All this gleaming white! And there's so much of it! It's magnificent!
FROBISHER: Who's been putting flowers and baskets of fruit everywhere? I can hardly find the door switch... Ah.
(The TARDIS doors shut.)
PEPIN: But surely then, you must have come from heaven after

all?

FROBISHER: No, Pepin...

PEPIN: But look at it! At all this! ...You really are angels!

FROBISHER: Listen, bud. It's as the Doc said. We're just travellers. There's no such place as heaven, okay?

(Lots of switches and buttons are pressed. There are a few bleeps. Muttering to himself:)

The TARDIS still isn't working properly. Or not wanting to work. Typical. ...What's the matter?

PEPIN: *(brokenly)* No heaven at all?

FROBISHER: *(awkwardly)* Well, no. Not that I've ever seen.

PEPIN: But there has to be a heaven. Or else what's the point of anything? What's the point of living at all?

FROBISHER: Hey, look... perhaps there is a heaven. Who knows? The universe is big enough. Perhaps the TARDIS just hasn't landed there yet. Don't take my opinion as gospel or anything... Come on, give me a hand moving this stuff.

(And he thumps about on the console.)

PEPIN: You must not touch the fruit and flowers. They are tributes to decorate the altar.

FROBISHER: That isn't an altar. It's a central console. A machine. It allows us to travel anywhere in time and space.

(He stabs a button. It gives a very half-hearted bleep.)

When it isn't on strike, that is...

PEPIN: Tell me again. This central console... it is the source of your temple's power? And it allows you to communicate with other worlds?

FROBISHER: Yes. In a way.

PEPIN: Then we agree after all, my friend. For that is exactly what an altar is.

Scene 18: INT.

The scribe's bedroom. We hear some pages being leafed through.

DOCTOR: Fascinating. So what you've got here is your good old-fashioned polytheistic religion, but with a monotheistic structure. You can worship lots of gods, but only one at a time. Must get rather confusing for you all.

SCRIBE: It did get a bit complicated a couple of centuries ago, when the royal family went down with a lethal dose of chicken pox. Gods were popping up and dropping down quicker than you could say 'heretic'.

DOCTOR: Indeed.

SCRIBE: In the end, though, I think the only one who gets really confused is me. The people are quite happy to worship whichever god they're told to. But I'm the poor chap who has to keep up with all the paperwork. Would you like a drink? I'm sure I've got some somewhere...

(Thumps and clatter.)

DOCTOR: And how many gods have you chronicled? How many of these books are yours?

SCRIBE: Oh, Doctor, I've no idea. To tell you the truth, I've lost count. Ah, here we are! Now. Do you like your hot water weak or tepid? *(The pouring of water into a mug. And then another. Over this the conversation continues.)*

DOCTOR: But you must remember which of these texts you were personally responsible for. This one here, Clothaire the Great. Is he one of yours?

(We hear a heavy volume being picked up.)

SCRIBE: Oh, Clothaire, he's one of my favourites! Oh no, I couldn't have written that one. He lived hundreds and hundreds of years ago. Except...

DOCTOR: ...Except what?

SCRIBE: Well, it is hard to be sure. I've read and reread all these books so many times I feel I might as well have written them. Certainly Clothaire seems as alive to me as young Pepin does now.

DOCTOR: *(closing a book with a snap)* You know, Eugene. There's something odd about this. Something that doesn't add up.

SCRIBE: You mean the handwriting?

DOCTOR: *(eagerly)* Oh, no, I hadn't noticed that! What about the handwriting?

SCRIBE: Well, it doesn't matter how old the book is. The handwriting is always the same.

DOCTOR: Let me see.

(Books being picked up eagerly.)

SCRIBE: *(slurping his drink)* I've always thought that was rather strange. I suppose it's because my father taught me how to write, and his father taught him, and so on.

DOCTOR: No, that doesn't make sense at all.

SCRIBE: *(cheerfully)* I didn't think it did! Tell me, Doctor. Which part of these texts doesn't make sense to you?

DOCTOR: You say that every time a god dies, you start writing in a completely new book?

SCRIBE: Yes, of course. The death invalidates the whole Bible. I have to start all over.

DOCTOR: Quite so. But every single one of these volumes... the god dies on exactly the last line of exactly the last page. No blank sheets at the end, nothing has been ripped out. How do you explain that?

SCRIBE: I don't know. Divine providence?

DOCTOR: Possibly. But I'd have thought that any god worth his salt would have more concerns than economising the stationery. Let me see your new Bible, the one you're writing for Pepin.

(With a grunt, the SCRIBE rises and passes him a book.)

SCRIBE: Here.

DOCTOR: But this is hardly a book at all! It's so thin it's practically a pamphlet.

SCRIBE: It's just the first text that came to hand...

DOCTOR: *(amiably)* Tell me, Eugene. Do you know something about the life expectancy of the emperor that I don't?

(There is a bang at the door.)

Are you expecting anyone?

SCRIBE: No. No-one ever comes here.

CLOVIS: *(outside)* Open up in there!

(The SCRIBE picks his way through the mess, knocking things over as he does so.)
SCRIBE: Yes, yes, of course. There's a lot of clutter for me to clamber over. Just don't break down the door. I've only just replaced it...
(The door opens.)
Good lord. It's the high priest.
DOCTOR: Really? How extraordinary. Do the upper clergy often make house calls?
CLOVIS: The two of you will accompany me at once.
(The sound of clatter as the DOCTOR rises.)
DOCTOR: And where are you taking us, may I ask?
CLOVIS: To see your new master.

Scene 19: INT.
The dungeons.
(Nothing but the dripping of water, and painful breathing. A few seconds of this. Then we hear footsteps on stone - slow, deliberate, and getting closer. The high heels of LIVILLA. The prisoner catches her breath - then calls out hoarsely.)

BERENGARIA: What? Who's there? Is that you, guard? Have you come to feed me already?
LIVILLA: *(softly)* No.
BERENGARIA: I should think not. I haven't even begun to starve yet. When I was empress, we knew how to torture prisoners.
LIVILLA: *(closer, deliberately)* As you say. Late empress Berengaria.
BERENGARIA: So who are you then? Move the candle a little closer.
(Another footstep on stone.)
...Ah. So it is you. Lady Livilla, my successor. Come to kill me already, have you?
LIVILLA: No.
BERENGARIA: I thought not. You'd want an audience, you're the sort. So what is it? Here for a bit of gloating? Why not, I did. I gloated over my mother-in-law a full month before I cut her down to die.
LIVILLA: I want your help.
(BERENGARIA's chains rattle as she reacts with surprise.)
BERENGARIA: My what?
LIVILLA: I want you to do something for me.
BERENGARIA: The only thing I'll do for you is die.
LIVILLA: And nothing else?
BERENGARIA: If you're lucky, I might scream with pain as I go. I may have been goddess, but I never said I was perfect.
LIVILLA: And yet it's such a little thing I ask.
(A short pause. Then the chains rattle again.)
BERENGARIA: I'm curious. What could I give you?
LIVILLA: You had two sons. Pepin, my husband, the legitimate heir to the throne. And Childeric.
BERENGARIA: What of it?
LIVILLA: I want you to say you made a mistake, you mixed them up. I want you to say that Childeric is the true God. And that Pepin is the illegitimate one.

Scene 20: INT.
The TARDIS console room.

FROBISHER: Pepin, I think I know why the TARDIS brought us here.
PEPIN: You do?
FROBISHER: It's always landing us in the middle of trouble. Seems to have a knack for it. The Doctor thinks there might be something philanthropic in the circuits, always taking us to places where we have to right wrongs and defeat evil in the nick of time.
PEPIN: Defeating evil. Just like real gods are supposed to do...
FROBISHER: Me, I just think it's being bloody-minded. But this time it's come here for the attention. It's got garlands of flowers all over its console, it's being worshipped as the holy church of a living god. I bet you're having the time of your life, aren't you? Even the background hum sounds smugger than normal.
(And the hum rises a little in tone, then returns to what it was before.)
PEPIN: We won't be allowed to hide in our humming temple forever, Frobisher.
FROBISHER: What do you mean?
PEPIN: Sooner or later the people will come for me. They'll expect me to make proclamations and judgements and that sort of thing. It's going to be horrid.
FROBISHER: Doesn't sound that bad...
PEPIN: One of my first commandments will be to execute one tenth of the population for heresy.
FROBISHER: What?
PEPIN: Tradition. Fair's fair, they are all guilty. Last week they all worshipped my father. They'll have to be punished somehow.
FROBISHER: Why? You're the god, aren't you? Tell them you forgive them. Tell them you just won't do it!
PEPIN: But the people demand it. They won't let me stand against tradition. There's no point in having a god if he isn't a bit vengeful now and again. Either their god kills them, or they will kill their god. That's what religion's all about.
(A cry of jubilation from outside.)
What's that?
FROBISHER: Let's find out.
(He operates the scanner. The jubilant cry is more distinct. We hear the smashing of rubble.)
FROBISHER: I thought you said your subjects were happy.
PEPIN: They are.
FROBISHER: Then what's all the vandalism for? Just high spirits? They've just torn down a thirty foot statue!
PEPIN: The statue was of my father.
FROBISHER: Oh.
PEPIN: They will desecrate his image wherever it can be found. The portraits will be burned, the mosaics smashed. By now a mob will have been to the mortuary, found his corpse, and ripped it apart.
(Short pause. We hear another cry of jubilation.)
FROBISHER: That's obscene.
PEPIN: *(flatly)* They feel betrayed. He said he would oppress them forever. And he lied. And I have to ask myself whether I will lie

to them as well.
(More wreckage as something bigger is torn down.)

Scene 21: INT.
The dungeons. As before. As BERENGARIA talks, we hear her chains rattle faintly.

BERENGARIA: I really loved him. He was the only man I ever loved. I picked him to father my bastard simply because he was the only one of my husband's guards that didn't smell. But in return he loved me, and gave me a boy, even though he knew that by tradition he would be executed for treason. When he was hanged it took him sixteen hours to die. I know, I counted every one. But he was Childeric's father. Not Pepin's.

LIVILLA: One word from you, and Childeric will be crowned. And I can be his goddess instead. Do this for me, and when I kill you, it will be painless.

BERENGARIA: No.

LIVILLA: Please.

BERENGARIA: No. *(Short pause, then she laughs.)* Get off your knees! How dare you abase yourself to a prisoner, manacled to a dungeon wall! You are pathetic. Are you an empress or aren't you?

LIVILLA: *(spitefully, desperately)* All right then! All right, you evil old bitch! Help me and I'll let you live! How about that? I'll give you your life!

BERENGARIA: You can't do that. My survival is against the constitution.

LIVILLA: And if your life will make Childeric god, don't you think he'll change that? Help me and live!

BERENGARIA: But I don't want to live.

LIVILLA: ...What?

BERENGARIA: For years I've been waiting for my husband to die. I had got so very tired of being all-powerful, of being feared and hated.

LIVILLA: That shan't happen to me.

BERENGARIA: Perhaps not. But I doubt it. It will take a greater imagination than yours to stave off the tedium of undeserved divinity.

LIVILLA: If you do not choose to help me, I can make you do so. You understand me?

BERENGARIA: Oh yes. I was wondering when the threats would come. *(And we hear a punch. It is loud, brutal. And another. And another. A pause, then another.)*

LIVILLA: *(out of breath)* Now. What do you say?

(Silence. And then we hear BERENGARIA spit. Hoarse, but with strength:)

BERENGARIA: ...When I came here to torture my mother-in-law. When I came to gloat. With a small blunt knife I would cut her face. Every day I would do it, hack another piece off. By the time I had her executed there was no face left, just her eyes so she could see the moment of her death. And never once did she cry. Did you even bring a knife?

LIVILLA: No.

BERENGARIA: You are not fit to follow in her footsteps or mine. Unless you are prepared to hurt me properly, leave here at once.

121

LIVILLA: Very well, Berengaria. If that is your wish...
(*And we hear her footsteps recede. The slow, deliberate click of her high heels on stone. Four or five paces, then they stop. We hear only the dripping of water and the heavy, guttered breathing of BERENGARIA. Then we hear something heavy and metal being picked up from the ground. And the high heels quickly skipping over the stone floor, and a hideous thump of a hideous thump hitting flesh. Involuntarily BERENGARIA gives a loud gasp of agony. And another weaker sound as the bar hits her again. But when she is hit for the third time, we hear nothing from her. And now we hear the heavy, excited breathing of LIVILLA. She drops the metal bar on the stone floor. And then she runs away.*)

Scene 22: INT.
The vaults.
(*We hear a door opening.*)

DOCTOR: Is this it?
CLOVIS: Both of you. Inside.
DOCTOR: You take us all the way down a whole series of wet, dark corridors just to bring us to a wet, dark room. I had been hoping for something a little more climactic.
(*The door is slammed behind.*)
CHILDERIC: Ah, Clovis. I see you have brought our guest. Welcome. Let me shake your hand.
SCRIBE: (*nervously*) Thank you.
CHILDERIC: I trust that your invitation here hasn't inconvenienced you.
DOCTOR: No, not at all. Frankly, I'm delighted to be here. Sooner or later the enemy always wants to meet me. Which suits me fine, because sooner or later I want to meet the enemy. You are the enemy, I take it?
CHILDERIC: Clovis, what did you bring this idiot for?
CLOVIS: He was with the scribe. I couldn't very well leave him behind.
DOCTOR: Less of the idiot. I can't be so stupid if you realised I needed capturing, now can I?
CLOVIS: But we didn't want to capture you. We wanted to capture Eugene Tacitus.
CHILDERIC: You're of no interest to us whatsoever.
DOCTOR: Oh. Rather an oversight on your part. You should count yourself lucky you've got me captured anyway. Now, why don't we all sit down and you can tell me what nefarious schemes you're concocting.
CHILDERIC: That is exactly what I plan to do.
DOCTOR: Excellent. Well, let's get the introductions out of the way. I'm the Doctor, Eugene you already know. No doubt you're the half-brother who intends to usurp the throne, and this is the high priest prepared to betray his god to help you.
CLOVIS: Correct.
DOCTOR: And who's that in the corner? Hello? What's your name then?
(*He takes footsteps towards him.*)

CHILDERIC: Don't speak to him, Doctor. He won't be able to answer you.
DOCTOR: And why's that then? Henchman shyness, I suppose? It's all right, old chap, I won't bite...
(And ARNULF gives a grunt of pain and misery.)
Oh my word...
CHILDERIC: He hasn't got a tongue.
(Short pause. The DOCTOR is suddenly quieter, more serious. He takes a few deliberate paces before he speaks.)
DOCTOR: And did you do that?
CHILDERIC: I did.
DOCTOR: Why?
CHILDERIC: Believe it or not, he volunteered. It's a requirement of his job. Arnulf would have done it himself, but cutting out one's own tongue is trickier than you might imagine. So I was happy to oblige.
DOCTOR: But what is it for? What job could require such mutilation?
CHILDERIC: If you will come with me, I'll show you.

Scene 23: INT.
The TARDIS console room.
(We hear a group of men all chanting 'heave' faintly.)

FROBISHER: Well, that's one statue they're not going to be able to topple. Look at the size of it. It must weigh tons.
(And we hear it crash. Loud shouts of joy, chants.)
Oh. Your subjects are stronger than they look, aren't they?
PEPIN: *(dully)* And that's the last one. It took fifteen years to finish, and twelve men died in its construction. It was a masterpiece.
FROBISHER: And now it's in rubble over the throne room floor. This is insane.
PEPIN: *(softly)* Oh, give them time, they'll build one of me just as magnificent.
(Underneath, we hear the crowd begin to chant 'Pepin'.)
And then one for my successor, and then one for his. The same stones used over and over again.
FROBISHER: Pepin? Are you all right?
PEPIN: By now every trace of my father will have been wiped away. Very soon I shall forget what he looked like.
(Short pause. The scanner is operated. The chanting is silenced. For a few seconds, we hear nothing but the hum of the TARDIS.)
FROBISHER: *(awkwardly)* I'm sorry.
PEPIN: I believed in him. I worshipped him. I followed all of his laws, revered all of his doctrines. I thanked him every time he beat me, and smiled when he said I was unworthy to be his son. Because I was unworthy, you see, Frobisher? Because he was my everything. He was my god.
FROBISHER: *(gently)* You're the god now.
PEPIN: I could believe in him. I can't believe in me. ...I can't hide here any longer. My people will be expecting me.
FROBISHER: And what will you tell them?

PEPIN: The truth.

FROBISHER: And they'll kill you.

PEPIN: Can't be helped though. Better to get it over and done with now before they start building any statues of me.

FROBISHER: Pepin... Look. Whether you're a god or not... you're the boss, aren't you? You're the one in charge. You could try to change things. Liberate your people or something, start a revolution! ...I know that may not be as easy as it sounds...

PEPIN: I can't.

FROBISHER: *(angrily)* If you don't, who else will?

PEPIN: My father might have been able to. But I'm sorry, my friend, I'm just not strong enough. I'm leaving the temple now.

FROBISHER: I just think you might serve your people better alive than dead. I just think you should consider that!

PEPIN: Don't worry. I shan't let them harm you. Open the doors.

(A hesitation. And then the doors open.)

Scene 24: INT.
The vaults.
(As the party move down stone steps:)

CHILDERIC: No-one really believes in God any more. That's what makes Pepin's honesty at the coronation all the more pathetic - no-one expects him to become immortal and rule forever. Oh, they'd kill him for saying so, of course, the laws against heresy are without mercy. But there is no true faith any more, the people commit heresy secretly every day in their hearts. The laws by which their ancestors feared for their lives have become empty rituals, without number and without meaning.

DOCTOR: *(gently)* Childeric. It's inevitable. No matter how fundamentalist a religion might be at its root, it gets compromised sooner or later. It happens to every belief in every nation on every planet. The extremists die out, and what's left is something woolly and fuzzy.

CHILDERIC: Come through this doorway, all of you. And down these steps.

CLOVIS: Where are you taking us, Childeric?

CHILDERIC: Are you frightened, Clovis? The lower we go into the catacombs?

CLOVIS: You know I am.

CHILDERIC: You have little faith. What a high priest you turned out to be. But it's not your fault. As the people began to doubt, so even the gods who lived amongst them became corrupted. They began to believe that they were fallible, that they were not the beginning and the end. And as the gods grew more corrupt, so the people who worshipped them were corrupted even further. High priests used to burn with the passion of their faith. Not like Clovis here, who's frightened of the dark.

CLOVIS: It's not just the dark I'm frightened of. Are you saying you really expect me to believe in god? But no-one in the church has done that for centuries!

CHILDERIC: But you will soon, Clovis. It's a vicious circle that must be broken.

DOCTOR: It's a fact of life which must be accepted. A consequence of civilisation. Eugene, are you all right?
SCRIBE: Doctor, I'm frightened. No-one ever goes down into the castle vaults. There's nothing in any of my texts about this.
DOCTOR: To tell you the truth, I'm frightened too.
CHILDERIC: You can all rest now. This is the deepest recorded level of the castle.
(And the footsteps come to a stop.)
SCRIBE: *(nervously, boldly)* Why have you brought us here?
CHILDERIC: I decided long ago that I would become god. But I would not be the weak and tepid god that this religion has made. When I rule, I will be all-powerful, and I really will reign forever. Doctor. Press this stone.
DOCTOR: Very well.
(Scratching on stone as the DOCTOR stoops. And then we hear the stonework move. Behind we hear distant wind. The rest of the scene is spoken over it.)
  A secret passageway?
CHILDERIC: Hidden for centuries. And down there, in the pitch black, the steps continue. Deeper and deeper into the bowels of the castle.
DOCTOR: And what is down there?
CHILDERIC: Hidden alone since birth. Untainted and pure. My son. And your new messiah.
(And the wind grows louder, then fades into:)

Scene 25: INT.
The throne room.

CROWD: All hail Pepin! All hail our god!
(And on. Over this:)
PEPIN: *(softly)* Frobisher. I'm frightened.
FROBISHER: I'm not surprised. They'll lynch you.
PEPIN: It's not that. I just hate public speaking. *(And louder, over the tumult:)* My people! Listen to me! *(And the crowd falls quiet.)* I thank you from the bottom of my heart. No emperor has been so honoured by his people.
A VOICE: Let's build him a statue!
(A roar of approval.)
PEPIN: No, please! No statues, I beg you! I only wish I deserved one. But I tell you I am no god. I am as mortal as the rest of you.
(A deathly silence, finally broken by one plaintive voice:)
A VOICE: But we need a god! How shall we survive without a god?
PEPIN: My friends, you have a god. Someone of great wisdom and courage. Someone who will watch over us and our children for the rest of time.
(Short pause)
A VOICE: Well, where is he then?
PEPIN: My people, this is Frobisher. He who came from another world to bring salvation to us all.
FROBISHER: What?
CROWD: All hail Frobisher! All hail the big talking bird! All hail Frobisher! All hail the big talking bird!

(And FROBISHER's words to himself are almost lost as the cries grow louder and louder.)
FROBISHER: *(softly)* Oh... my god.

End of Part Two

PART THREE

Scene 25, partial recap:

CROWD: All hail Frobisher! All hail the big talking bird! All hail
Frobisher! All hail the big talking bird!
(And, over this, hissing:)
FROBISHER: Where I come from, this is known as passing the buck.
PEPIN: But you are a god! I know that you're the only one with
the vision to bring salvation to my people.
FROBISHER: Thanks to you, I think I will have my work cut out just
trying to stay alive.

Scene 26: INT.
The vaults. As before. We hear the wind in the background.

CLOVIS: *(nervously)* Sire. I did not know that you had a son.
DOCTOR: Do you really mean to say that you are keeping a small
child imprisoned down there?
CHILDERIC: Oh, 'imprisoned' is such a perjorative word, Doctor. It is
true he can't leave his little cell. But he shall be grateful to me. I am
the means of his immortality. My actions are turning him into a god.
DOCTOR: And how long have you been this generous to him?
CHILDERIC: From the moment of his birth, Doctor. Or else there
would have been no point. He's been there these five years now.
CLOVIS: Childeric. Why didn't you tell me?
CHILDERIC: No-one has known. Except me, and Arnulf here, who
feeds him daily.
(ARNULF gives a grunt.)
DOCTOR: And that's why you cut out his tongue? To protect your
disgusting secret?
CHILDERIC: No, not at all. To protect the messiah. If he heard even a
single word from a mortal, his transformation would be threatened. On
no account must he be corrupted by the language of man, its cynicism,
its complacency. In his innocence he will have devised a language of his
own, a language without doubt and the taint of what man has become, a
language which is perfect and pure. A language from heaven itself. And
to safeguard that, even the servant who slides the food under the door
of his cell must be physically incapable of speech.
       (Affectionately:) You're a good man, Arnulf.
(ARNULF gives a pleased grunt.)
CLOVIS: We thought you couldn't have a child. Your wife
disappeared all those years ago, and you have refused to marry since.
CHILDERIC: But my wife never disappeared. I know precisely where
she is.
CLOVIS: You murdered her?
DOCTOR: Oh, not at all, Clovis. I'm sure her usefulness simply
came to an end. Isn't that right, Childeric?
CHILDERIC: As she was giving birth to my son, I cut out her tongue
so that even as she cursed during the agony of childbirth she could not
taint him. She was allowed to feed the baby down there for a few

months. And then, when she ran dry, I had her walled up.

DOCTOR: All to create the perfect being.

CHILDERIC: As you say, Doctor. I am a godmaker.

DOCTOR: So why don't you just let him out then? This god you have made?

CHILDERIC: He is still a child. I do not intend him to be released for another twelve years yet. Then, when he is an adult, he shall have the maturity to rule by my side, and teach me how to be perfect like him.

DOCTOR: And it's all gone wrong, hasn't it? Your father died earlier than you expected.

CHILDERIC: My son has become a god before I am ready for him to be one. Which is why I need you, scribe.

SCRIBE: (slightly in the distance, faintly) Oh. I had rather hoped you'd all forgotten about me...

CHILDERIC: I must know what has happened to him. For years you and your fathers have chronicled the lives of generations of false gods. Now you are to be privileged. You shall write an account of a real one. (Footsteps on stone. We hear the wind blow a little louder.)

SCRIBE: ...You're going to lock me down there?

CHILDERIC: Until he is of age, you will sit with him and observe him in every detail. What you write shall form the basis of our new Bible. Your tongue will be cut out, of course.

DOCTOR: Of course it will. And shall my tongue be cut out too?

CHILDERIC: There is no need, Doctor, since you will never see the messiah.

DOCTOR: Jolly good. So you'll be letting me off scott free, I assume?

CHILDERIC: I think I'll cut out your heart instead. (He laughs. And ARNULF joins him in his own hideous parody.)

DOCTOR: (suddenly sober) You are aware that you're utterly mad, aren't you? (The laughter stops from both of them.)

CHILDERIC: Oh yes. At the moment I am only mad. But soon I shall be divine.

Scene 27: INT.
The throne room.

(The chanting continues.)

PEPIN: Now you must speak to the people and make assurances of your divinity.

FROBISHER: No way, bud. I'm going back to the TARDIS. (The TARDIS door shuts. FROBISHER bangs on it in frustration.)
Hey! Let me in! Open this door at once! (The chanting subsides. We hear the chainmail heavy marching of SEJANUS.)
...Who's that man coming towards me?

PEPIN: That is Guard Captain Sejanus. (A sword is drawn.)

FROBISHER: And why is he drawing his sword? (As the footsteps stop:)
...Look, this has all been a big mistake...

128

CAPTAIN: *(smoothly)* I lay down my sword before my new lord.
(A clank of sword against stone.)
FROBISHER: What? Oh. Yes. Good.
CAPTAIN: Hail the big talking bird.
(And the crowd take up his words, and chant them once, with fervour.)
CROWD: Hail the big talking bird!
FROBISHER: I wish you wouldn't call me that... Oy! And you can stop kissing my flipper too.
CAPTAIN: I am yours to command, your omnipotence. What are your orders?
FROBISHER: ...Well, I don't have any at the moment. Why don't you just do what you normally do?
CAPTAIN: *(picking up his sword)* And smite your enemies wherever they are found?
FROBISHER: Yes. If you like.
CAPTAIN: Very good, sire. Right, come along, you.
(Chainmail footsteps begin to sound.)
FROBISHER: Where are you taking Pepin?
PEPIN: They're going to execute me, Frobisher.
CAPTAIN: He is a false god and a heretic. He must be destroyed.
FROBISHER: No, stop. Wait.
(The footsteps come to a halt. Expectant pause.)
        ...I forbid it.
PEPIN: You can't forbid it, my friend. It's the constitution. I must be put to death.
CAPTAIN: The lying blasphemer speaks the truth, your majesty.
FROBISHER: Well, I pardon him. How about that? What if I pardon him?
CAPTAIN: It's never been done before.
FROBISHER: Well, I'm doing it now.
(We hear him step forward, clear his throat.)
        Pepin, I hereby pardon you, yadda yadda yadda. There. Done.
PEPIN: Erm, are you sure about this? I have no purpose any longer. Honestly, perhaps it would be better if I just went off with the guard captain here and let him hack me to pieces. Might be better all round...
CAPTAIN: I'd have thought so...
FROBISHER: You want a purpose? Fine. I'll make you... I'll make you my high priest. There. I hereby appoint you...
CAPTAIN: But he's a heretic!
FROBISHER: Nonsense. I don't think anyone more fully believes I am a god than Pepin here. So he's the ideal man for the job.
CAPTAIN: But you can't do that! It makes a mockery of our history and tradition...!
FROBISHER: Silence! Am I your god or not? You shall obey me in everything.
(A dangerous pause. Then a clank as the sword is lain back on the stone.)
SEJANUS: My lord.
PEPIN: ...So you really are our god, after all?
FROBISHER: It seems I have to be.
PEPIN: Then speak to the people. They await your blessing.

(Pause. We hear him take a few steps forward. Then the cheering begins again. FROBISHER clears his throat.)
FROBISHER: My people!
(The cheers fade. They let him speak. Quieter:)
>...My subjects. Listen to me. Are you sure you want me as your new god?
(Raucous cheers.)
>Okay. Okay then, I accept. But listen up.
(The cheers die down again. Deliberately:)
>There are going to be a few changes.

Scene 28: INT.
A cell. Faint background dripping on stone. The odd sound of chains clanking throughout the scene.

SCRIBE: I don't expect they'll keep us waiting.
DOCTOR: No, I imagine not.
(We hear some chains being pulled.)
>Your manacles not too tight, I hope?
SCRIBE: Oh no. No, I'm almost comfortable.
(And he pulls his chains too.)
>For what it's worth, I don't imagine I shall outlive you very long.
DOCTOR: No offence, Eugene, but that isn't very much comfort.
SCRIBE: I'm an old man. I can't see myself surviving twelve years locked in a small cell with a superbeing. If I'm lucky, I might last a few months. But to be honest, it's a predicament likely to scare me quite literally to death. It's such a pity to die. As a historian, I want to know how everything turns out.
DOCTOR: What will happen to your Bible now?
SCRIBE: Well, the post is hereditary. So I expect my son will carry on the good work.
DOCTOR: You have a son?
SCRIBE: Oh, I expect I must have. Otherwise he couldn't very well succeed me, could he? Stands to reason.
(Short pause)
DOCTOR: *(softly)* Tell me about your son.
SCRIBE: Why? What about him?
DOCTOR: Oh, I don't know. What does he look like, for example?
SCRIBE: I don't know. He looks a bit like me. I'd have thought.
DOCTOR: Does he?
SCRIBE: Oh yes. The mirror image. I expect. But younger. I don't know. Doctor, does it really matter?
DOCTOR: Yes, I think it does.
SCRIBE: Well, I don't want to discuss it.
DOCTOR: *(insistently)* Do you remember him at all? Eugene? Can you remember your own son?
SCRIBE: *(with surprising anger)* He's not very important! That's all! That's all there is to it!
DOCTOR: Eugene...
SCRIBE: All that is important is recorded in the old texts! He'll be just another scribe, a scribbler, a penpusher like me. No scribes have

130

ever appeared in the pages they've written! We just don't matter enough! Do you understand?

DOCTOR: I think I'm beginning to.

(A heavy sound of chains, as SCRIBE turns away. Softly, to himself:)

SCRIBE: All of us. We're worthless.

Scene 29: INT.

The vaults.

(LIVILLA's heels click smartly on stone as she paces angrily. A creak as a door opens.)

LIVILLA: Childeric! How dare you keep me waiting like this?

CHILDERIC: I have been busy. But I'm sure when Arnulf here caught you, he would have put you in a comfortable cell. And, see, it is comfortable, isn't it? Well done, Arnulf.

(A pleased grunt from ARNULF.)

LIVILLA: He didn't capture me. I came to see you of my own free will. And I find it disgraceful the way you treat me, a potential ally locked up as a prisoner...

CHILDERIC: A potential ally?

LIVILLA: You see? I knew that would get your interest.

CHILDERIC: To be strictly honest, I'm more amused than interested. Why are you here, Livilla? What do you want of me?

LIVILLA: Isn't it obvious? I want you to give me a taste of your power.

CHILDERIC: *(chuckling)* Believe me, it is by no means certain I shall even give you your life. You do realise I could kill you in a moment? Show the empress your knife, Arnulf.

(ARNULF grunts. We hear a knife being drawn.)

LIVILLA: *(bravely)* You wouldn't kill me. Not before you hear what I have to offer.

CHILDERIC: I wouldn't count on it. Frankly, I'm too busy at the moment with my own plots and schemes to want to waste time listening to yours.

LIVILLA: You're going to take the throne, aren't you? You're going to kill my husband and take the throne.

CHILDERIC: Of course.

LIVILLA: When you do, I want to be your consort. I want to sit by your side and rule forever.

CHILDERIC: I take it then that you're not here to plead for your husband's life?

LIVILLA: Of course not. You are my only god.

CHILDERIC: I would have more respect for you if you were.

LIVILLA: I can offer you my beauty.

CHILDERIC: And you would give that beautiful to a man as ugly as I am?

(And he laughs. ARNULF joins in. LIVILLA, nervously, gives an awkward laugh of her own.)

LIVILLA: But you're not ugly, my love... No, not at all...

(The laughter stops dead. And we hear a heavy slap. LIVILLA gives a gasp of pain.)

CHILDERIC: *(quietly, intensely)* Look at me. Look right into my face.

Is this the face of god?

LIVILLA: (*frightened, barely audible*) ...Yes.

(*And we hear CHILDERIC step away from her. He begins to pace deliberately on the stone.*)

CHILDERIC: You are indeed beautiful, my dear. Unfortunately I have little taste for it. Living in the shadows as a renegade all these years has seen to that.

LIVILLA: (*nervously*) You could make me ugly if you wished it. Batter me, bruise me, whatever suits your pleasure. If you will make me a goddess.

CHILDERIC: What do you think, Arnulf? Shall we mark her now?

(*ARNULF gives a short burst of his laugh.*)

I'll consider it. What else can you offer?

LIVILLA: I'll give you a child. An heir.

CHILDERIC: Indeed. You must know that my son is my prime concern.

LIVILLA: But if you want to be god, you must act now.

CHILDERIC: I have been patient many years, Livilla. I can be patient a while longer.

LIVILLA: My husband has abdicated. And another god rules in his place.

(*The pacing stops. Short pause*)

CHILDERIC: What?

Scene 30: INT.

A cell. Chains rattling, as before.

DOCTOR: When you've been locked up for execution or torture as often as I have, you'll find the worst thing is all the hanging around waiting for them to get on with it.

SCRIBE: Speaking as a novice, I've got to say they can take as long as they like.

(*We hear a door creak open.*)

DOCTOR: I'm sorry, Eugene. It seems that they're ready for us.

(*Slow footsteps towards them. The menace is undermined when CLOVIS clears his throat awkwardly.*)

CLOVIS: Right. I have the knife here. Now. Who would like to go first?

DOCTOR: Is that a clumsy attempt at sadism? Because I'm telling you, I've heard better.

CLOVIS: Not at all, Doctor. I have no wish to cause either of you any more discomfort than is necessary. I am as unhappy with this situation as you are.

DOCTOR: Mmm. Probably not quite as unhappy.

SCRIBE: I don't mind going first. Give the Doctor a few more minutes of life.

CLOVIS: Very well.

(*We hear chains being steadied.*)

DOCTOR: That's very good of you, Eugene.

SCRIBE: Well, if there's one thing that being a historian has taught me, it's that death and torture are bound to happen sooner or later to all of us. Best just to grin and bear it.

CLOVIS: If you could open your mouth for me, please. As wide as possible, that's it.
(A little grunt from the SCRIBE.)
           Oh yes, I see it. Now, this may prick a little...
DOCTOR: If you're so unhappy with this situation...
CLOVIS: I am. I'm a holy man, not a butcher. For generations my family have been high priests, always betraying their god in some doomed rebellion or other. It's tradition. But none of them ever killed anybody. The only blood they spilt was their own when they were captured and executed.
DOCTOR: And that makes sense to you?
CLOVIS: This is not the sort of rebellion I was expecting. What usually happens is a glorious attack on the emperor, followed by humiliating defeat by his guards. None of this talk about new messiahs. Basic treachery isn't as simple as it was in my father's day.
DOCTOR: Clovis. You know that your leader is quite insane.
CLOVIS: Yes.
DOCTOR: Take the knife out of Eugene's mouth.
(A little grunt from the SCRIBE, as if in agreement.)
CLOVIS: I can't, Doctor. I'm sorry. I don't understand what's going on, but I know my role. I'm the high priest who rebels against the rightful god. It's hereditary. ...Now, hold still.
(A gasp from the SCRIBE.)
           And I'll have that tongue out in a jiffy.
(And we hear the door burst open, quick footsteps into the room.)
CHILDERIC: You can stop now, Clovis. Our plans have changed.
(And we hear a rattling gasp of relief.)
CLOVIS: Yes, lord.
DOCTOR: Are you all right, Eugene?
SCRIBE: Ahh... A bit of lockjaw, that's all.
CHILDERIC: You may be more useful alive after all, Doctor. It seems you have friends in high places.
DOCTOR: I have?
CHILDERIC: The big talking bird has usurped the throne and made himself god.
DOCTOR: How very enterprising of him. Frobisher, what have you been up to?
CLOVIS: And the scribe's tongue?
CHILDERIC: Can stay in his head. We can't afford to be cautious any longer. Ready or not, we shall have to release my son from the vaults immediately.

Scene 31: INT.
The throne room. We hear gentle snoring.

PEPIN: *(softly)* Am I disturbing you, your majesty? May I approach the throne?
FROBISHER: ...What? Sorry, I was just taking a nap. Being a god is certainly draining, isn't it?
PEPIN: How right you are, my lord. But what you say is always right.
(FROBISHER yawns and stretches.)

FROBISHER: Please don't fawn, Pepin. I'm Frobisher. Same guy I always was.
PEPIN: If you say so, your supreme and unquestionable omnipotence.
FROBISHER: *(sighing)* Well. I think I've made good progress anyway.
PEPIN: Excellent progress.
FROBISHER: Excellent progress, yes. I've introduced the people to parliamentary democracy, religious toleration and the concept of equal rights.
PEPIN: All in half an hour.
FROBISHER: And how are the elections for prime minister going?
PEPIN: Well, that's why I'm here, sire. Your subjects are ready to cast their votes, as you instructed them.
FROBISHER: Good.
(We hear a sheet of paper being studied.)
PEPIN: And they've asked me to ask you. Which candidate would you like them to choose?
(Short pause)
FROBISHER: For my next speech, Pepin, remind me to bring up the subject of free will.
PEPIN: Whatever you command shall be done. Your wish is all that matters.
FROBISHER: What of the Doctor?
PEPIN: There's no trace of him, your majesty. Or of the scribe we need to chronicle your great edicts.
FROBISHER: You'll continue to look for him, won't you? Maybe he got outside the castle...
PEPIN: *(puzzled)* Outside the castle?
FROBISHER: Yes. You know. Lowered the drawbridge or something.
PEPIN: I'm sorry, sire, I don't understand...
(And we hear battering at the door.)
FROBISHER: *(alarmed)* What is it?
PEPIN: The door's giving way...
(And as he says this, it breaks apart. Quick chainmail footsteps into the room.)
FROBISHER: What is this? Who dares disturb my great thoughts? Get out!
PEPIN: Sejanus!
SEJANUS: If you truly are an immortal god, you shan't feel the bullets when I shoot you.
(The gun is cocked.)
FROBISHER: *(irritably)* Oh, not another assassination. Get out.
SEJANUS: *(taken aback)* What?
FROBISHER: You heard me. Go on, get out.
SEJANUS: But, your majesty. It's my job. This is what I do...
PEPIN: Be fair, your majesty. It's what he does.
FROBISHER: What's the point? Your gun's loaded with blanks anyway...
(The gun is fired. A bullet ricochets around the room.)
PEPIN: Since the Doctor complained about the injustice of the ritual, the order was given for live ammunition to be used.
FROBISHER: Thanks a lot, Doc...

134

SEJANUS: To death! Or to life eternal!
(A gunshot.)

Scene 32: INT.
The vaults. We are in a larger room, so there is more echo.

CHILDERIC: Arnulf has been told to bring the child to us here directly. We shall wait for them.
LIVILLA: What is this talk of children? I thought we were going to usurp the throne!
CHILDERIC: Believe me, Livilla. The hour is at hand.
DOCTOR: Pardon me for pointing out the blindingly obvious, but isn't this terribly dangerous? If your experiment has been successful, and you have created a god, how can you dare release it as a five year old child who has been locked in a cell all his life?
CHILDERIC: It is a risk we have to take. I could have handled Pepin on my own. But this talking bird is an unknown quantity. I do not know the extent of his powers.
DOCTOR: Listen, Childeric. Frobisher may be a very unusual chap, but I assure you. He is no god.
CHILDERIC: Good. Then our struggle against him will be all the easier.
(We hear a stone doorway open. And heavy footsteps.)
CLOVIS: Arnulf is coming.
CHILDERIC: Bringing his new master, sleeping in his arms. Remember this, scribe. It will be a most poetic start to your new Bible.
(The footsteps stop.)
SCRIBE: *(cold horror)* Doctor! Look at the child's face...!
DOCTOR: What is it, Eugene? It's just a perfectly ordinary face. A little pale, I admit, but that's no surprise considering...
SCRIBE: No! It's the face... I've seen it before! Come back to haunt me...
CHILDERIC: Let me hold the boy.
(We hear him take the baby from ARNULF.)
SCRIBE: *(louder)* You mustn't wake him up! If you do, it'll be the death of you all!
CLOVIS: His eyes are opening...
SCRIBE: No!
CHILDERIC: I command you. Awake. And begin your reign here and now.
(And we hear the gentle innocent yawn of a baby. Short pause - then he begins to talk. When the BOY speaks, the voice has a sinister maturity. It is a higher pitched treatment of a particular member of the cast.)
BOY: Father. You have released me at last.
CHILDERIC: *(startled)* It's impossible... You know our language!
BOY: Of course I know your language. I know everything. Am I not your god?

Scene 33: INT.
The throne room.

PEPIN: I knew that you were a god.

FROBISHER: *(breathless)* But it isn't possible...

PEPIN: What are the limits of possibility to a god like you?

FROBISHER: The bullet passed straight through me. Look! Look at the hole it left in the throne behind me!

PEPIN: It's a miracle, lord. No doubt we shall see many such miracles in the aeons to come.

SEJANUS: Excuse me. But when do I get my imperial coin?

FROBISHER: Pay him outside, Pepin. And leave me. I need to think about this.

PEPIN: If I had any doubts before, my friend, they have been dispelled. You are a shining beacon of hope, and have come to save us all!

(As we hear the chainmail footsteps get fainter:)

FROBISHER: Oh, Doc. Where are you?

Scene 34: INT.
The vaults. Echo, as before.

BOY: Who are these people? Are they my subjects?

CHILDERIC: They are your slaves, your playthings.

LIVILLA: Well, I'm certainly not!

(We hear her high heels as she walks forward.)

Childeric, what is this? I thought I was going to give you a son!

CHILDERIC: As you can see, Livilla, I already have one. I need no other.

LIVILLA: But I am going to be a goddess, aren't I? I am going to be all-powerful? I've waited all my life to be all-powerful, and now I'm nearly there, I refuse to play second fiddle to a precocious brat!

BOY: May I have her, father? Can she be my plaything?

CHILDERIC: Of course, son. Let's see what a god can do.

BOY: Look at me, plaything. Look into my eyes.

LIVILLA: No... What are you doing?

(She falters on the stone floor, the high heels scraping.)

BOY: My doll. My toy.

LIVILLA: Please... Get out of my mind!

BOY: There's not much room in here. You see power as baubles and trinkets and pretty jewellery. You see power as spite and greed. You are wrong.

(And underneath this, we hear the sound of air being compressed...)

LIVILLA: What's happening to me...?

CLOVIS: My God... She's changing...

CHILDERIC: *(interested rather than concerned)* She's getting younger!

BOY: There is nothing petty about my power. My power is blind terror and death. I pity you. Show us what you really are.

LIVILLA: No!

(And her screams subside into the wails of a baby.)

BOY: She is an infant, nothing more. She is unworthy to be my slave.

SCRIBE: *(hissing)* Doctor, do you see? Do you see now what

136

we're up against? That face, always the same face...
DOCTOR: (*softly*) Quiet, Eugene. Don't make a sound.
(*The baby's cries are suddenly broken off, as its neck is snapped.*)
BOY: That plaything was no good, father. It's broken. I want another.
CHILDERIC: Not now, my son. There will be time for that later.
BOY: But I'm still hungry! I want to kill another!
CHILDERIC: I really think you've had enough, don't you? Now be a good boy.
(*Short pause. Then the BOY begins to cry. Harsh, angry sobs.*)
   Stop that at once. Is that any way for a god to behave?
BOY: (*viciously*) I want to kill! I want to kill! I want to kill!
(*And under his lines we hear the rush of a great wind.*)
CLOVIS: What's happening?
DOCTOR: The mental force of that child is incalculable. He's just throwing a little tantrum.
SCRIBE: What are we going to do?
DOCTOR: I suggest we run.
(*And we hear them do so, underneath the wind.*)
CHILDERIC: Where are you going? All of you, come back!
CLOVIS: Childeric, come on! We have got to get out of here!
CHILDERIC: (*fighting to be heard above the wind and the shouts of the BOY*) No! I shall stay with my son!

Scene 35: INT.
A tunnel off the vaults. We hear the wind behind us in the distance.
(*The DOCTOR races after the SCRIBE, panting. We hear them both running on the stone floor.*)

DOCTOR: Stop, Eugene! I need to talk to you!
SCRIBE: (*ahead of him, frantically*) No, Doctor! I have to get away from here!
DOCTOR: But you know what this thing is. You must tell me.
SCRIBE: (*closer, now the DOCTOR has reached him*) I know so many things, all written in the old texts...
DOCTOR: (*angrily*) No! Not in the old texts! You've seen this before.
(*They stop running. Gently:*)
   Haven't you?
SCRIBE: (*weakly*) ...It's the face. Always the same face. Always on a different child.
DOCTOR: What is it, Eugene? What's it doing here?
SCRIBE: It's come for me. It wants to revenge itself on me.
DOCTOR: And only you?
SCRIBE: How can it keep coming back, Doctor? The face. I killed it. I keep killing it. Why won't it go away?
(*Short pause. Then we hear the DOCTOR walking away in the direction he's just been running from. Our point of view stays with the SCRIBE.*)
   Where are you going?
DOCTOR: I think I know what the child is. I must try to make it see sense.
SCRIBE: Do you really think you can succeed?

DOCTOR: (*stopping for a moment, a distance from him*) If it's what I think it is, I haven't got a chance. So. We'll just have to hope I'm wrong.
(*And he resumes walking.*)

Scene 36: INT.
The vaults.

(*The wind and screams continue.*)
CHILDERIC: I said enough!
(*There is a loud slap. And the storm and cries stop abruptly.*)
BOY: (*surprised*) You slapped me.
CHILDERIC: Yes.
BOY: For that I should make your hand drop off.
CHILDERIC: Do you promise to be a good boy? Well. Do you?
BOY: (*sulkily*) Maybe.

Scene 37: INT.
Somewhere within the upper castle.

FROBISHER: What is it you want to show me, Pepin?
PEPIN: There, sire. Right ahead of you. ...No, look up.
FROBISHER: Crikey.
PEPIN: Your first statue.
FROBISHER: What, already? That's incredible.
PEPIN: And this is the sculptor.
FROBISHER: Very well done. Especially impressed with the eyebrows.
SCULPTOR: Please don't put me to death, sire. I have a wife and family.
FROBISHER: Why should I put you to death? I'm just impressed you could knock one out so soon...
PEPIN: Look at the nose, your majesty.
SCULPTOR: (*terrified*) I couldn't get the nose right.
FROBISHER: It's called a beak, actually, guys. Oh, it isn't that bad...
PEPIN: There's practically nothing of it. It's much smaller and far less grand than your divine nose, sire.
SCULPTOR: Your nose is so vast, my lord, I wasn't prepared. And there wasn't enough stone to go round...
FROBISHER: He would be executed for this?
PEPIN: It is a sort of treason, your excellency. A slur on the imperial visage.
FROBISHER: Well, I'll see to that.
(*Shapeshifting sound effect.*)
PEPIN: My lord! You've... changed!
FROBISHER: Mesomorphed is the word. My beak should now match the statue exactly. And the sculptor can be congratulated on a most accurate piece of work.
SCULPTOR: Thank you, sire, thank you...
FROBISHER: (*coldly*) Listen, Pepin. No-one is to die because of me. No-one. Is anyone else awaiting execution?
PEPIN: Just one woman, sire.
FROBISHER: Then we shall release her at once.

Scene 38: INT.
The vaults.

CHILDERIC: You cannot rule openly. I shall be your regent until you come of age.
BOY: Why?
CHILDERIC: Because you're only a child. No-one would accept you.
BOY: We shall reign together, father and son.
CHILDERIC: Exactly.
BOY: But my way. I shall enter your mind.
CHILDERIC: *(warily)* As you did with Livilla?
BOY: Oh, don't be frightened. I could never hurt my father. I shall become you. And we shall be each other, joined in one body.
CHILDERIC: You can do that?
BOY: Oh, father. You cannot conceive just how much I can do. ...I want to kill. I'm hungry. I want to kill.
CHILDERIC: There's no-one here to kill, you'll have to be patient. But when we are on the throne, then you can execute all the heretics you like!
BOY: What about him?
CHILDERIC: Arnulf's not a heretic. He's our good and loyal servant. We shall need servants like him.
BOY: We shall need no-one. No-one at all. ...He has no tongue.
CHILDERIC: I plucked it out to ensure your divinity.
BOY: Come here, Arnulf. Come closer.
(We hear heavy dragging footsteps.)
        That's it. I shall give you back your speech.
(ARNULF grunts - and out of the grunting comes a voice.)
ARNULF: The pain... It's stopped! I can talk again! I can talk!
BOY: But of course. I had to give you your tongue back, so I could find out what your dying words would be.
ARNULF: Please, my lord... No! I have looked after you! Let me live, do not hurt me! No!
(He gags, and dies. His body slumps to the ground.)
BOY: I'd been hoping for something more profound than that. How very disappointing.
(We hear deliberate footsteps.)
DOCTOR: *(boldly)* When is all this killing going to end?
CHILDERIC: Doctor! Why have you come back here? I thought you had run away with the other unbelievers.
DOCTOR: Oh, I believe in your son only too well. Tell me. What will you do with your great powers?
CHILDERIC: I shall be emperor and everyone will do exactly what I say.
DOCTOR: Not you. Him. Well? What will you do?
BOY: Kill.
DOCTOR: And what else?
BOY: Destroy.
DOCTOR: What else?
CHILDERIC: We cannot just kill and destroy, son. Or who will be there to worship us?
DOCTOR: *(insistently)* And what else?

BOY: There is nothing else. After I have destroyed everyone in the castle, I will destroy the castle. And I shall be alone with my father.
DOCTOR: And what about outside the castle? Will you kill all the people out there too?
CHILDERIC: What do you mean, outside?
DOCTOR: Out through the front doors, Childeric. Into the rest of the world.
CHILDERIC: There are no front doors, Doctor. The castle is our world.
BOY: The castle is the world.
DOCTOR: As I thought. You call this an empire? You call yourself a god? A god of one single building, you might as well call yourself a landlord! So I ask you again. What is the point of such great power now?

Scene 39: INT.
The dungeon. We hear the dripping, as before. From a distance we hear feet coming down the steps. The voices get louder as they approach.

FROBISHER: Are all the dungeons as dark as this? I can't see my flipper in front of my eyes...
PEPIN: It's just as well we can't see. There's probably all sorts of bones and blood stains down here...
FROBISHER: Wait! There's a body over there. Shine the candle a little closer.
(And scuffling on stone as they bend down.)
...Who is it?
PEPIN: It's Berengaria. It's my mother.
FROBISHER: She's lost a lot of blood. I think we're too late.
PEPIN: You're a god. You can heal her.
FROBISHER: Pepin, look at her!
PEPIN: Just touch her, and redeem her. And all shall be well.
FROBISHER: What?
PEPIN: Please. I believe in you.
FROBISHER: Very well. For all the good it can do...
(He touches her. We hear a tingle. And then, over it, a desperate gasp of air.)
FROBISHER: She's breathing!
BERENGARIA: What's happening? Am I still alive?
PEPIN: You've saved her!
FROBISHER: *(softly)* I am a god.

Scene 40: INT.
The vaults.

CHILDERIC: You are trying to confuse us, Doctor. What you say makes no sense.
DOCTOR: I know what this place is. And why the TARDIS brought me here.
CHILDERIC: I should have killed you when I had the chance.
DOCTOR: Oh, Childeric. You wouldn't have been able to. What you

are can't harm me or Frobisher.

CHILDERIC: But could my son?

DOCTOR: *(quietly)* Yes.

BOY: Come, father. Be at one with me. Let me enter your mind and soul. And we shall have absolute power.

CHILDERIC: Yes. I am ready.

(And their bodies merge. A humming sound.)

Yes! I can feel it! I am becoming a god at last!

BOY: What? What is this? You are not my father!

(And the humming becomes harsher.)

CHILDERIC: Of course I'm your father! I've had you incarcerated since birth! Who else but a father would do that?

BOY: You are not my father! You have betrayed me!

CHILDERIC: No! Stop! You're tearing me apart...

(With accompanying grisly sound effects...)

BOY: You shall die!

(CHILDERIC screams, and is silent. Wet slap as his body falls on the ground. Gently, as a small innocent child:)

I want my father. Doctor. Are you my father?

DOCTOR: *(softly)* No.

BOY: Please. I must know. Who is my father? Tell me who my father is.

DOCTOR: Lower your voice. Speak like the adults do.

(And the treated voice is lowered. Not enough though.)

BOY: Like this?

DOCTOR: Even deeper than that. And we shall hear who your father is.

BOY/SCRIBE: Well, Doctor? Who is it? Do you recognise this voice?

DOCTOR: *(hushed)* So it was you all the time...

BOY/SCRIBE: I see that you know! So tell me! Who is my father? Who is the man who created god?

End of Part Three

PART FOUR

Scene 40, recap:

BOY: Who is my father? Tell me who my father is.
DOCTOR: Lower your voice. Speak like the adults do.
(And the treated voice is lowered. Not enough though.)
BOY: Like this?
DOCTOR: Even deeper than that. And we shall hear who your father is.
BOY/SCRIBE: Well, Doctor? Who is it? Do you recognise this voice?
DOCTOR: *(hushed)* So it was you all the time...
BOY/SCRIBE: I see that you know! So tell me! Who is my father? Who is the man who created god?
(A dangerous pause.)
Well?
DOCTOR: *(carefully)* I know what you are. And you are not a god.
BOY/SCRIBE: I have complete power over this world. I can destroy every being in it.
DOCTOR: In this castle, yes. But you are not a god.
BOY/SCRIBE: Then what am I. Doctor? Tell me what I am.
DOCTOR: You are a torture device. Designed to torture one specific person.
BOY/SCRIBE: *(angrily)* Who is my father? Tell me who he is!

Scene 41: INT.
The dungeons. Background dripping of water.

BERENGARIA: The pain has stopped. Why don't I feel any more pain?
PEPIN: Another miracle you have performed, o lord.
BERENGARIA: I'd think I was in heaven, except I've already been a god. And know that heaven can't exist.
FROBISHER: How are you feeling? It's hard to tell in this darkness...
BERENGARIA: My wounds have healed over. My breathing is normal, my pulse steady... What is the meaning of this? What's going on?
PEPIN: I'm sorry, mother, really, I thought that you...
BERENGARIA: Oh, is that my pathetic son Pepin? I should have guessed you'd be behind this. And who's the figure next to you? Shine the candle closer to his face. I see, a big talking bird. Help me to my feet. *(A rattle of chains as they do so.)* And now, would you both like to explain to me what you think you're playing at?
FROBISHER: Listen, lady, I don't know how I did it, but I just saved your life...!
BERENGARIA: And who asked you to? If you hadn't interfered, I'd have been happily dead by now!
PEPIN: But, mother...
BERENGARIA: I was just beginning to feel my life ebb away when you two come in and ruin everything.
FROBISHER: But surely you can't want to die?
BERENGARIA: I am the wife of a dead god. I have no purpose any longer. I am an anachronism.
(A touch kindlier:)
Pepin, you are a god. However spineless you were as a mortal, you should know better now.

142

PEPIN: No, mother. I abdicated. Frobisher here is god.
BERENGARIA: Impossible! He's not even in the family!
PEPIN: I'm now the high priest.
BERENGARIA: Fallen gods don't get to be their successors' high priests! Like me, Pepin, you have no function now. The rituals say we should be dead.
PEPIN: Mother, Frobisher believes that the rituals are wrong. He believes that we can think for ourselves, make our own choices, and find happiness!
BERENGARIA: Well, big talking bird. Is that what you think?
FROBISHER: *(awkwardly)* Well, it did seem like a good idea...
BERENGARIA: The rituals by which we run our lives are sacrosanct. They are the only things which give our existence any meaning.
FROBISHER: But they don't make any sense.
BERENGARIA: Of course they don't make any sense. Otherwise they wouldn't have to be rituals - we'd be doing them without a second thought. But they bring a continuity, a certain security. You, Pepin, as high priest. Do you intend to betray your bird god here?
PEPIN: Of course not. He's my friend.
BERENGARIA: But the high priest always betrays his god. That's what he's for. It's tradition, don't you see? When you don't, everyone will get confused.
FROBISHER: But when they see that treachery and murder aren't the way it has to be, that you can make your own decisions...
BERENGARIA: Then what? You do my people no favours by giving them free will, bird god. The king will still be king, the slave will still be slave. At least they knew that before. And they knew that persecutor or persecuted, their time would come, and each of them, like me, will one day die a heretic's death in a dungeon somewhere. All of us, we're all executed eventually. How long have you been a god? How long has it taken you to wreck our society?
FROBISHER: Well. I started this afternoon, actually.
BERENGARIA: I don't want you to save me, bird god. I want to die, as I should have done. If you touch my wounds again, can you take away my life as freely as you saved it?
FROBISHER: I don't think so. I'm sorry.
BERENGARIA: Then what is your divinity worth? Leave us. I would be alone with my son one last time.

Scene 42: INT.
The vaults. Echo.

BOY/SCRIBE: You say I have been constructed?
DOCTOR: Yes.
BOY/SCRIBE: As a killing machine?
DOCTOR: Killing. Torturing. Inflicting pain.
BOY/SCRIBE: Do you think I would be good at it, Doctor?
DOCTOR: I imagine you would.
BOY/SCRIBE: Then you should be very frightened of me.
DOCTOR: *(sincerely)* Oh. I am. I am.
BOY: *(back to the child voice)* Do you think I'd be the bestest torturer in the world? Do you think my father would be proud of me? *(Short pause)*

Well? Would my daddy be proud? Would he bounce me

on his knee and chuck me under the chin, would he give me a kiss and put me to bed and read me a little story before I fall asleep? Do you think he would? ...Who is my father?

DOCTOR: I cannot tell you.

BOY: Why not?

DOCTOR: Because he is the man you have been constructed to kill.

BOY: You are wrong, Doctor. I do not want to kill my father.

DOCTOR: You don't?

BOY: No. I want to beg his forgiveness.

DOCTOR: Forgiveness for what?

BOY: ...I don't know. There must have been a good reason he killed me. ...Tell me who my father is, Doctor.

DOCTOR: I won't.

(And there is a sudden gust of wind. The DOCTOR winces in pain at the suddenness of it. The wind continues under the scene:)

BOY: You know I can invade your mind. You know I can extract the information. You know I can tear you apart to find it.

DOCTOR: Yes.

BOY: You know that I am your god. And I move in very mysterious ways.

DOCTOR: I know that here you're all-powerful. But you are no god.

(The wind blows stronger. And then over it, the sound effect as earlier, as the BOY enters the DOCTOR's mind. The DOCTOR screams.)

BOY: You shall show me the truth. Does it hurt, Doctor? As I look through your memories?

DOCTOR: Yes!

BOY: Does it hurt a lot? Will daddy be proud?

(And the humming grows still more intense. The DOCTOR cries out.)

...What is this? What trick is this? All these places. You call them... seas. Oceans. Planets, stars... Galaxies! Am I god of all this? How can I be god of all this?

DOCTOR: *(with difficulty)* It's the universe...

BOY: No! This castle is the universe! There is no other! And I am god of it all!

DOCTOR: *(painfully)* Can you find your father? He's there somewhere...

BOY: The millions of people you have known! Millions upon millions upon millions! Are all these my subjects? Must I kill them all? No! It's a lie, a dirty lie, you're a dirty liar! The castle is the universe, and my father is the centre of it!

(The sound effect fades. Both the BOY and the DOCTOR are weak.)

I can't find my father, not amongst so many people. Tell me who he is!

DOCTOR: *(weakly)* You'll have to find him for yourself.

BOY: Then I will! Then I will!

DOCTOR: And how long will that take? You may be a god, but you're still just a little boy. With little legs. You've got maybe two miles of steps to climb, and I'm not going to carry you.

BOY: Don't laugh at me! I'll find him! I'll find him, and ask his forgiveness, and we'll rule forever! And then you'll be sorry!

(He vanishes.)

DOCTOR: ...He's gone... He's just gone... Of course, I'm a fool. He must be able to move anywhere in the castle at will! With mental powers of that scale... well, a bit of instant teleportation isn't going to give him too many problems. This is his world... And within it, he can do just about anything he likes.

(Slow footsteps, as he drags himself across the floor.)

Two miles of steps. I must find Frobisher. I just hope there's time.

Scene 43: INT.
The dungeon. As before.

(PEPIN gives a grunt, and the chains fall loose.)

PEPIN: There, mother. You're freed from your chains.

BERENGARIA: I didn't ask for that.

PEPIN: *(gently)* I took the skin off my hands doing it. A thank you would have been nice, you know...

BERENGARIA: I don't understand it, Pepin. You always seem to expect some affection from me.

PEPIN: Well, after all these years, I think 'expect' is a little strong...

BERENGARIA: Quite why you feel that my being your mother should earn you a place in my heart is beyond me. You made my belly swell up for nine long months and you ruined my figure forever. At best, I should find the inconvenience of your birth rather irritating.

PEPIN: I'm sorry...

BERENGARIA: At worst, your constant apologising aggravates my gout. Did you really hope I'd be happy to be alive, if it meant I had to see you again?

PEPIN: I only wanted some attention from you and father. It didn't have to be good attention. But even when you both hit me, you were looking the other way...

BERENGARIA: You're not the only one who couldn't get attention from your father. Though I must admit, as the years went by, I began to see the advantage in it. Your father and I despised you, Pepin.

PEPIN: Yes. I know.

BERENGARIA: It was nothing personal. The imperial family always despises its offspring. It's tradition. When you have children, you'll see. You won't be able to stand them any more than we could stand you. It will make you a man.

PEPIN: I'd hoped you'd be pleased we had saved your life...

BERENGARIA: It isn't ever talked about, but at your age your father was as pathetic as you.

PEPIN: But he was such a monster...

BERENGARIA: He was a stammering fool, a congenital idiot who couldn't string two words together without dribbling. His father made him that. And you, the moronic son he hated, made him what he became, every inch the tyrant god. You see, I know. As empress, I know what this society is - and it's obsessed with fathers hating sons following fathers hating sons, it's all that it cares about.

PEPIN: What are you saying?

BERENGARIA: If you were still emperor, Pepin, you would have become like your father. Your son would have turned you into a god. It's what fathers and sons have done to each other, ritually, over the centuries. It's tradition.

PEPIN: It's too late for that now, mother.

BERENGARIA: And tradition has been broken. From what you've told me, as soon as that blue temple appeared in the throne room it destroyed all that we hold dear.

(We hear the rattle of chains gently as she picks them up.)

     I'd have preferred to have stayed in these chains. But they're broken now.

(And she drops them with a clatter on to the ground.)

Scene 44: INT.
A tunnel off the vaults.

(Running footsteps, tired but determined.)

DOCTOR: *(panting)* These tunnels all look the same... Well, they always do, don't they? So long as I keep going up... I just hope I'm not too late...

(And then, overlapping those footsteps, we hear some others from the other direction.)

CLOVIS: Doctor!

(The DOCTOR stops dead.)

DOCTOR: Who is that? ...Oh. Clovis. It's you.

CLOVIS: Doctor! I need your help!

DOCTOR: No time for that. You're just getting in my way.

CLOVIS: I've been hiding in these tunnels for my very life. We have to destroy that creature down there, but we'll stand no chance alone. Together we may yet be able to defeat it!

(Purposeful footsteps.)

DOCTOR: Clovis, at the first opportunity you'd sell me out. In fact, that's already your plan, isn't it? You want to offer me to the child in exchange for your life.

(The footsteps stop. Then they slowly walk back the way they came. Short pause)

CLOVIS: How did you know?

DOCTOR: It's what you do. You were created by a man with a limited imagination and a taste for the melodramatic. I'm sorry, Clovis. I can't trust you. I won't take you with me.

CLOVIS: *(musing)* I don't want to betray anybody. I don't think my father or my grandfather did either. It just feels like something I have to do, I can't help myself. I'd really much rather be a good man. But I'm not, am I, Doctor?

DOCTOR: I'm afraid not.

CLOVIS: What's the matter with me?

DOCTOR: I really don't think you'd understand.

CLOVIS: Please try.

DOCTOR: There's really very little time for this...

CLOVIS: I don't want to be this way! I've been trying to puzzle it out for years. Please.

DOCTOR: ...You're a stereotype.

CLOVIS: A stereotype?

DOCTOR: I'm afraid the man who created you had very little interest in giving you any real depth or personality. You behave in a series of predictable responses to the events around you.

CLOVIS: The man? Our creator?

DOCTOR: Your creator, Clovis. And the creator of your world. This

146

place, and all that is within it, is a fiction. You are a fiction. Nothing you say or do counts for anything, because it's already been predetermined.

CLOVIS: But that's what our religion has always taught us, Doctor. That we have no free will.

DOCTOR: I can't take you with me, Clovis. I cannot trust you. It's not your fault, I feel sorry for you. You're not even the lead villain, just a sort of sidekick henchman.

CLOVIS: Goodbye, Doctor. And good luck. When the creature kills me I shall try to die nobly, against my nature.

DOCTOR: I'm sorry. Good luck.

(Footsteps running off. We hear the nervous breathing of CLOVIS.)

CLOVIS: Right. Right. Think noble. Think noble.

(And the same sound effect used when the BOY vanished.)

Oh God. You've found me. It's too early, I haven't found a way to be noble yet...!

BOY: Are you my father?

CLOVIS: Be brave. Think noble. Try and act against my nature...

BOY: I said, are you my father?

CLOVIS: Keep away from me! Don't hurt me!

BOY: Father? Is that you?

CLOVIS: Don't kill me! I'll tell you anything you want! The Doctor, are you looking for the Doctor? He's just run that way! You can still catch him!...

(And the merging sound effect. CLOVIS screams with pain.)

BOY: Hush, little man. You don't need to tell me anything. I can take what you know for myself.

(And the scream freezes.)

...Ah, this is better. A much easier mind to digest.

Scene 45: INT.
The throne room.

FROBISHER: I need to think about all this... I can do it better from the comfort of my own throne. If you've got to think, might as well do it in the most comfortable chair in the castle...

(And a heavy door opens and closes. As it does so, we hear a frightened shriek, and someone scurrying away.)

Hey, you! Yes, you! What are you doing in my throne room? No-one is allowed in here without my permission!

SCRIBE: Keep away from me...

FROBISHER: Do you know who I am? I'm God, that's who! And there's no use hiding under the throne either. Oy! I can still see you!

SCRIBE: It's coming to find me, don't let it find me...

FROBISHER: Wait a moment. You're the scribe. The one who was with the Doctor!

SCRIBE: I'm Eugene Tacitus. Only Eugene Tacitus...

FROBISHER: Where is the Doctor?

SCRIBE: The Doctor's dead.

FROBISHER: What?

SCRIBE: He must be, he went back there, he'll never have survived. But it doesn't matter, you see, it doesn't matter...

FROBISHER: What are you talking about?

SCRIBE: Leave me alone...

FROBISHER: Come out from under there! I'll pull you out if I have to. Right...
(And we hear him pull the SCRIBE with a grunt. He slides across the floor. The throne topples over.)
SCRIBE: No, please...! Leave me somewhere to hide!
FROBISHER: What do you mean, the Doctor's dead? Tell me!
SCRIBE: He would have died anyway. You are all going to die anyway. It's coming for me now, and it'll kill everything in its path.
FROBISHER: What is it? What's wanting to kill you?
SCRIBE: Oh, it won't kill me. That's not the way it works. I'll kill it. I always kill it, over and over again. I'm so sick of it...
(Screams outside.)
FROBISHER: What's that?
SCRIBE: You're all going to die for my sins. I'm only Eugene Tacitus. I'm nothing. Who would have thought I was worth such carnage?

Scene 46: INT.
Elsewhere in the castle. A background of screams, of fear and pain.

BOY: Where is my father? Are you my father? No, then die! *(He laughs.)* I like the smell of death, I like the sound it makes. My daddy would be proud if he could see me. I'm a murderer now, just like him. If my daddy were here, we would make the people die together! I want my father!

Scene 47: INT.
The throne room.

(Continuous to the above scene, the screaming becomes an undercurrent. The SCRIBE appears to be narrating over it.)
SCRIBE: He will appear out of thin air and kill at random. The blood flows down the castle walls, the very air is dark with death - oh my god, so much death, so much... Who would have thought I was worth it? Who would have thought an old man had so much blood in him?
FROBISHER: What can we do to stop it? ...Look at me!!
SCRIBE: Nothing. He has come for me, as he always does, as he always will. And before he finds me, he likes to destroy my little world.
(The throne room doors burst open.)
SEJANUS: Your majesty!
FROBISHER: What is it, Sejanus?
SEJANUS: Your people are being slaughtered! What are your orders?
FROBISHER: My orders?
SEJANUS: Save us, sire! Save your good and loyal subjects!
FROBISHER: I'm sorry. I don't know how!
SEJANUS: ...But you're our god. You're supposed to know. You're supposed to know everything.
SCRIBE: He isn't a god!
SEJANUS: What?
SCRIBE: That child out there, that is your only god. And his name is death. There is no hope, Sejanus! No hope at all!
(Heavy chainmail footsteps. A sword is drawn.)
SEJANUS: *(coldly)* We believed in you. We had faith in you.

FROBISHER: *(softly)* I'm sorry.
SEJANUS: The people are hugging on to your statues, hoping it might save their lives. But they're cut down all the same.
(Short pause. Then the sword is sheathed. And the footsteps walk away.)
FROBISHER: Where are you going?
SEJANUS: If I had the time I would chop off your feathered head and stick it on a spike. But I must try to save the people you betrayed.
SCRIBE: There is no hope. You will all die.
SEJANUS: I know. But I would sooner die defending their lives than his.
(The door slams shut.)
FROBISHER: We must help him!
SCRIBE: Barricade the door. You'll never see him again.
(A background clatter as FROBISHER drags furniture over to the door. Our point of view stays with the SCRIBE, who speaks softly, almost in sing-song:)
    Why could I not love my child? My own child, I tried so hard, I really tried, but I couldn't, I failed, I couldn't. My own son, it's normal to love your son, it's natural. Why can't I be normal like that? *(And loud:)* I promise to love you, son! Whatever you want, I promise! So long as you stay away from me!

Scene 48: INT.
The dungeons.

BERENGARIA: Leave me now, Pepin. I would be on my own when I die.
PEPIN: But Frobisher healed you.
BERENGARIA: Yes, thanks to him it'll probably take weeks for me to starve to death. But I'll starve eventually.
PEPIN: Come with me, mother. You're free. There's nothing to stop you.
(A rattle of chains.)
BERENGARIA: I shall wrap these around me. And pretend I'm still manacled to the wall.
PEPIN: Come with me. back to the court. Live, and break tradition.
(Short pause)
    Goodbye, mother.
(And we hear his footsteps. And then, over them, a faint echo of the SCRIBE's voice.)
SCRIBE: Why could I not love my child? My own child, I tried so hard...
BERENGARIA: *(almost dreamlike, picking up on it straight after it has faded)* Why could I not love my child? My own son, it's normal to love your son. It is normal, it is what should be. Why can't I be normal like that?
(The footsteps stop during the above.)
PEPIN: *(uncertainly)* Mother? What are you saying?
BERENGARIA: I don't know... I don't know where that came from... Have I been wrong all these years?
PEPIN: Mother. I don't want you to die.
(And now the echo of the SCRIBE's desperate scream.)
SCRIBE: I promise to love you, son! Whatever you want, I

promise!

BERENGARIA: (*carefully*) Pepin. My own child. I understand what you want from me. I understand it now. But I'm not sure I can give it. That's all. I'm not sure I know how to love.

PEPIN: (*firmly*) I won't leave you, mother. You can starve here if you must. But I won't leave your side.

BERENGARIA: And what about your god? Don't you love him?

PEPIN: I love you.

(*Short pause*)

BERENGARIA: Then stay. And who knows, perhaps you'll do the impossible. And teach me after all.

(*And we hear the BOY appear. And the buzz of an intense light.*) It's so bright! I can't see...

PEPIN: What is it, mother? Covered in so much blood...

BERENGARIA: I don't know. But I imagine it's come here to kill us.

BOY: (*innocently*) Are you my father?

PEPIN: (*bravely*) Keep back! This is my mother, and I shall protect her!

BERENGARIA: Pepin!

PEPIN: Stop! I tell you to stop!

BOY: I'm looking for my father. Do you know where he might be?

PEPIN: I shan't let you hurt her.

BOY: I shall find out if you are my father. And if you are not, you shall die.

PEPIN: (*laughing*) I don't care! Do what you want! Don't you understand? I'm not frightened of anything any more!

(*Their bodies merge, but PEPIN doesn't scream. The sound effect fades, and the body hits the floor.*)

BOY: He didn't scream. I like it when they scream.

BERENGARIA: (*flatly*) You killed my son just as I was getting to know him.

BOY: You can't be my father.

BERENGARIA: Hardly.

BOY: I thought you weren't. I'm looking for my father. Tell me where he is and I will let you live.

BERENGARIA: Will you?

BOY: (*thoughtfully*) No. But tell me anyway. And when I find him I shall be god and rule forever.

BERENGARIA: You're no god of mine.

BOY: (*petulantly*) I certainly am your god! There's no-one half as godly as me! Get down on your knees and worship me!

BERENGARIA: And I shan't worship you.

BOY: Why not?

BERENGARIA: Free will. I choose not to.

BOY: You choose?

BERENGARIA: I choose. Maybe the bird was right after all.

BOY: If you don't worship me, I shall kill you! I've killed lots and lots of people!

BERENGARIA: I believe you. But I choose not to live in a world where you are the master.

BOY: Then die!

(*And the merging sound effect again. Over it, with relief:*)

BERENGARIA: At last. I've been waiting so long.

Scene 49: INT.
The throne room.

SCRIBE: (*softly*) They'll all be dead now, Frobisher. That's always the way it happens. And it'll come for you soon enough...
FROBISHER: You know, you're really not helping...!
SCRIBE: (*ignoring him*) And then it'll just be me. And I'll have to kill it. And go through it all over again, always, all over again...
(Underneath this, there is a banging at the door.)
FROBISHER: There's someone out there!
SCRIBE: (*stubbornly*) Not possible. All dead. Everyone.
(FROBISHER runs to the door.)
SCRIBE: No! You mustn't open it!
(A clatter as FROBISHER destroys the barricade.)
FROBISHER: If there's a chance anyone's still alive... Can you hear me out there?
SCRIBE: I won't let you open it! No!
FROBISHER: Get off me!
SCRIBE: I'm not ready to kill again!
FROBISHER: Get off! I don't want to hurt you, but I'm a private eye, and I can protect myself!
(And a crash as the SCRIBE is thrown, presumably into the furniture.)
      Sorry, but I did warn you.
(And the door swings open.)
SCRIBE: No! Don't let it in!
DOCTOR: Well, you took your time.
FROBISHER: Doctor! I thought you were dead!
DOCTOR: Don't bother closing the doors, Frobisher.
FROBISHER: But we had barricaded ourselves in...
DOCTOR: There's no point. What we're up against can bypass doors or walls at will.
FROBISHER: What are we up against?
SCRIBE: It can't be! You should be dead! It always kills everyone before it comes for me!
DOCTOR: Ah, Eugene. I wondered where I would find you.
SCRIBE: Keep away from me!
(And he runs and hides himself amongst the furniture. We hear the clatter.)
FROBISHER: He's scared out of his wits, Doc. And frankly, underneath my cool penguin exterior, I'm getting a little rattled myself. Am I pleased to see you!
DOCTOR: What happened to your beak? It looks blunter somehow...
FROBISHER: Oh, that's not the half of it. Some homicidal child is out there killing my subjects, and I seem to have become immortal.
DOCTOR: Come now, Frobisher. Things may be pretty grim, but you're not a god. The universe can take some comfort from that.
FROBISHER: The bullets passed right through me, Doc! I was shot at point blank range and I wasn't even scratched!
DOCTOR: This place is a fiction, Frobisher. A very elaborate fiction, I grant you, but no more substantial. And it is populated by fictitious people. They can't hurt us.
FROBISHER: What? This is all make-believe? But it seems so real...
DOCTOR: That's the idea.

FROBISHER: Well, if they can't hurt us, then we're okay, aren't we? Everything's all right.

DOCTOR: Everything is very far from being all right. We're not the only two real people here. There's still the author of this fantasy. And the killer out there trying to find him.

FROBISHER: What author?

DOCTOR: Who do you think? Who's been writing it all along?

FROBISHER: You mean that little man is responsible for all this?

DOCTOR: In a way, yes. He created all the people here, and the pointless rituals by which they ran their lives.

FROBISHER: Right. Come out from that pile of furniture. I've got a few bones to pick with you...!

(And we hear the clatter as he pulls out the SCRIBE.)

SCRIBE: No! Please don't hurt me...

DOCTOR: Take it easy, Frobisher. I think if he ever knew he was the author, he's long since forgotten. Look at him!

SCRIBE: Please don't let it find me... I can't go through it all again!

DOCTOR: I'm sure that's part of the punishment. To create a world for yourself, and only be a servant in it. To be a god, but never know it.

FROBISHER: The punishment?

DOCTOR: He didn't create the world out of choice, Frobisher. This is a prison. There's no escape from it.

FROBISHER: A prison? What, all of this castle's a prison?

SCRIBE: That's right.

FROBISHER: Just for one prisoner? Just for you? It's a bit big, isn't it?

DOCTOR: Oh, I don't think so. I imagine, from the outside, it looks no bigger than a blue police box.

Scene 50: INT.
Elsewhere in the castle. The sound of destruction in the background.

BOY: *(exultant)* Father! Father, can you see me? I have destroyed all the people you made. Aren't you proud? And now I shall destroy your world.

(And we hear the sound of walls tumbling, rocks falling. And replaced by a peculiar static buzz - the same sound heard on the TARDIS scanner in part one.)

Scene 51: INT.
The throne room.

(A heavy throne is righted by the SCRIBE, babbling.)

SCRIBE: Must set my throne straight. It's my throne, and I must sit on it.

DOCTOR: Eugene...

SCRIBE: No, Doctor! I'm the god now. I'm the one responsible for all this!

FROBISHER: His mind's completely gone.

DOCTOR: It's hardly surprising. He's probably been trapped here for hundreds of years.

FROBISHER: It's not possible...

DOCTOR: Just think about it. A prison cell bigger on the inside than it is on the outside. Where time and space have no meaning, where you can build an entire world with centuries of history. And live through all those centuries, until you forget you're not part of the illusion.

FROBISHER: That's obscene?

DOCTOR: And every once in a while something is sent in. To destroy the world completely. And make him relive his crime in every horrific detail.

FROBISHER: The little boy he's been talking about?

DOCTOR: This time, yes. This time it took the shape of a five year old boy used in a cruel religious experiment. Next time it could be the high priest, or the queen consort. Or any character within this fiction of his.

SCRIBE: And always with that face! Always with the same face!

FROBISHER: How long have you known?

DOCTOR: Not long. But I've always had my suspicions about this place. I knew there must be some reason the TARDIS brought us here after you interfered with the dimensional controls. She was drawn to something which had similar properties. An artificial environment in which she could recuperate.

FROBISHER: I thought it had brought us here because it quite fancied being a temple.

DOCTOR: I'll have you know, Frobisher, that like her owner, the TARDIS has her ego fully under control.

(Underneath the last few lines the sound of the static has been introduced gradually. It's now much more noticeable.)

FROBISHER: Doctor, look! Outside the door - there's nothing there! Just... static...

DOCTOR: It's what the TARDIS saw when we first landed. The child must have almost finished its work, and destroyed the prisoner's creation.

FROBISHER: Which means it's nearly ready for us?

DOCTOR: I'm afraid so.

(A clatter as the SCRIBE rises.)

SCRIBE: My world! What's happened to my world?

DOCTOR: Eugene. Eugene, listen to me. The child is coming. Your son will soon be here. You've seen this before, what happens next?

SCRIBE: There's nothing left out there! What good will my histories be now?

FROBISHER: None of it's real. None of it was ever real!

DOCTOR: Except for the child. The child who comes back to haunt you.

SCRIBE: Yes, that's right... Always the same face... I kill it, but it keeps coming back! What does it mean?

DOCTOR: That's the punishment, don't you see? You create a world. The child destroys it. Then you destroy the child. Then you create the world. Over and over again. Don't you see, Eugene?

SCRIBE: I'm beginning... to remember...

FROBISHER: What's happening?

DOCTOR: Now that the fantasy's broken down, there's nothing left to distract him...

SCRIBE: I remember who I am! I remember! Oh my god...

DOCTOR: What happens next, Eugene?

153

SCRIBE: Is that who I am? Oh my god...
(The BOY appears.)
FROBISHER: Doctor...!
DOCTOR: Not now, Frobisher!
FROBISHER: The child is here! It's covered in blood...
DOCTOR: I said, not now! Tell us, Eugene!
BOY: Are you my father?
DOCTOR: Keep back, Frobisher! Look at the boy, Eugene!
BOY: Father?
SCRIBE: No...
DOCTOR: What did you do to this child?
SCRIBE: I murdered him. I murdered my son.
FROBISHER: Oh no...
SCRIBE: I created this world, a perfect place to live, everything ordered, everything ritualised. And for a while I can forget what I did. I can live in peace, without the guilt. And then the history stops making sense, and the face comes back, the same face comes back to remind me!
BOY: Father! Tell me! Are you my father?
SCRIBE: But don't worry. I have a knife. I'll kill it again! I'll save you both!
DOCTOR: No, Eugene...
SCRIBE: I'm the only one who can stop it!
DOCTOR: But that's what you always do, Eugene, isn't it? The child wants you to kill it. It's trying to make you act out your crime again!
BOY: Are you my father? Are you my murderer?
DOCTOR: Kill him and you'll be killing him again and again forever. Break the ritual!
SCRIBE: I can't...
DOCTOR: Set yourself free!
SCRIBE: I'm frightened.
DOCTOR: Look around! There's nothing left! Even the throne room has disappeared! There's nothing left of your fantasy except your dead son. Speak to him. You have no choice.
(Indeed, underneath the last few lines, the static has been getting louder. Short pause)
BOY: Are you my father?
SCRIBE: Yes.
BOY: Really and truly?
SCRIBE: Yes. ...What are you doing? Why are you on your knees?
BOY: To ask you forgiveness.
SCRIBE: My forgiveness? No, please, don't say that...!
BOY: I must have done something very wrong, daddy, for you to have killed me like that. What did I do?
SCRIBE: Oh, my poor boy... I don't remember...
BOY: You do, daddy. You remember everything now. Why did you do it?
SCRIBE: I remember you were sleeping. Still on your bed, peaceful. And I took the knife. And I held it over you for a while, trying to work out if I could go through with it... to work out if I could stop myself...
BOY: *(crying)* Why did you kill me?

SCRIBE: (*brokenly*) Because I'm insane. My poor boy. Because I'm quite, quite mad. My poor beautiful son. How could I ever think of harming you?

BOY: You're holding a knife. Are you going to kill me again?

DOCTOR: Don't do it, Eugene! You've got to break this cycle!

SCRIBE: No, I can't...

DOCTOR: Throw away the knife! Just throw it away!

FROBISHER: Eugene! No, don't give it to the child...!

SCRIBE: Not this time. You're going to have to be very brave...

FROBISHER: No! What are you doing?

DOCTOR: Eugene, stop this!

SCRIBE: Take the hilt, like that...

BOY: I take the hilt...

SCRIBE: And hold the blade against my chest...

FROBISHER: You've got to stop this! Doctor, do something!

DOCTOR: I'm trying! I can't touch them! I can't pull the knife away! My fingers are going straight through...!

SCRIBE: This is my world, Doctor. This is my fiction. And I choose not to make you part of it.

DOCTOR: Eugene! Don't do this! There has got to be a better way!

BOY: Shall I push the knife into your chest, father?

DOCTOR: Don't let this happen! I can take you away from here! I can set you free!

SCRIBE: But I remember it all, Doctor! Who I am, and what I have done. Please, I can't go through it all again...

FROBISHER: Eugene, stop!

SCRIBE: Only I can set myself free.

BOY: I am ready, father.

SCRIBE: And push the knife in. ...That's it.

BOY: I love you, daddy.

SCRIBE: I love you too, son. And I'm so sorry.

DOCTOR: (*weakly*) No...

FROBISHER: Look at the boy, Doctor! He's ageing!

BOY: (*his voice matures into that of the SCRIBE*) I love you, daddy. But it's all over now. It's all over now. It's all over.

DOCTOR: His mirror image. He's killing himself.

BOY/SCRIBE: Daddy? You were a god to me. And I thought we would rule forever.

(*Silence, except for the static of the void.*)

DOCTOR: (*quietly*) He didn't have to do that. He didn't have to do that.

FROBISHER: They've gone. They've both gone.

DOCTOR: The child's purpose was over.

FROBISHER: And there's nothing but the void.

DOCTOR: The void and the TARDIS. Come on.

Scene 52: INT.

The TARDIS console room. We hear the familiar sound of the doors opening, then closing. The usual blips and bleeps from the console as the Doctor pushes buttons.

DOCTOR: (*quietly*) Everything should be back to normal. The TARDIS should be fully recovered.

FROBISHER: All the fruit and flowers on the console. They've gone.

DOCTOR: Everything's gone. Gone forever.

FROBISHER: And all those people? They were killed, just to punish Eugene? ...That's terrible.

DOCTOR: If it's any consolation, they were never actually real in the first place.

FROBISHER: No, Doc. That's no consolation. They thought they were real, didn't they?

DOCTOR: *(sighing)* Just like the fish in the swimming pool. They felt pain, they felt fear. And more than that, they had hopes and dreams and families. ...Yes, it is terrible. But that's what comes of travelling in the TARDIS. All the people you meet, all the planets you see... you know they won't last forever, and our next journey could be to a time when they'll have been long forgotten. Such little lives. And we can feel like gods, set apart from them all.

FROBISHER: And that's supposed to make me feel better, is it?

DOCTOR: No. Not at all.

FROBISHER: For a while back there, Doc, I actually felt I could do some good. I actually felt I could save them all.

DOCTOR: *(heavily)* I know, Frobisher. Believe me. I know. ...Come on. Let's get away from here.

Scene 53: The void.

(The TARDIS dematerialises. And all that is left is the static.)

End of Part Four

A TASTE OF MY OWN MEDICINE

By Gary Russell

One of the utter joys of being the script-editor for the Big Finish *Doctor Who* audios is that I have the opportunity to work with the writers quite closely to tweak and rationalise and modify and… well, I imagine, rather annoy them as I take their hard work and tell 'em, 'Yes, that's all very good but what if…?'

Therefore, let me explain the bare bones of the process as it usually goes. Script arrives. I read it through. I make little notes, checking for things that may conflict with the current direction we're going in for a particular TARDIS crew or inconsistencies in the script, or moments where a character appears to act in direct contrast to how they acted two episodes earlier, or pointing out plot holes a bus could be driven through and so on. The writer then does a rewrite or three and once everyone is happy (including lovely Jacqueline Rayner, who has been busy checking the Doctor doesn't gratuitously rip someone's head off, or Nyssa doesn't have sex with someone or Evelyn doesn't use a certain four-lettered word etc.), it goes to the director.

And this is where the perk of my job lies. Having seen the scripts first, having worked reasonably closely with the writer on reshaping them, I can go, 'Oh, I'd like to do that one myself!' Now, I should hurriedly point out that the ones I don't direct are not, in my eyes at least, in any way lesser scripts – indeed, given the chance I'd direct everything – but the Briggses and Peggs and suchlike of this world would complain. Loudly. So I have to share 'em out. Bah!

So what makes me select the ones I do? Firstly, casting – I do believe that half the audio director's job is done if the casting is good, and thus when reading scripts I often find myself thinking, 'Oh, that's a part for Actor A' or 'This would be a great role for Actor B'. Secondly, the event – if something big and important occurs and there's some good pacing leading to it, that fires me up. I'm still at heart a massive fan of *Doctor Who* and if in reading scripts I still get that thrill of 'I want to know what happens next' that I used to get watching the telly, I'm hooked. And thirdly, if it's a script which I suggested an idea for in the first place.

Which is very odd, as in the case of *The Fires of Vulcan*, absolutely none of the above criteria really came into play. Steve Lyons suggested a historical, which I liked 'cos I like historicals, especially when the fantasy elements are at a minimum. He delivered a script that required as few tweaks as you could imagine: it was the right length, it hit all the right peaks and troughs for drama, the characters spoke dialogue that could be said out loud (it's amazing how many script submissions I get in which someone has written prose for their characters to say rather than dialogue) and it made me laugh and feel sad in the right places.

Yet I hadn't a clue about casting, it didn't take months to knock into shape, I'd given him no 'moments' to build to. I suppose, however, I have to admit there was one, overriding reason, above and beyond the fact that it was a great script.

Bonnie Langford.

Three things I wanted to achieve when we got the audio range going: involve

Janet Fielding, Paul McGann and Bonnie Langford.

Still working on the first of those.

But the chance to work with Bonnie, and to create a version of Melanie Bush ('known as Mel') that would still be recognisable as the character from Season 24 but without the one or two little nuances that might get peoples' backs up, was too good to pass up. How delightful to find out in studio then that Bonnie, on reading the script, had noticed that effort. Our Mel does not scream, she asks intelligent questions and flaunts her brains.

She was very complimentary about Steve's script, and justifiably so. And working with her, watching her bring Mel back to life alongside Sylvester McCoy, was an ambition fulfilled.

But what about *Neverland*? (Oh, and if you don't know the story stop reading this waffle now, and read the script, then come back, otherwise the adventure may be spoiled for you.) Well, now, that really was the exact opposite.

Pity poor Mr Alan Barnes. How sure he was that resolving the Charley Pollard arc wasn't going to be his problem. How wrong he was. And not only that, but the veritable shopping list of instructions he was given would, for many writers, have had them throwing up their hands in anguish and screeching, 'If you want all of this, why don't you write the blasted thing?'

Instead, being the gentleman he is, Alan graciously took all my lists on board and still managed to weave a story full of incident, emotion and resolution that I could never have come up with in years.

And that list? Amongst it all was:

Resolve the Charley storyline

Rassilon

Time Lords but not Gallifrey

Romana

Vansell's death

Add something to the mythos

The last line must be 'I am not the Doctor! I am Zagreus!!'

Not much to ask for, was it? Of course, Alan ended up writing lots. And we recorded it all. But one day came a plaintive cry from Brighton, home of technical wiz Alistair Lock. 'It doesn't fit on two CDs.' Thus some editing and reworking with the available material was required. If the other three scripts in this book represent the favourites for each Doctor, as voted for by readers of *Doctor Who Magazine*, *Neverland* is here by virtue of the fact that, pulling producer's rank, it's my favourite of the Eighth Doctor run so far. Although I honestly don't think the final release suffered from losing the exorcised lines you'll find here, it is a good opportunity to show them to you.

I've been professionally involved with *Doctor Who* in one way or another now for just on twenty years. Don't think I've ever had as much fun as I had sitting down with Alistair whilst doing the final mix-down of *Neverland* and hearing the end result of all the plotting, forward-planning and back-referencing of the previous two years come to fruition. I cheered as Paul McGann and India Fisher delivered that final denouement, turned to Alistair and said, 'I wonder how we get out of that, then?'

THE FIRES OF VULCAN

By Steve Lyons

It wasn't my idea to send the Seventh Doctor to Pompeii. I wanted to write a science-fiction story for the Sixth Doctor. I had it all worked out – but I never even got the chance to mention it. When I begged Gary Russell to let me write a *Doctor Who* audio, the first thing he said was that he had more than enough Sixth Doctor science-fiction stories already. But he did have a slot for a Seventh Doctor/Ace historical. The only problem was, I couldn't think of a new setting for a historical story at all. Hadn't everything been done already?

Fortunately, a friend of mine who was studying history gave me a page full of ideas that *hadn't* been done. Colditz Castle immediately caught my eye, but Big Finish had just done a few stories set in recent centuries and Gary wanted something in a much earlier time period. He'd also said no Romans – a fact that completely slipped my mind as I saw, there at the top of the list, Pompeii, and realised how perfect it was. A small, walled city doomed to destruction – I could hardly believe that the Doctor hadn't turned up there and been separated from the TARDIS before (although there was that minor incident in the 1976 *Dalek Annual*, of course).

So, I emailed Gary with the basic idea for *The Fires of Vulcan*, and tried to emphasise Pompeii's Greek roots and its Egyptian gods. I also promised to avoid typical Romanesque elements such as mad emperors, chariot races and gladiatorial combats (although I later broke the last third of that promise when stuck for a subplot). And fortunately, Gary liked the setting too, and agreed to let me use it.

At first, I based the structure of *The Fires of Vulcan* on that of *The Massacre*, in which the Doctor and his companion also have to get back to their ship before a preordained disaster occurs. The story, I imagined, would end with the eruption of Mount Vesuvius, whereupon the Doctor and Ace would rush into the TARDIS a moment before it was engulfed in molten lava. As I read up on what actually happened in AD 79, though, I learned that there was no lava involved. I had been misled: shockingly, the details in that old *Dalek Annual* were wrong!

This, I must point out, was not Terry Nation's fault. It wasn't until the 1980s that vulcanologists began to revise their theories of exactly what happened when Vesuvius blew its top. However, as I read up on ash showers and pyroclastic flows, I realised that the Doctor could feasibly survive for many hours in Pompeii *after* the eruption began. And I realised that, if nothing else, that would make for some great sound effects! So, I brought the 'main event' forward to the beginning of Part Four (I thought about making it the Part Three cliffhanger, but didn't think I could sustain that level of tension for a full 25 minutes), where I hoped it would come as a bit of a surprise to a few people.

One big change to *The Fires of Vulcan* came about at a late date. Bonnie Langford asked to do a Big Finish play, and Gary was keen to use her as soon as possible, so he asked me to write Ace out of my script and replace her with Mel. Now, at this point, I'd written almost three episodes, the deadline was looming and I was also busy turning my Sixth Doctor science-fiction proposal into an Eighth Doctor novel called *The Space Age*. So, my first thought was, 'I can't possibly do that, I don't have the time!' My second thought was that actually, I really, really wanted to write for the Seventh Doctor and Mel. And my third thought was, 'I can't possibly do that, I don't have the time!'

To cut a long story short, Gary got his script late.

At first, the prospect of swapping Ace for Mel was quite daunting. On the face of it, they're very different. I was also disappointed that I hadn't been able to work out what I wanted to do with the character of Mel – much maligned from her TV appearances but with a lot of unrealised potential, I thought – and build a story around that. I felt that giving Bonnie a last minute rewrite of a script intended for someone else was doing both her and her character a disservice.

In the end, though, the changeover was easier – and worked far better – than I expected. I would have wanted to emphasise Mel's strengths anyway – rather than emphasising her weaknesses as so often seemed to be the case in the past – so, for the most part, she slipped easily into the space left by the strong-willed Ace.

There were a few problems, though. I knew that Mel would never attack a Roman legionary as Ace did in Part Three, so I had to give that task to the slave girl Aglae instead. A lot of the story also hinged on a white lie that Ace told in Part One – and, as we all know, Mel is as honest as they come. I had to do a lot of work to justify this uncharacteristic act on her part, which is why she's still agonising about her behaviour in Part Three! Gary also pointed out that Mel would be more understanding than Ace of the nature of the time paradox that has trapped her – so, rather than just blindly kicking against it as Ace originally did, she had to be more logical in her approach.

As for the Doctor… My original idea was to have the all-powerful, manipulative later version of the Seventh Doctor trapped by time and to see how he reacted. As it turned out, he reacted – in my script, at least – by reverting partly to his less sure, bumbling Season 24 self. Which was a nice coincidence for me, because it meant that it didn't take too much work to turn him into the Season 24 Doctor proper.

In this book, for the first time, you can see what *The Fires of Vulcan* – Part One, at least – would have been like if Bonnie hadn't come on board. Many of the changes are cosmetic, with Ace making the same points that Mel would end up making, only in her own characteristic style. I did, however, cut Scene Two altogether, because it would have required a complete overhaul to make it work and because the script was overrunning anyway.

A few other changes will be noticeable in the non-Ace scenes. Although I considered this draft pretty final at the time, I still did some tinkering before I sent it off. Gary also requested, and made, a few amendments; it was he who asked for an extra scene before the final one to give him something to cut away to. And he altered the gender of 'Beggar Woman' so as to be able to take this plum role for himself.

You may also notice that, at this stage, Captain Muriel Frost of UNIT is anonymous. Gary later asked me to give the character a name for the sleeve notes, so I suggested Captain Moran. Imagine my surprise when I read on an Internet news group that *The Fires of Vulcan* was to feature a character from the *Doctor Who Magazine* comic strip! I thought this was a really nice touch, though – a continuity reference that's completely inaudible to the casual listener – and, for a while, I really fancied the idea of doing an eighties UNIT story, just to use Ms Frost again.

Gary also named Eumachia's slave Tibernus. Now, in his email asking me to write this introduction, he encourages me to slag off any changes of his that I didn't like, so I'll stick my neck out and say that I was none too keen on that one. The characters in Vulcan are all based on real-life Pompeians - although with very little being known about Murranus, Eumachia, Celsinus, etc. beyond a few details graffitied on to the city's walls, I was able to flesh them out as I wished. The locations I used - Valeria's inn, the Lupanar, etc. - were also real. I'd left the slave without a name because I couldn't find one for him, and I felt that giving him a fictional identity spoiled things a bit. Gary also cut down a scene in Part Three, where the Doctor is trying to work out where the TARDIS might be by pumping Valeria Hedone for information about the politics of Pompeii. The shorter version is better (the original dumps a lot of irrelevant information into the story), but I don't think the Doctor's reason for going to Valeria's tavern is now as clear as it should be. But then, Gary also added the Vegetaria joke, which vastly improved what was, at the scripting stage, my least favourite scene.

No matter how many times I rewrote that dinner party conversation at Eumachia's house, I couldn't make it work. It didn't help that, although it's the longest scene in the story, it's one of the least eventful ones. Originally, Ace was to have stormed out of the meal after yelling at Eumachia and Celsinus and revealing information about the future. That's not Mel's style at all, so all that material went - but I couldn't lose the scene altogether as I needed it to set up later events. To me, the dialogue felt awkward and stilted - a fact not helped by the fact that the Pompeian characters talk, throughout the play, in that weird kind of formal, mock old-fashioned English that tends to pass for ancient languages in this type of drama.

In fact, the idea of hearing actors performing my lines at all was quite nerve-wracking. I was particularly worried about hearing Sylvester McCoy and Bonnie's performances, because I'd written the script with their voices in mind. I knew precisely how I wanted their lines to sound, and I expected that, in reality, they were going to sound different and somehow wrong to me.

So, I arrived at the studio and waited for a break in the recording, feeling all self-conscious. And soon enough, Gary invited me into the booth to watch what was going on - before announcing that he was about to record that dinner party scene! I made an excuse and stayed outside, until a part of the play that I was a bit more comfortable with came along.

My fears, of course, were unfounded. Sylvester and Bonnie may not have sounded *exactly* as I'd imagined they would all the time, but it didn't matter because they were so natural and right in their roles. And the wonderful supporting cast made those strange language constructions sound believable. The characters came to life in such a way that it didn't feel as if I'd written their words at all. And the dinner party scene came out really well!

Finally, a word about the production of *Vulcan*. When I was writing the script, I kept trying to imagine a lavish, expensive setting. I had the characters walk down lots of different roads, and suggested small ways in which they could sound distinct from each other. But no matter what I did, when I tried to visualise the story, I saw a typical *Doctor Who* style indoor set, slightly redressed and shot from different angles for each scene. When I listen to it now, I imagine it on a cinema screen, blessed with a multi-million-dollar budget. Like the actors' performances, that won't come across in the following pages. So if, upon reading this script, you suddenly realise that *The Fires of Vulcan* isn't half as good as you thought it was, that's because so many other people did such an incredible job on the finished product.

The Fires of Vulcan

CAST

THE DOCTOR	Sylvester McCoy
MEL	Bonnie Langford
PROFESSOR SCALINI	Anthony Keetch
CAPTAIN MURIEL FROST	Karen Henson
TIBERNUS	Robert Curbishley
POPIDIUS CELSINUS	Andy Coleman
VALERIA HEDONE	Nicky Goldie
MURRANUS	Steven Wickham
EUMACHIA	Lisa Hollander
AGLAE	Gemma Bissex

163

Part One

1. THE RUINS OF POMPEII, 1980

WE HEAR THE OCCASIONAL CRIES OF SEAGULLS, THROUGHOUT THIS AND ALL OTHER DAYTIME EXTERIOR SCENES UNTIL NOTED. PROFESSOR SCALINI, A (MALE) ARCHAEOLOGIST AND CAPTAIN MORAN, A (FEMALE) UNIT OFFICER APPROACH US ACROSS RUBBLE, IN MID-CONVERSATION.

SCALINI: ...walls and columns came tumbling down. Tumbling down, I tell you! Some buildings lost whole storeys. Our people are working to prop up what's left of Pompeii, but the damage, the damage!

MORAN: *(BORED)* I can see it must be frustrating for you, Professor.

SCALINI: Frustrating? It's disastrous! An archaeological disaster! Pompeii is our window on the Roman world, you know, Captain. A window! Thanks to the eruption of Vesuvius, this city was preserved like no other, just waiting for us to learn its secrets. It has survived looters, tourists, vandals... and now, for nature itself to do this...

MORAN: I'm sure you're doing everything you can, Professor. *THEY COME TO A HALT.* But this, I assume, is what we're here for.

SCALINI: Yes, yes, this is the artefact. We haven't completed our excavations of this region, you see. The artefact was uncovered by the earthquake. It –

MORAN: Could somebody have put it here? As some sort of prank?

SCALINI: Oh, goodness, no. As you can see, it is still partially buried under volcanic ash. No, the only way it could have arrived in its present position is if it was placed there before Mount Vesuvius erupted.

MORAN: Which was when, exactly?

SCALINI: AD 79. Almost two thousand years ago – which, as you can see, is impossible. Quite impossible.

MORAN: Indeed. OK, Professor, I'm taking custody of this artefact. I'll have men down here within the hour.

SCALINI: You intend to dig it out? But–

MORAN: I have to ask you not to speak to anyone about this. You will be required to sign a declaration to that effect. A representative of your government will be in touch shortly.

SCALINI: I don't understand. Is the artefact dangerous?

MORAN: I'm sorry, Professor Scalini, but this is UNIT business now. *(SHE MARCHES AWAY)* If I were you, I'd forget I ever saw anything.

SCALINI: But... but...

MORAN: *(CALLS BACK TO HIM)* Thank you, Professor!

SCALINI: *(FORLORNLY)* But what's so special about an English police telephone box?

2. A POMPEIAN BACK STREET

THE TARDIS MATERIALISES. THE DOCTOR AND MEL EMERGE. MEL STEPS HEAVILY INTO A PUDDLE.

MEL: *(DISGUSTED)* Oh, Doctor! I've just soaked my best shoes.

DOCTOR: Our first clue, Mel. Wherever we've landed, the drainage system isn't as advanced as you're used to. I think we should keep to the pavements.

MEL: I think you're right. It smells awful.

DOCTOR: You'll get used to it. We're on Earth, I think.

MEL: It certainly looks like it. Those buildings are Roman, aren't they?

DOCTOR: Roman or Greek.

MEL: We must have come a long way into the past.

DOCTOR: Millennia, from your point of view. *(THOUGHTFULLY, TO SELF)* This could be one of the older, residential parts of the city...

MEL: City? What city, Doctor? You said you didn't know where we were.

DOCTOR: I don't. The old girl wouldn't tell me where we've landed.

MEL: Oh, Doctor, you don't need to make it sound so sinister. The TARDIS malfunctioned, that's all. It's always happening. I don't know why you don't–

DOCTOR: Ssh.

SILENCE FOR A FEW SECONDS.

MEL: *(WHISPERS)* What is it, Doctor?

DOCTOR: *(SAME)* I don't think we're alone.

A SCRAPING SOUND, AS A SLAVE TRIES TO SLIP AWAY QUIETLY.

(CALLS) It's all right, don't worry, we aren't going to hurt you.

SLAVE: *(TERRIFIED)* My lord, my lady, I beg your forgiveness, I did not mean to intrude upon your conference.

MEL: You weren't intruding.

DOCTOR: You, ah, saw us arriving?

SLAVE: Take my eyes if you wish, lord, but I witnessed the arrival of your chariot from the heavens. I was fetching material for my owner and... and a sound,like a hundred elephants...

MEL: You mean somebody "owns" you?

DOCTOR: He's a slave, Mel. See that belt he's wearing? It's inscribed with the name of his mistress.

MEL: *(READING)* Eu-mach-ia.

DOCTOR: *(TO SLAVE)* We aren't going to punish you.

MEL: No, we certainly are not.

DOCTOR: We are simply, ah, messengers.

SLAVE: Is Isis then displeased with our offerings?

DOCTOR: Oh, no, no, nothing like that. However, we would like to keep our presence here a secret – if you could perhaps...?

SLAVE: I swear, lord, I will speak of this to nobody.

DOCTOR: Splendid. Well, run along now... No, wait! One more thing... We've been travelling for some time, and... *(AN EMBARRASSED LAUGH)* it's silly I know, but we seem to have lost track of the date...?

SLAVE: Why, it is the day of the Vulcanalia, my lord. The tenth before the Calends of September.

166

DOCTOR: *(SUDDENLY DISTRACTED)* I see. Thank you.
THE SLAVE SCURRIES AWAY.
MEL: What did he mean, Doctor?
DOCTOR: *(SOMBRELY)* He said it's the twenty-third of August.
MEL: You should have asked him the year.
DOCTOR: I'm afraid I already know.
HE WALKS AWAY QUICKLY. MEL HURRIES TO KEEP UP WITH HIM.
MEL: What are you talking about, Doctor? Doctor! How can you know?
DOCTOR: We can cross the road on these stepping stones. Be careful.
MEL: Where are we going?
DOCTOR: *(WALKING AHEAD OF HER NOW)* Do you want to explore or don't you?
MEL: What's wrong, Doctor? Where are we? *(HE PULLS AWAY FROM HER; SHE CALLS AFTER HIM, FRUSTRATED)* Doctor!

3. A POMPEIAN STREET
THE DOCTOR WALKS ON, WITH MEL A SHORT WAY BEHIND HIM. THERE ARE A FEW PEOPLE AROUND; WE HEAR THEM WALKING AND SOMETIMES TALKING. AT SOME POINT, AN IRON-WHEELED CART MIGHT TRUNDLE PAST, DRAWN BY TWO HORSES.

DOCTOR: *(MUTTERS SADLY TO SELF, AS IF CONFUSED)* So, this is it. The final journey. I had hoped for a while longer. Time to prepare. Time, slipping away from me. Only just arriving, but we've already stayed a lifetime. Too many lifetimes. Withering like roses.
WE HEAR FOOTSTEPS AS MEL CATCHES UP WITH HIM.
MEL: *(OUT OF BREATH)* All right, Doctor, what's going on?
DOCTOR: I'm sorry, Mel.
MEL: *(FRUSTRATED)* What for?
THEY STOP WALKING.
Tell me, Doctor!
DOCTOR: *(SIGHS, COMPOSES HIMSELF)* The year is AD 79. The Roman Empire is under the short-lived rule of Titus. We are in the city of Pompeii, a prosperous trading centre on the Bay of Naples. If you look between the buildings over there, you can see a mountain by the name of Vesuvius.
MEL: The volcano!
DOCTOR: Yes. The volcano.
MEL: I've never seen a real volcano before. *(LAUGHS NOSTALGICALLY)* I remember, we made a model of that particular one in primary school, out of *papier mache*. We had red liquid pouring out of the top like lava.
DOCTOR: *(MUTTERS)* Actually, that's not quite what will happen.
MEL: *(SUDDENLY WORRIED)* When will Vesuvius erupt, Doctor?
DOCTOR: I think it might be better if we just leave.
MEL: What?
DOCTOR: Leave. Go back to the TARDIS.
MEL: Why?
DOCTOR: Because you aren't dressed for this time and place.

Because, beneath their sophisticated veneer, the Romans are a quite barbarous people. Because we have a habit of attracting trouble. And because this is your history, and no good can come of our meddling in it.

MEL: *(SIGHS)* It's all right, Doctor. I get the idea. You want to go.

DOCTOR: No. It's your decision, Mel. It has to be your choice.

MEL: Well... can't we at least have a quick look round first? I mean, there's no reason why we should go rushing straight off, is there?

DOCTOR: None whatsoever.

MEL: I wish you'd tell me what's wrong.

DOCTOR: Nothing's wrong, Mel. Quite the opposite. Events are proceeding precisely as I expect they should.

MEL: And Mount Vesuvius?

THE DOCTOR SETS OFF WALKING AGAIN.

DOCTOR: *(DOURLY)* Will erupt, burying Pompeii and killing thousands of its people, at approximately midday tomorrow.

MIX INTO MUSIC

4. THE STREET OF PLENTY

A FEW MINUTES LATER. THE DOCTOR AND MEL WALK INTO A BUSY SHOPPING CENTRE. WE HEAR LOTS OF VOICES AND LAUGHTER.

DOCTOR: *(CHEERFULLY)* The Via dell'Abbondanza. The Street of Plenty.

MEL: There are certainly plenty of people about.

DOCTOR: They're celebrating, Mel. If I remember my history – or rather, yours – correctly, we've arrived during the Festival of the Divine Augustus.

MEL: I see they've invented graffiti by now. It's everywhere! Now, let me see. I did a bit of Latin at school. That one says... 'Polycarbus runs from... *(CORRECTS HERSELF)* ran from... his opponent...'

DOCTOR: 'In shameful fashion.'

MEL: Referring to a gladiator, I assume.

DOCTOR: You can learn a great deal about a culture from its writings.

MEL: *(DISTASTEFULLY)* On walls, though!

DOCTOR: There's a time and a place for everything, Mel.

MEL: So long as we don't have to see any of these gladiators.

DOCTOR: The Amphitheatre will be closed for the festival. Thankfully. We could take in a poetry recital, if you'd like.

MEL: Yes, that could be quite interesting. *(BEAT)* Doctor? Do you see that man behind us? Quite young, dark hair... Do you think he's following us? It's just that he keeps looking over here and...

HER VOICE TRAILS OFF, AND THE SOUND OF THE CROWD GROWS LOUDER. SHE HAS LOST HIM.

(WORRIED) Doctor? Where are you?

BEGGAR WOMAN: Spare some asses, dear?

MEL: *(A STARTLED GASP)*

BEGGAR WOMAN: Some coins for a homeless old woman?

MEL: Oh. Oh, I see. I'm sorry, I don't have any money.

BEGGAR WOMAN: *(ANGRILY)* What? You dare claim poverty? You, with your clean face and your neat hair and your clothing of strange fabrics?

MEL: I don't. Really, I just –

BEGGAR WOMAN: You think yourself better than me, but you are no more than a base dissembler!

MEL: I'd help you if I could. But I've only just arrived here. I... I'm a messenger. From Isis. I'm here to –

DOCTOR: To honour the Divine Augustus with a quiet drink.

MEL: *(RELIEVED)* Doctor!

DOCTOR: So, if you'd excuse us...?

MEL: Where were you?

THE DOCTOR CHIVVIES MEL AWAY. WE STAY WITH THEM.

BEGGAR WOMAN: *(SHOUTS AFTER THEM)* You have not even the decency to cover your head. You are shameless, woman. Shameless!

DOCTOR: I don't think it's a good idea to encourage that particular rumour.

MEL: I don't like lying, obviously – but I didn't know what else to say. We can't tell the people of the first century AD about the TARDIS, can we?

DOCTOR: You should leave the talking to me in future.

MEL: *(OFFENDED)* Oh, Doctor! I only repeated what you told that slave – or rather, what you let him believe.

DOCTOR: He saw the TARDIS materialising. I had no choice. Believe me, Mel, making claims of that nature can be very unwise indeed. You're drawing enough attention to us already.

MEL: I'm drawing attention?

DOCTOR: Your clothing is anachronistic. Women should keep their heads covered, and pink stripes are definitely out of season.

MEL: Whereas question mark pullovers are the height of discretion, I suppose.

DOCTOR: I think we should find somewhere a bit more private.

THEY WALK AWAY FROM US, AND WE RETURN TO THE BEGGAR WOMAN. SHE IS APPROACHED BY POPIDIUS CELSINUS; HE IS TWENTY-SIX YEARS OLD; A WEAK MAN IN A POSITION OF POWER.

CELSINUS: Well? What have you learned?

BEGGAR WOMAN: That you must like the aspect of this stranger a good deal that you, *(WITH MOCKING GRANDEUR)* Popidius Celsinus of the municipal council, would pay for the favour of such as I.

CELSINUS: You try my patience, woman. What did she tell you?

BEGGAR WOMAN: A more precious secret, perhaps, than can be bought with the few coins you have promised.

CELSINUS: I offer fair recompense for a simple deed, hag! Would you have me talk to the aediles and have you run out of this city?

BEGGAR WOMAN: *(AMUSED, TAUNTINGLY)* I merely find it strange that you know not the answer to your question already.

CELSINUS: Why say you that?

BEGGAR WOMAN: The woman comes from Isis, decurione. She is a messenger of the goddess. Now, how can it be that you, of all in Pompeii, were not aware of that fact?

5. VALERIA HEDONE'S INN

A SMALL BAR CROWDED WITH REVELLERS, SOME OF THEM DRUNK AND QUITE ROWDY. ITS FRONT IS OPEN TO THE STREET, SO THE SOUNDS FROM OUTSIDE CAN STILL BE HEARD. THE BAR IS RUN BY VALERIA HEDONE, A TOUGH, FORTHRIGHT GREEK WOMAN.

VALERIA: *(CALLS INTO THE STREET)* Come, handsome stranger, feast here with your chambermaid. Valeria offers the lowest prices for hot food and the finest garum in all Rome.

DOCTOR: Yes, yes, thank you, I think we will.

THE DOCTOR, MEL AND VALERIA MOVE INTO THE BAR TOGETHER.

MEL: Thank you. But I'm not his –

DOCTOR: You keep an interesting establishment here, er...?

VALERIA: Valeria Hedone at your service. You are a stranger to Pompeii, but a man of good standing I can see. It will be Falernian wine for you, I'd wager. I ask but four asses for the drink of the emperors.

DOCTOR: Very reasonable... Ah. But not just yet, I'm afraid. I appear to have left my coins at home.

MEL: *(EMBARRASSED)* Oh, Doctor!

VALERIA: *(ICILY)* Then perhaps you should fetch them, stranger, before you waste any more of my time.

SHE WALKS OFF.

MEL: What was that you said about drawing attention?

DOCTOR: *(BITTERLY)* Why are you humans so obsessed with money? *(MUTTERS THOUGHTFULLY)* Money, money, money...

MEL: I don't think it's a good idea to eat here anyway. Those fish aren't even cooked. They're rotting!

DOCTOR: They're not for eating, Mel.

MEL: So, what are they for?

DOCTOR: Throwing back into the river.

MEL: I think it's a bit late for that.

DOCTOR: It's a ritual, Mel. Remember what that slave told us? Today is the Vulcanalia. The fish are an offering to Vulcan, the Roman God of Fire and Furnaces. *(MUTTERS THOUGHTFULLY)* I always did wonder how that particular custom originated.

MEL: You mean it's Vulcan's feast day as well as the Festival of the Divine Augustus? I knew the Romans had a lot of holidays, but two at once!

DOCTOR: They treat their gods very seriously.

MEL: As a serious excuse to get drunk, from what I can see.

DOCTOR: *(HAPPILY)* Ah! I think I've just seen the answer to our problem.

HE LEADS MEL OVER TO A TABLE AT WHICH FOUR PEOPLE ARE PLAYING WITH DICE MADE OUT OF BONE. ONE IS MURRANUS, A GLADIATOR: LOUD, ARROGANT AND QUICK TO ANGER. WE MUST HEAR VOICES OF ALL FOUR AS THEY PLAY.

MEL: *(LOWERS HER VOICE, UNEASILY)* Are you sure, Doctor? They don't look very friendly.

DOCTOR: *(AT NORMAL SPEAKING VOLUME)* Gladiators, I expect. But don't worry, Mel, they're only wielding dice, not swords. Excuse me, gentlemen, I wonder if you might be able to accommodate one more player?

MURRANUS: You have coins to stake?
DOCTOR: Ah, no. But I thought you might have a use for... *(HE ELONGATES 'FOR' AS HE RUMMAGES THROUGH HIS POCKETS)* this silver, er... *(DISAPPOINTED)* yo-yo. No, no, that won't do at all, will it?
MURRANUS: We play for coins or nought. Now, leave. You disturb us.
MEL: I think he means it, Doctor.
DOCTOR: Yes, yes, but there must be something I can interest you in.
MURRANUS: *(LAUGHS)* I am Murranus, stranger, the greatest mirmillo ever to do battle in Pompeii's Amphitheatre. What could you offer to me?
DOCTOR: *(FEIGNING DELIGHT)* Ah, Murranus! Delighted to meet you. I've heard your name spoken, of course. The most courageous swordsman in the whole of the Empire, they tell me.
MEL: Much braver than Polycarbus.
MURRANUS: You hear right. Why, in the latest games, I vanquished my opponents with ease. Even Crescens, 'the people's darling' could not withstand my sword.
THE DOCTOR PULLS BACK A CHAIR AND SITS DOWN.
DOCTOR: Indeed. And it would be a great honour to dice with the renowned Murranus. I'm the Doctor, by the way.
MURRANUS: *(THREATENINGLY)* I did not give you leave to sit.
DOCTOR: *(HE'S SUDDENLY THOUGHT OF SOMETHING)* My maidservant!
MURRANUS: What madness afflicts you now?
DOCTOR: My maidservant. She must be worth... oh, two thousand sesterces at least, wouldn't you say?
MURRANUS: The girl?
MEL: *(HALF-LAUGHING, NOT SURE IF HE'S JOKING)* Doctor!
DOCTOR: The girl! What's wrong, Murranus? My wager too rich for Pompeii's finest warrior? I will stake the girl against just thirty sesterces.
MURRANUS: Then you are a fool, Doctor. You must know the gods will favour he who fights and wins in their name.
DOCTOR: Then you accept?
MEL: *(IN AN URGENT WHISPER)* I hope you know what you're doing.
MURRANUS: Aye, Doctor. I accept!
DOCTOR: Splendid, splendid. Well, then... perhaps you'd like to make the first roll?

6. THE HOUSE OF EUMACHIA
EUMACHIA, AN ARROGANT NOBLEWOMAN, REMONSTRATES WITH HER SLAVE.

EUMACHIA: *(ANGRILY)* Speak, slave! I require an answer. I would know how it is that you should take so long about a simple errand.
SLAVE: *(AFRAID)* Forgive me, Mistress Eumachia, I am pledged not to say.
EUMACHIA: To whom? To whom would you show greater fealty than to your mistress; to she who feeds and clothes and houses you?

SLAVE: Only to the gods, I swear it.

EUMACHIA: Ah! Then 'twas the Gods who obstructed your work. Were my husband still alive, he would flog you for such lies!

SLAVE: It was... (*MUMBLES, ALMOST INAUDIBLY*) their messengers.

EUMACHIA: Do not mumble so!

SLAVE: Their messengers, mistress. It is the truth, I swear it. I would scarce have believed it myself, and yet I saw their temple as it descended from the heavens.

EUMACHIA: What temple is this, that a priestess of the true religion knows nought of it?

SLAVE: It was sent to us by Isis, mistress.

EUMACHIA: Ha! The foreign goddess! Then these messengers be false prophets indeed.

SLAVE: My lady?

EUMACHIA: Their deceptions may fool one such as you – but they will not long stand in the light of the true faith.

7. VALERIA HEDONE'S INN

A CROWD OF ONLOOKERS HAS GATHERED, AND THE BAR IS QUIETER THAN BEFORE. TWO BONE DICE ROLL ACROSS A TABLE, AND A COLLECTIVE GASP IS RAISED.

DOCTOR: I believe we agreed on thirty sesterces?

MURRANUS: (*BITTERLY*) By Jupiter, Doctor, the Lares smile upon you today.

DOCTOR: Apparently so.

HE PULLS A NUMBER OF COINS ACROSS THE TABLE. THE ONLOOKERS BEGIN TO RESUME THEIR CONVERSATIONS.

And now, if you'll excuse me...?

MURRANUS: What is this? Surely you will not take your gains and leave so soon?

DOCTOR: Well, time is pressing.

MURRANUS: (*THREATENINGLY*) That is not the way of a sportsman, Doctor. I would test your fortune further. You will agree, I feel sure, that I should have the opportunity to recover what I have lost?

DOCTOR: Oh, very well then, just a little longer... (*CALLS*) Valeria? Valeria, I wonder if you could do me a small favour? I'm sure you've noticed how my, ah, maidservant here is dressed. Most inappropriate. I wonder if you could, ah...?

HE HANDS SOME COINS OVER.

VALERIA: For this price, Doctor, I will clothe the girl in the finest robes.

WE FOLLOW VALERIA AS SHE MOVES THROUGH THE CROWD TO AGLAE, A SHY GREEK TEENAGER.

I have one more task for you, Aglae. Take these coins to Vesonius and purchase a stola for the Doctor's maidservant. I would say she has your build.

AGLAE: But, my lady, it is the Festival. My mistress expects my return.

VALERIA: You will do as I say, girl. Asellina will not miss you for a few minutes more.

AGLAE: *(COWED)* As you wish.
VALERIA MOVES AWAY. AGLAE MAKES FOR THE DOOR, BUT MEL INTERCEPTS HER.
MEL: Hello. You're Aglae, aren't you? I'm Melanie Bush – Mel to my friends. I'd like to come with you, if I may.
AGLAE: *(SURPRISED)* Will your master allow you to leave his side?
MEL: You must be joking! Anyway, he seems to have other things on his mind at the moment – and I'm attracting just as much attention here as I would be outside. So, let's go!
MEL HEADS FOR THE STREET, AND AGLAE FOLLOWS.
AGLAE: *(GIGGLING)* I will enjoy your company, Mel.
MEL: Well, there's nothing like a bit of shopping to relax, is there?

8. THE STREET OF PLENTY / THE LUPANAR
MEL AND AGLAE APPROACH US IN MID-CONVERSATION.

AGLAE: And you say this Doctor has... changed since you met him?
MEL: *(LAUGHING)* Oh Aglae, you don't know the half of it. *(WISTFULLY)* I was beginning to think he didn't need me any more – but, since we arrived in Pompeii, he's been acting very strangely. All quiet and brooding. It's not like him at all. I wish he'd tell me what's wrong.
AGLAE: You are a very compassionate woman, Mel.
MEL: *(TOUCHED)* Oh, I just try to help when I can.
THEY STOP OUTSIDE A BUILDING.
So, this is where you live, is it?
AGLAE: Yes, this is the Lupanar.
MEL: It's nice and central – right on the Street of Plenty.
AGLAE: We do good trade. Come inside, Mel. You may change in my room. With luck, my lady Asellina will have no need of me for a time yet.
MEL: Thanks, Aglae. What did you call this toga thing again – a stola? *(BEAT)* Hey, just a minute!
AGLAE: What is it, Mel?
MEL: Those... those things up there. On the sign. They can't be what I think they are... *(UNCERTAINLY)* can they?
AGLAE: *(PUZZLED)* As you say, Mel, it is a sign. It bespeaks the nature of the Lupanar.
MEL: But they look like... *(WITH AN EMBARRASSED LAUGH)* well, I don't really like to say... they... *(REALISES)* Oh. Oh, does that mean you're a...? Oh.
AGLAE: Do you not also serve your master in this manner?
MEL: I most certainly do not! And you shouldn't – *(BEAT, THEN GROANS)* Oh no! Don't look now, Aglae, but there's that man again: the one who was watching me before. I think he's coming over here.
AGLAE: *(GASPS)* Mel, that is Popidius Celsinus. He is a decurione: a member of the municipal council.
MEL: I don't really care, actually. Let's just get inside.

173

AGLAE: But Mel, you should be honoured that he seeks you out.
MEL: I can do without that particular honour, thank you.
MEL PULLS AGLAE INTO THE LUPANAR AND SLAMS THE DOOR.
(*LAUGHS HOLLOWLY*) Oh, wonderful! Just wonderful!
AGLAE: Does something vex you?
MEL: (*SIGHS*) No, Aglae, not really. It's just that the local creep makes a beeline for me, so what do I do? Run straight into the nearest brothel! Talk about giving somebody the wrong idea!

9. VALERIA HEDONE'S INN
THE DICE ROLL. MURRANUS'S THREE FRIENDS LAUGH UNKINDLY.

MURRANUS: (*MOCKINGLY*) Once more, Doctor, you throw the caniculae. The fates have truly deserted you.
DOCTOR: As you said, Murranus, the gods favour those who honour them in battle.
MURRANUS GATHERS UP HIS COINS. THE DOCTOR PUSHES BACK HIS CHAIR AND STANDS.
And now, I really must bid you good day.
MURRANUS: Hold!
DOCTOR: You have won all my coins, Murranus.
MURRANUS: Thirty sesterces did you take from me. A mere ten have you staked in return.
DOCTOR: Ah, yes. Well, I had to buy clothes for my companion, you see.
MURRANUS: (*THREATENINGLY*) You will find something to wager! If you have nought else, then the clothes from your back may fetch an as or two.
DOCTOR: Perhaps they would. But –
MURRANUS: (*EAGERLY*) Better yet, I should like another chance at winning your servant.
DOCTOR: I'm afraid that was a one-time-only offer, Murranus. And, as you said, my luck really isn't holding out. Your, ah, skill with the dice is a little too great for my liking.
MURRANUS JUMPS TO HIS FEET AND UNSHEATHES HIS SWORD.
MURRANUS: (*LOUDLY AND ANGRILY*) Do you accuse Murranus of cheating? I will run you through where you stand!
SILENCE FALLS.
DOCTOR: (*UNFLUSTERED*) It's all in the wrist action, of course. No point in having a loaded die if you don't know how to roll it properly. But don't worry, I shan't hold a grudge. I just wish to find my companion –
MURRANUS HURLS THE TABLE ASIDE TO GET TO THE DOCTOR. THE SILENCE IS BROKEN, AS ONLOOKERS REACT WITH FEAR AND ASTONISHMENT.
MURRANUS: You seem well versed in the ways of the cheat, Doctor. Could it be that it is you who have won your coins unfairly?
VALERIA INTERCEDES.
VALERIA: (*FORCEFULLY, AFRAID*) Stop this, gentlemen!
MURRANUS: It will stop when I have satisfaction, not before!
THE DOCTOR PUSHES A CHAIR OVER AND RUNS. MURRANUS LEAPS ON HIM, SNARLING. WE HEAR GRUNTS AND GROANS FROM BOTH AS

A SCUFFLE ENSUES.
VALERIA: *(SHOUTS)* I will not have this brawling in my inn, do you hear?
THE DOCTOR GASPS AS MURRANUS GETS AN ARM AROUND HIS NECK.
MURRANUS: Worry not, Valeria. This imp will trouble us no more – not once I have crushed the life from his body!
A STRANGULATED CRY FROM THE DOCTOR.

10. THE LUPANAR/THE STREET OF PLENTY
MEL AND AGLAE CLATTER DOWN A FLIGHT OF WOODEN STAIRS.

MEL: Am I wearing this the right way round? It's not very comfortable.
AGLAE: You should not wear your old garments beneath the stola, Mel.
MEL: I don't want to lose them.
AGLAE: At least you will draw less attention now. If fortune favours you, then Popidius Celsinus will not spy you again.
AGLAE OPENS THE DOOR ONTO THE STREET OF PLENTY. THEY EMERGE TO FIND THE CROWD SILENT, APART FROM A FEW AWE-STRUCK GASPS AND MURMURS.
MEL: What's happening out here?
AGLAE: I do not...*(EXCITEDLY)* Oh! Oh, look Mel! Look over there!
MEL: *(IN A HORRIFIED WHISPER)* Vesuvius!
AGLAE: Is it not magnificent? Smoke rises from the very mountain. It can only have come from the furnace of Vulcan himself.
MEL: *(TO HERSELF, NUMBLY)* The God of Fire and Furnaces. Oh no...
A DISTANT RUMBLING STARTS UP. IT GROWS LOUDER.
AGLAE: He acknowledges Pompeii's offerings to him. Perhaps we are not so out of favour with the gods as we have feared.
MEL: No. No, it can't be. Not yet. *(BEAT; THEN, WORRIED)* Aglae... Aglae, something's happening.
THE CROWD REACTS AS THE RUMBLING GROWS LOUDER STILL AND THE EARTH BEGINS TO SHAKE.
    Aglae! *(PANIC)*

11. VALERIA HEDONE'S INN
THE TREMOR CONTINUES. POTS SMASH ON THE FLOOR. PEOPLE REACT FEARFULLY, AS ON THE STREET. THE DOCTOR BREAKS FREE.

MURRANUS: *(A GRUNT OF PAIN AND SURPRISE)*
DOCTOR: *(A GASP OF RELIEF)*
MURRANUS FALLS ONTO A TABLE AND BREAKS IT.
DOCTOR: *(A LITTLE SHAKILY)* Oh dear, you seem to have slipped.
VALERIA: Enough, I say! Is it not trial enough that the earth betrays us, without that you continue this behaviour?
MURRANUS: *(FURIOUSLY)* Confound you, cheat! The gods themselves keep me from snapping your neck – but they will not save you twice.
VALERIA: You! Get out of here, now!

175

DOCTOR: Delighted to.

VALERIA: Go on, run! *(WARNINGLY)* No, Murranus, I care not about your reputation. If you wish to settle your differences, then you will find a place other than mine in which to do it, or you will settle them with me!

MURRANUS: I shall do just that, once this infernal tremor has ended.

12. THE STREET OF PLENTY

THE TREMOR CONTINUES, PROBABLY FRIGHTENING A HORSE OR TWO.

AGLAE: *(SHOUTS, IN A STRAINED VOICE)* Be not afraid, Mel. Hold on to me. This earth tremor is not such a bad one, I think. It will soon end.

MEL: *(SAME)* You mean this happens a lot?

AGLAE: It is the gods' way of showing us their displeasure.

THE QUAKE SUBSIDES. PEOPLE PICK THEMSELVES UP, WITH A GENERAL OUTPOURING OF RELIEF.

     You see? There has been no real damage. This was but a warning. We shall have to honour our gods more diligently.

MEL: You're not making sense, Aglae. A minute ago, you were telling me how pleased Vulcan was with you. Now you're saying the gods are angry?

AGLAE: It is true, I fear, that the earth shakes more often and more violently these past weeks. None can remember such ill omens since the upheaval of seventeen years since.

MEL: Then why doesn't somebody do something? Doesn't anyone realise what's happening?

AGLAE: We observe the rituals, we make offerings, we pray to be forgiven. What else can we do?

MEL IS DUMBFOUNDED. THEN THE DOCTOR BREEZES PAST.

DOCTOR: Ah, there you are, Mel. Yes, very fetching. Thank you for your help, Aglae. Come along, Mel.

MEL: Doctor?

DOCTOR: *(HE HAS PASSED HER NOW; HE CALLS BACK)* There are at least two very good reasons why we ought to be somewhere else.

MEL: *(CALLS BACK)* Wait for me then. *(TO AGLAE)* Well, er... thank you for everything, Aglae. It's been lovely meeting you, but it really does look like I've got to go.

AGLAE: I understand, Mel. Your master has need of you.

MEL: *(SIGHS)* Something like that.

13. A POMPEIAN STREET

IN A QUIETER AREA, MEL CATCHES UP WITH THE DOCTOR.

MEL: It's the volcano, isn't it, Doctor? Causing the tremors? *(HE DOESN'T ANSWER)* It's horrible! This city... these people... Aglae! Valeria! They're all going to die, aren't they?

DOCTOR: Many of them, yes.

MEL: Can't we do something?

DOCTOR: Against Nature? No. Against Time? Certainly not. This happened a long time ago, Mel. We can't change it.

MEL: It doesn't seem fair.
DOCTOR: Time never is.
THEY COME TO A HALT.
(GENTLY) Are you ready to leave now?
MEL: *(THINKS CAREFULLY, THEN)* Yes. Yes, I think I am.

13A. VALERIA HEDONES INN
VALERIA GREETS MURRANUS AS HE RETURNS.

VALERIA: Murranus! So, you did not find your foe?
MURRANUS: *(BITTERLY)* I did not. This is your fault, Valeria. You should not have kept me from him.
VALERIA: You have caused enough damage here you and the gods between you. I hope you have returned to help put things aright.
MURRANUS: I will do that, Valeria. And I will put things right with this Doctor also. If he has any wit about him, he will leave Pompeii before I can find him for I swear he will not have the chance after.

14. A POMPEIAN BACK STREET
A FEW PEOPLE MILL ABOUT AND TALK IN CONCERNED TONES.
HEAVY STONES ARE BEING SHIFTED. THE DOCTOR AND MEL
APPROACH.

MEL: ...so, you did cheat, then?
DOCTOR: Only on that first roll. I observed our gladiator friend's technique and used it – and his own dice against him.
MEL: *(WITH MOCK DISAPPROVAL)* Well, it sounds like cheating to me.
DOCTOR: It's only cheating if you get caught.
MEL: Whereas you got clean away with it, I suppose. Well, if you want to know what I think – *(SEES SOMETHING AND IS SUDDENLY WORRIED)* Doctor... Doctor, what's going on?
DOCTOR: *(MURMURS, UPSET)* No. No, this can't be how it ends.
THEY RUN FORWARDS TOGETHER.
MEL: We are in the right place. I know we're in the right place.
DOCTOR: I should have known. We should have turned back as soon as I realised...
MEL: It was the earthquake, wasn't it? It brought that building down, and the TARDIS... the TARDIS was right underneath it!
DOCTOR: ...but how could I? Time marching on. The future laid out before me. We've already stayed a lifetime.
MEL: Doctor, tell me we can get the TARDIS back. I mean, it's just a bit of concrete, right? Look – those slaves are already clearing the wreckage. We can dig it out, can't we? We can get away before... before...
DOCTOR: I'm sorry, Mel.
HE WALKS AWAY SLOWLY. MEL HESITATES FOR A SECOND,
STUNNED, THEN RUNS AFTER HIM.
MEL: Now wait a minute! What do you mean, you're 'sorry'? Doctor!
DOCTOR: It's Time, don't you see? Time, working against us.

MEL: No. No, I don't see. What's wrong with you?
DOCTOR: I'm sorry for dragging you into this, Mel. I should have known. I did know. I found out a long time ago.
MEL: Found out what? *(HE DOESN'T ANSWER)* Doctor!
DOCTOR: I've seen the future, Mel. I know what will happen. What must happen. *(HE COLLECTS HIMSELF AND EXPLAINS)* In the year 1980, the TARDIS will be discovered. Dug out of the ash that will rain upon this city tomorrow.
MEL: *(SHOCKED)* You don't mean...?
DOCTOR: We can't escape it, Mel. No matter what we do, Time already knows. We've already lost.
MEL: But –
DOCTOR: We won't see the TARDIS again. Nobody will see it. Not for almost two thousand years.

END PART ONE

Part Two

14 (CONTINUED FOR RECAP)

DOCTOR: I'm sorry for dragging you into this, Mel. I should have known. I did know. I found out a long time ago.
MEL: Found out what? *(HE DOESN'T ANSWER)* Doctor!
DOCTOR: I've seen the future, Mel. I know what will happen. What must happen. *(HE COLLECTS HIMSELF AND EXPLAINS)* In the year 1980, the TARDIS will be discovered. Dug out of the ash that will rain upon this city tomorrow.
MEL: *(SHOCKED)* You don't mean...?
DOCTOR: We can't escape it, Mel. No matter what we do, Time already knows. We've already lost.
MEL: But –
DOCTOR: We won't see the TARDIS again. Nobody will see it. Not for almost two thousand years.
MEL: I don't understand. What are you talking about, Doctor? Two thousand years... How can you know that? Doctor?
HE WALKS AWAY FROM HER.
Doctor! Where are you going?

15. A POMPEIAN STREET
THE DOCTOR HAS WANDERED TO A FAIRLY BUSY AREA. MEL CATCHES UP TO HIM AND TACKLES HIM. THEY KEEP WALKING TOGETHER, LEAVING THE SOUNDS OF THE BUILDING SITE BEHIND THEM.

MEL: I wish you'd talk to me, Doctor. *(BEAT)* Well? Come on, Doctor! You knew we'd lose the TARDIS, didn't you? How did you know?
DOCTOR: *(SUBDUED, DISTANT)* It was a long time ago, Mel. I was in my... fifth body, I think. I visited your world – this world – in the early nineteen-eighties. I was contacted by an organisation called UNIT. They're a –
MEL: I know who UNIT are, Doctor.
DOCTOR: Of course you do, of course... *(BEAT)* They'd found my TARDIS. In Italy. An earthquake had revealed it, beneath the volcanic ash that covered Pompeii. Only my TARDIS was still sitting at Hyde Park Corner, where I'd left it.
MEL: They'd found your TARDIS – but it was the TARDIS from the future, right? I mean, from the past... No, hold on, I mean –
DOCTOR: It's one of the perils of time travel, Mel. I was given a glimpse of the one thing no one should ever see. My personal future. My destiny. Perhaps my own death.
MEL: Death?
DOCTOR: I don't know, Mel. I didn't want to know. The UNIT people had taken the TARDIS into storage. I refused to see it. The less I knew about the circumstances in which I was fated to lose it, the better. But I couldn't forget what I had already learned.
MEL: That the TARDIS would end up buried here.

179

DOCTOR: I didn't know that for sure. There were other possibilities.

MEL: Such as?

DOCTOR: That UNIT hadn't found the TARDIS at all, but rather some sort of replica. That it may have found itself beneath the ash in some other way. I even considered that, one day, I might have chosen – might choose – to retire to your world, in this time. I might abandon my ship here in Pompeii, expecting it not to be seen again. I pushed my suspicions to the back of my mind, Mel. The important thing was that I didn't know for certain what the future had in store.

MEL: Until we landed here, the day before the eruption of Vesuvius.

DOCTOR: And then I knew. *(A LONG, REFLECTIVE PAUSE)* The old girl tried to keep it from me, to protect me. *(LAUGHS BITTERLY)* She hates farewells as much as I do.

MEL: That's what I still don't understand. If you knew – or even suspected – that we might lose the TARDIS here, then why didn't you do something? *(HE DOESN'T ANSWER; SUSPICIOUSLY)* Doctor?

DOCTOR: I think we should find somewhere to have a proper talk

16. OUTSIDE THE BATHS

EUMACHIA WAITS FOR CELSINUS ON A BUSY STREET.

EUMACHIA: Popidius Celsinus!

CELSINUS: *(STARTLED)* Eumachia!

EUMACHIA: I sent in a slave to fetch you.

CELSINUS: I sent him away. Can a man not take his bath in peace?

EUMACHIA: The afternoon has near gone while I have waited for you to bathe, decurione. Had you idled longer, I would have come into the tepidarium in search of you, men's hours or not.

CELSINUS: You have no sense of decorum, Eumachia.

EUMACHIA: And 'tis clear that you have no sense of responsibility. Are you unconcerned with the events of the day? Have you not heard of the arrivals in our city?

CELSINUS: I saw a fair young stranger. What of it?

EUMACHIA: And does this woman claim to have come from your goddess?

CELSINUS: What does it concern you? You have no love for Isis, Eumachia.

EUMACHIA: And she has no love for you, so the rumours have it.

CELSINUS: *(ANNOYED AND A LITTLE ALARMED)* Of what rumours do you speak?

EUMACHIA: *(ENJOYING THIS)* Had you spent more time abroad this aft, you would have seen the writings yourself. The citizens ask how it is that Isis should send her messengers to Pompeii and yet they do not visit her temple, nor seek out he who takes credit for it.

CELSINUS: Isis well knows how I rebuilt her temple, after it was felled by the earthquake.

EUMACHIA: Ha! Your father paid for it to be built in your name, when you were but a child of nine. He bought you a future, and your seat on the Curia.

CELSINUS: *(ANGRILY)* I have earned the goddess's favour!

EUMACHIA: Then should you not know why she spurns you?

CELSINUS: If you seek to turn me against Isis, Eumachia, then it will profit you nought.

EUMACHIA: That you worship the foreign deity of the lower classes says much of you, Celsinus – but I do not seek to question your faith.

CELSINUS: No. But you would denounce these messengers.

EUMACHIA: Test them, perhaps. I am not so proud, decurione, that I could not be persuaded yet to welcome your Isis into my heart.

CELSINUS: I doubt our loving goddess could stand to enter that shrivelled chamber.

EUMACHIA: 'Tis rather you who has reason to disprove these strangers' claims, I think. For, if they hold, then all will know that your goddess disdains you, Celsinus. What price your position, or your father's wealth, then?

CELSINUS: *(AFTER A LONG, THOUGHTFUL PAUSE)* What would you have me do?

17. VALERIA HEDONE'S INN

THE DOCTOR AND MEL HAVE JUST ENTERED. VALERIA IS SERVING.

VALERIA: By rights, Doctor, I should not serve you. I want no more trouble.

DOCTOR: Good. Then we're agreed. And, er, Murranus...?

VALERIA: He has gone. But I would place scant value on your life, should he return – especially when he espies the fresh writings on my wall.

DOCTOR: Yes, so I see. "The mighty Murranus was outfought by..."

MEL: Go on. What does it say?

VALERIA: "By a mightier dwarf."

MEL: *(LAUGHS)* Oh, Doctor!

VALERIA: *(WITH A SIGH OF RESIGNATION)* Well, I expect the mirmillo has returned to his barracks by now, to sleep off his libations.

DOCTOR: Excellent! In that case, I shall have two cups of your ordinary wine please, Valeria.

MEL: Do you think it's a good idea to be drinking, Doctor?

VALERIA STARTS TO POUR THEIR DRINKS.

DOCTOR: I'm afraid they don't serve carrot juice, Mel. Don't worry, the wine will be diluted with water, honey and... *(WORRIED)* Ah.

MEL: What's wrong?

DOCTOR: Coins. I appear to be rather short again.

MEL: *(RELIEVED)* As the graffiti says. Here, Doctor. Change from the clothes.

SHE HANDS A FEW COINS TO THE DOCTOR, AS VALERIA PUSHES TWO CUPS ACROSS THE BAR.

VALERIA: A mere two asses if you please, Doctor.

THE DOCTOR HANDS THE COINS OVER.

DOCTOR: Thank you, Valeria. Come along, Mel, I see a table.

THEY MAKE THEIR WAY THROUGH THE CROWD, PULL BACK CHAIRS AND SIT DOWN. THERE IS A SHORT PAUSE.

MEL: All right then, Doctor. I'm waiting.

DOCTOR: It's difficult, Mel.

MEL: Well, I'll try to understand.

DOCTOR: As soon as I realised where we were, I knew what was likely to happen. I wanted to leave, but I couldn't.

MEL: Why not?

DOCTOR: Because the loss of the TARDIS, its excavation in 1980... it's all part of history.

MEL: How can it be, if it hasn't happened yet?

DOCTOR: It will happen, Mel.

MEL: But there's still time to stop it.

DOCTOR: No. I've already seen it. We can't stop it.

MEL: What if we'd just dematerialised as soon as you realised where we were? That would have changed things, wouldn't it?

DOCTOR: Yes. But think, Mel. If I'd done that – if I'd used my foreknowledge to alter events – what do you think would have happened?

MEL: Well, the TARDIS wouldn't have been buried, for a start.

DOCTOR: Precisely. The TARDIS wouldn't have been buried. It wouldn't have been dug up in two thousand years' time. I wouldn't have been told of its discovery, and I would have arrived in Pompeii without any foreknowledge.

MEL: So, you'd have acted as normal, left the TARDIS behind and... and it would have been buried?

DOCTOR: Time cannot abide a paradox.

MEL: No, neither can my brain. So, what you're saying is, we've just got to accept what's happening? We can't even try to get out of here?

DOCTOR: I'm saying that history has already taken account of our actions – and it's shown us their outcome.

ANOTHER TREMOR, MUCH SHORTER AND LESS VIOLENT THAN THE LAST. CUPS RATTLE, AND THERE ARE MURMURS OF CONCERN.

We can't cheat Time, Mel.

A LONG PAUSE, DURING WHICH THE TREMOR SUBSIDES.

MEL: *(WITH FRESH DETERMINATION)* No. No, I'm sorry Doctor, I can't accept that.

DOCTOR: Please listen to me, Mel.

MEL: *(SHE STANDS UP)* You might think you know what's going to happen in the future, but all I know is that we aren't beaten yet. I mean, what if UNIT were wrong? Or... or what if the TARDIS will end up in Pompeii one day but just not yet?

DOCTOR: *(IMPLORING)* Mel!

MEL: I'm going to find a way out of this, whatever it takes. Are you coming with me or not?

DOCTOR: I'm sorry.

MEL: *(SIGHS)* So am I. But I can't give up, Doctor... even if you can.

SHE MARCHES OFF, DETERMINEDLY.

18. THE STREET OF PLENTY
EUMACHIA AND AGLAE ARE ARGUING.

AGLAE: *(FRIGHTENED)* But, Mistress Eumachia, I know no more than I have told already.

EUMACHIA: *(ANGRILY)* Do not lie, child! I paid Asellina well to take you from your chores for a time, and I will know what you are hiding!

AGLAE: I hide nothing, I swear. I did talk to Mel, it is true, but she said nought of Isis.

EUMACHIA: She must have spoken of herself.

AGLAE: She did speak of strange worlds and times, but I understood so few of her words.

EUMACHIA: Liar!

SHE SLAPS AGLAE, WHO SHRIEKS. MEL RUNS ONTO THE SCENE.

MEL: Hey, leave her alone!

AGLAE: *(GASPS, HORRIFIED)* Mel!

EUMACHIA: And who might you be, girl, that you presume to speak so to a priestess of the Capitoline Triad?

MEL: I'm her friend, that's who. Come on, Aglae, we're getting out of here.

AGLAE: But Mel...

MEL: I said, come on!

AGLAE: *(TEARFULLY)* No, Mel, I cannot... I must not...

MEL: You're not a... a piece of furniture, Aglae. She doesn't own you!

AGLAE: *(APPALLED)* You must show proper respect, Mel. Oh, mistress, please forgive my friend her rudeness. She knows not our ways.

MEL: I can speak for myself, thank you very much.

EUMACHIA: *(COLDLY)* Go back to Asellina, child.

MEL: Don't do it, Aglae.

AGLAE: I must, Mel. My mistress has been kind to me.

MEL: By making you sell yourself?

EUMACHIA: I gave you an order, girl.

AGLAE: *(WEEPING OPENLY)* I must not see you again, Mel. You will bring the gods' just punishment down on us both.

AGLAE FLEES.

MEL: *(CALLS AFTER HER, HURT)* Aglae!

EUMACHIA: Your friend has denied you, girl. And you – do you still make claim to have been sent by the foreign goddess?

MEL: I don't think that's any of your business, actually.

EUMACHIA: Know this, stranger: that I shall do all in my power to expose your deceit.

MEL: *(SCORNFULLY)* And you should know that you don't scare me like you did that poor girl.

SHE WALKS AWAY.

EUMACHIA: *(LAUGHING TO HERSELF)* Oh, Celsinus... I fear this is almost too easy.

19. VALERIA HEDONE'S INN

THE DOCTOR AND VALERIA TALK.

VALERIA: You are too kind of heart, Doctor.

DOCTOR: *(GLUMLY)* Am I, Valeria?

VALERIA: Your maidservant is quick to disobey you –

DOCTOR: That's certainly true.

VALERIA: – yet you choose not to punish her. You would do well to sell her to a stricter master, for the girl's own good. She is still young, she will fetch a handsome price at market.

DOCTOR: Mel is far more precious than money, Valeria. If she gets hurt —

VALERIA: — then 'twill be her own doing. She has too strong a spirit. She is too quick to do what she ought not to do.

DOCTOR: No. She wants to do what she can't do. That's the problem.

VALERIA: If it troubles you, Doctor, then you should seek the counsel of Isis. A sacrifice is to be made to her this very hour.

DOCTOR: Sacrifice?

VALERIA: Our farmers would know why ill fortune besets them: why the earth shakes, and why their crops fail on the mountainside.

DOCTOR: On the slopes of Vesuvius, I presume.

VALERIA: They pray that Isis will offer them hope for the future.

DOCTOR: And in return they offer her death.

VALERIA: You disapprove?

DOCTOR: It's not for me to judge your culture, Valeria. I cannot interfere.

VALERIA: Today the priests give but an animal to Isis. But I would gladly surrender my life to her should she desire it. Would you do less for your god?

DOCTOR: *(MUTTERS)* The trouble is, Valeria, it's not just my life.

20. A POMPEIAN BACK STREET

WORK CONTINUES AT THE SITE OF THE COLLAPSED BUILDING. STONES ARE BEING SCRAPED ALONG THE GROUND; WORKERS MIGHT SHOUT TO EACH OTHER. MEL IS HERE. AGLAE APPROACHES AT A RUN.

AGLAE: Mel! Mel!

MEL: Aglae! What are you doing here? What about your–?

AGLAE: Trade is slow today. Asellina sent me to find custom. I came in search of you instead.

MEL: Well, good for you.

AGLAE: Oh Mel, I regret my harsh words earlier, but I feared for us both.

MEL: That's all right, Aglae.

AGLAE: For all that I am discomfited by your strange manner, you are my friend. I will not desert you.

MEL: *(TOUCHED)* Well, thank you Aglae. *(SIGHS, DISHEARTENED)* It's beginning to look like I might be around for a while too.

AGLAE: You help to rebuild this house?

MEL: I... lost something under the rubble, that's all. I did try to clear some of it away, but it's no use.

AGLAE: I am sure your possession will be recovered in time.

MEL: *(SIGHS)* In a couple of thousand years, maybe.

AGLAE: Pardon me?

MEL: *(FRUSTRATED)* I haven't got time, Aglae! I just haven't.

AGLAE: *(RESOLUTELY CHEERFUL)* Then we must seek assistance. I know of one who could ease your burden.

MEL: Really?

AGLAE: Aye, Mel, I do: one who has offered help to many a troubled soul. *(SHE LEADS MEL AWAY, EAGERLY)* Come, friend Mel, come!

21. OUTSIDE THE TEMPLE OF ISIS
A PRIEST ADDRESSES AN ATTENTIVE AUDIENCE, AS SOMEONE PLAYS A SIMPLE, SOLEMN TUNE ON A REED PIPE ACCOMPANIED BY A RATTLE. HOWEVER, THESE SOUNDS ARE FAIRLY DISTANT; WE ARE AT THE BACK OF THE CROWD, WHERE A FEW PEOPLE CONDUCT MURMURED CONVERSATIONS. MEL AND AGLAE ARE HERE; AFTER A FEW SECONDS, THEY START TO TALK OVER THE PRIEST IN HUSHED TONES (IT DOESN'T MATTER IF WE CAN'T HEAR EVERYTHING HE SAYS).

PRIEST: Great Isis, we implore with you to hear your faithful followers. These men, who have toiled long and hard in the fields without our city, would know why the earth shakes so; why the fruit of the seeds that they have so diligently sewn is taken from them. It is our fear that Pompeii has earned the disfavour of the gods. We ask you, sweet goddess, how might we atone for our sins? We render unto you this sacrifice, and hope that you might look with kindness upon our humble plea.

MEL: Oh, Aglae! This person you said could help me – you were talking about your god, weren't you?

AGLAE: Have I done wrong, Mel, in bringing you to the temple of Isis?

MEL: No offence, Aglae, I just don't think standing in a courtyard and listening to some priest talking about farmers is going to help.

AGLAE: But Eumachia told me you serve our goddess.

MEL: Eumachia was wrong, I'm afraid.

THE PRIEST FINISHES HIS SPEECH ABOUT NOW, TO MURMURS OF ANTICIPATION.

AGLAE: E'en so, Mel, you should take your troubles to her. She may yet choose to favour you.

MEL: I don't think so.

FROM UP NEAR THE PRIEST, WE HEAR A DISTRESSED GOAT. THE CROWD IS QUITE EXCITED NOW, AND MEL AND AGLAE TALK AT NORMAL SPEAKING VOLUME.

What's happening now?

AGLAE: See, Mel! The priests make an offering to Isis. They bring our sacrifice to her out onto the steps of the temple, to the altars.

MEL: That's horrible!

AGLAE: *(SURPRISED)* The goddess requires an offering, Mel.

MEL: That's no excuse to slaughter an innocent animal.

AGLAE: *(AFRAID)* Oh, please do not speak out!

MEL: I should, you know. I should go up there and give that man a piece of my mind. *(SIGHS, TO SELF)* But that wouldn't change anything, would it? And it might be just the action that keeps me here forever.

AGLAE: Mel?

MEL: I'm sorry Aglae, I can't watch this.

WE FOLLOW THEM OUT ONTO A QUIET STREET (ALTHOUGH WE CAN STILL HEAR THE CROWD IN THE COURTYARD), WHERE THEY BUMP INTO CELSINUS.

        (GASPS, STARTLED)

CELSINUS: You leave so soon, my lady?

MEL: You again!

CELSINUS: Popidius Celsinus, devoted servant to Isis. I have heard much of your visit to our city. I watched you earlier, as you perused our shops.

MEL: Yes, so I noticed.

CELSINUS: *(MILDLY OFFENDED)* I serve on the municipal council, my lady. It is natural that a fair young stranger in our city should interest me.

AGLAE: May I present Mel, my lord.

MEL: *(ARCHLY)* It's Melanie, actually.

CELSINUS: Perhaps, fair Melanie, I might show you the inside of our temple, for which I paid myself?

MEL: I'd rather not, if you don't mind.

CELSINUS: Then at least do me the honour of dining with me. Your travelling companion is also welcome. We have much to discuss, I fancy.

MEL: I don't know about that.

AGLAE: Mel! You cannot decline such an honour.

MEL: An honour? *(BEAT)* Of course! You're a councillor, right?

CELSINUS: I am one of Pompeii's decuriones.

MEL: So, if I wanted some work doing – say, some rubble shifting – then you could speed things up for me?

CELSINUS: It would please me to render what assistance I may. Will you then accept my invitation?

MEL: What do you think, Aglae? Are you hungry? *(BEAT)* Oh, I see. Not good enough to eat with the upper classes, is she? Well, in that case –

AGLAE: It matters not, Mel, really. I must return to my work at the Lupanar. Asellina will wonder what has become of me.

AGLAE LEAVES.

CELSINUS: So, Melanie?

MEL: *(TAKES A DEEP BREATH TO STEEL HERSELF)* All right then, Celsinus, you win. I'll have dinner with you.

CELSINUS: You are most gracious, lady.

MEL: And do you know why? Because, under normal circumstances, it's the last thing in the world I'd dream of doing. And that's a good thing right now... *(UNCERTAINLY)* I think.

CELSINUS: And your companion?

MEL: I left him at Valeria Hedone's inn.

CELSINUS: Come then, Mel. We shall fetch him as we walk.

22. THE HOUSE OF EUMACHIA

A SLAVE SHOWS THE DOCTOR, MEL AND CELSINUS INTO A SMALL ROOM WITH A TILED FLOOR, WHERE EUMACHIA GREETS THEM. OTHER SLAVES ARE BUSTLING IN AND OUT OF THE ROOM, SETTING A TABLE FOR DINNER.

186

CELSINUS: My friends, may I introduce the mistress of the house.
EUMACHIA: Eumachia, at your service.
DOCTOR: Ah. Delighted to meet you.
EUMACHIA: And I, you.
DOCTOR: I'm the Doctor and this is my friend, Melanie.
MEL: We've met, actually. *(TO CELSINUS)* I thought you said we were eating at your house?
CELSINUS: *(SURPRISED)* It was not my intention to mislead you. I thought you would be honoured to dine with a priestess.
MEL: Are you telling me the truth, Celsinus? This wouldn't be some kind of a trap, would it?
EUMACHIA: *(LAUGHING)* Fear not, girl. Eumachia holds no grudge for ill words chosen in haste. Doubtless you knew not to whom you were speaking.
MEL: I was rather more concerned with what you were doing.
DOCTOR: *(HURRIEDLY)* That's, ah, very gracious of you, Eumachia. *(ASIDE)* You can tell me about it later, Mel.
EUMACHIA: The sky is overcast; I fear the evening will not bring clement weather. We shall eat, then, here in the triclinium.
DOCTOR: An excellent idea. Come along Mel, let's take our places, shall we?
THEY MOVE INTO THE ROOM.
(ASIDE, TO MEL) We lie down on the couches.
MEL: *(ASIDE)* I can't eat lying down.
DOCTOR: When in Rome, Mel... or at least in the Roman Empire. And we eat with our hands.
THE FOUR DINERS LOWER THEMSELVES ONTO COUCHES AROUND THE LOW CENTRAL TABLE, WHICH THE SLAVES ARE STILL SETTING.
EUMACHIA: It pleases me to entertain you, Doctor, Melanie. There is much I would know of these strangers about whom the whole of Pompeii speaks.
DOCTOR: *(LAUGHING)* I hope we aren't a disappointment. You know how rumours can get out of hand.
EUMACHIA: Indeed. So, is it true you are a holy man, Doctor?
DOCTOR: *(GUARDEDLY)* I have the utmost respect for your beliefs.
EUMACHIA: And for the cult of the foreign goddess?
CELSINUS: Foreign Isis may be, Eumachia, but she is as wondrous and kind as any member of the Triad.
DOCTOR: We are simply travellers.
EUMACHIA: Come now, Doctor. You are plainly more than that.
DOCTOR: You, ah, have a beautiful house here, Eumachia. I particularly admire some of your paintings.
MEL: Even if they don't leave much to the imagination.
EUMACHIA: Thank you, Doctor. I come from a family of good standing.
CELSINUS: The Eumachii own Pompeii's wool market.
DOCTOR: I see.
EUMACHIA: And what of you, Doctor? Are you a wealthy man?
DOCTOR: In some respects. I always find money to be a little overrated.
BY NOW, THE SLAVES HAVE FINISHED THEIR WORK AND LEFT.

CELSINUS: *(ENTHUSIASTICALLY)* You keep a splendid table, Eumachia.

DOCTOR: Yes, very appetising. *(ASIDE)* You might wish to avoid the roasted thrush, Mel.

MEL: *(BEMUSED)* Thanks for the warning.

EUMACHIA: Well, eat heartily my friends! By the grace of the Venus Pompeiana, our stomachs will be full tonight.

CELSINUS: And let us each drink to the health of our host, and to that of the Emperor Titus.

DOCTOR: Indeed.

THEY DRINK, AND THEN BEGIN TO EAT (WITH THEIR HANDS, AS NOTED). CELSINUS EATS LOUDLY AND APPRECIATIVELY.

CELSINUS: These lark's tongues are delicious, Eumachia!

MEL: *(ASIDE, WITH HER MOUTH FULL, DISGUSTED)* Oh, Doctor!

EUMACHIA: Is the food not to your liking?

MEL: It's... you see I'm a vegetarian and -

EUMACHIA: Veget... *(THINKS)* No. No, I am not familiar with the name. Is this Vegetaria a province far from here?

MEL: No, it's -

DOCTOR: It's a long way from here indeed.

(PAUSE)

CELSINUS: Melanie, you said you are in need of assistance?

EUMACHIA: Oh?

CELSINUS: A small matter of a... lost treasure, was it not?

DOCTOR: *(WITH A FALSE, WORRIED LAUGH)* It really isn't important.

MEL: Yes it is, Doctor. Celsinus might be able to help us.

DOCTOR: *(ASIDE)* I don't think so, Mel.

MEL: *(SAME)* It's worth a try, isn't it? Why have you given up?

EUMACHIA: Perhaps you should tell us what vexes you. It may be that we can offer aid.

DOCTOR: *(TO EUMACHIA AND CELSINUS)* I mislaid a little something of mine. But it needn't concern you.

EUMACHIA: Might this be the temple of which people speak?

A LONG PAUSE; EVEN CELSINUS STOPS EATING.

I see I have disconcerted you, Doctor. Such was not my intent.

MEL: It sounded to me like you knew exactly what you were saying.

EUMACHIA: You should know that the citizens of Pompeii believe you both to have come from Isis; to be her messengers.

DOCTOR: As I said, rumours can get out of hand.

MEL: *(QUIETLY)* Yes. I thought we came from Vegetaria now.

EUMACHIA: And the servants of a goddess may wish to keep their secrets.

DOCTOR: We have not come from Isis, I assure you.

CELSINUS: *(SCANDALISED)* But Melanie herself said it was so!

EUMACHIA: Then there is some confusion, is there not?

DOCTOR: You must have misunderstood.

EUMACHIA: Or perhaps you fear we could see through your

deceptions, as a simple slave and a beggar woman could not.

DOCTOR: Really, I –

EUMACHIA: *(FORCEFULLY)* You are a liar, Doctor – and, if you are not, then this girl surely is.

MEL: *(INSULTED)* I'm as honest as they come!

DOCTOR: *(WARNINGLY)* Mel!

MEL: *(ASIDE)* Why don't we just tell them, Doctor?

DOCTOR: *(SAME)* We can't do that.

MEL: But it wouldn't change anything, would it? No one can stop the... what's going to happen. And they might be able to do something for us.

DOCTOR: It wouldn't do any good, Mel.

HE STANDS, ABRUPTLY.

    (TO THE OTHERS) You should disregard what my companion says. Too much wine, I expect.

MEL: *(INSULTED)* Doctor!

DOCTOR: Thank you for your kind hospitality, but we really ought to leave.

CELSINUS: Please stay, Doctor. Tell us more of –

EUMACHIA: *(SCORNFULLY)* No, Celsinus. Can you not see it? They flee from the light of truth!

DOCTOR: You were right, Mel. These people never had any intention of helping us.

HE HURRIES MEL OUT OF THE ROOM.

23. VALERIA HEDONE'S INN

THERE ARE FEW CUSTOMERS LEFT NOW, AND THE STREET OUTSIDE IS QUIET. VALERIA IS AT THE BAR WHEN MURRANUS ENTERS.

VALERIA: Murranus! I did not expect your return.

MURRANUS: I am in need of wine, Valeria.

VALERIA: Then fortune is not with you. I shall serve no more today. I have but to remove these last few drunkards, and I shall take my rest.

MURRANUS: *(BANGS HIS FIST ON THE BAR, ANGRILY)* Wine, woman! The finest gladiator in Pompeii will not be denied! By Jupiter, has my reputation fallen so far in so short a time?

VALERIA: *(SIGHS)* Very well, Murranus. I shall pour you one cup, and no more.

MURRANUS: Well must you know you what drives me to drink, Valeria. Why, even your wall tells of my disgrace – and who is responsible for that, I wonder?

VALERIA FILLS A CUP.

VALERIA: My inn has been full through the festival, Murranus. I cannot see all that occurs within.

MURRANUS: I would see how the culprit fares against my sword, if his only weapon be the words of a coward.

VALERIA PLACES THE CUP IN FRONT OF HIM.

VALERIA: I will not countenance another fight here.

MURRANUS: *(TAKES A LARGE GULP OF WINE)* But my first concern must be the restoration of my honour. The stranger! The cheat! The... the...

VALERIA: Doctor.

MURRANUS: The Doctor, aye! He is responsible for my shame.

VALERIA: You know it is said that the Doctor and his friend are from Isis?

MURRANUS: The prattling of the masses! Besides, it matters not to me. This Doctor impugned my honesty –

VALERIA: He but told the truth.

MURRANUS: – and used trickery and fortune to outfight me.

VALERIA: You attacked him.

MURRANUS: *(SAGGING)* You know of my past, Valeria. You know the crime for which I was sent to the Amphitheatre. The aediles thought they had sentenced me to die. They knew not that I should prove so mighty a warrior. I live for the contest now, for the glorious battle. But still I live for so long as I have the respect of the people, and no longer.

VALERIA: And for so long as you are victorious.

MURRANUS: Even Murranus cannot always be victorious. And, when a fight is lost, he must depend, like all gladiators, on the mood of the crowd. *(BECOMING ANGRY AGAIN)* Should I lose their favour, should they think me so easily brought down by a... a deceitful stranger, an impertinent imp... then they shall not vote to spare me again.

VALERIA: I do see why you are troubled, Murranus.

MURRANUS: It is a matter of life and death to me, Valeria – and I swear, it will be the Doctor's death that safeguards my life.

24. A POMPEIAN STREET

EVENING IS DRAWING IN (SO, NO SEAGULLS). THE DOCTOR AND MEL SIT BESIDE A FOUNTAIN.

MEL: *(DISCONSOLATORY)* Well, that was a complete waste of time!

DOCTOR: *(SYMPATHETICALLY)* It wouldn't have worked, Mel. There's nothing you could have done.

MEL: I thought I could get somewhere with Celsinus; that he'd help us get the TARDIS back. I just made things a hundred times worse, didn't I?

DOCTOR: You mustn't give up.

MEL: Why not? You already have!

DOCTOR: Perhaps I did. But not any more.

MEL: You said –

DOCTOR: I know what I said, Mel. But you were right. There may still be a chance. And, so long as there is, I can't abandon the TARDIS.

MEL: *(RELIEVED)* I knew you'd come round in the end. So, what do we do first?

DOCTOR: *(GRIMLY)* I didn't say there was a good chance. *(HE TAKES A LONG PAUSE)* I want you to leave here.

MEL: What?

DOCTOR: I can't risk your life as well as my own. I want you to leave Pompeii before it's too late.

MEL: No!

DOCTOR: Don't make this difficult, Mel.

MEL: I'm not leaving you, Doctor.

DOCTOR: It's too dangerous for you here. You said it yourself:

190

Eumachia bears a grudge against you.

MEL: And you too, now. You'll need me here.

A HORSE AND CART APPROACHES.

DOCTOR: What I need, Mel, is for you to be safe. I got you into this. I can't be responsible for... for...

MEL: *(SUSPICIOUSLY)* You think this is it, don't you? You don't expect to get the TARDIS back at all. You think you're going to die here! And you want me to be somewhere nice and safe, far away, when it happens.

THE DOCTOR DOESN'T ANSWER. SECONDS LATER, THE HORSE AND CART ARE RIGHT ON TOP OF THEM. EUMACHIA IS IN THE CART.

EUMACHIA: Stop the cart. Stop! That is the girl, there.

MEL: What's going on now?

THE HORSE STOPS. EUMACHIA GETS OUT OF THE CART, ALONG WITH TWO MEN.

EUMACHIA: You cannot run from justice, vile thief! I would know where you have taken my precious jewels, that my poor dead husband gave to me. And if you will not tell me, then you will tell these men.

MEL: I don't know anything about your jewels.

DOCTOR: I'm sure there's been some mistake.

EUMACHIA: Liar! I invited you into my house in good faith, and you have stolen from me. My slaves bear witness to it. Take her away, Centurion!

THE MEN MARCH FORWARD AND SEIZE MEL.

MEL: Get off me! Both of you, get your hands off me!

EUMACHIA: The aediles will have the truth from you if I cannot.

MEL: Can't you see she's lying? She's trying to frame me. Doctor!

EUMACHIA: They will not take his word against that of a priestess.

DOCTOR: Another attempt to discredit Isis, Eumachia?

MEL STRUGGLES, BUT IS MANHANDLED INTO THE CART.

EUMACHIA: Your friend will serve my purpose well, Doctor.

MEL: *(SHOUTS)* Doctor, do something!

EUMACHIA: There is nought he can do, child. It will go better for you if you but speak the truth.

MEL: *(SHOUTS, ANGRILY)* The truth? Oh, you don't want to know the truth, I promise you.

DOCTOR: *(SHOUTS, URGENTLY)* This won't do any good, Mel!

THE CART PULLS AWAY; MEL'S VOICE RECEDES.

MEL: *(PANICKING)* You can't lock me up. You can't! Don't you realise? You'll kill me! This time tomorrow, we're all going to be dead! Do you hear me? We've got to get out of Pompeii before it's too late. *(YELLS IN DESPERATION)* Doctor!

END PART TWO

Part Three

24 (RECAP)

EUMACHIA: I invited you into my house in good faith, and you have stolen from me. My slaves bear witness to it. Take her away, Centurion!
THE MEN MARCH FORWARD AND SEIZE MEL.
MEL: Get off me! Both of you, get your hands off me!
EUMACHIA: The aediles will have the truth from you if I cannot.
MEL: Can't you see she's lying? She's trying to frame me. Doctor!
EUMACHIA: They will not take his word against that of a priestess.
DOCTOR: Another attempt to discredit Isis, Eumachia?
MEL STRUGGLES, BUT IS MANHANDLED INTO THE CART.
EUMACHIA: Your friend will serve my purpose well, Doctor.
MEL: *(SHOUTS)* Doctor, do something!
EUMACHIA: There is nought he can do, child. It will go better for you if you but speak the truth.
MEL: *(SHOUTS, ANGRILY)* The truth? Oh, you don't want to know the truth, I promise you.
DOCTOR: *(SHOUTS, URGENTLY)* This won't do any good, Mel!
THE CART PULLS AWAY; MEL'S VOICE RECEDES.
MEL: *(PANICKING)* You can't lock me up. You can't! Don't you realise? You'll kill me! This time tomorrow, we're all going to be dead! Do you hear me? We've got to get out of Pompeii before it's too late. *(YELLS IN DESPERATION)* Doctor!
AS THE CART TRUNDLES INTO THE DISTANCE, A HUGE THUNDERCLAP HERALDS THE START OF A SEVERE STORM. RAIN LASHES DOWN.

24A. VALERIA HEDONES INN
THE SHUTTERS ARE CLOSED (SO THE ROOM IS NO LONGER OPEN TO THE STREET), BUT WE CAN HEAR RAIN BEATING DOWN ON THEM. MURRANUS HAS FALLEN ASLEEP AT THE BAR, AND IS SNORING.

VALERIA: Murranus? Murranus! *(SHAKES HIM ANGRILY)* Murranus!
MURRANUS: *(STIRS, BUT DOESN'T WAKE)*
VALERIA: *(SIGHS)* Well, slumber if you will, mirmillo but I will not be here to attend to you when you finally wake. You can haul your own drunken carcass out onto the street. It is late, it will be another busy day tomorrow, and I am in dire need of sleep.

25. A POMPEIAN BACK STREET
THROUGH THE STORM THE DOCTOR AND AGLAE WALK TOWARDS US.

AGLAE: I must confess, master –
DOCTOR: Doctor, please.
AGLAE: I must confess... Doctor... that I am perplexed. Why do you ask me to walk with you, so late at night, and in such weather?
DOCTOR: I need your help, Aglae. I'm running out of time.

(DISTANTLY) Less than twelve hours left now...

AGLAE: Master?

DOCTOR: I've been a fool, Aglae. I've been trying to recover a... an object of mine.

AGLAE: From the site of the collapsed building?

DOCTOR: Yes. But I was wrong.

AGLAE: Mel also tried to recover your possession.

DOCTOR: I thought it was her best chance. Find the TARDIS. Rescue her. Leave. Defy our destiny. But I've wasted time. Time, working against me. I have to do something about Mel, while there's still time.

AGLAE: *(WORRIED)* Mel? Is she in trouble?

DOCTOR: I'm afraid so, Aglae. And I've only made things worse. It seems I've overlooked something rather obvious.

26. A PRISON CELL

WE CAN STILL HEAR THUNDER AND RAIN BEATING DOWN OUTSIDE. MEL IS HERE. FOOTSTEPS APPROACH ALONG AN INTERNAL CORRIDOR, AND KEYS JINGLE IN THE DOOR LOCK.

MEL: Doctor? Doctor, is that you?

THE DOOR OPENS AND CELSINUS ENTERS.

CELSINUS: No, Melanie. It is I, Popidius Celsinus.

MEL: Oh. What do you want?

CELSINUS: I could not sleep.

MEL: You couldn't sleep? You try being locked up for the night!

CELSINUS: You haunted my thoughts.

MEL: I hope this isn't another chat-up, Celsinus.

CELSINUS: I desire only to know more about you, Melanie. The aediles will judge you on the morrow, and I felt we should speak first.

MEL: Well, I'm not sure I should speak to you.

CELSINUS: You must accept that your plight is of your own making.

MEL: I don't think so. You don't know me very well, do you Celsinus? I could never steal anything!

CELSINUS: Eumachia swears –

MEL: Eumachia framed me – and as far as I can see, you helped her.

CELSINUS: *(INDIGNANTLY)* You are speaking of a priestess!

MEL: Oh, come on Celsinus. You were with me the whole time I was in Eumachia's house. Did you see me take any jewellery?

CELSINUS: I... did not. But –

MEL: There you are, then.

CELSINUS: Yes... Yes, you are right, Melanie. I had thought perhaps... but no... I swear, none of this was my doing.

MEL: It was you who tricked me into going to that house!

CELSINUS: I was also tricked, I fear. I see now that Eumachia used me to discredit the goddess herself.

MEL: Well, that's pretty clear. But it's not your goddess I'm worried about. She didn't end up in a prison cell.

CELSINUS: *(SCANDALISED)* You cannot care so little about Isis.

MEL: It's not that, Celsinus. I just happen to have more pressing concerns at the moment.

CELSINUS: You made claim to have come from Isis yourself.

MEL: *(EXASPERATED)* Well, I was lying, obviously. *(BEAT)* Oh, I'm sorry Celsinus, I had no choice. I didn't think anyone would believe the truth.

CELSINUS: Of what truth do you speak?

MEL: Trust me, you don't want to know.

CELSINUS: No, Melanie. It is time you trusted me! There is something... different about you. I have sensed it from the start. I do not think you to be evil, despite your dishonesty.

MEL: Well, thank you very much.

CELSINUS: Confide in me, and I can help you. I can plead with the aediles to show you mercy.

MEL: I'd like to, I really would. I just don't know...

CELSINUS: You need but speak the truth, and I will have you free of this gaol within days. And then, perhaps we... *(BEAT)* Melanie? Melanie, have I said ought to offend you?

MEL: *(SADLY)* 'Days', Celsinus? *(A LONG PAUSE; THEN, SIGHS)* I think you'd better leave.

CELSINUS: But I would –

MEL: Just go! Please, Celsinus, leave me alone. I don't think you can help me.

CELSINUS: *(RELUCTANTLY)* As you wish, then. *(HE HESITATES AT THE DOOR)* But I shall pray to the goddess, my lady – that, though you have turned your back on her, she may not so hastily abandon you.

HE LEAVES, CLOSING AND LOCKING THE DOOR BEHIND HIM.

MEL: *(TO SELF)* I don't think it's Isis I need. Where are you, Doctor?

27. THE GUARD ROOM

CELSINUS ENTERS, TO FIND THE DOCTOR STOOPED OVER A SLEEPING – AND SNORING – GAOLER.

DOCTOR: *(TO GAOLER, SOFTLY)* That's right. You just sleep. Let me take care of everything. That is... if I can find where you keep your...

CELSINUS: What in the name of the goddess occurs here?

DOCTOR: *(STARTLED)* Ah, Mister Celsinus. *(RUEFULLY)* Oh. So, you have the keys to the cells, I see.

CELSINUS: Doctor! What business do you have in this place?

DOCTOR: Just, ah, visiting my companion.

CELSINUS: At this hour?

DOCTOR: *(VAGUELY)* Well, who keeps track of time?

CELSINUS: What has happened to the gaoler?

DOCTOR: *(AS IF SURPRISED)* Oh, yes. Well, it's the long hours, I expect. Working through the night... er, do you think it's wise to wake him?

CELSINUS: I will not accept such slothfulness!

DOCTOR: *(WITH MOCK INDIGNATION)* Quite right. Why, anybody could have walked in here –

CELSINUS: I shall have the wretched fellow flogged.

DOCTOR: – and released your prisoners.

194

CELSINUS:	Indeed.
DOCTOR:	Although...
CELSINUS:	Although?
DOCTOR:	It must be a great responsibility.
CELSINUS:	What concern is that of mine?
DOCTOR:	And, as you said, it's late –
CELSINUS:	It is late.
DOCTOR:	– and I should think he's very tired.
CELSINUS:	You're right, Doctor. I am tired.

DOCTOR: Tired of all the responsibility. In fact, you're tired of everything, aren't you, Celsinus? Tired of being a good councillor to the people. Tired of being a good servant to Isis. Tired of having to solve everybody else's problems. It's late, Popidius Celsinus, and you want to rest, don't you?

CELSINUS: I would like to rest. But –

DOCTOR: Hand over the responsibility. Let somebody else take care of it.

CELSINUS: *(DROWSILY)* Somebody else... *(HE SITS DOWN HEAVILY)*

DOCTOR: *(SOOTHINGLY)* That's right. Just sit down. Rest. Let somebody else take the responsibility. Let somebody else take the... keys...

HE EASES THE KEYS CAREFULLY FROM CELSINUS'S GRASP.

CELSINUS: *(STIRRING)* No, wait. The prisoner... Melanie...

DOCTOR: There's no need to be concerned. You don't have to worry about anything. *(HE WAITS UNTIL CELSINUS IS ASLEEP)* I'll take good care of your prisoner.

28. A POMPEIAN STREET

THE DOCTOR AND MEL RUN OUT INTO THE RAIN, TO WHERE AGLAE WAITS WITH A RESTLESS HORSE AND A WAGON.

MEL: I knew you'd rescue me, Doctor.

DOCTOR: I'm touched by your faith – but we aren't out of danger yet.

AGLAE: *(CALLS FROM HORSE)* Mel!

MEL: Aglae! What are you doing here?

AGLAE: Your friend came to see me, Mel. He asked that I bring my mistress's horse and wagon.

MEL: You mean you've stolen them?

DOCTOR: I've assured Aglae she won't get into trouble. I think Asellina will have other things to worry about tomorrow, don't you?

MEL: Oh... I see what you mean. Well, I suppose we do need to get out of Pompeii, don't we?

DOCTOR: Not 'we', Mel. Just you.

MEL: No, Doctor!

DOCTOR: There's no time to argue. I want you to hide in the wagon until you're safely out of the city. Then you and Aglae should get as far away from here as possible.

MEL: And what about you?

DOCTOR: I told you before, if there's a chance of finding the TARDIS –

MEL: Then I'm not leaving either.

DOCTOR: (IMPATIENTLY) The best way to change history, Mel, is to do something unexpected; something totally out of character; something you would never have done if it wasn't for your knowledge of the future.

MEL: Like what?

DOCTOR: Like doing as I tell you for once!

MEL: But you said if we make a deliberate attempt to change history –

DOCTOR: (EXASPERATED) Just do it, Mel. Please!

MEL: Well... OK, Doctor... if you're sure it's the right thing to do. (CLIMBS INTO THE WAGON) But I'm still not happy about this.

DOCTOR: This isn't goodbye, Mel.

MEL: It feels like it. You'll never dig out the TARDIS in time.

DOCTOR: I don't have to.

MEL: What do you mean?

DOCTOR: It isn't buried. Somebody moved it before the building collapsed.

MEL: How can you possibly know that?

DOCTOR: I should have seen it much earlier, Mel. That part of the city was excavated long before 1980. If the TARDIS really was beneath that rubble, it would have been discovered then.

MEL: So, who do you think moved it?

DOCTOR: I don't know, but I intend to find out. And I'll find you, Mel, I promise – with or without the TARDIS. I don't intend to die here.

MEL: (STERNLY) You better hadn't, Doctor.

A LONG PAUSE, THEN THE DOCTOR WALKS TO AGLAE.

DOCTOR: She's ready to go now, Aglae.

AGLAE: Goodbye, Doctor. Thank you for your kindness.

DOCTOR: Goodbye, Aglae. It's been a pleasure knowing you.

THE HORSE SETS OFF; HE WAITS UNTIL IT'S SOME DISTANCE AWAY.

(TO SELF, SADLY) Goodbye, Mel.

29. THE CITY GATE

A LEGIONARY IS ON GUARD. THE HORSE AND CART APPROACHES.

LEGIONARY: Hold!

THE HORSE AND CART STOPS.

Why, you are but a slave! Where is your mistress, girl?

AGLAE: (TRYING IN VAIN TO CONCEAL HER NERVOUSNESS) She is abed, sir. She sent me out on an errand of some urgency.

LEGIONARY: It is an uncommon time of night for a young maidservant to be travelling out of the city. What manner of errand might this be?

AGLAE: I am to fetch supplies from Herculaneum. For Valeria Hedone. She requires fresh amphorae of wine.

LEGIONARY: (AMUSED) So, Valeria's inn has been drunk dry? Aye, it has been a good feast indeed!

AGLAE: Please... I must return with the supplies before dawn.

LEGIONARY: Then you may pass, girl... once I have checked your wagon.

AGLAE: (AFRAID) My wagon?

LEGIONARY: It will be empty for the outward journey, will it not?
AGLAE: It is a most urgent errand. Please, open the gate.
LEGIONARY: Dismount, girl.
AGLAE: *(COWED)* As you wish, sir.
AGLAE DISMOUNTS AND FOLLOWS THE LEGIONARY ROUND TO THE BACK OF THE WAGON.
LEGIONARY: Now, what's in the back here –
HE PULLS BACK THE CLOTH.
MEL: *(WEAKLY)* I expect you're surprised to find me here.
AGLAE HITS THE LEGIONARY ON HIS NECK/SHOULDERS WITH A STICK (IT MIGHT CLANG AGAINST HIS HELMET TOO), KNOCKING HIM OVER.
LEGIONARY: *(GRUNT OF PAIN)*
MEL: *(SHRIEKS)* Aglae!
AGLAE: *(HORRIFIED)* Oh Mel, what have I done?
MEL: *(ASTONISHED)* You've knocked him out, that's what. What did you hit him with?
AGLAE: This... It is an arm, from that statue... the earthquakes must have shaken it loose...
MEL: I know I told you to be a bit more assertive, Aglae, but I didn't mean –
AGLAE: *(TEARFULLY)* When the aediles hear of this, I will go the lions for my sins.
MEL: *(DETERMINED)* No! No you won't, Aglae. Not if they don't catch you. Get back on that horse, go on. Let's get out of here!
AGLAE: But, Mel, the gate is still closed.
LEGIONARY: *(GROANS AS HE BEGINS TO STIR)*
MEL: Well, there's no time to open it – and I don't like the look of that legionary's sword.
SHE JUMPS OUT OF THE WAGON.
That wagon wasn't very comfortable anyway. It looks like we're on foot from now on. Come on, Aglae.
THEY RUN TOWARDS THE GATE.

30. VALERIA HEDONE'S INN
THE RAIN HAS STOPPED. WOODEN SHUTTERS ARE DOWN OVER THE FRONT OF THE INN. SOMEBODY KNOCKS ON THEM FROM WITHOUT, WAKING MURRANUS.

MURRANUS: *(GROANS)* What in Jupiter's name –?
THE KNOCKING COMES AGAIN, MORE URGENTLY.
DOCTOR: *(FROM OUTSIDE)* Valeria!
VALERIA ENTERS DOWN A FLIGHT OF WOODEN STAIRS.
VALERIA: What is that infernal racket? Murranus! Are you still here?
MURRANUS: *(BLEARILY)* My lady... I must have fallen asleep at your bar.
VALERIA: You did indeed, mirmillo – and it is time you stirred yourself and returned to your barracks. It is almost dawn.
THE DOCTOR KNOCKS AGAIN.
DOCTOR: Valeria!
VALERIA: *(CALLS, IRRITATED)* Be gone with you! Can you not see

197

the shutters are up? Festival or no, I am entitled to some sleep.
DOCTOR: Valeria, I must speak to you.
VALERIA: Doctor?
MURRANUS: *(SUDDENLY ALERT)* Doctor?
A TENSE PAUSE.
VALERIA: Hold, Doctor. I have to... adjust my clothing.
MURRANUS: *(ASIDE, SO THE DOCTOR CAN'T HEAR)* The Doctor –
here! Oh, but the fates are kind to me this morning. The source of my
shame has walked into my grasp.
VALERIA: *(SAME)* I will have no fighting in my bar, Murranus, I
warned you of that last night.
MURRANUS: He must pay for his treachery!
VALERIA: *(SHARPLY)* Murranus!
MURRANUS: *(IGNORING HER)* Damn you, Valeria. Damn you for
plying me with your wine.
VALERIA: I heard no complaints at the time.
MURRANUS: I am not yet ready for this. My head aches. My stomach
feels as if Vulcan himself has stoked his fire within.
VALERIA: Then I shall send him away. It is a simple matter.
MURRANUS: No! No, let him enter. I shall take cover in your back
room until I have had time to think. And you, Valeria... *(HAS AN IDEA)*
Yes, yes, with your assistance, I shall see my honour restored.
VALERIA: I want no part of this, Murranus.
MURRANUS: *(ANGRILY)* Your wants do not concern me, woman. My
life is at stake. If you obstruct my mission, then know that you will be
my sworn enemy – and you will suffer the same fate as the Doctor.

31. INSIDE A TOMB
*MEL AND AGLAE HAVE TAKEN SHELTER HERE. MEL OPENS THE
HEAVY DOOR A CRACK TO PEER OUTSIDE. IT IS MORNING, AND WE
HEAR THE CRIES OF SEAGULLS AGAIN.*

AGLAE: *(IN A FEARFUL WHISPER)* Do you see ought, Mel?
MEL: Only that the sun's coming up. It looks like being a
beautiful morning. A lot warmer than it is in this old crypt, anyway.
AGLAE: But what of the legionary?
MEL: No sign of him, thank goodness.
SHE CLOSES THE DOOR.
AGLAE: I was certain he had followed us into the necropolis. I
even feared he had spied us as we entered this tomb.
MEL: Well, he isn't out there now, and this place is giving me
the creeps.
AGLAE: Oh Mel, you ought not to be afraid of the spirits of our
ancestors. So long as we are respectful to them, they can only assist
us.
MEL: All the same, I'd rather not spend any more time than I
have to with their bones. I think we should be making a move now.
AGLAE: *(DISTRESSED)* No, Mel, I cannot. We will surely be seen.
We have passed beyond the city walls. Is that not enough?
MEL: No, Aglae, it isn't. You heard what the Doctor said. We
have to get as far away as possible. And now that we don't even have a
horse...

AGLAE: *(TEARFULLY)* Oh, Mel, I have brought this misfortune
upon us.
MEL: No you haven't, Aglae. You've done the right thing, I
promise.
AGLAE: When the Doctor came to me last night, he made it
sound so right, so necessary, that I should flee Pompeii. Now, in the
light of dawn, I look on what I have done and I see how foolish it was. I
have earned the gods' wrath.
MEL: Not necessarily. We've got a chance, if you'll take it.
AGLAE: Asellina will be rising now. She will see I am not about
my chores. Soon, everyone will know my shame.
MEL: Believe me, Aglae, it won't matter soon. Now are you
coming or not?
AGLAE: I –
MEL OPENS THE DOOR AGAIN.
MEL: No one's going to catch us, Aglae, and the gods certainly
aren't about to punish us. We're just doing what we can to save our –
(GASPS IN SHOCK)
THE LEGIONARY APPEARS IN THE DOORWAY.
AGLAE: *(SHRIEKS)* Mel, no!
LEGIONARY: So, this is where you thought to hide from me?
MEL: *(RUEFULLY)* I may have spoken too soon.

32. VALERIA HEDONE'S INN
THE DOCTOR AND VALERIA SIT AT THE BAR.

VALERIA: Are you certain you will not take a drink, Doctor?
DOCTOR: *(DISTRACTEDLY)* Hmm? Oh, no, no thank you, Valeria.
There's no time. I need to keep a clear head... to think. To look for
patterns...
VALERIA: I shall pour you one anyway. You may change your
mind.
SHE FILLS A CUP WITH WINE.
DOCTOR: So, remind me: Pompeii is under the rule of two duoviri,
right?
VALERIA: They answer to the Emperor, of course.
DOCTOR: Of course. And beneath them...?
VALERIA: The aediles, Doctor, and one hundred decuriones beneath
them.
DOCTOR: Like Celsinus. And the elected magistrates beneath
them. A lot of the graffiti in the city refers to electoral candidates.
There must be some in-fighting? People trying to climb the political
ladder?
VALERIA: The writings are old. The elections were more than a
month since.
DOCTOR: Of course.
VALERIA: Must we speak of this now, Doctor? It is past dawn, and
an uncommonly hot morning it looks like becoming. I will have
customers here soon. I have much to prepare.
DOCTOR: *(DEEP IN THOUGHT)* Dawn... dawn, yes... there was a
ceremony in progress at the Temple of Isis. Greeting the new day. *(TO
SELF, SADLY)* The last day. *(TO VALERIA)* What do you think of Isis,

Valeria?
VALERIA: She is a most benevolent goddess.
DOCTOR: And what about your rulers?
VALERIA: I see what you imply, Doctor, but you are wrong. Foreign Isis may be, but she is tolerated and even embraced. Her cult has spread so that even the decuriones now worship at her altar.
DOCTOR: *(THOUGHTFULLY AGAIN)* Yes, Rome always did incorporate the cultures of the people it conquered into its own. *(TO VALERIA)* But there must be some dissenters? Eumachia, for example.
VALERIA: Eumachia is a bitter old widow, who fears only that her own power will diminish. You are aware that she is a priestess of the Capitoline Triad?
DOCTOR: Which is Jupiter, Juno and Minerva?
VALERIA: Although she worships many gods, as we all do.
DOCTOR: *(REMEMBERING)* Venus Pompeiana...
VALERIA: Aye, the official goddess of Pompeii. She brings us fortune and prosperity. And the Emperor, of course, the only god who may walk on this Earth. Are you sure you will not drink, Doctor?
DOCTOR: *(SIGHS)* I shouldn't be doing this, Valeria.
VALERIA: I do not understand.
DOCTOR: I shouldn't be here. Talking to you. Trying to find my ship. If it weren't for my foreknowledge, I'd still be in that back street, trying to shift debris, letting time run through my fingers.
VALERIA: You make no sense to me, Doctor.
DOCTOR: Best not to think about it. But how can I ignore it?
VALERIA: You need sleep.
THE DOCTOR STANDS.
DOCTOR: No time to sleep. I must find the TARDIS.
VALERIA: Then at least take this drink.
SHE PUSHES THE FULL CUP ACROSS THE BAR TOWARDS HIM.
          I cannot help you with your arduous task, Doctor, but I can ensure that you are refreshed for it.
DOCTOR: *(UNCERTAIN FOR A MOMENT, THEN)* Yes. Yes, I think I will. Thank you, Valeria. *(HE DRINKS)*

33. A PRISON CELL
MEL AND AGLAE ARE IMPRISONED HERE. MEL BANGS FRANTICALLY ON THE DOOR.

MEL: *(SHOUTS)* Hello? Can you hear me?... I know there's somebody out there. I want to see my friend... Hello?
AGLAE: It is no use, Mel. The guard will not come.
MEL: I can't believe I'm right back where I started. Back in Pompeii. Back in this cell.
AGLAE: *(SELF-PITYING)* We have transgressed against the gods.
MEL: *(GROANS)* Please, Aglae, not again. What time do you think it is?
AGLAE: I know not, Mel, but the morning grows long.
MEL: Yes, that's what I was afraid of. And it's getting a bit too warm for my liking too.
AGLAE: I have stolen from my mistress and run from her. I have attacked a soldier of the Empire. I deserve to be punished.

MEL:　　　　Well, you might be punished a bit more harshly than you expected if we don't get out of here soon. *(BANGS ON THE DOOR; SHOUTS)* I know you can hear me out there. I demand to see somebody in charge. Hello? *(GIVES UP WITH A SIGH)* The worst thing is, the Doctor doesn't even know we're back here. We can't count on a rescue from him this time. We've got to do something for ourselves.

AGLAE:　　　He will learn of our plight soon enough. The whole of Pompeii will hear of our actions. There will be much talk.

MEL:　　　　*(GLOOMILY)* I don't know if that's comforting or worrying.

AGLAE:　　　But the Doctor, I fear, can do nought to help those who have offended the gods.

MEL:　　　　*(SIGHS)* OK then, Aglae, you've convinced me. There's only one thing for it – more's the pity.

AGLAE:　　　Mel?

MEL:　　　　*(BANGS ON THE DOOR; SHOUTS)* Listen to me! I want you to take a message to someone – and I'm sure he'll be very cross with you if you don't. *(TAKES A DEEP BREATH)* Tell Popidius Celsinus I want to see him, please.

34. VALERIA HEDONE'S INN

THE DOCTOR'S DRINK WAS DRUGGED. MUCH AS HE TRIES TO RESIST IT, HE IS FALLING ASLEEP.

DOCTOR:　　　*(DROWSILY)* Valeria, what have I been drinking?

VALERIA:　　Only the finest local wine, Doctor.

DOCTOR:　　　(STRUGGLING TO TALK) Tired... so tired...

VALERIA:　　It is to be expected. You have been up all night.

DOCTOR:　　　Drugged... the wine.. Valeria...

VALERIA:　　I'm sorry, Doctor.

MURRANUS ENTERS.

MURRANUS:　*(TAUNTINGLY)* Why, Doctor, you ought to show our host some gratitude. She flavoured your drink with a concoction of herbs that will aid your relaxation... at my suggestion, of course.

DOCTOR:　　　*(ONE LAST GASP BEFORE HE SUCCUMBS)* Murranus!

MURRANUS:　You have done well, Valeria.

VALERIA:　　*(SCORNFULLY)* I have done your dirty work for you, Murranus, and may the gods curse me for it.

MURRANUS:　*(MOCKINGLY)* You are most kind.

VALERIA:　　Oh, Murranus, when will you see? This Doctor isn't your enemy. You don't need to kill him to make your point.

MURRANUS:　It is my life at stake, Valeria. I shall be the judge of what I must do.

VALERIA:　　If that is the case, then you will take yourself away from this inn, Murranus. You are no longer welcome here.

MURRANUS:　I go gladly, Valeria – so long as I take my prize with me.

35. A POMPEIAN STREET

IT IS LATE MORNING, AND THE STREET IS FAIRLY BUSY. MEL AND CELSINUS WALK TOGETHER, TRAILED BY SEVERAL SLAVES.

MEL: Oh really, Celsinus, are all these slaves necessary? I'm hardly going to overpower you and run away, now am I?

CELSINUS: You have escaped before, Melanie. I cannot take the risk that it will happen again. It was difficult enough to persuade the aediles to release you into my care, so we could talk like this.

MEL: *(AGGRIEVED)* Yes, and it took you long enough too – and poor old Aglae's still locked up in that awful cell.

CELSINUS: I have done all I can, Melanie – and you must return to that gaol yourself.

MEL: Oh Celsinus, I'm grateful for your freeing me, of course. But I wish you'd believe what I've told you. We're running out of time.

CELSINUS: I know not, Melanie. Your story is incredible, and your prophecy goes against what Isis herself has promised.

MEL: What's Isis got to do with it?

CELSINUS: You saw how the farmers went to her temple yesterday. She gave them her blessing. She decrees that better days will come; that the mountainside will again be fertile.

MEL: It's lies, Celsinus. Superstitious lies! Why can't you see that? *(HE IS AGHAST; SHE TRIES TO MOLLIFY HIM)* I'm sorry, but I'm telling you the truth, I swear. I don't know how much trouble I'll get into for it, but I am telling you the truth.

CELSINUS: I want to believe you, Melanie, but you have lied before.

MEL: I told you, I didn't think I had a choice. You've got to believe me, Celsinus, it just isn't like me to tell lies. *(RUEFULLY)* And after all the damage it's caused this time, I'll be even less likely to do it in future.

CELSINUS: I could speak to the aediles this afternoon—

MEL: *(FRUSTRATED)* By this afternoon, we'll be dead!

CELSINUS: *(ANGUISHED)* How can I believe that the gods would so abandon Pompeii? You speak of the mountain erupting, girl, but Vesuvius is no volcano. Why, our people have farmed its slopes for generations.

MEL: Then they're about to get a big surprise, I'm afraid.

CELSINUS: But why would Vulcan send his fire to destroy us now? He was so pleased with our offerings yesterday.

MEL: I don't know how to prove it to you, Celsinus, and by the time I can it will be too late for any of us. You've just got to trust me.

CELSINUS: And the oracles of Isis; why did they not foresee this doom?

MEL: *(DESPERATELY)* Can't you give me the benefit of the doubt? Just for a couple of hours? After that, if it turns out I was lying to you, you can lock me up and throw away the key! Just a couple of hours, Celsinus.

CELSINUS: *(STILL SUSPICIOUS)* What do you want from me?

MEL: Somebody took something from us – from the Doctor and me.

CELSINUS: This is the temple of which Eumachia spoke?

MEL: I suppose so, yes. But it's not a temple.

CELSINUS: A blue box carved from wood, Eumachia said, painted with signs that made no sense... *(FALTERINGLY)* 'Po... Po-lick-ay...'

MEL: *(SPELLING IT TO HERSELF)* Pol.. P-O-L... yes! 'Police

Box'! Eumachia told you that?

CELSINUS: Is that not correct?

MEL: No! I mean, yes. Yes it is. It's absolutely correct. *(THOUGHTFULLY)* But how did Eumachia...? Unless... *(SUDDENLY ENTHUSIASTIC)* That's it! That's got to be it! Oh Celsinus, I could kiss you.

CELSINUS: My lady?

MEL: Don't you see? Eumachia couldn't have described the TARDIS in such detail unless she'd seen it herself. She took it, she must have done!

CELSINUS: But, Melanie, the strange manner of your arrival here has been the talk of the city.

MEL: *(THINKING HARD)* Maybe. But... but how many people actually saw it? And how many can read – or even recognise letters? Not many of the slaves, I'll bet... No, it makes sense. Eumachia must have seen the TARDIS. And she wants to discredit Isis. So, if she thought the Doctor and I were her messengers come to Pompeii in some... some magical temple...

CELSINUS: *(TRYING TO KEEP UP)* You blame Eumachia for your loss?

MEL: Yes, Celsinus, I do. *(TO SELF, EXULTANTLY)* I do. I've actually done it! I've found out where the TARDIS is. We can't be destined to lose it here. *(TO CELSINUS)* I want to go back to Eumachia's house.

CELSINUS: Is that wise?

MEL: She's got the TARDIS, Celsinus, I know she has. And that's the one thing that can save my life... all our lives... right now.

36. THE AMPHITHEATRE

THE AMPHITHEATRE IS CLOSED TO THE PUBLIC, BUT MURRANUS HAS CARRIED THE SLEEPING DOCTOR TO THE CENTRE OF THE ARENA. HE POKES THE DOCTOR WITH HIS TOE, STIRRING HIM.

MURRANUS: Wake, Doctor! Come on, wake! I am eager for our final confrontation.

DOCTOR: *(BLEARILY)* Mmm? What...? Where am I? The Amphitheatre? How did...? Murranus! Murranus, you tricked me.

MURRANUS: As you also tricked me yesterday, Doctor. You fought without honour. Now you will pay for that.

DOCTOR: You talk of fighting with honour? You had Valeria drug me. *(SUDDENLY WORRIED)* Wait! Wait, how long have I been unconscious?

MURRANUS: Several hours, Doctor, but worry not: when next you sleep, it will be for much longer. *(LAUGHS CRUELLY)*

DOCTOR: *(PICKS HIMSELF UP; ANGRILY)* You idiot, Murranus. Do you have any idea what you've done?

MURRANUS: *(WITH EQUAL ANGER)* I have done what is necessary to regain what you stole from me. You cannot take the coward's way out this time, Doctor. My comrades in arms guard the exits from this arena.

THE MEN GROWL ACCORDINGLY

Now choose your weapons, and we shall settle our

differences like men.

DOCTOR: You're forgetting something, Murranus. The Amphitheatre is closed. You have no audience here.

MURRANUS: It matters not. Word will spread that I have bested you. They will talk of my great victory for months.

DOCTOR: And that will please you, will it? Killing me will make you happy?

MURRANUS: Here, Doctor! You have the build of a retarius. You can fight with the net and trident of one.

THROWS THE IMPLEMENTS TO THE DOCTOR

DOCTOR: I'm not going to fight you, Murranus. Kill me if you must, but it will have to be in cold blood as I stand here before you, defenceless.

MURRANUS: *(UNDAUNTED)* Then so it shall be.

ANOTHER QUAKE BEGINS, QUIETLY AT FIRST BUT BUILDING.

37. A POMPEIAN STREET

THE QUAKE CONTINUES TO BUILD. IT'S A BAD ONE. THIS ISN'T A VERY POPULOUS AREA, BUT THOSE WHO ARE PRESENT REACT AS BEFORE.

MEL: *(FRIGHTENED)* Do you see what I mean now, Celsinus? It's starting. It's starting already!

CELSINUS: Calm yourself, Melanie, it is but another earthquake. Pompeii has suffered many. The gods must remain displeased.

MEL: Can't you see? Can't you see what's happening here?

CELSINUS: Just hold on to me. With the assistance of Isis, we can withstand this trial.

MEL: I don't think Isis is going to get help you this time.

38. THE AMPHITHEATRE

THE QUAKE CONTINUES. THE GLADIATORS WHO GUARD THE EXITS MAKE DISCONCERTED NOISES.

MURRANUS: Once again, the gods come to your aid – but this time they cannot do enough to spare you from me.

DOCTOR: *(URGENTLY)* I don't have time for this, Murranus!

MURRANUS: You have no more pressing appointment than with Death, Doctor. It matters not how fierce the quake becomes; we shall have our reckoning.

39. A POMPEIAN STREET

THE QUAKE SUBSIDES. FROM THIS POINT ON, WE HEAR NO MORE SEAGULLS.

CELSINUS: There, Mel, do you see? The quake has ended. There is nought to fear from our gods.

MEL: Then... then why has the water stopped flowing from that fountain?

CELSINUS: *(PUZZLED)* Why, I do not –

MEL: And look! Look over there – that bird fluttering in its cage. Like it knows what's going to happen. *(GASPS IN REALISATION)*

And listen! Listen, Celsinus. Can you hear any seagulls?

CELSINUS: The gulls have left the sky? But surely –

MEL: That sundial. What does it say? What time is it?

CELSINUS: It is near the sixth hour.

MEL: It's midday, isn't it? Of course it is. I can tell by the position of the sun. Can't you feel it, Celsinus? It's going to happen. It's going to happen any minute now.

CELSINUS: *(UNCERTAINLY)* I... do feel something... but, if anything, it is an unnatural calm. Surely...

MEL: *(IN A HORRIFIED WHISPER)* It's too late!

40. THE AMPHITHEATRE

DOCTOR: *(URGENTLY)* Fighting won't solve anything, Murranus. We've all got more important things to worry about.

MURRANUS: Pick up the net and trident, Doctor, or you will be defenceless.

DOCTOR: There has to be another way to settle this.

MURRANUS: Fight back or not, Doctor, I will slaughter you either way. I have given you a chance to defend yourself; my conscience is clear. But I will have satisfaction. If you will not take the weapons, then you will die all the sooner.

DOCTOR: *(FURIOUSLY)* You think you'll reclaim your honour this way, but your honour will be worth nothing when you're reduced to ashes!

MURRANUS: Die, Doctor, with a coward's plea on your lips!

END PART THREE

Part Four

40 (RECAP)

DOCTOR: *(URGENTLY)* Fighting won't solve anything, Murranus. We've all got more important things to worry about.

MURRANUS: Pick up the net and trident, Doctor, or you will be defenceless.

DOCTOR: There has to be another way to settle this.

MURRANUS: Fight back or not, Doctor, I will slaughter you either way. I have given you a chance to defend yourself; my conscience is clear. But I will have satisfaction. If you will not take the weapons, then you will die all the sooner.

DOCTOR: *(FURIOUSLY)* You think you'll reclaim your honour this way, but your honour will be worth nothing when you're reduced to ashes!

MURRANUS: Die, Doctor, with a coward's plea on your lips!

41. A POMPEIAN STREET
THERE IS AN UNNATURAL SILENCE. A FEW PEOPLE ARE MUTTERING APPREHENSIVELY, AS IF THEY CAN FEEL THAT THINGS AREN'T RIGHT.

MEL: Do you trust me now, Celsinus?

CELSINUS: I feel I must – and yet how can I accept that Pompeii has seen its final dawn? There must surely be hope.

MEL: Of course there's hope. Plenty of people will escape. You can settle down somewhere else; start a new life.

CELSINUS: Then the gods have judged us already? They have decided which of us should live or die?

MEL: No, Celsinus, it's in our hands as well. It's up to us to do whatever we can to help ourselves... *(MEANINGFULLY)* and each other.

CELSINUS: You wish something of me.

MEL: I want you to let Aglae out of gaol.

CELSINUS: I know not if –

MEL: You must, Celsinus. If she's locked in there when the volcano erupts, she'll die! She doesn't deserve that. She's only in this mess in the first place because she tried to help me. You've got to set her free. Then you've both got to get away.

CELSINUS: You are not coming with us?

MEL: There's something I've got to do first.

CELSINUS: You still mean to visit Eumachia.

MEL: I have to. I remember the way, don't worry.

CELSINUS: But the aediles –

MEL: I thought you said you trusted me.

CELSINUS: I... yes, Melanie. Yes, I do trust you.

MEL: Then will you do as I ask? Please, Celsinus!

42. THE AMPHITHEATRE

MURRANUS: Prepare to die, Doctor. Prepare to –

VALERIA RUSHES IN, PUSHING PAST THE GLADIATORS.
VALERIA: No, Murranus! Stop this!
DOCTOR: *(RELIEVED)* Valeria! Am I glad to see you.
MURRANUS: Valeria Hedone, this is no concern of yours. The Doctor and I have a score to settle.
BY NOW, VALERIA HAS MARCHED UP TO MURRANUS.
VALERIA: *(DETERMINEDLY)* You are wrong, Murranus, it is my concern It was I who delivered this man to you; this man who has done nought to warrant your vengeance, who may even be a servant of our goddess. Slay me if you wish, but it is only thus that you will get to the Doctor.
DOCTOR: I'm very grateful, Valeria, but this really isn't–
MURRANUS: *(DISMISSIVELY)* Begone, woman! You have no place here.
VALERIA: I had not the courage to stand against you before, Murranus, but I will not back down again. I will not have the Doctor's blood on my hands.
MURRANUS: Then you leave me no choice, Valeria.
THE DOCTOR LEAPS ON MURRANUS.
MURRANUS: *(AN INCOHERENT ROAR OF RAGE)*
VALERIA: Doctor!
THERE IS A BRIEF STRUGGLE.
DOCTOR: *(URGENTLY)* Thanks for the distraction, Valeria. Now, get behind me!
MURRANUS: You fight like a coward, Doctor, attacking from behind.
DOCTOR: I don't wish to fight you at all – but I have your weapon now, Murranus. If I were you, I'd keep your distance from us.
MURRANUS: *(SCORNFULLY)* Why? You can barely lift my sword, let alone wield it. I could kill you with my bare hands.
DOCTOR: *(MUTTERS)* Yes, I think you probably could. *(TO MURRANUS)* Here, catch!
HE THROWS THE SWORD TO MURRANUS.
VALERIA: *(ALARMED)* No, Doctor, not the sword!
THE DOCTOR SCRAMBLES FOR THE DISCARDED NET OF THE RETARIUS AND FLINGS IT OVER MURRANUS, ENTANGLING HIM.
DOCTOR: You can try this net for size too. *(URGENTLY)* Now, Valeria, while he's entangled.
MURRANUS: *(SCREAMS ANGRILY)* I will kill you for this!
DOCTOR: So you keep saying. But you seem to be a little tied up at the moment. Come on, Valeria, run!
VALERIA: *(FRIGHTENED)* But... but the other gladiators...
THE DOCTOR TAKES VALERIA'S ARM AND PULLS HER AWAY. THE GLADIATORS RUN TO CUT THEM OFF.
DOCTOR: Towards the audience seating. We can climb out that way.
VALERIA: *(SHRIEKS AS SHE STUMBLES)* Doctor!
DOCTOR: Valeria!
HE HELPS HER UP.
VALERIA: No! Save yourself, Doctor. I do not deserve your aid. It is the gods' will that I should die here.
DOCTOR: I wish it was that simple. Can you still walk?
VALERIA: It is too late! You have doomed yourself, Doctor. The gladiators surround us.

MURRANUS HAS FREED HIMSELF. HE APPROACHES THEM ANGRILY.

MURRANUS: A fair attempt, Doctor, but I told you: no power on Earth or in the heavens themselves can save you from me. My comrades will not let you pass. Now you will pay the price for your defiance. And you, Valeria... much as it grieves me, you must be punished also.

VALERIA: Forgive me, Doctor. I have brought these woes upon us.

DOCTOR: *(GRIMLY)* Don't worry, Valeria. If I'm correct, we're about to benefit from a bigger distraction than even Murranus can anticipate.

A HUGE, OMINOUS RUMBLE OF THUNDER.

43. MOUNT VESUVIUS
THE VOLCANO ERUPTS, DESTROYING ITS OWN PEAK IN A TREMENDOUS EXPLOSION.

44. A POMPEIAN STREET
A LIGHT RAIN OF HOT ASH AND PUMICE STONES BEGINS TO FALL. SHOCK TURNS TO PANIC; PEOPLE SCREAM AND WAIL AS THEY RUN FOR SHELTER. ANIMALS ARE PANICKING; IN THIS AND THE FOLLOWING SCENES, WE MIGHT HEAR HORSES, DONKEYS, BIRDS AND DOGS. THE LEGIONARY GRABS MEL AND BUNDLES HER UNDER THE COVER OF A PORTICO.

MEL: *(PANICKING)* What are you doing? Get off me! Get off!

LEGIONARY: I am escorting you to shelter.

MEL: To the shelter of a prison cell, you mean. Of all the luck, running into you again.

LEGIONARY: I know not what you mean. You seemed helpless and afraid. I thought only to do my duty as a legionary and protect you from the storm.

MEL: Oh. Oh, I see. Well, thank you for the thought, but it really wasn't –

LEGIONARY: *(SLOWLY REALISING)* However, your face is familiar to me. You... you are one of the girls who assaulted me at the gate. Can you have escaped gaol once again?

THE SHOWER INCREASES IN INTENSITY, AND HEAVY STONES BOUNCE OFF THE CANOPY ABOVE THEM.

MEL: Look, I know how this must seem – but it was Popidius Celsinus who let me out of gaol. You can ask him if you like. Only I can't stop to discuss it with you now. I've got to be somewhere else.

LEGIONARY: How can you travel, when hot rocks and ash fall from the sky?

MEL: But you don't understand. I'm almost there. *(HER INSISTENCE DRAINS AWAY AT THE SIGHT OF THE FALLING STONES)* I almost... *(SIGHS, DISPIRITED)* I almost found my way home.

LEGIONARY: *(MOURNFULLY)* The gods cleanse our city with fire. We can only hope that they have no want to take our lives as well.

MEL: You're right. And... and thank you. Thank you for saving me. I could have been scalded or... or suffocated out there.

LEGIONARY: With the blessing of Isis, this trial may soon be over. We can go about our business again. Until then, we can but wait.

MEL: *(IGNORING HIM; TO SELF, MISERABLY)* And even if I

had got to the TARDIS, I couldn't have got inside it without the Doctor. Now I can't even get out of the city. It's too late.

45. OUTSIDE THE AMPHITHEATRE
THERE AREN'T TOO MANY PEOPLE HERE, BUT WE CAN HEAR SCREAMS FROM NEARBY STREETS. THE DOCTOR AND VALERIA RUN TOWARDS US, AND TAKE SHELTER.

VALERIA: *(OUT OF BREATH)* Here, Doctor, here! We can take cover beneath the portico of the house of Julia Felix.
DOCTOR: *(SAME)* Yes, yes, an excellent idea, Valeria. *(STOPS; TRIES TO GET HIS BREATH BACK)* How's your foot now?
VALERIA: It feels much better.
DOCTOR: Good – because we can't stay here for long.
VALERIA: Murranus and the other gladiators have not followed us.
DOCTOR: It's not Murranus I'm worried about.
VALERIA: *(AFTER A SHORT PAUSE, AWED)* It is scarcely believable, Doctor. The ash, the fire... that great cloud covering the sky. You... you are all that has been claimed of you.
DOCTOR: *(STARTLED)* I'm sorry?
VALERIA: That the mirmillo's attack upon you should bring such divine wrath down upon our heads.
DOCTOR: This has nothing to do with me, Valeria, I promise you. This is an entirely natural phenomenon.
VALERIA: Natural? How can it be natural? It is the middle of the day, and yet a great darkness has descended. Fire falls from the sky. Vesuvius must be a gateway to the underworld itself.
DOCTOR: It's a volcano, Valeria. Just a volcano.
VALERIA: No, Doctor. We have lived beneath the mountain's slopes for generations. Pompeii was settled –
DOCTOR: Pompeii was built on an outcrop formed by lava from the volcano's last eruption, a thousand years ago. Vesuvius has been dormant for a long time, Valeria – but it's making up for it now.
VALERIA: You cannot stop it?
DOCTOR: I haven't come from Isis. The eruption has nothing to do with me. I just seem to be in the wrong place at the right time, as usual. Nature will run its course, as it always does. Nobody can stop it.
VALERIA: Then we are truly doomed.
DOCTOR: You mustn't think like that. Listen to me. I can explain what's happening; what will happen. I can give you – give both of us – a fighting chance to survive this.
VALERIA: I fear that may not be possible.
DOCTOR: You're wrong, Valeria. This downpour will continue for twelve hours. It will bury Pompeii in a layer of ash six feet deep. Many people will abandon their homes and flee. Many others will stay, taking shelter indoors. They're the ones who will die.
VALERIA: How can that be?
DOCTOR: They can survive the ash – but they won't survive what happens next: a pyroclastic flow, a virtual river of boiling hot rock, pouring down the mountainside at a speed of one hundred miles per hour. It will engulf the city, killing everyone it touches. We can't outrun it, Valeria. We can't hide from it. Thousands will die in Pompeii alone.

VALERIA: But if the ash is to fall until then, how can we flee? We will suffocate on the very air, if we are not scorched or beaten to death by stones.
DOCTOR: It won't be easy, but it's our only hope.
VALERIA: You say you are not a messenger of the gods, Doctor. How is it that you know so much of their intentions?
DOCTOR: I know the workings of Nature, Valeria, and of Time. I know that, twelve hours from now, this city will no longer exist.
VALERIA: Then this is Pompeii's fate: to be judged by the gods and found wanting; to be removed from the face of the earth.
DOCTOR: Pompeii will rise again, Valeria, one day.
(*MOURNFULLY*) But that day will be many years from now, I'm afraid. None of you – none of us – will live to see it.

46. A POMPEIAN STREET
THE VOLCANO IS STILL BELCHING OUT ASH, BUT THERE ARE FAR FEWER STONES NOW. MEL MAKES TO BREAK COVER.

LEGIONARY: My lady, what are you doing?
MEL: I've made up my mind. I can't just stay here – no matter how hopeless it seems.
LEGIONARY: You must.
MEL: I suppose I'm under arrest, am I?
LEGIONARY: What does it matter now? You cannot survive out there.
MEL: I've got to try. Look, I'm grateful for your concern, really I am, but I've got to go. I know it's dangerous, but I'll just have to take that risk.
LEGIONARY: How will you see? The sky is black and the air thick with ash.
MEL: I can find my way... I think. (*TRYING TO CONVINCE HERSELF*) It's not too far now. Just around that corner and across one road. I can stay under shelter for most of the way. And there aren't as many stones falling now. I can put this stola up over my head and make a run for it.
LEGIONARY: This is madness.
MEL: You're probably right. (*TAKES A DEEP BREATH*) So, you'd better wish me luck, hadn't you?
SHE MAKES A RUN FOR IT.

47. A POMPEIAN STREET
THE DOCTOR AND VALERIA RUN THROUGH THE STREETS, BUT COME TO REST BENEATH ANOTHER PORTICO.

VALERIA: (*COUGHING*) It is no use, Doctor. I cannot keep going. This ash blinds me. It claws at my throat so I can hardly draw breath.
DOCTOR: (*OUT OF BREATH*) There won't be a better chance than this, Valeria. There aren't as many pumice stones now, but the volcano will keep belching out hot ash. Stay here for a few minutes. Rest. But then we must move on.
VALERIA: (*SAME*) You would do better without me to slow you down.
DOCTOR: There's no point in trying to be noble. I need you. I need

your knowledge of this city. You have to steer us towards a gate.

VALERIA: I must return home first.

DOCTOR: There isn't –

VALERIA: *(INSISTENTLY)* You say that Pompeii will be buried. What of my house? What of my possessions?

DOCTOR: They aren't important, Valeria. Not compared to your life.

VALERIA: *(THINKS, THEN DRAWS A DEEP BREATH)* Very well. I trust you, Doctor. I will do what you think is best.

DOCTOR: *(RELIEVED)* So, where to now?

VALERIA: This way. We will go down to the shore.

DOCTOR: No. The tide will be against us.

VALERIA: But if a boat cannot carry us away from this, what can? No horse could be calmed enough to brave this storm.

DOCTOR: We'll have to remain on foot, I'm afraid.

VALERIA: But… do you not have a boat yourself? A… a ship. You spoke of it at my bar. It seemed important to you.

DOCTOR: It is. More important than you can know. But I don't know how to find it. I've run out of time. So, I only have one option. I promised a friend I wouldn't die here. I'm going to try to keep that promise. *(TO SELF, SADLY)* I only hope she got far enough away from Pompeii to return the favour.

48. THE HOUSE OF EUMACHIA

WE CAN STILL HEAR THE ROAR OF THE VOLCANO AS ASH RAINS DOWN OUTSIDE. INSIDE, MEL CONFRONTS EUMACHIA.

EUMACHIA: *(ANGRILY)* How dare you burst unannounced into my house! Why are you not still in gaol?

MEL: Well, perhaps not everyone is taken in by your lies.

EUMACHIA: I know not what you speak of, girl.

MEL: I've come to get our property back.

EUMACHIA: I have nothing of yours. Rather, it is vice versa.

MEL: You're not fooling anyone, Eumachia. It's just you and me now, and you know precisely what I mean. The blue box. The Doctor's 'temple', as you keep calling it. You moved it, didn't you? What have you done with it?

EUMACHIA: Oh, but you have some nerve, to come here and hurl your accusations at me. Do you not care that your sins and your blasphemous lies have brought this rain of fire upon our city?

MEL: You're unbelievable! You're trying to blame the Doctor and me for all this?

EUMACHIA: You are to blame. You and all the heathens who have turned their backs upon the true religion for the sake of the foreign interloper. *(SHRILLY)* This is what your Isis brings to Pompeii. Damnation and death!

MEL PUSHES PAST HER.

What are you doing, girl?

MEL: I've had enough of this. I'm searching your house.

EUMACHIA: You have no right! I will call my slaves. I will have you thrown from my premises. Stay out of –

A PUMICE STONE PENETRATES THE ROOF AND HITS THE GROUND

211

NEXT TO HER.

(A SHRIEK OF TERROR; THEN, STRIDENTLY) Do you see? Do you see now? The gods observe the evil that you do in this house; they send the boiling stones even through my own roof to punish you.

MEL: I think you'll find that stone fell a lot closer to you, actually.

EUMACHIA: My gods will protect me, girl. You cannot say the same.

MEL: Just show me where the TARDIS is, Eumachia, and I'll get out of your way – before the 'gods' do any more damage to your roof.

EUMACHIA: You will not find it here.

MEL: But you did take it, didn't you?

EUMACHIA: I took your temple, aye. But I was not so foolish as to bring that blasphemous object into my house.

MEL: So, where did you hide it?

EUMACHIA: I will not tell you.

MEL: Your wool market! No, that would be too public. It must be somewhere else. Somewhere like... *(REALISES)* somewhere like the necropolis, outside the city walls. Your family's tomb! *(SEEING EUMACHIA'S REACTION)* I'm right, aren't I? You hid the TARDIS in your family's tomb.

EUMACHIA: Believe that if you wish, girl. But the gods will strike you dead before you can cross even half of Pompeii.

MEL: We'll just have to see about that, won't we?

49. A POMPEIAN STREET

THE STREET IS PACKED WITH PEOPLE TRYING TO ESCAPE. THE DOCTOR AND VALERIA ARE AMONG THEM. THEY HAVE TO SHOUT OVER THE CROWD AND THE ROAR OF THE VOLCANO – AND THEY HAVE SOME DIFFICULTY BREATHING.

DOCTOR: Come on, Valeria, keep going. How far to the gate now?

VALERIA: We are almost upon it. But we must still cross the fields beyond, and there will be no buildings there; no shelter if we falter. And my foot is slowing me... both of us down!

DOCTOR: One problem at a time. Concentrate on reaching the gate. You're doing well, Valeria.

THEY RUN INTO CELSINUS AND AGLAE.

CELSINUS: Doctor!

DOCTOR: Mr Celsinus. I'm glad you had the sense to leave.

VALERIA: Decurione.

AGLAE: Doctor! It is good to see you again. I feared you dead.

DOCTOR: *(WORRIED)* Aglae... what are you doing here?

AGLAE: We tried to do as you instructed, Doctor, but we couldn't get out of the city. We were captured and brought back here.

CELSINUS: The girl is with me. I swore to your friend Melanie that I will see her come to no harm.

DOCTOR: Where is Mel? What's happened to her?

CELSINUS: She went in search of Eumachia.

DOCTOR: I've got to find her.

212

VALERIA: Wait, Doctor. You cannot go back.
DOCTOR: I must, Valeria. I have to find Mel.
VALERIA: You ignore your own advice. If your friend is sensible, then she will have fled Pompeii by one of the other gates.
DOCTOR: Unless she thinks she can find me. Or the TARDIS.
CELSINUS: *(APOLOGETICALLY)* I did not wish to leave her, Doctor, but she is very –
DOCTOR: I know, Celsinus. It's all right.
CELSINUS: I will come with you.
DOCTOR: There's no need, really.
CELSINUS: But perhaps it is for the best. Our city is being destroyed. Perhaps it is the gods' will that we should die with it.
DOCTOR: No, Celsinus. And that goes for all of you. This isn't the end. I know it doesn't seem like it, but life will go on. Even Pompeii will be rebuilt, on a different site. I want you all to promise me that you'll be here to see it.
VALERIA: But Doctor –
AGLAE: The Doctor is wise, mistress. We ought to do as he says.
DOCTOR: Thank you, Aglae. Keep running. Don't turn back.
VALERIA: Good luck, Doctor.
CELSINUS: May Isis bring you the best of fortune.
THE DOCTOR IS ALREADY STARTING TO HURRY AWAY.
DOCTOR: Goodbye, all of you. And good luck to you too.

50. THE HOUSE OF EUMACHIA
AS MEL HURRIES THROUGH THE ENTRANCE HALL, SHE IS INTERCEPTED BY EUMACHIA'S SLAVE (FROM SCENE 2).

SLAVE: *(FURTIVELY)* My lady! My lady!
MEL: What? Oh, it's you. You're Eumachia's servant, aren't you? You saw us arriving yesterday.
SLAVE: I saw your temple, yes, my lady – and I know where it is now.
MEL: You do? Where is it? Is it in Eumachia's tomb?
SLAVE: That is where the mistress had us take it, my lady, concealed in a wagon – but then she changed her orders. She feared that, were someone to look inside the tomb and find the temple, her guilt would be clear.
MEL: So, what did you do with it?
SLAVE: We took the temple to the tomb of another family.
MEL: Which one? Please tell me.
SLAVE: I know not, my lady, for I am but a poor slave. I cannot read the –
MEL: *(URGENTLY)* Can you show me?
SLAVE: I must not. Eumachia has commanded all her servants to remain with her.
MEL: She's keeping you all here? She can't!
SLAVE: I must go, my lady. Eumachia would flog me if she knew I was even speaking to you.
MEL: The gods won't protect her, you know. She'll die, and she'll take everyone who stays in this building with her.
THE SLAVE IS ALREADY BACKING AWAY NERVOUSLY.

SLAVE: *(AFRAID)* I must go, my lady.

MEL: *(INSISTENTLY)* Why don't you stand up to her? Just walk out. You don't want to die for her sake, do you?

SLAVE: The tomb you seek is near the Nucerian gate, my lady. Now, I must return to my mistress. *(BEAT; THEN, HESITANTLY)* I hope you may speak well of me to Isis.

HE FLEES BACK INTO THE HOUSE PROPER.

MEL: *(TO SELF, DESPONDENTLY)* Oh, I wish I could. I wish I could help you. I wish there was time to help everyone.

SHE LINGERS FOR A SECOND LONGER, THEN TURNS AND RUNS OUT OF THE HOUSE.

51. THE GLADIATORIAL BARRACKS

WE CAN STILL HEAR THE VOLCANO OUTSIDE. MURRANUS ADDRESSES A CROWD OF GLADIATORS (SIXTY-TWO, TO BE PRECISE).

MURRANUS: Hear me, my fellow gladiators. Many of you have had your say as to what should be done; now I, Murranus, shall have mine. There is no doubt that the gods have turned against Pompeii. They send fire from the sky to cleanse the sin from our city. But I tell you, this is no more than a test!

SOME GLADIATORS REACT WITH SUPPORTIVE CHEERS; SOME AREN'T SO SURE, AND THERE MURMURS OF DISCONTENT.

The gods would know who is worthy to serve them; who has faith enough to stand strong. Well, I tell you this: we, of all Pompeians, have nought to fear. Have we not served our gods well? Have we not entertained them and honoured them with displays of skill and courage?

GENERAL PROUD AGREEMENT.

Some of you speak of abandoning our great city; of joining the craven masses who flee like frightened cattle. Well, I tell you this: your cowardice will bring disgrace upon our proud profession!

THERE ARE MORE CHEERS THAN JEERS AT THIS.

Some of us have braved the ashes already to return here to the barracks. We have proven that there is nought to fear for the bold of heart and strong of limb. Here, then, we should stay – and, when this catastrophe is spent and the citizens return, ashamed, to their homes, they will say at least that their gladiators had faith and courage enough to weather the storm. They will honour us and respect us as is our due.

A MORE STRIDENT ROAR OF AGREEMENT.

If anyone here disputes that – if anyone would still turn tail and flee – then let him speak now. *(IN A LOWER, THREATENING GROWL)* Let him argue his case with me.

NOBODY SPEAKS UP.

52. THE CITY GATE

CELSINUS AND AGLAE, STILL PART OF A LARGE AND FRIGHTENED CROWD, REACH THE GATE.

AGLAE: Decurione! Decurione, where is Valeria Hedone? We have lost her. We have lost her!

CELSINUS: I cannot see her, Aglae – but, with the ash and the crowd, she could be mere inches away. You must not trouble yourself. Valeria will do as the Doctor has said: she will leave Pompeii to its fate. We must do the same.

AGLAE: But what if she has turned back? What if she has chosen to find the Doctor and Mel?

CELSINUS: We cannot concern ourselves with her, child. Here: we have attained the gate at last. We may survive this ordeal yet.

AGLAE: But there is still far to go, decurione, and the ash fills my mouth and pulls at my feet. I do not think I can go on.

CELSINUS: I will not leave you behind.

AGLAE: I will only slow you down. Why would a man such as you risk your life for one such as I?

CELSINUS: I made a promise, Aglae. I swore to Melanie that I would see us both safe. And I will keep that promise... whatever it takes.

THEY STRUGGLE ONWARDS.

53. THE HOUSE OF EUMACHIA

EUMACHIA RUNS FRANTICALLY THROUGH HER HOUSE AS STONES CRASH THROUGH THE ROOF.

EUMACHIA: My slaves! My slaves, attend me! The stones burst through my very roof. Look! Look at the damage they have wrought to my statue. You! Yes, you! I ordered you to carry this down to the cellar, where it would be safe. Now see what your indolence has caused. Take it. Take it now and you, you must rescue my precious paintings. If more harm is done, then I will take it out of your hides!

SLAVES SCURRY AROUND HER FEET, LIFTING PRECIOUS ITEMS AND CARRYING THEM AWAY.

SLAVE: *(NERVOUSLY)* Should you not take shelter yourself, mistress?

EUMACHIA: I need no protection.

SLAVE: But mistress...

EUMACHIA: Our city has been found wanting. Pompeii welcomed in the foreign goddess and we have been damned for it. But I have remained faithful. I worship the true gods. Jupiter, Juno and Minerva will not abandon Eumachia to die with the heathens. I will be spared as all around me becomes dust!

ANOTHER STONE CRASHES THROUGH THE ROOF. WE CAN HEAR THE VOLCANO VERY CLEARLY NOW.

54. OUTSIDE THE TEMPLE OF ISIS

THERE AREN'T MANY PEOPLE LEFT THIS DEEP INTO THE CITY. MEL STUMBLES BLINDLY THROUGH THE STREETS.

MEL: *(CHOKING AND SPLUTTERING ON ASH)* Help! Help! Can somebody help me? You, over there! No, please come back. Help me! It's too dark. I can't find my way. Somebody, help me! *(SURRENDERS TO A COUGHING FIT)*

THE DOCTOR APPROACHES AT A RUN.

DOCTOR: Mel! Mel, is that you?

MEL: *(SPLUTTERS)* Doctor?

HE REACHES HER.
                    (RECOVERING; ENORMOUSLY RELIEVED) Oh, Doctor!
It's so good to see you.
DOCTOR: You too, Mel. You too.
MEL: We couldn't get away. We reached the gate, but the
guard –
DOCTOR: I know, Mel.
MEL: Doctor... I know where the TARDIS is.
DOCTOR: You do?
MEL: It's in a tomb, outside the Nucerian gate... wherever that
is.
DOCTOR: I think it's over in this direction. No, wait a minute... if
this is the Temple of Isis... and the Forum is over that way...
MEL: *(BECOMING DISPIRITED AGAIN)* It's no use, is it
Doctor? We'll never find our way through all this – and even if we did,
we'd have to search all the tombs to find the right one. It's too dark, I
can hardly breathe and the ash is already knee deep. You were right,
Doctor. History's working against us. This is the end, isn't it?
DOCTOR: It's the end for Pompeii, Mel. *(BECOMING DISTANT,
REFLECTIVE)* Inside that temple now, the priests of Isis are sitting
down to their last meal: one final tribute to a goddess who won't save
them. That's how they'll be found, many years from now, their corpses
petrified, preserved by the ash, their food still laid out on the table.
MEL: And us? Will they find our bodies too, Doctor?
DOCTOR: *(SNAPPING OUT OF IT)* There's always a chance, Mel.
You told me that, remember?
HE HURRIES OVER TO THE WALL OF THE TEMPLE COURTYARD.
MEL: What are you doing?
DOCTOR: *(HIS VOICE STRAINED AS HE REACHES UP)* Just
borrowing this hanging-lamp from the temple wall. I don't think they'll
be needing it any more, do you?
*HE RUMMAGES IN HIS POCKETS, FINDS A MATCH, LIGHTS IT AND
LIGHTS THE LAMP FROM IT.*
                    There. At least now we can see a little better.
MEL: Until the ash puts out the flame.
DOCTOR: If that happens, we'll just re-light it. I was wrong, Mel.
You were right. You had hope. Sometimes, that's the most important
thing of all.
MEL: So, what do we do now?
DOCTOR: Whatever it takes, Mel. Whatever we can, to find the
TARDIS and escape from Pompeii.
MEL: And the Laws of Time?
DOCTOR: We'll worry about them later. *(SPIRITEDLY)* Come along
Mel, we've no time to lose.
MEL: *(GLADLY)* I'm right behind you, Doctor.
*THEY RUN INTO THE DISTANCE TOGETHER. THE SCREAMS OF THE
POMPEIANS FADE AND, FOR A WHILE, WE HEAR JUST THE SOUNDS
OF THE CONTINUING ERUPTION UNTIL THEY FINALLY FADE INTO...*

55. THE RUINS OF POMPEII, 1980
AS SCENE 1. THE DOCTOR AND MEL STROLL TOWARDS US.

MEL: It's hard to believe it was all so long ago, isn't it?

DOCTOR: Two thousand years do seem to have gone by in a flash.

MEL: You know what I mean, Doctor. You saw the Street of Plenty back there – and Valeria's inn, still standing. Well, more or less.

DOCTOR: Pompeii was buried, Mel; protected from the elements for centuries. People forgot about it – forgot its name, even. It was only in the middle of your eighteenth century that excavation work began. Pompeii is still being rediscovered – unearthed and restored – one piece at a time. It is a moment of history preserved like no other.

MEL: They can bring back the buildings – but they can't bring back the people, can they?

DOCTOR: No. They can't.

MEL: There was nothing we could have done for them, was there?

DOCTOR: We were too late, Mel. It had already happened.

MEL: *(SIGHS)* Yes, I know. I suppose we should just be grateful that it didn't happen to us too. For a while there, I thought we were never going to find our way back to the TARDIS. *(BEAT)* Do you think they survived, Doctor? I mean, Aglae and Celsinus and Valeria.

DOCTOR: I don't know, Mel. Many people died. Thousands of bodies were found within the city walls, preserved in cavities in the ash. They told the historians of your time far more about their Roman ancestors than they could ever have hoped to learn otherwise.

MEL: But those were the ones who stayed, weren't they? Thousands more must have evacuated. What happened to them?

DOCTOR: They were fighting their way through a heavy shower of volcanic ash, Mel. Some would have been lucky. Others would have died. From this point in time, there's no way of knowing the fate of any one of them. *(GENTLY)* I prefer to believe the best until I see proof to the contrary.

THEY WALK ON IN CONTEMPLATIVE SILENCE FOR A FEW SECONDS.

MEL: *(TAKES A DEEP BREATH; TRIES TO BE CHEERFUL)* I must say, it is nice to get out in the open air again, after – how long was it; three days almost? – cooped up inside the TARDIS.

DOCTOR: Yes, I meant to explain that to you.

MEL: There's no need, Doctor. I understand perfectly. We had to wait for the ash to well and truly harden around us before we could dematerialise, leaving a police box-shaped hole –

DOCTOR: – into which I could then guide the TARDIS one thousand, nine hundred and one years later –

MEL: – in time for it to be uncovered by the earthquake of 1980. This year.

DOCTOR: After that, it was simply a matter of waiting for the archaeologists to move away from their 'impossible' discovery –

MEL: – and then we could come outside. So, UNIT will be called in after all. They'll take the TARDIS away –

DOCTOR: – they'll tell my former self about it –

MEL: – and then, when all the fuss has died down –

DOCTOR: We'll simply stroll into UNIT's Italian headquarters and take my ship back without fear of creating a paradox.

MEL: It's still cheating though, isn't it? I mean, we've still used our foreknowledge to change things.

DOCTOR: But we haven't altered the events that created our foreknowledge. That's the important difference.
MEL: If you say so.
DOCTOR: As I said, it's only cheating if you get caught.
MEL: *(GROANS WITH MOCK DISAPPROVAL)* Oh, Doctor!
DOCTOR: *(CHEERFULLY)* Come on, Mel. Let's explore.
MEL STOPS HIM.
MEL: *(IN A HUSHED VOICE)* Ssh! Doctor, I think there's someone coming.
THEY TAKE COVER AS TWO PAIRS OF FOOTSTEPS APPROACH ACROSS RUBBLE. PROFESSOR SCALINI AND CAPTAIN MORAN ARE IN CONVERSATION, PRECISELY AS IN SCENE 1.
SCALINI: ...walls and columns came tumbling down. Tumbling down, I tell you! Some buildings lost whole storeys. Our people are working to prop up what's left of Pompeii, but the damage, the damage!
MORAN: *(BORED)* I can see it must be frustrating for you, Professor.
SCALINI: Frustrating? It's disastrous! An archaeological disaster!

THEME

NEVERLAND

By Alan Barnes

My name is Alan Barnes, and I don't know what I'm doing.

I was reminded of this enduring truth most recently by my mother. Having heard the first half of *Neverland* – 'I'm sure it's all terribly clever,' she said, disarmingly – she picked up on the 'metal forest' scene, where Charley first meets and gets menaced by the Never-people. 'Burnham Beeches!' she exclaimed, recognising the incident I'd dredged up from my childhood and prostituted for the sake of *Doctor Who*'s latest thrilling adventure in time and space. 'Poor thing, you must have been terrified!'

Well, I was. It was exactly how Charley describes it – six or seven, family outing, wandered off into the woodland, found myself alone, started running, calling out, ran further, got more and more lost. Probably the first and only time I've ever experienced blind panic – literally unable to see the wood for the trees. Write what you know, the textbooks say, and I was quietly chuffed by how well the scene came across on the finished disc – how much of my remembered terror was there.

'What *did* those boys do to you?' she continued.

I beg your pardon? I just got lost, didn't I? At least, tha–

'Don't you remember?' she asked. 'Really? You know, with the monsters doing the chasing, and the bit when they catch up with her?'

It turns out that what actually happened was, I was brought out of the forest they'd later use as the location for *State of Decay* by two rough-looking teenage boys. I'd been lost for about twenty or thirty minutes, apparently. The boys said they'd found me crying, and my grateful father had given them a pound note – a lot of money in those days – for their trouble. Only the thing was, on the way out an hour or so later, my mother had seen the same two boys presenting another 'lost' child to vastly relieved parents – parents who, like mine, were only too happy to show their gratitude by opening their wallets.

What these boys were up to, she reckoned, was deliberately chasing children through the woods, getting them lost in order to get rewarded when they led the sobbing tot back to safety some time later. 'I tried to get you to tell me what had happened to you in there,' she said, 'but you wouldn't say a single word about it.' And I can honestly say that I've got no recollection whatsoever of two rough-looking older boys in there with me – I must have blanked it from my mind. My *conscious* mind, at least, because listening back to *Neverland* now I can hear that I've written about not just being lost, but about being menaced by strange, scary children in the woods. 'Memories fade, but the scars still linger,' as Tears For Fears put it.

All of which means that I find myself slightly wary of writing about how *Neverland* came to be. For years now, I've been writing books and features confidently attributing this or that film, or book, or play as the source for this or that bit of this or that script; when my first *Doctor Who* audio, *Storm Warning*, came out, I was appalled, really, to see reviews and so on claiming that scene x was clearly a swipe from film y – a film I'd never even *heard* of, let alone seen. This is known as getting a taste of your own medicine; the boot being on the other foot, etc. I even got a terribly earnest letter from a religious-minded chap pointing out how the three sides of the Triskele race were actually a metaphor for the Holy Trinity, and complimenting me for writing a play about how intellectual advancement is nothing in the absence of God (or something). Er…

That's the trouble with this writing lark: once you let your words run free, you lose any and all control over their interpretation (assuming, of course, that you knew exactly what it was you were doing in the first place). For me, *Storm Warning* was about the end of the British Empire, and those valiant adventurers and entrepreneurs of the early years of the last century who fought against reason to keep the flame burning in every sphere of achievement: like Scott in the Antarctic, or Mallory and Irvine on Everest, or the passengers on the *Titanic*, or the whole generation of boys who willingly gave their lives for Flanders mud. The *R101* airship, it struck me, was the very last of these terrible and magnificent endeavours. And yet still people bang on about how Charley calls herself an 'Edwardian Adventuress', when Edward VII had been dead for twenty years. It *must* have been a mistake … mustn't it?

Neverland, on the other hand, is about dying young; it's about how we remember those who are lost before their time. My daughter, Isabella, died the day she was born. It wasn't long after Isabella that I started on the story that turned into *Neverland*, and it became very obvious to me in the course of things that I was writing about what had happened to me, to *us* - not writing about Isabella directly, but certainly about my grief, and dealing with my anger. Before I really knew it - subconsciously, again - I'd constructed a story about a girl whose short time is borrowed, who can never grow up, and about the forgotten children of Gallifrey who are using her as a means to revenge themselves on the living.

Like Charley says, we measure our lives in love - and I was writing about how we can only grieve for the times we *have* had, not for those times we've been denied. I was also writing a *Doctor Who* story, and once I'd realised where a lot of *Neverland* was coming from, I was tempted to withdraw completely, to write something less personal - but if you're not going to write from within yourself, from the heart, you may as well not bother writing at all.

So there you have it - that's where all those long, long dialogues between Charley and the Doctor came from, where the scene in which Romana meets the childhood friends she can't remember originated. There's more to *Neverland* than that, and I hope it functions as an exciting adventure story, too. Looking back at the script now, it seems to me that the only bit where I'm preaching got cut for time - that's midway through Part Three, where Vansell exchanges Romana for Rassilon's casket and Romana tells him, and the listener, how she believes the world works. It's a bloody good speech, it balances out the Romana/Vansell dynamic, and Lalla Ward delivered it beautifully in studio - but for all that, it's me talking, I think.

I guess I should explain about the cuts. There were quite a few, as you'll see, and still the damn thing filled two CDs. I thought, when I delivered it, that *Neverland* was slightly over-length - four half-hour episodes, rather than 25 minute ones. This was, as it turned out, a spectacular miscalculation. There are a lot of long, earnest and involved speeches in *Neverland*. There isn't much snappy dialogue. Speeches take longer; performers slow down, chew the words a bit, make the most of what they've got. The *Neverland* script was only ten pages or so longer than the *Storm Warning* script, but that's not a reliable guide.

So stuff had to go – cliffhangers and reprises first, hence the two-part format of the finished play. The first cliffhanger was brilliant because it was a blatant crib from one of Scott Gray's *Doctor Who Magazine* comic strips – I swiped it from an episode of *Ground Zero* (sorry, Scott). The third was a bit rubbish – virtually identical to *Storm Warning* Part Three – so no loss there. Looking back at my original outline, I see that I'd intended for the cliffhangers to be the Anti-Charley appearing on the command deck of the Time Station (Part One) and the Time Station launching on its way back to Gallifrey, leaving the Doctor and Romana behind (Part Three). My timing was going awry, even then.

Another big cut comes in Part One, where the Doctor sees a battle-ravaged future Gallifrey inside the Matrix. There's a whole scene set inside a field hospital here, with the Doctor being forced to donate unused lives to help regenerate the Imperiatrix's fallen troops. It's a slightly cheesy idea, and I'm not sure I like it. All these Gallifrey scenes were leftovers from an abandoned first draft storyline, which had an amnesiac Doctor waking up in a hospice in Gallifrey's past, like Ralph Fiennes in *The English Patient*. It was called *The Web of Time* at this stage, and the Doctor was known only as 'Puzzle' – a nod to C.S. Lewis's *The Last Battle*, because there's a huge, Armageddon-like war raging in the background. At this stage, I'd convinced myself that the world was ready for the *Doctor Who* equivalent of the *Book of Revelations*. It wasn't.

If you thought the plot of *Neverland* was convoluted, then *The Web of Time* was something else – it had Romana sending Battle-TARDISes into Rassilon's era, because she's been convinced that all of Gallifreyan history is a sort of Ouroboric loop beginning and ending with a war with an entity known as Zagreus (which, as in the finished thing, is all an elaborate con-trick… or is it?). I decided that the Gallifrey setting was inessential – it had all been done before, and better, in books like Marc Platt's *Time's Crucible*. Marc's character, the Pythia, was involved in this draft – she had the Juliette Binoche role, playing the nurse who the Doctor is telling his story to. I like the fact that *Neverland* is now a Time Lords story, not a Gallifrey story. It's weird how fans talk about 'Gallifrey stories' when we don't talk about 'Skaro stories' or 'Telos stories' – the Time Lords are really interesting, but their planet is actually very, very dull. The whole point of the Doctor running away from Gallifrey in a stolen TARDIS is that it's the most boring place in the universe.

You'll probably see lots of other little cuts here and there – nips and tucks, really. The only thing I do regret losing was a significant little fig-leaf of exposition at the end of Part Three where the Anti-Charley, Sentris, explains exactly what the 'planetoid' that the action takes place on actually *is*. There's a plot hole left gaping without it!

Neverland is a very strange story – the villain doesn't appear until the final scene for a start (and for most of the length of the play, he doesn't exist at all). I'd like to think that it goes into places that *Doctor Who* normally doesn't – although, that said, I can only agree with Dave Owen's comment in his *Doctor Who Magazine* review, in which he said that *Doctor Who* shouldn't be like this *all* the time. I can't honestly believe that it'll be as exciting to read as it is to listen to – I'm very fortunate to have had performers of the calibre of India Fisher, Paul McGann, Lalla Ward and Don

Warrington to bring it to life. Also, if you compare the printed page to the disc, you'll notice that the editing and sound design were truly exceptional; I got away with what might, very easily, have been a total disaster from beginning to end.

All the same, it's not usual for a script to still be revealing its secrets to its author nearly two years after he wrote it. I told you, I don't know what I'm doing, but I do know that there's definitely something special going on in *Neverland*. And maybe, like that Burnham Beeches scene, I'll discover more that's buried in there, as time goes by.

Neverland

CAST

THE DOCTOR	Paul McGann
CHARLEY	India Fisher
ROMANA	Lalla Ward
RASSILON	Don Warrington
MATRIX VOICES	Jonathan Rigby
	Dot Smith
	Ian Hallard
CO-ORDINATOR VANSELL	Anthony Keetch
KURST	Peter Trapani
LEVITH	Holly King
EMPEROR	Alistair Lock
UNDER-CARDINAL	Lee Moone
RORVAN	Mark McDonnell
TARIS	Nicola Boyce

PART ONE

1. THE MATRIX

(FX: STRANGE, ECHOING AMBIENCE. BRING UP INCOMPREHENSIBLE BABBLE OF HUNDREDS OF VOICES. BRING UP VOICE 1 - MALE, DEEP)

VOICE 1: Humanian Era. Earth. October the fifth, 1930. Airship R101 crashes in France ... Humanian Era. Earth. January the thirtieth, 1933. Adolf Hitler appointed Chancellor of Germany ... Humanian Era, Earth. December the tenth, 1936. Abdication of King Edward the Eighth ...*(FX: NOW BRING UP VOICE 2 BELOW - FEMALE, STRIDENT. VOICE 1 FADES OUT UNDER:)* Humanian Era. Earth. September the first, 1939. German forces invade Poland ... Humanian Era. Earth. May the twenty-seventh, 1940. Evacuation of Dunkirk begins ... Humanian Era. Earth. December the seventh, 1941. Japanese bomb Pearl Harbour ... *(ETC)*

VOICE 2: Sensorian Era. Peladon. Second quarter, 3894. Peladon granted membership of the Galactic Federation ... Sensorian Era. Fifth Galaxy. Fourth quarter, 3932. Zephon overthrows the Embodiment of Gris ... Sensorian Era. Central City. Third quarter, 3950. Mavic Chen elected Guardian of the Solar System ... *(FX: NOW BRING UP VOICE 3 BELOW - MALE, YOUNG, FALTERING. VOICE 2 FADES OUT UNDER:)* Sensorian Era. Kembal. First quarter, 4000. Representatives of Outer Galaxies meet with the Daleks ... Sensorian Era. System 4X Alpha 4. Fourth quarter, 4949. Dalek and Movellan battle fleets locked in stalemate ... Sensorian Era. Andromeda. Second quarter, 5132. Star Pioneers consumed by Wirrn ...

VOICE 3: Rassilon Era. Karn. 5725 point three. Time Lords ambush the Cult of Morbius ... *(STRAINING)* Rassilon Era. Gallifrey. 5892 point nine. Files on Doomsday Weapon stolen by - by ... *(DETERMINED)* Rassilon Era. Outer Planets. 6241 point one. Chancellor Goth visits Terserus ... *(WEAKENING AGAIN)* Rassilon Era. Etra Prime. 6776 point seven. President Romana vanishes on routine mission ... Rassilon Era. Gallifrey. 6796 point eight. D-Dalek invasion force repelled by President Romana - I ... R-Rassilon Era ... Interstitial space. 679 ... I - I can't ... 6798 point two. Dalek Time Fleet captured in Vortex and — and ... *(WHISPERED)* I can't remember. Dalek Time Fleet captured in — *(PANICKING)* I can't remember! Captured and — I can't remember. *(LOUDER)* I can't remember! *(SCREAMING, ELONGATED)* I ... can't ... rememberrrrr!!!

(FX: HOLD. ECHO. FAST CUT TO:)
(OPENING THEME)

2. INT. TARDIS

(FX: THE TIME ROTOR)

CHARLEY: So that's it, Doctor? No more Daleks, ever?
DOCTOR: That's it, Charley! Trapped in their own time pocket! Caught by the, er —
CHARLEY: — plungers?

225

DOCTOR: Plungers, yes! *(BEAT)* Do you know, I don't think even Dalek ingenuity can get them out of a paradox that tangled. A few million years in limbo, I suppose, and the Emperor might swallow his pride, call on the Time Lords …

CHARLEY: The Time Lords? Why? They'd never let the Daleks out?

DOCTOR: Oh, it's possible. The Daleks' total obliteration might cause terrible ructions in the Web of Time. History turns on several of their machinations. But it's not our job to work that one out, is it? And besides, President Romana has her own score to settle with the Daleks. She'll let them stew for - well, twenty years, at least. *(UPBEAT)* Now. Things to do. *(FX: LEVERS AND SWITCHES ON CONSOLE)* Where exactly are we? *(FX: 'WHOOSH' OF CEILING SCANNER)* The Acteon Galaxy! I've not been round these parts since I was an old man, probably! See? Spiral nebulae …asteroids made of mercury … a gas giant and a red dwarf … bo-o-oring! No, I've got a much better idea …
(FX: MUCH LEVER-PULLING AND SWITCH FLICKING)

CHARLEY: What's the whirling Dervish impression in aid of?

DOCTOR: Places to go! People to see! *(BEAT)* It's a surprise. You'll like it. Not a lot, but you'll like it …*(FX: MORE SWITCHES)* *(TO HIMSELF)* Let's see. Sumaron Era, dateline 9235 point three …

CHARLEY: *(SARCASTIC)* Oh, don't mind me. I'll just stand here at the back, quiet as a mouse, looking pretty and pouting? *(LOUDER)* I said, I'll just stand here at the back, quiet as a mouse, looking —

DOCTOR: *(DISTRACTED)* Good idea!

CHARLEY: Do you know, Doctor, sometimes you get right on my … wick. *(BEAT; THEN, GRANDLY)* I am going for a bath. I may be some time.

DOCTOR: *(STILL DISTRACTED)* Mmm! *(TO HIMSELF)* Now, is that before or after the Megaluthian Slimeskimmers explode the third planet? Think, think …

CHARLEY: *(STILL LOUD)* And after my bath, I've invited some people round for tea. The Emperor Caligula, Lucretia Borgia, the Mountain Mauler of Montana and the Terrible Zodin. Charming couple, the Zodins, but their table manners leave a lot to be — *(BREAKS OFF)* Doctor. *(BEAT; THEN, URGENTLY)* Doctor!

DOCTOR: *(STILL NOT PAYING ATTENTION)* Good! Fine! Whatever!

CHARLEY: No, Doctor — look! *(FX: DISTANT MATERIALISATION SOUND)* Up on the scanner, just there to the right — that dull grey box — is that a TARDIS?

DOCTOR: Sorry, what!?!
(FX: ANOTHER DISTANT MATERIALISATION. AND ANOTHER. AND ANOTHER)

CHARLEY: And there's another — and another — and another! Are they coming for the Daleks, do you think?

DOCTOR: *(TO HIMSELF)* No no no - not yet! Not just yet!
(FX: MORE MATERIALISATIONS)

CHARLEY: More of them! Well, it's best they go in mob-handed, I suppose…

DOCTOR: *(TO HIMSELF)* Just like before. Battle-TARDISes in an escort formation. *(TO CHARLEY)* Charley, I don't think it's the Daleks the Time Lords are after — it's us!

3. INT. TIME STATION (CONSOLE CHAMBER)

(FX: A VAST AREA OF BLEEPING HIGH TECHNOLOGY - HALFWAY BETWEEN AIR TRAFFIC CONTROL AND THE CONNING TOWER OF A SUBMARINE. CALM COMPUTER VOICE RUNNING OVER)

COMPUTER VOICE: All systems fully operational. Time Station readied for flight. All units to their posts. Repeat, all units to their posts. *(BEAT, THEN REPEAT:)* All systems fully operational. Time Station readied for flight. All units to their posts. Repeat, all units to their posts ... *(ETC)*

(FX: SWISHING OF ELECTRONIC DOORS)

ROMANA: *(HURRIED)* Co-ordinator Vansell! Am I to assume that the Agency has located the Doctor?

VANSELL: *(SMOOTHLY)* Madam President. May the Star of Rassilon guide you, His Wisdom inform you and His Sash be your protection in the vastness of your duties—

ROMANA: *(TETCHILY)* Yes yes yes. Can we just dispense with the pomp? *(BEAT)* Where is he?

VANSELL: The Type Forty Time Capsule known to have been misappropriated by the Doctor is currently — *(FX: BLEEPS)* — drifting in the Acteon Galaxy, co-ordinates 7729 gamma seven, nineteenth span. TARDISes with full offensive capabilities are blocking all entrances to the Vortex across five million consecutive years. Doubtless the Doctor will be twisting like a Slithery Nematode - but he shan't be wriggling off this hook this time.

ROMANA: You have a tortured way with metaphor, Co-ordinator. How soon can this Time Station be within range?

VANSELL: A mere seven microspans, Madam President.

ROMANA: Then make it so. *(TO HERSELF)* Oh, Doctor. Of all the countless billions of people in the whole of space and time — why did it have to be you?

4. INT. TARDIS

(FX: ATMOS AS BEFORE. MORE MATERIALISATIONS. MORE SWITCHES)

CHARLEY: But why the panic, Doctor? Surely the Time Lords won't harm you, of all people!

DOCTOR: On past form, I wouldn't like to bet on that. Excuse me. *(BEAT)* Thank you. Look, Charley - another seven TARDISes! What a reception.

CHARLEY: Should be flattered, really. I mean —

DOCTOR: Ssh sh sh! Listen - there's a message coming through!

VOICE: *(DEEP, OMINOUS, TRANSMITTED VIA TARDIS CONSOLE)* Calling occupants of rogue time capsule. The High Council of Gallifrey demands you power down your vessel and await further instructions. Repeat, power down your— *(CUTS OFF DEAD)*

DOCTOR: Yes yes yes, power down your vessel, yadda yadda yadda. Don't think we need to hear any more, do we?

CHARLEY: You never know, it might be something important ...

DOCTOR: Important? The Time Lords? Oh no. It's bound to be something really ... dreary. *(MOCKING PONDEROUS GERIATRIC)* 'We, the dull men in big collars, have convened an enquiry into the matter of your involvement in the recent Nimon assault on planet Earth and expect you to submit evidence of your actions in detail so stultifyingly unnecessary it will make your head bleed.' *(LOUDLY)* Well, I won't do it!

CHARLEY: So there.

DOCTOR: Exactly. Now, let's see if there isn't a way past this little blockade ...

CHARLEY: Doctor ...

DOCTOR: Mm?

CHARLEY: Doctor, what's that TARDIS doing - that one, there?

DOCTOR: *(CASUALLY)* Oh, that one. Well, that halo effect is what you get, you see, when a battle-TARDIS opens up its warp silos just prior to the launch of a cluster of precision-targetted Time Torpedoes. *(BEAT)* Time Torpedoes?!? They wouldn't dare!

(FX: TIME TORPEDOES LAUNCHING - A NOISE LIKE WHOOSHING DARTS, BUILDING IN PITCH AS THEY CLOSE IN ON THE TARDIS)

CHARLEY: *(DRILY)* I think they just have.

DOCTOR: Action stations! Action stations! *(TO CHARLEY)* That's right, stand there.

CHARLEY: Shouldn't we be taking, um, 'evasive action' or something?

DOCTOR: Oh no. Evasive action is exactly what they'll be expecting us to take — so that's exactly what we won't do!

CHARLEY: ... and so we're just going to sit here and get blasted across the spaceways? Oh, good plan, Doctor!

DOCTOR: Charley, Charley, Charley — *(WITHOUT TAKING A BREATH)* the Time Lords want us to take evasive action because they know that the second the TARDIS dematerialises in whatever direction they'll be ready to pluck us out of the vortex and reel us in to who-knows-where. Twenty-nine seconds to impact! *(BEAT - THEN, GABBLING)* On the other hand, if the Time Torpedoes hit we'll be frozen in a microsecond of space-time for several centuries, long enough for the Time Lords to over-ride the TARDIS's entrance protocols and drag us out to who-knows-where. *(BEAT)* Eighteen seconds!

CHARLEY: Doctor, if they've got us where they want us whatever we do, can't we just avoid all the unpleasantness of being hit by those really rather large and alarming missiles and just, well, give ourselves up?

DOCTOR: Absolutely not! Nine seconds!

CHARLEY: Why?!?

DOCTOR: Because I'm the Doctor — and whatever happens, whatever the odds, I never, ever, never give up! Brace yourself, Charley — *(FX: AND SUDDENLY THE ROARING OF THE TIME TORPEDOES, WHICH HAS BUILT TO AN ABSOLUTE CRESCENDO, SLOWS, SLIPS — THE SOUND REVERSING, HICCUPING)*

CHARLEY: Is that it?

DOCTOR: I don't underst— Oh yes I do! Hear that? *(BEAT)* Some sort of time slippage crossing the torpedoes' trajectory — sliding through space-time, stealing whole seconds, chewing up moments and regurgitating them, infected, back into the continuum! It's snared the torpedoes, just before impact! *(BEAT)* Hang on, it's moving again! *(FX:*

THE TORPEDOES REGAIN THEIR MOMENTUM) Charley, Charley — that lever, quick!

CHARLEY: What, this one here?

DOCTOR: That one there! Come on! The torpedoes are about to h— *(FX: MASSIVE, WEIRD-SOUNDING EXPLOSION OF TORPEDOES. AS IT DIES AWAY, WE HEAR THE AFTER-ECHOES OF THE TARDIS DEMATERIALISING ... AND INTO:)*

5. INT. TARDIS

(FX: THE SOUND OF THE TARDIS' DEMATERIALISATION CONTINUES ON, BUT BEGINS TO PICK UP SPEED ... AND THEN SLOWS ... SPEEDS UP AGAIN, REVERSES, CONSUMES ITSELF - SIMILAR TO THE EFFECT RUN OVER THE SOUND OF THE TIME TORPEDOES PREVIOUSLY. FOLLOWING DIALOGUE SHOULD ALSO BE TREATED IN THE SAME WAY. SUGGEST MUSIC TRACK SHOULD BE A STRONG STEADY, CONTINUING MOTIF - SO IT DOESN'T SOUND LIKE THE LISTENER'S CD IS SKIPPING!)

CHARLEY: Waaah! Doctor, what's happening to us?

DOCTOR: The TARDIS is riding the tail of the time slippage we experienced. The Time Lords won't be able to predict our path — we just have to sit it out until we're washed up wherever the phenomenon ends! Don't worry, Charley — it's perfectly — *(FALLS)* Gaaah!

CHARLEY: Doctorrrrrrrrrrrrrrrrrrrrrr *(FX: CUT FX WITH A BUMP. REGULAR CONSOLE NOISES)* Oh. It's all over. *(DOCTOR GROANS)* Doctor! Are you alright? Have you broken anything?

DOCTOR: I nearly broke an intergalactic pudding-eating record on Maruthea a few bodies ago, but right now — no. Well, nothing a hot bath and a king-sized tub of liniment won't cure.

CHARLEY: What happened back then?

DOCTOR: Oh. Right. As I was saying — ow! — the TARDIS was riding the tail of the time slippage we experienced. The Time Lords won't have been able to predict our route — terribly jumbled co-ordinates, you see, that's why it feels like we've been tumble-dried. And now —

CHARLEY: Yes?

DOCTOR: — now, we've been beached up in the wake of the slippage — *(GETS UP, CROSSES TO CONSOLE, FLICKS SWITCHES)* — so let's just see where and when that might be ...

CHARLEY: *(TO HERSELF)* Well, I may be none the wiser, but I dare say I'm better informed.

DOCTOR: *(TO HIMSELF)* Vectors stabilising ... a-ha! That's only a few hundred light-years off-course! *(TO CHARLEY)* Now. Before I was so rudely interrupted, I promised you a surprise. Tell me, Charley, how long have you been travelling with me in the TARDIS?

CHARLEY: It's not all that easy to keep track - but, well, a good six months, I suppose.

DOCTOR: Which means ... ? *(BEAT)* Something that's terribly overdue? Something extra-special? Oh, come on, Charley!

CHARLEY: *(DRY)* I haven't got the faintest idea, but I'm sure you're going to tell me.

DOCTOR: It means that it really is way past time we ... I mean, it must be round about ... Oh, look: it's like this. *(BEAT)* Happy birthday, Charley.

CHARLEY: *(INCREDULOUS)* Happy birthday?!?

DOCTOR: Happy birthday! And what tends to happen on birthdays, hm? *(BEAT)* Parties! Parties! I like parties, don't you? And I happen to think that the best assistant in the Universe deserves the best party in the Universe - so that's where we're going!

CHARLEY: I'm sorry, you've lost me. Could we start again?

DOCTOR: *(OBLIVIOUS)* Sumaron Era, dateline 9235 point three! The Jovian Fold! The Millennium Mardi Gras! You see, the Jovians - a lovely race of people, trust me - decided to celebrate the billionth span of their civilisation with a party lasting a thousand years inside a very discreet little space-time fold - which, quite coincidentally, the Time Lords know absolutely nothing about. And just as well! It's the party to end all parties and we don't want killjoys in the kitchen! The most exclusive event in history - and guess who's got an invite? *(BEAT)* You, Charley, you! You are going to have a ball. I'm actually quite jealous.

CHARLEY: I'm going to this amazing shindig - and you're not?

DOCTOR: Only one invite, I'm afraid. I told you it was exclusive. Besides ... you don't want a neurotic old nine-hundred-and-fifty-something cramping your style! Let your hair down! Go wild! There's a suite booked at the best hotel in town - I'll pick you up in a year or so!

CHARLEY: One year!?!

DOCTOR: Not long, I know, but it was the best I could do at such short notice. *(BEAT)* Oh, cheer up! You'll love it - I promise?

CHARLEY: *(SARCASTICALLY)* So what will you be doing while I'm whooping it up in the back of beyond?

DOCTOR: Ah. Well. Things. Nothing for you to worry about.

(LONG PAUSE)

CHARLEY: *(COLD)* You're going to see the Time Lords, aren't you?

DOCTOR: No, no, of course not! Why in the Seven Galaxies—

CHARLEY: *(CUTTING IN, ANGRY)* Don't lie to me, Doctor! It's written all over your face!

(BEAT)

DOCTOR: *(FLATLY)* Is it? *(BEAT)* Oh, Charley - don't turn away. It's for the best. I just have to go and sort things out with President Romana, see what all this is about. It won't take long. And then, well, I'll be back and —

CHARLEY: This is about me, isn't it? The break in the Web of Time caused by me surviving the crash of the R101. It's not over, is it? It's nothing to do with the Nimon, or the Daleks — it's me, and you know it!

DOCTOR: I don't know it, Charley. But I'm very much afraid that's what the Time Lords might think. They've been tracking the TARDIS for some time now, you see - hovering on the fringes of the Vortex, waiting for their chance to pounce. I couldn't understand why they didn't just haul us back to Gallifrey. But they're scared, you see — scared of any random factor, any tremor in causality — and they don't want any of that back home, oh no. They have to preserve the Web of Time and any chink in the Web, however slight, they fix it. It's their job.

CHARLEY: You think they'll put me back on the R101, don't you?

DOCTOR: I think that they might think that was the simplest option, yes. But I won't allow that to happen. I need to go to the Time Lords, talk to them — explain. I won't let anyone hurt you, Charley. Whatever it takes. Whatever the cost.

(BEAT)

CHARLEY: *(BITTERLY)* 'Happy birthday,' he says. 'Happy birthday, Charley.' Only it isn't my birthday, is it? It isn't my birthday because I'm not supposed to have any more birthdays. No more cake, no more candles, no more presents, not now, not ever. No more birthdays since—

DOCTOR: *(SADLY)* Oh, Charley ...

CHARLEY: — since I died. That's right, isn't it, Doctor? No more birthdays because I'm supposed to be dead, dead and burned in the wreck of an airship. Born on the day the Titanic sank, died on the R101. Poor, tragic little Charlotte Pollard, her life snuffed out before it had even begun — that's how it is, isn't it, Doctor? *(BEAT)* And now you want to hide me away in some knees-up at the end of the universe while you go and risk God-knows-what at the hands of the Time Lords on my behalf. Why's that, Doctor? Why? It's not your problem. It was me who wanted to see the world. It was me who stowed away on the R101. It was my choice, Doctor, my own stupid fault. Should have stayed at home that day, but I didn't. And that's that.

DOCTOR: But what if it isn't? What if it doesn't have to be like that?

CHARLEY: *(ANGRY)* But it is like that! *(BEAT; SOFT, SOOTHING)* Oh, you. You know who you remind me of? You're Peter Pan — the little boy who never grew up, who lived in Never-Never Land and fought with pirates and pixies. Nanny used to read me Peter Pan. I wanted to be Wendy. And now I am. Wendy Darling, having adventures in fairyland with the boy who never grew old. But, you see, Wendy grew up in the end. That's what's so sad. And poor Peter, poor little Peter, left all on his own —

DOCTOR: He didn't forget, Charley. He'd never forget. And he never left Wendy to face the crocodiles alone.

CHARLEY: You're so sweet, so kind, so caring. Too good to be true, like a dream. And all this is just dreaming. These adventures we've had, these scrapes and japes in Never-Never Land, with monsters and ray guns and magic — they've been wonderful. Better than my wildest dreams. But you can't hide in dreams. Everyone wakes up in the end. It's time to stop dreaming, Doctor. Time to grow up.

(LONG PAUSE)

DOCTOR: Charley, I — I don't know what — *(PASSIONATE)* I won't give up, Charley! Not now, not after all this time! Please, Charley — let me help you. Let me face this for you. Whatever it takes, I'll put it right and —

CHARLEY: *(INTERRUPTING, AS IF APROPOS OF NOTHING)* Doctor, remember this switch? The one marked 'Fast Return', the one I used to get us out of the Nimon problem? If I remember your description correctly, it sends the TARDIS back to its last spatio-temporal location.

DOCTOR: *(URGENT)* Charley, will you please just listen to m— *(THE PENNY DROPPING)* Fast Return. Don't touch that — Charley, no!

(FX: DEMATERIALISATION)

CHARLEY: Sorry, Doctor. It was my choice to get on board that airship. It's been a fantastic ride — but now it's time to get off. (SADLY) There is no alternative.

DOCTOR: NO!!! (FRANTIC SWITCH-FLICKING) Can't stop it! We're going back —
(FX: MATERIALISATION BEGINS)

CHARLEY: — back into the path of the Time Torpedoes. (FX: ROARING OF ENCROACHING TORPEDOES) I'm going to meet the Time Lords. Can't wait to see Gallifrey, at last.

DOCTOR: NOOOOOOOOOOOOOOOOOOOOOOOOOOOOOOOOOOOOOO
(FX: THE TORPEDOES HIT. EXPLOSION ECHOES OVER INTO —
— SILENCE.)

6. INT. TARDIS
(FX: TOTAL SILENCE. NO ATMOS)
(FX: METAL BLISTERING, BURNING)

KURST: (MALE, YOUNGISH, GUNG-HO, MUFFLED) Clear.
LEVITH: (FEMALE, CALM, OLDER, MUFFLED) Check.
(FX: A 'FWUMP' AS THE TARDIS DOORS ARE BLOWN IN. CLANGING OF METAL. RUSH OF AIR, TINGED WITH ETHEREAL EFFECTS. TARDIS CONSOLE BEGINS TO HUM INTO LIFE.)
(FX: KURST AND LEVITH STEP THROUGH, BOTH OBVIOUSLY WEARING SPACESUITS OF SOME DESCRIPTION - VOICES TINNY, MUFFLED)
KURST: We're through. Resealing doors.
(FX: CLANG OF DOORS)
LEVITH: Temporo-environment is — (FX: BLEEPS FROM METER) — stabilising. Relative time compression minus three point six.
KURST: Safe enough. (FX: CLUNKING AS HE RELEASES CATCHES ON HELMET OF SPACESUIT. DRAWS BREATH. NO LONGER MUFFLED) Better. I hate these suits.
(FX: LEVITH DOES THE SAME)
LEVITH: (UNMUFFLED) For a fully-trained Agency operative, Kurst, you seem unduly concerned with your comfort. (DEEP BREATH; CONSOLE EFFECTS CLEARLY HEARD) What has he done to the inside of this capsule?
KURST: Looks like an Ormelian brothel.
LEVITH: Like you'd know. (BEAT) Now, where —
KURST: Here, Levith. This him?
LEVITH: Dressed like a retrograde. Must be. (BEAT) How long has this capsule been frozen?
KURST: Only a few hundred years.
LEVITH: Seasoned traveller. Adjusts quickly. He's back with us, see?
DOCTOR: (WEAK, BEFUDDLED) I tell you, Lord Byron ... you're meddling with forces you don't understand — (TRAILS OFF)
LEVITH: He's ready for transport. Is that the Earth girl?
KURST: Yes. (FX: CHARLEY BREATHING) She looks almost intelligent. (BEAT) Must get lonely, rattling about in a capsule this old. You don't suppose he ... indulges?
LEVITH: Kurst, that's disgusting. (BEAT) You'll have to ask our Madam President.
KURST: She knows him?

LEVITH: You haven't heard? She went renegade for a while, travelled with him.
KURST: 'Travelled'?
LEVITH: Travelled. And that's all she did. If you know what's good for you, that is. *(BEAT)* The girl will live. Better bring the equipment in, hook her up to the time/space converter.
KURST: And the Doctor?
LEVITH: Yes, 'the Doctor'. The Doctor has a date with the President herself.

7. INT. TIME STATION (MATRIX CHAMBER)
(FX: ECHOING CHAMBER. SLIGHTLY ETHEREAL ATMOS)

DOCTOR: *(GROGGY)* Mary, Mary — you must believe me. That man is not your brother! He — *(BEAT; SURPRISED)* Oh! Oh. Not Switzerland, then. Some sort of ... chamber. Dark. *(FX: GETS UP. FOOTSTEPS ON METAL FLOOR)* Hello? Hello? *(FX: TAPS METAL WALLS)* Metal. Triple-bonded polyesium with tinclavic relief, if I'm not much mistaken. *(ALOUD, AS IF TO AUDIENCE)* Unusual composition. Very unusual. In fact, I'd go so far as to say it was specific to the hull of one particular Gallifreyan vessel - a Class Seven Supra-Orbital Time Station. *(BEAT)* Well? Am I right? *(ANGRY)* Show yourselves!
(FX: WHOMP! WHOMP! WHOMP! OF ARC-LIGHTS BEING ACTIVATED)
DOCTOR: Ah! Do you mind? Those lights really are terribly bright ...
VANSELL: *(HEARD FROM ABOVE LEFT)* Class Seven-C, actually, Doctor. But in all other respects you are, of course, infuriatingly correct.
DOCTOR: Oh, now there's a voice I recognise! *(FAIRGROUND BARKER PATOIS)* Come on! Don't be shy! Step forward Celestial Intervention Agency Co-ordinator Sevansellostophossius, hif yew pur-lease! *(MOCKING)* Oh, I'm sorry. I forget - you never were all that keen on the 'ostophossius' bit, were you? Terribly common. Prefector Zorac came up with something rather better, if I remember right...
VANSELL: If you really think I will be in the least bit affected by any sordid reminiscence relating to our time in the Academy all of six hundred years ago ...
DOCTOR: *(EXPLOSIVELY)* 'Nosebung'! That was it! Nosebung! Hm. Or was it 'Toastrack'?
VANSELL: *(PAINFULLY CONTROLLED)* That wasn't me, Doctor, and well you know it.
DOCTOR: You're quite right, Vansell. I do apologise. *(UNDER HIS BREATH)* No need to get sniffy. *(BEAT; ALOUD)* This isn't an impromptu reunion, then? No Ushas, no Koschei, no Jelpax or Magnus? No more of the Deca?
VANSELL: No, Doctor.
DOCTOR: *(RESIGNEDLY)* So what does the Agency want?
(FX: CLICKING AND WHIRRING OF ELECTRONIC DATA)
VANSELL: Charlotte Elspeth Pollard. Human. Born Hampshire, England, on the fourteenth of April, 1912. Died Bee-or-var-iss, France—
DOCTOR: — that's 'Beauvais', actually —
VANSELL: 'Beauvais', thank you. Died Beauvais, France, on the

fifth of October 1930, aged eighteen years, five months and twenty-one days.

DOCTOR: And?

VANSELL: And then: traced to deep space freighter Vanguard, 2503; Venice, Earth, 2294; the republic of Malebolgia, Earth, 2003; New York, Earth again, 1938; London, oh look, Earth ... et cetera, et cetera, et cetera. And all despite having died in Beauvais, France, on the fifth of October 1930, in the wreck of a dirigible known as the R101. What an intriguing anomaly.

(BEAT)

DOCTOR: On behalf of Charlotte Elspeth Pollard, I invoke the right clearly stated in the Archetryx Convention to be tried by an independently-assembled commission of the Temporal Powers. Harm one hair on her head in malice, Vansell, and I'll hound you to the end of reality.

ROMANA: *(FROM ABOVE RIGHT)* And I'll gladly assist you, Doctor. But there's no chance of it coming to that.

DOCTOR: *(PLEASED)* Romana! Or should that be Madam President? Whatever. Romana, will you kindly tell Co-ordinator Nosebung to stop sticking his snout in where it's not wanted?

ROMANA: It's not quite that simple, Doctor.

(BEAT)

DOCTOR: Oh, I get it. Bad cop, good cop; good cop, bad. Have you prepared my confession? Shall I sign it now?

VANSELL: *(TO ROMANA)* 'Good cop, bad cop'? This is an Earth colloquialism?

ROMANA: *(TO VANSELL)* It usually is. *(TO DOCTOR)* Doctor, I give you my promise: I will not sanction any random justice or injustice against your friend Charlotte Pollard.

DOCTOR: Friends call her Charley.

ROMANA: Charley, then. She's still in your TARDIS, and safe.

VANSELL: At least, as safe as anyone - now.

8. INT. TARDIS

(FX: TARDIS ATMOS)

CHARLEY: *(WOOZY)* What - where -

LEVITH: *(BUSINESSLIKE) (FX: BLEEPS OF EQUIPMENT)* Disoriented? Not surprising. You just sit tight in your nice Earth chair.

CHARLEY: Who are you? And — *(REALISING SHE'S STRAPPED IN)* — let me out of these straps! Where's the Doctor? What have you done with the Doctor?

KURST: *(TO LEVITH)* Thalia's bones! Are all humans this noisy?

LEVITH: *(TO KURST)* I've only met a few.

CHARLEY: Please! It's me you want. Wherever he is, whatever you've done to him, it's not his fault — it's mine. I'll do whatever you want so long as he's safe.

KURST: *(TO LEVITH)* Loyal, isn't she? Interesting, that.

LEVITH: Kurst, you're obsessed. *(TO CHARLEY, ENUNCIATING SLOWLY SO CHARLEY WILL UNDERSTAND)* Don't you worry, Earth girl. Your friend the Doctor is all right. My name is Levith, this is —

CHARLEY: *(JUST AS DELIBERATELY)* — Kurst, I know. I am not subnormal.

KURST: *(AMUSED, TO LEVITH)* Oho! Picked up some tricks from her master...

LEVITH: Drop it, Kurst. *(TO CHARLEY)* We represent the Celestial Intervention Agency. We're not going to do you any harm. We need to prepare you for a small ... procedure. So long as you don't resist, it won't hurt at all.

KURST: We can't guarantee that, you understand. But if it doesn't work, Earth girl, you won't live long enough to feel the pain.

LEVITH: Then again, neither will we.

CHARLEY: *(WAILING)* No!

9. INT. TIME STATION (MATRIX CHAMBER)

VANSELL: Doctor, tell us how you first escaped the Time Torpedoes?

DOCTOR: Ah. Well. You know. Improvisation, genius, a well-turned trouser, a rapier wit ...

ROMANA: *(REPROACHFULLY)* Doctor ...

VANSELL: A wave of time distortion, hm?

DOCTOR: Time distortion? Oh! You've brought me here to talk about time distortion? *(BRIGHTENING)* Well, I'm your man! I've been warped and flipped and slipped and spun through more temporal phenomena than a Mexxonian Dragon has had hot dinners!

VANSELL: But this particular type of time distortion - you have encountered it several times recently, have you not?

DOCTOR: *(CAREFULLY)* Time factors do seem to have played a large part in my life of late — but that sort of slippage, no. At least, I don't think so.

VANSELL: Then I suggest you pay closer attention to what's going on right beneath your ... nose. We at the Agency have observed that very form of slippage many times over the last few quarters. Gallifrey's scientists have been struggling to categorise it. In many ways, it behaves quite unlike any other form of causal disturbance ever before detected. But one possible explanation has presented itself in one of the more esoteric branches of academia. The research was suppressed, naturally.

DOCTOR: *(MOCKING)* Naturally.

ROMANA: The distortion fits a thesis which has been among the Thinking Circles for a long time — one which has never been accepted into our Codex of Disciplines. *(BEAT)* 'Anti-Time.'

DOCTOR: Ha! 'The spider in the Web of Time' - that old chestnut? Romana, 'Anti-Time' has been around longer than the Flat Galaxy Society, but it's given far less credence!

VANSELL: Officially.

DOCTOR: Now, how does it go? 'The Web of Time could not exist until the great Rassilon built the Eye of Harmony, the hitching-post of chronology, that which does not flux nor wither nor change its state ...'

ROMANA: 'The Eye of Harmony created a universe of 'positive' time, finite time. Gallifrey anchored the continuity of the universe. But just as matter has its counterpart in anti-matter, just as every action has an equal and opposite reaction, then, by all the immutable laws of the universe, positive Time - the Web of Time - must have its shadow ...'

DOCTOR: '"Anti-Time" ... as intractable and destructive a force to causality as anti-matter is to space. Something with no past, no present, no future ... a perpetuity of meaningless chaos, a now with no beginning or end.'*(BEAT)* Elegant, brilliant, thoroughly logical - and utter gibberish. I've been trolling about the Space/Time Vortex for a lot longer than any of you. If there really was another plane of cause and effect, don't you think that maybe, just maybe, after all these centuries, I might have noticed?

(BEAT)

ROMANA: The Web of Time is stretched to breaking. Observe the screens. *(FX: BUZZ OF ELECTRONIC DATA)* We see time slippage in the Sensorian, Humanian and Sumaron eras. The Fifty Years' War of the Kosnax and the Uhrai is now into its third century. In the Ring System of the Veta Worlds, stones, and not reptiles, are emerging as the dominant life form. Earth was barely stable until this nexus, when the wrong President was elected into executive control of this major land-mass ...

VANSELL: The Agency no longer has enough operatives to maintain continuity across the universe, despite a draft of the Temporal Powers. History is leaking like a sieve.

ROMANA: If we plot these slippages back, however, a remarkable pattern emerges. We see the earliest major wave of distortion centred around the planet Earth in the 1930s ... then deep space 2503; back to Earth in 2294, 2003, 1938, 1906 and so on; each outbreak sees the distortion expanding, sometimes trailing off, but most usually infecting histories wherever it goes.

DOCTOR: You talk like it's a virus.

ROMANA: Precisely.

DOCTOR: *(SLOWLY)* And you think ... Charley is the carrier?

ROMANA: Not exactly. But she might be Patient Zero. *(DARK)* If the universe of Anti-Time was real, Doctor, if it were an actual place, how do you suppose it might be accessed?

DOCTOR: I don't know. Some kind of gateway? A rip, a tear, a breach... a hole?

ROMANA: *(GRIMLY)* Go on.

DOCTOR: *(AGHAST)* Charley?

VANSELL: In itself, the Earth girl's survival is not the problem. She was nothing. She would amount to nothing. Her descendants would be nobodies. She's nothing special, Doctor. She wouldn't go on to cure a disease, or start a war, or discover a planet. By rights, her survival would be but the tiniest hiccup, easily made and easily mended. But her living was a rift, her very being a breach. Charlotte Pollard is a rip in the fabric of space/time, a breach with presence and physicality.

ROMANA: And it's through her we believe these distortions are flowing — a living conduit to a dimension which should never have met ours.

VANSELL: Well, Doctor? Have you nothing to say?

DOCTOR: *(LOST TO HIMSELF)* Charley ... oh, Charley. What have I done? I should have realised, should have seen it. *(BEAT)* Ramsay! Of course, he could sense it – as a Vortisaur, he wanted to feed from it.

236

That's why he became so unmanageable...

VANSELL: Doctor, please do pay attention. Time is short. Time, in fact, is running out. The Matrix, as you know, is a vast repository housing the combined intelligences of all Time Lords, past and present, living and dead. We have turned the entirety of the Matrix over to remembering all of history, as it should be recorded - so.

(FX: ELECTRONIC WHOOSH! - AND CUE BABBLE OF VOICES FROM Sc. 1)

MATRIX VOICES: *(SCREAMING)* Can't remember! I can't remember! *[ETC]*

(FX: ANOTHER WHOOSH! VOICES CUT OFF)

VANSELL: But as you can hear, the Matrix is cracking under the strain. And if the Agency can no longer determine the true course of recorded time, well ... *(TO ROMANA)* I think, Madam President, that the Doctor should see for himself.

ROMANA: If he must.

VANSELL: The chamber in which you have been standing is not a cell, Doctor. It is, in fact, a portal into the Matrix - an Eighth Door, if you will, over which you are currently positioned. There is a projected future, based on the likelihood of a continuing and incremental incursion of these Anti-Time phenomena into our universe. As ever, you will have an actual presence in the projection ... but there's no substitute for being there, eh, Doctor? Tell us what you see.

(FX: AN EVEN DEEPER ELECTRONIC WHOOSH!)

DOCTOR: No - wait - I'm not readyyyyyyyyyyyyyyyyyyyyy—

10. THE MATRIX (DARK GALLIFREY)

(MUSIC: BIG, SWEEPING, DARKLY MAJESTIC THEME)
(FX: UP CITY ATMOS. SPACESHIPS ROARING OVERHEAD. DISTANT EXPLOSIONS. CRACKLE OF FLAMES. SOUNDS OF SOBBING AND CRYING FOR HELP FROM OFF-MIC, LIKE LONDON IN THE BLITZ)
(FX: WHOOSH! AND THE DOCTOR IS DUMPED INTO THE SCENE WITH A THUMP)

DOCTOR: Whoa! *(TO THE SKY)* Thank you very much, Vansell! *(TO HIMSELF)* So where is this? *(BEAT)* A city, burning! And above it ... a vast, black citadel, hulking over the landscape! *(BEAT)* Hang on, those stars look just like ... the Kasterborean Borealis ... and there, Mount Cadon, her peak obscured by smog ... This — is this — *(QUIETLY, BOGGLING)* — Gallifrey?

OLD MAN: *(FROM NOWHERE) (SOLEMN, DIGNIFIED, POWERFUL TONES)* That word has not been used here in many, many years.

DOCTOR: *(SURPRISED)* Oh! I didn't see — Where did you spring from, by the way? *(BEAT)* You know, old man, your aspect is terribly familiar — like I've always known I'm going to know you, except not—

OLD MAN: *(CUTTING THE DOCTOR'S BABBLING DEAD, SORROWFUL)*
Gallifrey? O, Gallifrey ... Her forests are cracked and dead, the silver leaves of the Cadonwood trees withered and perished. The skies which once danced with lights - purple and green and brilliant yellow - now broil, heavy with the stinking exhalations of the charnel-house. Those of her people who are

237

not beaten and cowed have grown cruel, their hearts hardened to ice. This is the empire of Zagreus.

DOCTOR: Zagreus? Did you say — Zagreus?

OLD MAN: *(CRYPTICALLY)* There is no alternative.

DOCTOR: *(TO HIMSELF)* 'Zagreus sits inside your head/Zagreus lives among the dead'... and something else. Or someone. Think, Doctor, think! Brain like a ... *(SLOW, REMEMBERING)*... a spiral staircase ... I was with Charley, that's right, and —

(FX: THROUGHOUT, A SPACESHIP HAS BEEN ROARING OVERHEAD. THE BEGINNING OF THE LONG, LOW WHISTLE OF A BOMB FALLING...)

OLD MAN: My friend, might I suggest you move away?

DOCTOR: *(COMING OUT OF HIS REVERIE)* Sorry, what? I mean — *(IT DAWNS ON HIM THAT THE BOMB IS ABOUT TO STRIKE)* Oh no!

(FX: HUGE, WEIRD-SOUNDING EXPLOSION. CUT IN MATRIX 'WHOOSH!' AS OLD MAN TRANSPORTS HE AND DOCTOR TO AN INTERIOR — A FIELD HOSPITAL. MORE GROANS OF AGONY, WEEPING)

DOCTOR: The bomb — it — Ah. An unreal landscape, of course. *(TO OLD MAN)* You must be very powerful, to shift about the Matrix with such ease.

OLD MAN: If you say so.

DOCTOR: *(INTRIGUED)* I'm sorry? Do I know y—

(FX: COMMOTION. DOORS BURST OPEN — CASUALTY-TYPE SCENE. WOUNDED MAN BEING PUSHED THROUGH ON TROLLEY, SURROUNDED BY SHOUTING MEDICS)

MEDIC 1: Out of the way — casualty coming through! *(TO DOCTOR)* Come on, move! Yes, you! This is a hospital, not a loungearium!

DOCTOR: Oh, yes! Sorry — sorry!

MEDIC 2: *(JABBERING DETAILS SIMULTANEOUSLY)* Hearts rates falling fast! BP 228 over six! Blue corpuscle count — point nine four per hundred! We're losing him!

(FX: TROLLEY SQUEAKS TO A HALT. PINGING OF TECHNOLOGY. DOUBLE FLAT-LINE HEARD)

MEDIC 1: Not if I can help it! Nurse — the energy paddles! Quick!

(FX: ACTIVATING A SORT OF CARDiAC MASSAGER. WHINE AS IT CHARGES UP)

MEDIC 2: Charging!

MEDIC 1: Clear!

(FX: A DOUBLE 'WHUMP!' OF ELECTRICITY. GROAN FROM PATIENT)

MEDIC 1: Again!

(FX: THE DOUBLE 'WHUMP!' AGAIN. REPEAT IN B/G WHILE DOCTOR/OLD MAN DIALOGUE BELOW CONTINUES OVER.)

(ROUND-TROLLEY DIALOGUE ENDS WITH:)

(FX: DOUBLE FLAT-LINE CUTS DEAD)

MEDIC 2: Oh no — that's —

MEDIC 1: Wait for it. Wait for it — now!

(FX: BANG ON CUE, DOUBLE HEART-BEAT PINGS HEARD ON MACHINE)

MEDIC 1: I'm not losing anyone today!

(MEANWHILE:)

DOCTOR: *(TO OLD MAN)* Those injuries — they're five-dimensional! The poor devil — you can see those rents moving across his body! *(BEAT)* What's happened here? Why the devastation above —

and the carnage down here?
OLD MAN: This is war, friend.
DOCTOR: War? Gallifrey is at war? Who with? Who would dare? The Daleks? The Cybermen? The Sontarans? Or some other terrible enemy I've not yet encountered ...
OLD MAN: Oh, all of those. But most of all, this planet is at war with... herself.
DOCTOR: Herself? What do you mean, herself—?
(MEDIC 1 BUTTS IN FROM END OF PREVIOUS DIALOGUE)
MEDIC 1:   *(INTERRUPTING DOCTOR)* Hey! You, the Objector! I want you on tha gurney now!
DOCTOR: Who, me? *(HE'S GRABBED BY MEDIC 2)* Aah!
MEDIC 2:   What is it — got cold feet now it's time to deliver? You Objectors are all the same!
(FX: CRASH! AS THE DOCTOR IS SLAMMED DOWN ONTO TROLLEY)
MEDIC 1:   Hold him still! Prepare him for immediate chronoplasty! This patient won't be stable for long!
DOCTOR: *(STRUGGLING)* There's no need for all this ... violence. Tell me what it is you want!
MEDIC 2:   You're a Donor, you donate. *(TO MEDIC 1)* How many should I take?
MEDIC 1:   By the look of him, he can spare six.
DOCTOR: Six? Six what? *(REALISATION DAWNING)* Six lives?
MEDIC 2:   You know the rules. If you won't fight in the armies of our glorious Imperiatrix, if you Object — then you Donate, willingly or otherwise!
MEDIC 1:   This proud soldier has used up all his regenerations in the struggle against the forces which menace our people! You, you snivelling coward — the least you can do is surrender a few of your lives with good grace, so he might continue his service in the name of the Imperiatrix herself!
DOCTOR: You don't understand — this is my eighth body!
MEDIC 1:   *(SCATHINGLY)* Oh dear. *(TO MEDIC 2)* Proceed.
DOCTOR: Please, listen — I don't have six lives to spare!
MEDIC 1:   Then you should have been more careful, shouldn't you?
MEDIC 2:   Attaching Hadron socket now!
(FX: BUZZING SOUND)
DOCTOR: *(SCREAMS)*
MEDIC 2:   Socket in place!
MEDIC 1:   Drain him!
(FX: BUZZING STEPS UP A PITCH)
DOCTOR: *(AGONISED)* Stop — please — please!!! I — *(ROARING OUT LOUD — INTO THE SKY, NOT THE SCENE)* No! This is not my reality! Show me something else! Show me who's to blame for all this!
(FX: MATRIX 'WHOOSH!' AGAIN — AND NOW WE'RE INSIDE A VAST HALL: THE PANOPTICON. THRONGING, NOISY CROWD)
DOCTOR: *(TO HIMSELF)* Whoa! *(BEAT)* I'm not going to get used to this, am I, old m— *(BEAT)* Hey! Where's he gone? Hm. I can't help thinking that I knew you from somewhere — or maybe I will do. *(BEAT)* Where am I now — *(INCREDULOUS)* The Panopticon? Don't approve of the decor — and certainly not this nasty heads-on-spikes motif—

CRONE: *(INTERRUPTING)* Get out of the way, will you, Mad One — talking to yourself like some simple Shobogan!
DOCTOR: Sorry, I ...
CRONE: You are obstructing the view!
DOCTOR: View? — What, of that podium?
CRONE: Cretin!
(FX: A VAST FANFARE SOUNDS. CROWD NOISES UP IN PITCH, EXCITED CHEERS)
CRONE: She's here! She's coming!
TANNOY VOICE: Silence! Silence for your Imperiatrix!
(FX: CROWD NOISES DROP AWAY. NEAR SILENCE. A FEW COUGHS)
DOCTOR: *(TO CRONE)* So who is she, this Imperiatrix?
CRONE: Ssh! Do you want to get us both executed?
(FX: AHEAD, BESIDE A PODIUM ABOUT 100 FEET AWAY, WE HEAR A THRUMMING AS HUGE DOORS SLIDE OPEN ELECTRONICALLY. HEELED FOOTSTEPS OVER METAL)
DOCTOR: *(TO HIMSELF)* She seems — I don't know, familiar ...
CRONE: Ssh!
(FX: FOOTSTEPS DO PRECISE, SQUEAKY SWIVEL AND STOP)
(THE IMPERIATRIX PAUSES TO SURVEY THE CROWD, THEN SPEAKS IN CRACKED, HARD TONES. SHE IS, UNMISTAKABLY, ROMANA - A 'WICKED WITCH OF THE WEST' ROMANA)
IMPERIATRIX ROMANA: *(ADDRESSING CROWD)* My people. I am your Imperiatrix. Today, you will bear witness to a judgement on our enemies.
DOCTOR: *(TO HIMSELF, INCREDULOUS)* Romana?!? No, no — it can't be!
IMPERIATRIX ROMANA: *(CONTINUING ADDRESS)* We strive to attain unending glory for all our people — for the furtherment of our civilisation, the one true society. Yet there are those who challenge our beliefs — those who follow different paths, other timelines.
(STIR OF UNREST AMONG CROWD)
IMPERIATRIX ROMANA: Such beliefs cannot be permitted!
(CROWD CHEER)
IMPERIATRIX ROMANA: I am to communicate with a representative of one such group. *(FX: BLEEPS)* Observe the viewscreen. *(FX: DISTANT, STATICISED CRACKLE)* *(TO SCREEN)* Identify yourself to us.
EMPEROR DALEK: *(VIA VIEWSCREEN)* I ... am the Emperor ... of the Dalek race! Time Lady, I demand you authorise our release!
(ANGRY JEERS FROM CROWD)
IMPERIATRIX ROMANA: *(TO DALEK)* You dare demand anything of us? Emperor Dalek. We are proud to declare that you, and your entire fleet of Daleks — you are our prisoners!
EMPEROR DALEK: *(VIA VIEWSCREEN)* No. The Dalek fleet is held in a time pocket, here in the darkness of the Vortex. But you need us. Your continuity cannot survive without us. Release us now!
IMPERIATRIX ROMANA: You are an enemy of our people. Your request is denied! *(TO CROWD)* This creature, and the remaining battalions of its wretched race, we hold outside the realms of space/time. We now have the ability to extinguish these Daleks in an instant, crush them within the bounds of their prison. We have decided that this course

must now be carried out!
(ECSTATIC CHEERING FROM CROWD)
DOCTOR: No! No — this isn't how we do things!
EMPEROR DALEK: *(VOICE RISING IN PITCH)* Time Lady — you cannot exterminate the Dalek race!
IMPERIATRIX ROMANA: Oh yes I can.
(FX: BLEEPS. GATHERING, SWIRLING SOUND ON VIEWSCREEN, AS IF A
TORNADO IS WHIPPING UP AROUND THE EMPEROR)
EMPEROR DALEK: Please. Have … pi-ty.
IMPERIATRIX ROMANA: 'Pity'? *(BEAT)* I don't think so.
(FX: THE 'TORNADO' REACHES A CRESCENDO - AND THEN … BOOM!
PAUSE. STATIC FROM VIEWSCREEN)
IMPERIATRIX ROMANA: So. *(BEAT)* Does anyone else care to disagree with me?
(CUE HUGE CHEERING FROM CROWD)
DOCTOR: *(SHOUTING TO BE HEARD ABOVE THE CROWD)* This is terrible — terrible! Romana! Romana — the Web of Time! What about the Web of Time?
CRONE: What's wrong with you?
CROWD MEMBER 1: He challenges our Imperiatrix!
CROWD MEMBER 2: Traitor!
DOCTOR: But this isn't how things should be!
CRONE: Teach this traitor a lesson!
CROWD MEMBER 1: Kill him!
CROWD MEMBER 2: Rip his hearts out!
DOCTOR: What? Please, leave me — aaow!
CROWD: *(VARIOUSLY)* Traitor! Kill him! Rip his hearts out! *[ETC]*
DOCTOR: (STRUGGLING) No - please — no — I — I didn't—
AAAAAAAAAAAAAAAAAAAAAAAAAAAAAAAAA
(CONTINUE INTO:)

11. INT. TIME STATION (MATRIX CHAMBER)
(FX: THE BIG MATRIX WHOOSH! AGAIN. CHAMBER ATMOS)

DOCTOR: *(FROM END OF Sc 10)* AAAAAAAAAAAAAAAAAAAAAA
(BIG INTAKE OF BREATH. SHUDDERS)
VANSELL: I take it, Doctor, you found the projection - uncongenial?
ROMANA: That's enough, Vansell. *(TO THE WALLS)* Matrix Chamber - bring the Doctor up.
(FX: ELECTRONIC SKITTERING. HYDRAULIC THRUM)
DOCTOR: Whoa! The architecture reconfigures itself?
ROMANA: *(STEPPING FORWARD, NOW ON THE DOCTOR'S LEVEL)* Transcendentally.
DOCTOR: Very good, very good …
ROMANA: I know what you saw.
DOCTOR: Do you?
ROMANA: The projection never changes. The Web of Time in shreds. Time collapsing in on itself. The fall of Gallifrey, the corruption of the oldest civilisation. Chaos and anarchy loosed upon us all. A new order. A twisted one.
DOCTOR: Yes, I saw it. I saw what might happen to Gallifrey, to —

241

(BEAT) — her leaders. But if this vision is supposed to make me recant, to make me see the folly of my choices in the past, to approve the unmaking of a single life for the sake of order — Romana, I won't. The choice is yours. Go back in time; erase my deeds, the last few months of my life; blast me from the whole of history, even. Maybe I made a mistake, taking Charley with me; but I stand by my mistakes - and my promises too. If you destroy Charley, rightly or wrongly, then I won't let you do it with a clean conscience. There has to be another way. And while my hearts are still beating, I swear to you I'll find it.

ROMANA: I know that, Doctor. Even if I was prepared to sanction the intervention necessary, to avoid the breach being opened in the first place, it'd be too late. This distortion, this disturbance, has grown too large to be controlled. *(SLOWLY)* But what if there was another way?

DOCTOR: Then I'd take it.

ROMANA: It might be — dangerous. And the chances of success very slight.

DOCTOR: Oh, you know me, Romana - I like long odds.

VANSELL: And you'd go along with anything, to put things right, so long as no harm came to Miss Pollard?

DOCTOR: I think so, yes.

(BEAT)

ROMANA: *(FORMAL)* Very well. Doctor, our only realistic approach is to follow the time distortion to its source —

VANSELL: And destroy it. Lay waste to the scourge of Anti-Time at its root, before it lays waste to us. Always and forever.

DOCTOR: You want to cross over into a dimension which may or may not even exist — and wipe it out?

VANSELL: Oh, we have reason to believe the thinking is sound. There are — records, Doctor. Ancient records. But that's not important now. Will you join us? Will you help us?

ROMANA: *(TO THE DOCTOR)* Will you help me?

DOCTOR: Yes. Yes, you know I will. *(BEAT)* But how? How in the name of Rassilon are you going to transport yourselves into this universe of Anti-T— *(DRIES AS REALISATION STRIKES)* Ah.

VANSELL: Obvious, isn't it, Doctor? We'll be taking the same route as the time distortion. Through the space/time breach. Through Charlotte Elspeth Pollard.

12. INT. TARDIS

(FX: TARDIS ATMOS)
(FX: BLEEP OF HI-TECHNOLOGY)

KURST: That's the Space/Time converter installed and operational. Though whether or not it's fully compatible with this antique - well, who can say?

LEVITH: Then run through the data codes again, Kurst. We only have one chance to get this right, and I don't plan on being squashed to a singularity thanks to a faulty plug. *(TO CHARLEY)* Now, girl —

CHARLEY: That's 'Charlotte', thank you.

LEVITH: 'Charlotte'. *(BEAT; THEN, SOFTER)* Sorry. Tense. Pressure of work. This is the difficult bit. This device here is what we call a sub-proton accelerator - a special machine which, um... stimulates matter at the atomic level?

CHARLEY: I haven't the foggiest idea what you're talking about, but it looks a bit like one of those things they have in hospitals now - you know, a Z-ray thing.

LEVITH: An X-ray, you mean?

CHARLEY: X-ray, Y-ray, Z-beam - what's the difference?

LEVITH: Never mind. We're going to position these around you and soon - well, things will start to happen. You may feel yourself... changing.

CHARLEY: Changing? Changing how?

LEVITH: You're special, you see. Very special. There's more to you than meets the eye. Charlotte - I don't know how to tell you what you are. If I told you you were a unique cosmic phenomenon, a four-dimensional archway into a universe, anathema to our own, you . wouldn't understand me, let alone believe it. Be still.

CHARLEY: *(STRUGGLING)* What do you think you're — ow! *(BEAT)* If you see the Doctor afterwards, Levith — give him my love. If you'd understand that, of course.

LEVITH: *(TO KURST)* Activate!

(FX: A PULSING BEAM - FWUB, FWUB, FWUB ...)

CHARLEY: *(GASPS IN PAIN)* Uuuuuuh!

13. INT. TIME STATION (CORRIDOR)
(THE DOCTOR, ROMANA AND VANSELL, WALKING FAST)

DOCTOR: This is madness, Romana! If you're wrong —

ROMANA: Then the process should make no difference to Charley. It's an acceleration of matter — not all that different from a simple teleportation.

VANSELL: And how many times in all of your famous exploits have you had your atoms split, broadcast and reassembled in the name of derring-do, Doctor — hm?

DOCTOR: Lots, I suppose, but—

ROMANA: — but the point is, Doctor, you think we're right about her. You know what effect it's going to have on her. But it doesn't have to be for long — she'll restabilise once we're through, be her normal self again. And once we've discovered how to stem the flow of Anti-Time, there'll be no reason not to let she, and you, go. I'm sure that, under the circumstances, given your co-operation, Co-ordinator Vansell will be minded to turn a blind eye to an error in the CIA's — accounting.

VANSELL: The Agency might be — persuaded, yes.

DOCTOR: Romana, I wasn't sure about it at first, but I'm warming to your style of government.

ROMANA: I'll take that as a compliment, shall I? We're here.

(FX: SWISHING OF ELECTRONIC DOORS — AND DIRECTLY INTO:)

14. INT. TIME STATION (CONSOLE CHAMBER)
(FX: BUSY ATMOS, AS IN Sc 3)

DOCTOR: Now that's what I call a Time Rotor.

ROMANA: Oh, Doctor. You don't keep a trans-temporal space/time

station this size going with Meccano and a ball of string.
DOCTOR: Foul slur! I replaced those parts properly, in the end. *(BEAT)* Hm. Don't have too many shipmates, do we? Just a skeleton crew — the Under-Cardinal there, and a cohort of guards. Keep the secret mission secret, hm? Wouldn't do to spread alarm.
ROMANA: Do be quiet and take a seat. Vansell - are your people prepared?
VANSELL: Confirming now. *(FX: PUNCHING BUTTONS; INTO INTERCOM)* Levith, Kurst — all is ready aboard the Doctor's TARDIS?
LEVITH: *(FUZZY, THROUGH INTERCOM)* Running smoothly, Co-ordinator Vansell.
DOCTOR: *(TO VANSELL)* I want to speak to Charley.
VANSELL: Too late, Doctor. She's already in the acceleration field. *(TO LEVITH, VIA INTERCOM)* That is correct, Levith?
LEVITH: *(VIA INTERCOM)* Fully stabilised, now. Ready on your command.
ROMANA: *(TO THE DOCTOR)* As the breach is opened, Vansell's people will download details of its precise space/time co-ordinates to us, here in the console chamber. The Time Station will then dematerialise through those precise co-ordinates and — well, we'll see where we are when we get there.
DOCTOR: If we get there.
ROMANA: Doctor, she will be alright.
DOCTOR: She'd better be.
ROMANA: *(ALOUD, ECHOING THROUGH SPEAKERS)* Attention, crew of Time Station! Prepare for full dematerialisation! *(TO VANSELL)* Vansell, give the order.
VANSELL: *(TO LEVITH, VIA INTERCOM)* Calling Doctor's TARDIS. Begin sub-proton acceleration. *(BEAT)* Open the gateway!

15. INT. TARDIS
(FX: PULSING BEAM, AS BEFORE)
(CHARLEY MOANING SOFTLY IN BACKGROUND)

LEVITH: Confirmed. *(BEAT)* Ready, Kurst?
KURST: Ready.
LEVITH: This is it. Begin full proton acceleration.
(FX: PULSING STEPS UP A GEAR)
CHARLEY: *(SCREAMS)* AAAAAAAAAAAAAAAAAAAAAAAA

16. INT. TIME STATION (CONSOLE CHAMBER)
(FX: CHARLEY'S SCREAMS THROUGH INTERCOM)

DOCTOR: You're hurting her! Stop it! Stop it now!
VANSELL: *(INTO INTERCOM)* Levith! What's happening down there?
LEVITH: *(VIA INTERCOM, EXCITED)* The girl — Charlotte. She's rippling, like a stone thrown into a pond, changing, expanding ... It's happening! It's —
(FX: VIA INTERCOM, CHARLEY'S SCREAM TRANSMUTES INTO A HUGE, VIBRATING, WHIRLING SOUND - TINGED WITH TWINKLING, ETHEREAL EFFECTS. BURST OF STATIC. INTERCOM GOES DEAD)

DOCTOR: Charley!!!
VANSELL: *(INTO INTERCOM)* Levith! Levith, are you there?
(BEAT)
DOCTOR: No, no, no, no, no!!!
ROMANA: Doctor, I — I'm sorry. I —
(FX: BUZZ OF STATIC. INTERCOM BURSTS BACK INTO LIFE. THE WHIRLING IS GENTLER, MORE EVEN)
VANSELL: Quiet! Levith? Levith?
LEVITH: *(VIA INTERCOM, AWESTRUCK)* It's just — fantastic. She's whirling, dancing with colour and... You can see the universe through her. You can see — everything —
VANSELL: *(SOFTLY, TO HIMSELF)* 'And the gate of Zagreus opened before him/And all of the Antiverse was revealed to him/And its terrible beauty ached in his hearts ...'
ROMANA: There, Doctor. There is another way. There is — hope. *(ALOUD)* Under-Cardinal! Commence dematerialisation.
UNDER-CARDINAL:Yes, Madam President!
(FX: THE VAST, PONDEROUS TIME ROTOR VWORPING)
ROMANA: So the adventure begins.

17. INT. TARDIS
(FX: FULL 'GATEWAY' EFFECTS, AS BEFORE - MUCH LOUDER, ROARING)

KURST: Amazing. Just amazing ...
(FX: SUDDEN POPPING EXPLOSIONS FROM THE CONSOLE)
LEVITH: Kurst! The console!
KURST: Something's wrong — it's too much for this heap —
(FX: AND THE ROARING GATEWAY BEGINS TO VIBRATE, CHARLEY'S SCREAMING FADING IN AND OUT OF THE EFFECT)
LEVITH: The breach! It's changing back! It's —
(FX: BIGGER EXPLOSIONS FROM TARDIS CONSOLE)
(KURST AND LEVITH SCREAM)

18. INT. TIME STATION (CONSOLE CHAMBER)
(FX: MASSIVE ROARING OF TIME STATION ROTOR)
(FX: CHAOS IN TARDIS VIA INTERCOM - THE WOBBLING GATEWAY/SCREAMING CHARLEY BREAKING THROUGH)

VANSELL: Your TARDIS, Doctor — it's falling apart as it's being sucked through!
(FX: AND A SERIES OF BANGS AND FLASHES IN THE TIME STATION ITSELF. CRIES FROM CREWMEMBERS)
DOCTOR: Abort the mission! Charley can't take it! Neither time ship can take it! In all that's decent, Romana - abort!!!
ROMANA: Too late, Doctor! There is no alternative! The sequence has started — *(FX: SOUND REACHING A HUGE CRESCENDO)* — and it cannot be stopped! We're going in!!!

(END OF PART ONE)

PART TWO

(RECAP FROM:)

17. INT. TARDIS
(FX: FULL 'GATEWAY' EFFECTS, AS BEFORE - MUCH LOUDER, ROARING)

KURST: Amazing. Just amazing ...
(FX: SUDDEN POPPING EXPLOSIONS FROM THE CONSOLE)
LEVITH: Kurst! The console!
KURST: Something's wrong — it's too much for this heap —
(FX: AND THE ROARING GATEWAY BEGINS TO VIBRATE, CHARLEY'S SCREAMING FADING IN AND OUT OF THE EFFECT)
LEVITH: The breach! It's changing back! It's —
(FX: BIGGER EXPLOSIONS FROM TARDIS CONSOLE)
(KURST AND LEVITH SCREAM)

18. INT. TIME STATION (CONSOLE CHAMBER)
(FX: MASSIVE ROARING OF TIME STATION ROTOR)
(FX: CHAOS IN TARDIS VIA INTERCOM - THE WOBBLING GATEWAY/SCREAMING CHARLEY BREAKING THROUGH)

VANSELL: Your TARDIS, Doctor — it's falling apart as it's being sucked through!
(FX: AND A SERIES OF BANGS AND FLASHES IN THE TIME STATION ITSELF. CRIES FROM CREWMEMBERS)
DOCTOR: Abort the mission! Charley can't take it! Neither time ship can take it! In all that's decent, Romana - abort!!!
ROMANA: Too late, Doctor! There is no alternative! The sequence has started — *(FX: SOUND REACHING A HUGE CRESCENDO)* — and it cannot be stopped! We're going in!!!
(FX: FREEZE CRESCENDO. ECHO. FADE TO NOTHING)

19. INT. TARDIS
(FX: BRING UP TARDIS MATERIALISATION EFFECT - FALTERING, WARPED. WHEN IT REACHES ITS FINAL 'BUMP' IT SOUNDS SOMETHING LIKE A DEATH RATTLE)
(SIMULTANEOUSLY, CHARLEY GASPS HUGELY, AS IF SHE'S JUST SURFACED FROM A LONG SPELL UNDERWATER)

CHARLEY: *(SMALL, SHUDDERING)* Help me. *(BEAT)* Please ... won't somebody ... help me?
LEVITH: *(ABRUPT)* That's enough, Charlotte. *(GETTING TO HER FEET)* That ... could have been a smoother ride. Kurst. Kurst!
KURST: *(BEFUDDLED)* Levith? Aren't we dead yet?
(FX: LEVITH CROSSES THE FLOOR, KICKS KURST IN THE RIBS)
KURST: Oof!
LEVITH: Did you feel that in your ribs?
KURST: *(THINKS)* Er, yes.
LEVITH: Then you can't be dead, can you? On your feet. You, me

and Charlotte have got work to do.

KURST: The girl-? *(LOOKING AT CHARLEY)* The breach! It's resolved!

LEVITH: She was reverting to her natural state as this TARDIS was being dragged through.

KURST: *(UNCOMPREHENDING)* She was?

LEVITH: When the ship began to break up, the power to the proton accelerator must have shut down and Charlotte here began to stabilise mid-flight. It's a miracle we didn't end up a twisted mass of Earth girl and TARDIS, smeared across the vortex.

CHARLEY: *(ANGRILY)* Will you two stop blathering on and help me?

LEVITH: Untie her, Kurst. I have to check on the console.

(FX: BLEEPS FROM CONSOLE)

CHARLEY: *(TO KURST, PRIMLY)* Thank you.

KURST: How do you feel?

CHARLEY: Sick.

KURST: *(ALARMED)* Really? Because if you're about to disgorge a chunk of space/time —

CHARLEY: *(SHARPLY)* Not that sort of sick, stupid. *(BEAT)* Just … sick.

LEVITH: Kurst! Kurst! Look at this!

(FX: SOUND OF TARDIS' DESTINATION MONITOR WHIRRING FURIOUSLY)

KURST: The destination monitor! It's just going round and round and round —

LEVITH: Unable to settle. Unable to fix a space/time location. You know what this means, Kurst? *(AWESTRUCK)* We made it.

KURST: You mean …?

LEVITH: Nowhere, nowhen — at least, no place we can describe by our mathematics. No 'x', no 'y', no 'z', no 'n' — nowhere. Beyond those doors lies the universe of Anti-Time. *(FX: FLICKING SWITCHES)* Pressure readings indicate …*(READING OFF COUNTER)* … one point one three gees, point nine five atmospheres … air thick, but breathable … *(BEAT)* I think we should investigate. *(FX: ACTIVATES DOOR. HUM OF DOORS OPENING)* Come on. You too, Charlotte. Let's see what nothing looks like.

20. EXT. THE WILDERNESS (PLAIN)

(MUSIC: MASSIVE, PORTENTOUS HORROR MOVIE CUE)
(FX: HIGH, HOWLING WINDS. RUMBLING OF DISTANT EARTHQUAKES. THUNDER AND LIGHTNING. SHOOTING STARS. THROW EVERYTHING AT IT)
(CHARACTERS SHOUT TO BE HEARD OVER THE WINDS, EXCEPT WHERE SPECIFIED)

KURST: *(SOFTLY)* Rassilon protect us. What kind of blemishment have we landed in?

LEVITH: *(QUOTING)* 'And he set then his course/To a scar on the face of Creation/Where the stars lived and died in the churn of one night/Where the mountains might move in the blink of an eye/And decay was the only true constant …'

CHARLEY: Poetry, Levith?

LEVITH: Something I remember reading. Doesn't matter.

(FX: BLEEPS AS A HANDSET IS OPERATED. REGULAR PULSING SOUND CONTINUES OVER:)

CHARLEY: What's that you're doing?

LEVITH: Setting up a trans-temporal beacon to guide the Time Station to us — *(DARKLY)* — if they made it through the breach, of course, and if they can cross this broiling horizon...

CHARLEY: And if not?

LEVITH: Then get used to the view, because I don't think this TARDIS will be going anywhere for a very long time...

21. INT. TIME STATION (CONSOLE CHAMBER)

(FX: HARD CUT TO ROARING OF ROTOR AND JUDDERING ENGINES. EVERYONE SHOUTING OVER THE NOISE, VOICES SHAKEN, BUFFETED BY TURBULENCE)

DOCTOR: You're looking a little ... green, Vansell. Unsteady on your space legs. Whoa! You should ... take something ... for that!

VANSELL: *(QUEASILY)* Doctor ... do shut up.

(FX: AND CUT ROARING. ROTOR SLOWS TO A STEADY PURR.)

(BEAT)

ROMANA: We're through. *(BEAT; TO CREW)* Congratulations, everyone.

(FX: POLITE, DEFERENTIAL CHEER FROM CREW)

ROMANA: *(EMBARRASSED)* Yes, yes, yes.

VANSELL: *(TO HIMSELF)* Scanner screens are dead. *(TO UNDER-CARDINAL)* Under-Cardinal — please download a full survey of all 5-D flight readings into the central data pool.

(FX: CONTINUING MODEM-TYPE BLEEPINGS)

UNDER-CARDINAL: Downloading now, Co-ordinator!

DOCTOR: *(TO VANSELL)* Ah. I see the temperature in the Time Station's solarium dropped half a degree during the crossing, Vansell. What a useful fact.

VANSELL: All information gathered by our sensors is of immediate and urgent value in a situation as untried as this.

DOCTOR: Look around you! Are your arms and legs still there? Mine certainly are. *(BEAT; PATS SELF)* I think.

ROMANA: Do you have a point, Doctor? Or are you simply baiting my Co-ordinator once again?

DOCTOR: Oh, Romana - surely it's obvious? We have travelled into another universe, a dimension utterly alien to our own. Your cameras, your scanners, your sensors are recording data calibrated according to continuous, constant time - but they can't measure the sheer anarchy of this Antiverse. It's anathema to our science! *(FX: BLEEPINGS SLOW AND STOP)* See? Now you've flooded your data pool with nonsense, it's gone and overflowed. Well done!

ROMANA: So what do you suggest? How do we gather intelligence on the phenomena of Anti-Time minus our sensors?

DOCTOR: We use our eyes, our ears, our tongues, our noses, our fingers and toes. And then we put our heads together. *(TO UNDER-CARDINAL)* Under-Cardinal! Raise the shutters on the observation ports!

ROMANA: *(TO UNDER-CARDINAL, RESIGNEDLY)* Just do it.
UNDER-CARDINAL: Madam President.
(FX: THRUMMING OF VAST SHUTTERS BEING RAISED. UP SPOOKY COSMIC TWINKLING AMBIENCE FROM OUTSIDE)
VANSELL: There, Doctor. Space. Satisfied?
DOCTOR: Oh, far from it. *(BEAT; ENRAPTURED)* A comet - eating its own tail. Two nebulae, locked together in an accelerated dance. A star, swallowing a star, swallowing a star. Constant motion! You're witnessing the life and death and life of an entire universe taking place in an ever-changing instant.
ROMANA: That was always the theory, Doctor. Our academics put it in slightly less florid terms.
DOCTOR: There. See it? There!
VANSELL: It's just a planetoid, Doctor - some blackened rock, hanging in the sky —
DOCTOR: Yes, yes — but what else? *(IMPATIENT)* Oh, come on! *(BEAT)*
ROMANA: Of course.
VANSELL: Of course what?!?
ROMANA: The planetoid is static, Vansell. Don't you see? The only fixed point in this maelstrom - is there.
DOCTOR: Which suggests —
ROMANA: — that it doesn't belong here?
DOCTOR: A foreign body - just like us! *(BEAT)* Well, maybe. And if that's the case - whatever it is, it's not been consumed. I don't see any other safe location for a field trip, do you?
ROMANA: Conceded.
VANSELL: I ... see.
DOCTOR: And let's not forget — my TARDIS was dragged through into this place. My TARDIS, containing Charley —
ROMANA: Our only way out of this universe. The realisation hadn't escaped me. *(BEAT)* And if that planetoid is the only fixed point in the whole of Anti-Time ...
DOCTOR: ... then we would be mad not to head there, too. But more to the point, I daresay the TARDIS' displacement field would have kicked in as she passed through into this place - and she'd have materialised on the nearest solid ground - there.
(FX: A SMALL, TINNY, VERSION OF THE REGULAR, PULSING SOUND MADE BY LEVITH'S BEACON IN Sc. 20 IS HEARD)
VANSELL: *(SMUGLY)* Well, Doctor. It seems your deductive powers are indeed correct — but sadly redundant. That is a trans-temporal beacon: Kurst and Levith, I'll be bound. Our sensors are not entirely useless. *(BEAT; STUDYING INSTRUMENTS - BLEEPS)* And yes ... it is indeed emanating from that particular planetoid you picked out ... as is the signature of a TARDIS — too scrambled to identify, but —
DOCTOR: *(DEFENSIVELY)* Well, I daresay the old girl took a fair old battering. She's getting on a bit, you know.
ROMANA: Then that's settled. *(BEAT; ALOUD, TO CREW)* To your posts, everyone. Under-Cardinal — set course for the planetoid!

22. EXT. THE WILDERNESS (PLAIN)
(FX: BEACON PULSING)

LEVITH: *(TO HERSELF)* Hurry, Vansell. How long are we going to have to wait?
CHARLEY: Vansell? Your boss?
LEVITH: Our superior.
KURST: *(FROM 20 FEET AWAY)* Levith! Levith! Over here! *(CHARLEY AND KURST RACE UP RIDGE)*
LEVITH: My stars. A forest!
CHARLEY: Don't be silly. Those aren't trees. They're ... spikes. Metal spikes, or something. Thousands of them. *(BEAT)* I'm going to have a closer look. Last one there's a big old witch!
LEVITH: Hey! Stop!
(CHARLEY GIGGLES AS SHE RUSHES AWAY)
LEVITH: Well, come on, Kurst! *(FX: THE PULSING OF THE BEACON STARTS TO DISTORT - SLIPPAGE MOTIF)* That girl's our- *(BEAT)* Wait. Wait! Something's wrong.
KURST: What?
LEVITH: The beacon! It's - malfunctioning. The pulses are out of synch. *(FX: SHAKES BEACON)* Work!

23. INT. TIME STATION (CONSOLE CHAMBER)
(FX: ENGINES ROARING)

ROMANA: Range, Under-Cardinal?
UNDER-CARDINAL: Landfall in eight microspans, Madam Pres—
DOCTOR: Sh sh sh! Listen! *(FX: BEACON'S PULSING HEARD DISTORTING)* Something's affecting the beacon down there. *(OMINOUS)* I know what that is!
ROMANA: Time distortion!

24. EXT. THE WILDERNESS (SPIKE FOREST)
(FX: WIND PICKING UP AGAIN. SPOOKY)

CHARLEY: *(RUNNING, LAUGHING, SHOUTING BEHIND)* Can't catch me! *(TRIPS, FALLS)* Wah! *(BEAT)* Ow. *(TO HERSELF)* Careful, Charley - don't want to skewer yourself on these great rusty spike trees. *(BEAT, SHOUTING BEHIND)* Levith! Kurst! I'm over here! *(TO HERSELF)* Fog coming down. Can't see where — Oh, if only the Doctor was here. He'd be bound to have Galileo's compass in his pocket, or something. *(SHE LAUGHS NERVOUSLY TO HERSELF ...)*
(FX: ... AND HEARS A DISTORTED, ANTI-TIME ECHO OF HER LAUGHTER ABOUT TEN FEET AWAY)
CHARLEY: What was that —?
(FX: A RIPPLE OF ANTI-TIME LAUGHTER AGAIN; CLEARLY HER OWN)
CHARLEY: *(ALOUD)* Is there somebody there? *(LOUDER)* I said, is there somebody there? *(BEAT; TO HERSELF)* Brr. Spooky. Haven't felt like this since I was—
(A DISTORTED, ANTI-TIME VOICE: CHARLEY'S, BUT COLDER, DEEPER)
ANTI-CHARLEY: — six?
CHARLEY: *(SHRIEKS)* Aaah! *(BEAT; TO HERSELF)* Nothing there. There is nothing there. You're a grown-up now. So what do you do? You stay calm, retrace your steps, find the others — not sit here quivering at the slightest sound just because it reminds you a bit of the time you

were —

ANTI-CHARLEY: — six. You were six. Behind you, Charley. Don't be scared. Turn around. I won't hurt you. After three. One. Two.

CHARLEY: *(TO HERSELF)* This is madness. It's like I'm talking to mysel— *(HER WORDS DIE AWAY AS SHE TURNS)*

ANTI-CHARLEY: Three. There — that wasn't so hard, was it now?

CHARLEY: Y-you're me. Or a ghost of me. What—

ANTI-CHARLEY: I'm not you, Charley. But I know everything about you. I know about when you were six, about that time in Burnham Beeches. Such a long, lazy, late afternoon in the woods, running and laughing with Nanny, your brothers. Then you ran on ahead, and you hid in the bracken, and you waited and waited — but they never came. And it got darker and darker, and you called out for help, but they still never came. And the shadows got longer, so you called and you whoopped and you shouted and cried. Then you ran, but you only went deeper and deeper into the woods — became more alone. And the shadows got longer and longer and longer, touching your heels. And you fell in a clearing, with no-one in sight. And you thought you were lost, that you'd never be found, and the shadows would reach you and take you away. *(BEAT)* Oh, Charley. I've been on your trail for such a long time. Where you led, I followed. From France to Sebastian Grayle's Wycombe estate...

CHARLEY: *(DESPAIRING)* Who ... are ... you?

ANTI-CHARLEY: Me? I'm everyone who never was —

(ANOTHER ANTI-TIME VOICE - MALE, TO RIGHT)

ANTI-VOICE 1: — everyone who's never been —

(AND ANOTHER, FEMALE, TO LEFT)

ANTI-VOICE 2: — everyone who never lived —

CHARLEY: More of you?!?

(FX: A BABBLE OF SEVERAL MORE HISSING ANTI-VOICES)

ANTI-VOICE 1: — everyone who never died —

ANTI-CHARLEY: — and now, Charley, you're mine.

CHARLEY: K-keep back, all of you! Please! Please! Nooooooooooooooooooooooo!!!

(CUT TO KURST AND LEVITH, ABOUT A HUNDRED FEET AWAY)

KURST: Did you hear that?!?

LEVITH: The girl! Come on!

(BACK TO:)

(CHARLEY, STRUGGLING, CRYING. EXCITED SHRIEKS AND BABBLE FROM ANTI-PEOPLE)

CHARLEY: Please! I don't know what you want! I don't know what to do!

ANTI-CHARLEY: Oh, Charley. You don't have to do anything. Just hold still — and join us.

CHARLEY: Please!!!

(CUT BACK TO:)

KURST: There! She's there! Surrounded by — ghosts?

LEVITH: Whatever they are, let's see how they like - this!!!

(FX: BURST OF STASER FIRE)

(SHRIEKS FROM ANTI-TIME PEOPLE)

ANTI-CHARLEY: *(HISSING)* Time Lords!!!

LEVITH: *(SHOUTED)* Earth girl! Charley!!! While they're

distracted — run!!!
(FX: TWO MORE BURSTS OF STASER FIRE)
(BACK TO:)
(ANTI-PEOPLE SNARLING)
CHARLEY: *(TO HERSELF)* You heard the woman, Charley. Get up and - RUN!!!
ANTI-CHARLEY: Take them!!!
(TO:)
LEVITH: *(TO KURST)* Hold them off, Kurst. I'm going to get her!
KURST: Levith! Levith, wait! *(FX: FIRES STASER)* *(TO ANTI-PEOPLE)* Stay back, ghosts!
(CUT TO:)
CHARLEY: *(RUNNING)* Can't — can't run any more ...
(FX: STASER BURST)
LEVITH: *(TO ANTI-PEOPLE)* Back!!! *(TO CHARLEY)* Faster, girl, faster! This way - to the TARDIS!
(CUT TO:)
KURST: *(HOLLERED)* Levith! They're re-forming! Cut them down and they just start re-forming!
ANTI-CHARLEY: *(BESIDE HIM)* Do you really think you can do us harm, Time Lord — here, in our home?
ANTI-VOICE 1: You made us, Time Lord —
ANTI-VOICE 2: — here, we can unmake you.
KURST: W-what are you going to do to me?
ANTI-CHARLEY: We know you, Kursteliaphaestyxsan. A Cousin of the Patrex House. Under-assassin with the Celestial Intervention Agency, fast-tracked from the Chancellery Guard. You keep a striped pig-bear called Staser-snout, and feed him Promaze bars.
KURST: H-how do you ...?
ANTI-CHARLEY: Has yours been a good life, Kursteliaphaestyxsan? Will it nourish us for long?
KURST: Don't touch me! Please, don't touch me! NOOOOOOOOOOOOOO!!!

25. EXT. THE WILDERNESS (PLAIN)
(FX: PLAIN ATMOS. CHOPPY WINDS)
(FX: BRING UP PULSING BEACON)
(LEVITH AND CHARLEY, RUNNING. ANTI-PEOPLE SHOUTING BEHIND)

CHARLEY: They're gaining on us!
LEVITH: Not far now, Charley! Nearly at the beacon! A minute more and we'll be in the TARDIS—
(FX: CUE A GREAT RUMBLING, QUAKING IN THE GROUND)
CHARLEY: Levith, watch out! The ground's giving way!
(FX: RUMBLING GROUND. BEACON CRUNCHED - PULSE CUTS DEAD)
LEVITH: Aaaah!
CHARLEY: It's alright, I've got you! *(BEAT)* Whew. Tell your mother I saved your life.
(BEAT)
LEVITH: Oh. Oh no. No no no.
CHARLEY: What is it? What's wrong?
LEVITH: The beacon — the TARDIS — they've gone. The ground

cracked open and swallowed them!

26. INT. TIME STATION (CONSOLE CHAMBER)

(FX: ENGINES. BEACON PULSE NOW THE SINGLE NOTE OF A FLATLINING LIFE SUPPORT MACHINE - 'BEEEEEEEEEEEEEEEEEE' - AND FADES)

VANSELL: We've lost the beacon.
DOCTOR: What? Vansell, let me see! *(FX: ELECTRONIC BLIPS)* Nothing! Nothing!
VANSELL: Except the TARDIS signature. *(FX: A LOOPING 'SWISH', LIKE RADAR)* That's clearer now - no echo.
DOCTOR: No no, that's not right. I know my TARDIS better than anyone—
ROMANA: Doctor, Vansell - if you please. We're entering the atmosphere! *(BEAT)* Under-Cardinal - settle into a high orbit.
DOCTOR: Belay that, Under-Cardinal! *(TO ROMANA)* Romana, there's a layer of mist obscuring the surface. We cannot trust the instrumentation - we have to go lower! *(BEAT)* If the beacon is down, then Charley might be in trouble. And if Charley's in trouble, then so are we!
VANSELL: *(TO ROMANA)* An unnecessary risk, Madam President, founded as usual on baseless intuition and a flagrant disregard of the possible dangers —
DOCTOR: Oh, Vansell — there's no point in living if you can't live dangerously! *(BEAT; COYLY)* Under-Cardinal, if I could just —
ROMANA: Doctor, no!
(FX: TWO BLEEPS - AND THE NOISE OF THE ENGINES ACCELERATES, THE TIME STATION DROPPING THROUGH THE ATMOSPHERE)
DOCTOR: Sorry, slip of the fingers ...
VANSELL: *(SHOUTING, TO CREWMAN)* Level up! Level up!
DOCTOR: Too late now!

27. EXT. THE WILDERNESS (PLAIN)

LEVITH: We're trapped!
(FX: ANTI-TIME MUSIC. BABBLE OF SUDDENLY APPEARED ANTI-PEOPLE)
ANTI-VOICE 1: This is nowhere, Time Lord —
ANTI-VOICE 2: Here, there's nowhere to run.
LEVITH: You again! Where did you spring from?
ANTI-VOICE 1: We move as we like.
ANTI-VOICE 2: Here, we are free.
CHARLEY: *(TO LEVITH)* We could always try leaping into the rift in the ground ...
LEVITH: *(TO CHARLEY)* It's bottomless, Charley. Unless you're about to sprout wings —
ANTI-VOICE 1: Come to us.
ANTI-VOICE 2: Join us.
CHARLEY: *(SHOUTING)* Oh, Doctor — where are you!?!
(FX: EXACTLY ON CUE, WE HEAR THE ROARING ENGINES OF THE TIME STATION IN THE SKY. COMMOTION AMONG ANTI-PEOPLE)

ANTI-VOICE 1: What is this —
LEVITH: I - I don't believe it. The Time Station! They're coming!
CHARLEY: Coming straight for us, by the look of it.
(ALARM AMONG ANTI-PEOPLE)
LEVITH: The wraiths — they're scattering!
CHARLEY: It's going to crash!Don't just stand there gawping, woman - RUN!

28. INT. TIME STATION (CONSOLE CHAMBER)
(FX: THE PLUMMETTING ENGINES STEADYING SLIGHTLY)

ROMANA: Time Station steadying. Doctor, if you won't behave yourself I will have you restrained!
DOCTOR: Restrained? Me? Romana, I'm actually hurt. We've shared shackles everywhere from E-space to— *(SEEING SOMETHING BELOW)* There! There!!! People running, beside that crevasse! Is that Charley? *(BEAT)* Hang on, what's that beyond? A forest?
VANSELL: Detecting mass in our path. Density conforms with registered alloys ...
DOCTOR: A metal forest? No such thing! I warned you about those sensors, Vansell ...
ROMANA: *(SHOUTING)* Pull up now!
DOCTOR: Don't worry - we'll scrape the treetops at worst.
VANSELL: Impact imminent!
ROMANA: Doctor, I strongly advise you get dow-
(FX: THE BASE OF THE TIME STATION SKIMMING THE BARBS OF THE METAL FOREST. WRENCHING AND TEARING OF METAL)
(CRIES OF ALARM FROM EVERYONE)
DOCTOR: Oh. Metal trees. My mistake.
(FX: TREMENDOUS 'WHUMPS' AS THE TIME STATION'S BASE HITS GROUND, AND THE WHOLE THING SKIDS ACROSS THE SURFACE OF THE PLANETOID. ABSOLUTE BLOODY MAYHEM)

29. EXT. THE WILDERNESS (PLAIN)

LEVITH: She's down!
CHARLEY: Oh no. The Doctor! Come on!
LEVITH: No, Charley! Charley, wait!

30. INT. TIME STATION (CONSOLE CHAMBER)
(FX: SPARKS. STEAM. KLAXONS)

COMPUTER VOICE: Emergency. Time Station damaged. Hull integrity compromised. All units on crisis standing. *(BEAT; THEN REPEAT)* Emergency. Time Station damaged. Hull integrity compromised. All units on cri— *(FX: SWITCH. WORDS DWINDLE AS COMPUTER IS DEACTIVATED)*
ROMANA: Yes, yes, I think we get the point. *(COUGHS ON SMOKE; SLIGHTLY BREATHLESS)* *(INTO INTERCOM)* Power deck - report! *(FX: STATIC THROUGH INTERCOM)* Temporal reactors - report! *(FX: MORE STATIC)*
DOCTOR: *(COUGHING)* I think now might be a good time to say

'sorry'. Sorry, everyone...

ROMANA: Spare me, Doctor. Catastrophe follows in your footsteps, just as it ever did. But perhaps you could now concentrate your efforts on not making a disaster out of this crisis? Thank you. *(BEAT)* Where's Vansell?

(VANSELL MOANS)

DOCTOR: Over here. *(BEAT; OVER-ENUNCIATING)* Vansell? Nosebung Vansell? It's the Doctor. That's right. You've taken a bit of a knock. Nothing to worry about, probably.

VANSELL: *(QUOTING, WOOZY)* 'Zagreus waits at the end of the world/For Zagreus is the end of the world/His time is the end of time/And his moment Time's undoing ...'

DOCTOR: Do you know, that's the third time today old Zagreus has come up. He seems ever-so well-connected for a silly villain in a minor nursery rhyme.

ROMANA: Later, Doctor. If you'll allow me? *(BEAT)*

(ROMANA SLAPS VANSELL HARD ROUND THE FACE)

DOCTOR: *(SYMPATHETIC)* Ouch.

VANSELL: *(ALERT AGAIN)* What? Where — ? *(BEAT)* What's happened here? Doctor, what have you done? *(FX: BRING UP TWINKLING, COSMIC EFFECTS; ANTI-TIME MUSIC)* Careless, irresponsible, untrustworthy lackwit! You should have been removed from our histor—

ROMANA: *(URGENT)* Quiet, Vansell! There's something in here with us. Something —

ANTI-CHARLEY: — unwanted, Madam President? *(LAUGHS)* Welcome to the land of the lost.

VANSELL: Where did that come from?

DOCTOR: Charley? No — you're not Charley. Some kind of spectral entity that's taken Charley's form ...

ANTI-CHARLEY: A ghost? Doctor, you don't believe in ghosts.

DOCTOR: You're alive, then?

ANTI-CHARLEY: Not in your terms.

VANSELL: *(IMPATIENT, TO DOCTOR)* What is that thing?

DOCTOR: Isn't it obvious, Vansell? *(TO ANTI-CHARLEY)* You are a creature of Anti-Time.

ANTI-CHARLEY: A Never-person, if you please.

DOCTOR: You know us? All of us?

ANTI-CHARLEY: Intimately. I've visited your reality once or twice — but briefly, so as not to cause ... catastrophe.

DOCTOR: And there are more of you?

(FX: A RUSH OF NOISE. MULTIPLE TWINKLING SOUNDS. MURMURS, WHISPERS AND RHUBARBING OF OTHER ANTI-PEOPLE)

ANTI-CHARLEY: Oh yes, Doctor. Hundreds. Thousands. Some you may recognise from your recent sojourn to 1806 – I do apologise but I needed some nourishment when I got there.

DOCTOR: I don't see any... *(SUDDENLY VERY QUIET:)* Lucy? Lucy and Richard Martin... of course, all that time energy, must've attracted you like a beacon. Oh Lucy, I'm so sorry...

ROMANA: *(ALOUD, TO ROOM)* Keep away from them, all of you!

DOCTOR: *(FASCINATED)* Tell me, Never-person — where do you come from? Is it here?

ANTI-CHARLEY: An excellent question, Doctor.
(BEAT)
DOCTOR: Somewhere else, then. What do you want from us?
ANTI-CHARLEY: Why Doctor — we only want a little of your time.
(BEAT) Brothers, sisters — the vessel is ours. This Time Rotor is cracked. Let us feast on it.
(FX: EXULTANT ROAR FROM ANTI-PEOPLE. A SURGE. MULTIPLE SUCKING NOISES)
VANSELL: *(WHISPERED)* What are they doing?
DOCTOR: *(WHISPERED)* Draining temporal energy from the rotor — from this ship. Fascinating! They're becoming less translucent, more solid!
ROMANA: *(TO ANTI-CHARLEY)* This Time Station is the property of the High Council of Gallifrey! I demand you... you people evacuate my craft!
(ANGRY HISSES)
DOCTOR: Careful, Romana. No need to antagonise them...
VANSELL: *(ALOUD)* That's quite enough. You guards — ready stasers and — FIRE!!!
(FX: SEVERAL STASER BURSTS)
ANTI-CHARLEY: *(LAUGHING)* Oh, Vansell. Don't be so silly. *(BEAT)* The thing that you seek lies not far from here.
(BEAT)
VANSELL: What thing, Anti-creature?
ANTI-CHARLEY: The truth you came in search of, you foolish man. The truth about Zagreus.
VANSELL: *(AGHAST)* You know about Zagreus?
DOCTOR: Everyone seems to, today. Interesting, that.
ROMANA: Quiet, Doctor!
ANTI-CHARLEY: *(TO VANSELL)* There is a grotto in the hills not far away. There you will find the answers that you seek - and the object of your quest. *(BEAT)* Leave us to feed on your vessel — and go in search of the thing you came here for.
VANSELL: *(DECISIVE)* Guards, lower your weapons and follow me.
ROMANA: Stop! *(BEAT)* You over-reach your authority, Vansell!
VANSELL:
And there is a higher authority than yours, Madam President! Guards!
DOCTOR: *(WHISPERED)* Romana, I have absolutely no idea what's going on here, but you can't possibly consider abandoning the Time Station to these creatures — it's our only way out of this place!
ROMANA: *(WHISPERED)* Firstly — if you could be bothered to keep up with the latest developments in our technology, you'd know that this ship has a limited ability to regenerate itself — given time. And secondly — we do still have your TARDIS, Doctor.
DOCTOR: *(WHISPERED)* Wherever she is.
ROMANA: *(WHISPERED)* And we have to find your friend. My mind is made up. *(ALOUD)* Guards — form an escort. Co-ordinator Vansell and myself have a great and important mission to carry out.
VANSELL: We do.
(BEAT)
ROMANA: Well, Doctor?
DOCTOR: Romana, this is madness!

ANTI-CHARLEY: Go, Doctor. Go, all of you.
(BEAT)
DOCTOR: Well, whatever this great secret is, I only hope it's worth it
ROMANA: Doctor, it will be. *(ALOUD)* Guards — follow me!
(FX: SLIDING DOORS)
(GUARDS, DOCTOR, ROMANA AND VANSELL TRAMP THROUGH)
ANTI-VOICE 1: Can we not gorge ourselves on the Time Lords? All that temporal energy flowing through them...
ANTI-CHARLEY: Not yet, brother. They cannot escape us — not here, not now. First we feast on their machine — and once we're filled to bursting with their time, then we can consume them all.

31. EXT. THE WILDERNESS (PLAIN)
(FX: DISTANT CRACKLING FLAMES FROM TIME STATION)
(CHARLEY AND LEVITH, RUNNING)

LEVITH: *(PANTING)* Slow down, Charley!
CHARLEY: It's still in one piece! They might need help! *(BEAT; THEN, EXULTANT)* DOCTOR!!!
(CUT TO: JUST OUTSIDE TIME STATION)
DOCTOR: So come on, Romana. What exactly have we come here for?
ROMANA: The source of Anti-Time, Doctor. And we've found it.
DOCTOR: I know that. But please, please - what else?
CHARLEY: *(SHOUTING, ABOUT 50 YARDS DISTANT)* Doctor!!! Whoo-hoo! Over here! Doctor!!!
DOCTOR: Charley! Romana, it's Charley! Charley, I'm coming!
(RACES OFF)
VANSELL: *(TO ROMANA, SARCASTIC)* Such devotion to his companion. Oh, how touching. *(BEAT)* You know that if that 'Never-person' back there was correct - if the Books of Zagreus are proved to be true, and what we seek is indeed somewhere in this Anti-verse - then the Doctor will never approve.
ROMANA: The Doctor is full of surprises, Vansell. But his one abiding characteristic, whichever body he wears, whatever gibberish he speaks, however erratically he acts — is his unerring sense for what is right. I trust him, absolutely. And I always have.
VANSELL: And if he pits himself against you? Against the Time Lords? Against the thing we almost daren't believe might be here? Who will you place your trust in then, Madam President?
(CUT TO: A FEW FEET AWAY)
CHARLEY: Doctor! Oh Doctor — I was so afraid I'd never see you again!
DOCTOR: You don't get rid of me that easily! *(BEAT; INTIMATELY)* I told you, Charley — whatever it takes. I won't ever let you down, I promise. *(UP)* Come on — you have to meet Romana!
(BEAT) Romana, this is Charley, one of my best-ever friends. Charley, this is Romana, one of my best friends ever.
CHARLEY: *(SOURLY)* Hello.
ROMANA: *(AWKWARDLY)* Hello.
DOCTOR: *(OBLIVIOUS, EXUBERANT)* See - you're going to get

along just famously! Now, who's this?
CHARLEY: Oh, this is Levith. She ... helped me, I suppose.
LEVITH: Commander Levith. CIA.
DOCTOR: Never mind.
LEVITH: Co-ordinator ... Madam President. You should know —
there are creatures here. We lost Kurst when we met them. They've
vanished now, but they're dangerous—
ROMANA: Yes. The Never-people currently have control of the
Time Station, Commander.
DOCTOR: Not the best news, is it? *(DISTRACTED, WALKING
AWAY)* Hmm. Those spikes. I wonder ...
VANSELL: *(URGENT)* What about the local terrain, Levith? What
have you seen?
LEVITH: It's weird, Co-ordinator. There's a crevasse opened up —
and then there's this forest — and the blowholes we passed on the way
here —
VANSELL: Blowholes?
LEVITH: Entrances or something, in the ridges an foothills.
VANSELL: Really.
(CUT TO:)
CHARLEY: So what do you make of this forest, Doctor?
DOCTOR: Mm. Interesting. These spikes — there's something
about them. Nothing natural. It's almost like they've been
manufactured, then beaten out of shape, twisted beyond recognition.
Even the dust and the earth ... this is metal ore, see?
CHARLEY: Like iron filings?
DOCTOR: That's it, exactly! *(BEAT)* Exactly ...
(FX: DEEP RUMBLE OF THUNDER; SPOTS OF RAIN)
CHARLEY: Don't like the sound of that. *(SUDDENLY)* Yow!
DOCTOR: What's wrong, Charl — ow!
CHARLEY: Spots of rain.
DOCTOR: Acid rain.
CHARLEY & DOCTOR: (TOGETHER) Run!!!
(FX: GUARDS 'YOWING' DISCONTENTEDLY IN BACKGROUND)
ROMANA: *(SHOUTING FROM A FEW FEET AWAY)* Doctor! Charley!
We have to take cover! Over here!
*(FX: RAIN GETS HARDER. MORE THUNDER. DOCTOR AND CHARLEY
RUNNING OUT OF SCENE, 'OW'-ING AS THEY GO)*

32. INT. TUNNEL ENTRANCE
*(FX: CONTINUE RAIN, THUNDER EFFECTS OUTSIDE. HOLLOW
AMBIENCE)*
*(DOCTOR AND CHARLEY RUNNING INTO TUNNEL; ROMANA, VANSELL,
LEVITH AND GUARDS ALREADY THERE)*

ROMANA: Oh, do get a move on, Doctor!
DOCTOR: I know! I know! *(STOPS)* Whew. That stuff stings — and
where I'm going to find a tailor to mend this jacket in the whole of
Anti-Time, I don't know. *(BEAT)* You should get rid of that collar,
Romana. It's hardly practical — and we're not standing on ceremony
here.
ROMANA: Aren't we? *(MOVES OFF)*

CHARLEY: *(TO DOCTOR)* Is your Madam Icy-Drawers always so frosty?
DOCTOR: *(SCANDALISED)* What, Romana? No, not at all! But there's something here — something she's not telling me. Something big. Vansell's in on it, too — and that certainly bothers me. *(BEAT)* Tunnels.
CHARLEY: Blowholes, Levith said.
DOCTOR: No, too regular. Corridors, in fact. Leading left and right and straight ahead. *(LOST IN THOUGHT)* A network, forking off in all directions. There's light here, too. Dim light. Phosphorecence? No, no, no...
CHARLEY: Is this a pattern, on the walls? See, like big ellipses? *(BEAT)* There's something it reminds me of, but I don't know what.
DOCTOR: Hm. More filings. More rust. More decay. This is a very odd place we've landed up in, Charley.
LEVITH: *(DISTANT)* Here! Over here!
(COMMOTION AMONG GUARDS)
DOCTOR: *(GRIM)* Come on.

33. INT. CAVERN
(FX: HUGE SPACE. MASSIVE ECHO. CLATTERING FEET OF GUARDS)

LEVITH: It's incredible!
ROMANA: Guards — spread out. *(SCHOOLMISTRESSY)* And don't touch anything. *(TO VANSELL)* Well, Vansell?
VANSELL: This is it.
ROMANA: Possibly.
DOCTOR: *(ENTERING)* Come on, come on, let us through! *(STOPS DEAD)* Well, I'm impressed! It's vast — not so much a cavern, more a —
ROMANA: — a chamber, Doctor.
DOCTOR: Yes, yes, that's it! A chamber! *(MOVING FORWARD)* And what's this at the heart of it, hm?
CHARLEY: Doctor, this doesn't make sense. We've not come deep enough underground to be in a space like — *(AND SOMETHING DAWNING ON HER)* Oh. Oh, Doctor, don't you see what this is?
DOCTOR: *(GRANDSTANDING, MOVING AROUND)* Yes, Charley, I think I do! Metal spikes, piercing the earth all around us, twisted and blasted, encrusted with rust and decay... Tunnels, corridors leading to a huge chambers and vaults, perhaps some even bigger than this ... Everywhere, pitted circles in the walls ... And now here, at the core of the thing, a massive stalactite, connecting a fluted ceiling to a broad, hexagonal dais... We're not on an asteroid, some natural satellite. *(ACCUSINGLY, TO ROMANA AND VANSELL)* Are we, hm? *(BACK TO AWESTRUCK REVERIE)* This entire planetoid - this blasted lump of flotsam, spinning in the chaos of Anti-Time, this coal fallen from infinity's grate - the only fixed point in the whole of this swirling Anti-verse ... it doesn't belong here. It came from outside the bounds of the maelstrom, from — from...
ROMANA: Our world, Doctor.
DOCTOR: Our world, exactly.
CHARLEY: *(SLOWLY)* We've not come deep enough underground to

be in a space like this because ... because it's bigger on the inside than—

DOCTOR: — bigger on the inside than the out! No stalactite, then. A console. *(BEAT)* This whole world ... the shattered hulk of a fabulous machine, its dimensions ripped asunder, turned inside out, compacted, mapped onto itself ... *(LOUD, ALMOST EXULTANT)* This - is the wreck - of a TARDIS!

CHARLEY: I don't believe this.

DOCTOR: Romana, Vansell — you knew, didn't you? You've known all along. *(SADLY)* Oh, Romana.

ROMANA: The possibility was accounted for. I'm sorry, Doctor - I didn't quite dare believe it myself.

VANSELL: You see, Doctor — the question is not that this place is the remnant of an abandoned TARDIS. The question is not even how it came to be here. No, the question is — who brought it here? Whose TARDIS was this? *(BEAT)* Madam President - if you would permit me the honour?

ROMANA: The stage is yours.

VANSELL: Guards. The neutron staff — quick. Now, Doctor — let's see if we can shed a little light on the mystery. Out of the way of the console! *(FX: SCRAPING OF METAL)* The power receptors are still intact. Opening flux valves - now.

(FX: SPARKS. BLIPS AND BLEEPS. SHAKING. STEADY THRUM OF BUILDING POWER, EVOLVING INTO MAJESTIC TARDIS ATMOS)

DOCTOR: Amazing — I never imagined —

VANSELL: Just a spark of life, Doctor. One spark ... will be... enough!!!

(FX: SUDDENLY, A 'FWIP!'. TWINKLING SOUND)

CHARLEY: *(STARTLED)* Aah! Above the console - there's something forming ... A face — in the air!

DOCTOR: We call it a hologram, Charley. *(BEAT)* And I know that face. I saw it in the Matrix ... An old man, eternally sad and infinitely wise ... *(SUBDUED, ALMOST HORRIFIED)* It can't be.

VANSELL: *(QUOTING)* 'There to do battle with Zagreus, the Beast/Never resting as long as history is lasting/Until either or both are laid to waste ...'

CHARLEY: It's going to speak!

ROMANA: On your knees, Doctor — Miss Pollard. On your knees, all of you!

(AND THE HOLOGRAM SPEAKS - SLIGHTLY DISTORTING, SHAKING, BUT STILL FILLING THE AIR WITH DEPTH AND RICHNESS ... SOMETHING LIKE THE VOICE OF GOD)

OLD MAN: It has been a time beyond measuring - here, alone in the cold, adrift and aloof from my people, my home. Once, my name was hailed and feared in equal measure by friends and enemies alike. Know, then, that I am Conqueror of Yssgaroth, Overpriest of Drornid, First Earl of Prydon, Patris of the Vortex, Ravager of the Void ... and President of Gallifrey from the time of our empire's Great Foundation. I am the Lord Rassilon. At last, my children, you have returned to me.

(END OF PART TWO)

Part Three

(RECAP FROM:)

33. INT. CAVERN

VANSELL: Madam President — if you would permit me the honour?

ROMANA: The stage is yours.

VANSELL: Guards. The neutron staff — quick. Now, Doctor — let's see if we can shed a little light on the mystery. Out of the way of the console! *(FX: SCRAPING OF METAL)* Her power receptors are still intact. Opening flux valves — now.

(FX: SPARKS. BLIPS AND BLEEPS. SHAKING. STEADY THRUM OF BUILDING POWER, EVOLVING INTO MAJESTIC TARDIS ATMOS)

DOCTOR: Amazing — I never imagined —

VANSELL: Just a spark of life, Doctor. One spark... will be... enough!!!

(FX: SUDDENLY, A 'FWIP!'. TWINKLING SOUND)

CHARLEY: *(STARTLED)* Aah! Above the console - there's something forming ... A face — in the air!

DOCTOR: We call it a hologram, Charley. *(BEAT)* And I know that face. I saw it in the Matrix ... An old man, eternally sad and infinitely wise ... *(SUBDUED, ALMOST HORRIFIED)* It can't be.

VANSELL: *(QUOTING)* 'There to do battle with Zagreus, the Beast/Never resting as long as history is lasting/Until either or both are laid to waste ...'

CHARLEY: It's going to speak!

ROMANA: On your knees, Doctor — Miss Pollard. On your knees, all of you!

(AND THE HOLOGRAM SPEAKS - SLIGHTLY DISTORTING, SHAKING, BUT STILL FILLING THE AIR WITH DEPTH AND RICHNESS ... SOMETHING LIKE THE VOICE OF GOD)

OLD MAN: It has been a time beyond measuring - here, alone in the cold, adrift and aloof from my people, my home. Once, my name was hailed and feared in equal measure by friends and enemies alike. Know, then, that I am Conqueror of Yssgaroth, Overpriest of Drornid, First Earl of Prydon, Patris of the Vortex, Ravager of the Void ... and President of Gallifrey from the time of our empire's Great Foundation. I am the Lord Rassilon. At last, my children, you have returned to me.

DOCTOR: *(TO ROMANA)* I don't understand. Rassilon died on Gallifrey millions of years ago. Romana, I've been inside his tomb!

ROMANA: Quiet, Doctor! There's more of the simulacrum!

OLD MAN: *(CONTINUING)* A long time past, I helped end centuries of tyranny and bloodshed on my home planet, helped to usher in a great age of enlightenment. With faithful counsel from the wisest of my technomagi, I locked the space/time continuum with the great Eye of Harmony. But, in my declining years, I grew fearful that by constructing the one true Time, I might have brought into being its very opposite. The menace of what I termed Anti-Time — a vile poison which might yet spill out to contaminate and undo all I have sought to achieve

261

— filled me with horror and dread. I resolved to journey into the strange, uncharted fringes of space/time in search of my nemesis — and here, in this weird unreality, I found the neverworld of Zagreus, the corpus of chaos and no-when. I have battled this entity; it is dormant, docile now. My TARDIS shattered, my exit point shut, I am trapped in this place. But I leave this message in the hope that one day, my Time Lords will find a way to rescue me. My body, I have placed in a Zero Cabinet nearby, my life's breath suspended; if I live, my children, I should like you to revive me, and take me to Gallifrey... take me home.

(FX: REVERSE 'FWIP!' AS THE HOLOGRAM DISAPPEARS THEN: A HUSH)

CHARLEY: So ... I take it that was someone important?

DOCTOR: That's putting it mildly, Charley. *(BEAT; TO HIMSELF)* This is all wrong ...

ROMANA: *(TO EVERYONE)* You may stand. Well, Doctor. Now you know.

DOCTOR: Congratulations, Romana. You've discovered Rassilon. What do you call someone so powerful they rescue God?

ROMANA: There are no gods, Doctor — Rassilon least of all. Oh, we've given him the trappings of a god — sacred relics and recitals, myths of his achievements and creations. We even call him Father to our race. But he was just a man. A great and wise man — but a man, all the same. For millions of years, we've been busy venerating his name, garlanding him in glory — but how much do we actually know about him?

DOCTOR: Biographical information is thin on the ground, I'll admit, but—

VANSELL: So the great Doctor turns sceptic. Now I've heard it all!

DOCTOR: That's not the point, Vansell. We are in an environment we know next-to-nothing about — just conjecture and guesswork. There are ghost-like creatures back there — which we really don't know anything about — draining the Time Station dry. And now we find that the greatest of our heroes is not actually resting in peace in the Death Zone, but actually transported himself here I-don't-know-how in search of an I-don't-know-what called 'Zagreus'? *(BEAT)* Whew. Hasn't it been a long day?

CHARLEY: I think I understand who Rassilon was. But how did this lot know to find him here? And wasn't 'Zagreus' a character in a children's rhyme, or something? That's right — it came up in Singapore, remember?

DOCTOR: Oh, yes. *'Zagreus sits inside your head/Zagreus lives among the dead ...*

VANSELL: ... *'Zagreus sees you in your bed/And eats you when you're sleeping.'* Miss Pollard asks good questions, Doctor.

DOCTOR: It's a nursery rhyme, Vansell - tea-time terror for Time Tots! It doesn't mean anything — does it?

CHARLEY: *'Ring-a-ring-a-roses.'*

DOCTOR: What?

CHARLEY: Oh, Doctor — you know. *'Ring-a-ring-a-roses/A pocket full of posies/A-tish-oo/A-tish-oo/We all fall down.'* *(BEAT)* It's about the Black Death, isn't it? Sneezing was a symptom of bubonic plague, and 'all fall down' means — well, dying.

DOCTOR: Charley, you're right! So how does the second verse go? Think, think! *'Zagreus at the end of days/Zagreus ...'* (*BEAT*) No, it's gone.

VANSELL: Then let me refresh your straining memory, Doctor. *'Zagreus at the end of days/Zagreus lies all other ways/Zagreus comes when time's a maze ...'*

DOCTOR: ... *'And all of history's weeping.'* Yes, of course! It could almost be a metaphor —

VANSELL: — for what's happening to the Web of Time, yes. Intriguing, then, that 'Zagreus' should figure in the literature of other worlds — as a parable on Sparbarus and Finniam 4; as an epic of the Jxrxkrk-speaking peoples ...

DOCTOR: Well, don't quote that. The consonants alone could keep us here for weeks.

VANSELL: (*IGNORING HIM*) ... and can be found in the Black Library of an Earth sect, the Knights of St John the Beheaded. Commander Levith here borrowed this 'Book of Zagreus' in Earth's twentieth century — but it is known to have existed as far back as the twelfth epoch, and possibly beyond. Levith?

LEVITH: Co-ordinator. (*BEAT; CONTINUES STORY*) The book tells of a great hero, an alchemist and warrior who has struck a deal with the Gods to establish a marvellous empire in the heavens; his people are contented and happy, living in an enlightened, benevolent Utopia. But at night, this hero dreams of a terrible being who will rise to overthrow his people; his mirror-opposite, who will exact as awful a disestablishment of the hero's empire as its building was miraculous.

VANSELL: (*QUOTING*)*'Zagreus waits at the end of the world/For Zagreus is the end of the world/His time is the end of time/And his moment Time's undoing.'* Again, the parallel to the Web is quite remarkable.

CHARLEY: So what happens, to the hero?

VANSELL: He abandons his people. He builds a vast and mighty cosmic ship and goes in search of the land of Zagreus, a land he knows only to exist in dreams. (*QUOTING*) *'He set then his course/To a scar on the face of Creation/Where the stars lived and died in the churn of one night/And decay was the only true constant.'*

LEVITH: After many, many years, he is ready to give up his quest — when he imagines a huge gate in the clouds: (*QUOTING*) *'And the gate of Zagreus opened before him/And all of the Anti-verse was revealed to him/And its terrible beauty ached in his hearts.'*

DOCTOR: (*INTRIGUED*) Hearts plural? Really?

VANSELL: (*CONTINUING*)*'So through them he ventured/There to do battle with Zagreus, the Beast/Never resting as long as history is lasting/Until either or both are laid to waste.'*

DOCTOR: ... and they all lived happily ever after, I suppose? I accept, there are a few circumstantial connections to be made, but the evidence is hardly compelling. So what else?

ROMANA: The name of the hero, Doctor, is 'Azalon' or sometimes 'Razlon'; in some traditions, simply 'Ra'. These folktales share one other element: before the hero leaves home in search of Zagreus, he orders all records of his quest destroyed, for fear of undermining his Utopia. His people believe him passed away.

DOCTOR: And you believed it. All of it.

VANSELL: It explained why the idea of Anti-Time has always been discredited or suppressed — an enduring legacy of Rassilon's lieutenants — but a possible congruence between these tales and the heresy of Anti-Time has been noted for centuries.

ROMANA: Only recently have our students been brave enough to break with the Great Curriculum, to open their eyes to newer fields — sharing their knowledge with other of the Temporal Powers.

VANSELL: — An undertaking which my Agency has been happy to assist. But imagine if the great Rassilon were to be returned to us — he who began the Intuitive Revelation, who established the Eye of Harmony and anchored the space/time vortex. How much could we achieve? How much further could the Time Lords go?

DOCTOR: Well, you'll forgive me for stating the blindingly obvious, Vansell, but the question is entirely academic for the moment.

CHARLEY: Why's that, Doctor?

DOCTOR: Where is he, Charley? Where's Rassilon? Where's the body?

34. EXT. THE WILDERNESS (PLAIN)
(FX: HOWLING WINDS)

ANTI-VOICE 1: The Time Lords are all gathered together, sister, in the cavern. Can we not absorb them now — now, while their saga is stalled and their histories ripe for consumption?

ANTI-CHARLEY: Stay your appetite, brother. Will we squander an eternal banquet for the sake of a moment's hunger? Satisfaction will be ours. There is a phrase, known by the Earth girl — 'just desserts'. The Time Lords will be our just desserts — not only now, but forever. *(BEAT)* They procrastinate. It's time we intervened.

35. INT. CAVERN

DOCTOR: — but you're not listening to me, any of you! Our mythologies are not so widespread to have permeated the cultures of so many other worlds —

ROMANA: The legend of the Vampires did. There, Rassilon is cast in many guises: on Xerxes, as He-With-the-Bolts-of-Truth; on Earth, as Shandor, and Van … something, too.

DOCTOR: Well, yes, there is that.

VANSELL: In the Outer Wastes, the curse of the Pythia is recounted in the saga of their She-Serpent …

LEVITH: In the witch-lore of Casseiopeia, she is known as the Countess Bathori, or Baphmet.

ROMANA: So why not? Why should the tale of Rassilon's true fate not have escaped Gallifrey — especially if it were proscribed?

CHARLEY: Romana does have a point, Doctor.

DOCTOR: I know, I know — it's just that I'm certain something's wrong, and I don't know quite what …

LEVITH: Why are we debating this?

VANSELL: Indeed. *(TO ROMANA)* Madam President, the proof lies inside a Zero Cabinet, somewhere within the bounds of this planet — or

264

TARDIS, whatever.

ROMANA: Agreed. *(TO ALL)* We search, methodically — and find Rassilon's casket.

DOCTOR: If it exists.

(FX: BURST OF TWINKLING, COSMIC EFFECTS; ANTI-TIME MUSIC)

ANTI-CHARLEY: Oh, Doctor. Of course the casket exists.

DOCTOR: You again! Have you been listening in?

CHARLEY: *(TO DOCTOR)* Doctor! Have you met that, that — thing with my face already?

DOCTOR: *(TO CHARLEY)* Oh yes. And I know enough to be wary of it.

ANTI-CHARLEY: Well, Co-ordinator? Have you found what you came here for?

VANSELL: Only in part. Do you know where the casket is, Never-person?

ANTI-CHARLEY: We do.

DOCTOR: I don't like the way this conversation is going ...

ANTI-CHARLEY: We hold the casket. We wish to make an accommodation with you, for its return.

ROMANA: I'm sorry? Am I to take it you want to negotiate terms?

ANTI-CHARLEY: We know you, Time Lords. We know the effect that our limited excursions into your reality has had upon your continuity. We know, if you could, you would eliminate us utterly. But your time gives us being. Would you deny us our right to exist?

DOCTOR: A very fair point. Romana?

ROMANA: Doctor, I can't. What their very existence might do to the Web of Time — it's incalculable! You saw the Matrix projection.

DOCTOR: But who's to say that's not one of a billion alternatives? You — I mean, we — we Time Lords are a pretty conservative bunch; the minds in the Matrix even more so. The slightest tremor in their web sets their senses jangling. Of course the Matrix is in turmoil!

VANSELL: As much as the sentiment sticks in my throat, Madam President, the Doctor is right. The least we can do is hear their terms.

ROMANA: I will not be rushed, Vansell!

VANSELL: And I will not stand by while our greatest hero languishes at the mercy of these creatures, while our very reality is imperilled! *(COLD, DELIBERATE)* Sometimes, Madam President, I don't think you've the hearts for this job.

ROMANA: Is this insurrection, Co-ordinator? Take care. Take great care!

DOCTOR: Calm down, both of you.

VANSELL: *(BURSTING WITH ANGER)* I will not be calm! We have held ourselves back too long, bound by caution, tradition and deference. We are a joke! We maintain the universe, oh yes — we preserve it in amber, its injustices uncorrected. Aggressors go unpunished in the name of mediation. Doctor, you placed the Daleks — the Daleks, the most evil, ruthless, coldly calculating race to have ever stained our history! — in a time loop. We could crush them, now, ensure that the torments they visit upon every peoples they encounter never occur again! But will we? Will we? We could work with our allies — the Monan Host, the Warpsmiths of Phaidon, humanity even — to build a consensus for progress across all the galaxies, to be a radical force for the advancement of a common good!

ROMANA: Have you quite finished?

VANSELL: I haven't begun! So come on, Madam President. The Daleks. What will you do? Will you let them go eventually? Will you? Of course you will. You don't have the imagination for anything else!

ROMANA: This is hardly the time or the place for such a debate.

VANSELL: Why not? Do we have to argue whether or not we should negotiate the return of the architect of our race — a progressive, a hero who was unafraid to reach out to the unknown to further not just the glory of his people, but the security of the people of the entire universe! Our reality is falling apart, and yet you vacillate while the one man who might have the wisdom and power to resolve this crisis is within your reach!

(BEAT — BROKEN BY A SLOW HANDCLAP FROM THE DOCTOR)

DOCTOR: Good speech, Vansell — a postcard from Planet Nosebung. A nice place to visit, but you wouldn't want to live there.

VANSELL: I'll not take criticism from a deposed President, a convicted criminal — a feckless joyrider whose misplaced sentimentality caused the Anti-Time breach in the first place! You should have paid dear for your countless offences by now. A strong leader would have ensured it!

ANTI-CHARLEY: *(BOOMING)* Enough! These are our terms. We will return to you the casket containing your hero, the great Rassilon, whose thoughts and deeds have passed into legend. We will also return to you your Time Station. In exchange we require only that you undertake to establish a dialogue between the peoples of our realities. We hope to abide by the laws of your universe, in exchange for limited freedom to trawl your time stream for the energies which give us meaning. We anticipate, therefore, the construction of a permanent gateway between our realities ...

DOCTOR: What, using Charley as your back door? That's not on!

CHARLEY: Definitely not! *(ALMOST EMBARRASSED)* Well, don't I have a say in the matter?

ANTI-CHARLEY: *(CONTINUING, UNAFFECTED)* ... and so, as a show of good faith, we desire to retain one of your three leaders — the Madam President, the Co-ordinator, or the Doctor — who shall remain here, in our universe, until such an accord can be reached.

DOCTOR: Yes yes yes, but what about Charley?

(BEAT)

VANSELL: "What about Charley?" What about her? The time she has now is stolen — pilfered on her behalf by you, Doctor.

ROMANA: That is a very unkind reading of Miss Pollard's predicament —

VANSELL: *(CUTTING IN)* — but an accurate one! *(BEAT)* There is every reason to suppose that Rassilon himself may yet find a solution to this conundrum. After all, we don't yet know how he entered this Antiverse in the first place. *(BEAT; TO ANTI-CHARLEY)* We accept your terms, Never-person.

ANTI-CHARLEY: You volunteer yourself to remain behind, Co-ordinator?

(BEAT)

VANSELL: I do not. I nominate the Lady Romanadvoratrelundar,

President of Gallifrey and all its dominions. One president — for our first President. A fair exchange. Levith — escort the Lady Romana.

LEVITH: With pleasure, Co-ordinator.

ROMANA: I would have stayed behind all the same, Vansell. My choice will not be made at staser-point.

DOCTOR: So this is what you wanted, Vansell. Staff a Time Station with your CIA placemen, take your President into another universe and pull off a bloodless coup, returning in glory as Rassilon's right-hand man — and chosen heir, perhaps? *(TO ANTI-CHARLEY)* Do not take this man at his word, Never-person. He is more interested in his own political gain than the well-being of your people!

ANTI-CHARLEY: I do not agree, Doctor. We have been observing the Co-ordinator. He is a principled and honest man, who believes in his oath of office. We trust him. *(BEAT)* The casket awaits you on the plain outside. You will all join me there.

(FX: TWINKLING EFFECTS. THE ANTI-CHARLEY IS GONE)
(BEAT)

ROMANA: I'm disappointed in you, Vansell. I judged you loyal.

VANSELL: Oh I am. To my planet. To my people. To Rassilon. But to you, my lady? I don't think so.

CHARLEY: Well, I think turncoats like you get what they deserve!

VANSELL: Levith, keep these three covered. And if Miss Pollard so much as squeaks again — be sure to kill the Doctor. *(BEAT)* Now, we have just arranged a meeting, let's go. Come on, then — move!

36. EXT. THE WILDERNESS (PLAIN)
(FX: HOWLING WINDS)

VANSELL: *(SHOUTING INTO THE AIR)* We are here, Never-people. Where are you? *(FX: TWINKLING COSMIC EFFECTS. ANTI-TIME MUSIC)* What — just you again? Where is the casket?

ANTI-CHARLEY: Patience, Co-ordinator. *(BEAT)*

CHARLEY: Doctor, is she communicating with the others — you know, with telepathy or something?

DOCTOR: Possibly, Charley, very possibly. *(WHISPERED, TO ROMANA)* Romana, whatever happens, don't give up. Keep the faith. There's a way out of all this — I know there is!

ROMANA: *(WHISPERED)* Doctor, one day you'll fail to keep one of your promises. It'll come as a terrible shock to you when it happens.

VANSELL: Stop gossiping, you two. We're waiting.

ROMANA: I'm ready. *(TO ANTI-CHARLEY)* What do you want with me, Never-person?

ANTI-CHARLEY: You will cross to my position. The remainder will stay back.

ROMANA: Very well. *(BEAT/FX: TEN FOOTSTEPS' SPACE)* Will this do?

ANTI-CHARLEY: That will suffice.

ROMANA: *(SPONTANEOUSLY, ALOUD)* You know, you're wrong, Vansell. We Time Lords have a duty to all the people of the Universe, yes. But the Utopia you imagine is an anodyne and pointless paradise. How many things do you want us to set right? Do we intervene to ensure that no-one dies young? Do we change the course of history

267

when someone's heart is broken? Do we remove all predators from the timeline, rewrite the rules of natural selection? The Universe can be a cruel and savage place — but a wild garden can be beautiful. You'd concrete the galaxy if you pricked your thumb on a rose. We guard the inevitability of events. Sometimes, the hardest thing is not to act; the hardest thing is to watch, and learn. And the joy of life is in living it, good and bad the same.

VANSELL: *(SHOUTED BACK)* Oh, spare us the sophistry, Madam President, and make way for someone with nerve! *(TO ANTI-CHARLEY)* Never-person — where is it? Where is the casket?

ANTI-CHARLEY: Why, beneath your feet, Co-ordinator.

(FX: A LOW RUMBLING IN THE EARTH ...)

VANSELL: What? Where—?

DOCTOR: Watch your step, Charley!

CHARLEY: Waah! This happened before, when the TARDIS disappeared!

(FX: ... THEN A FEARSOME CRACK! HISS OF STEAM. A CRACKLING SOUND. AND THE BABBLE OF MANY MORE ANTI-PEOPLE)
(GASPS FROM GUARDS)

DOCTOR: *(TO HIMSELF)* Oh how very theatrical. An anti-funeral — phantom pallbearers dragging the casket with them from the ground...

ANTI-CHARLEY: Here is your hero, Co-ordinator.

(FX: A LOW CRACKLING FROM THE CASKET)

VANSELL: *(REVERENT, TO CASKET)* My Lord Rassilon. I can sense your power already.

DOCTOR: Yes, there's some sort of aura about it. Strange.

ANTI-CHARLEY: We will take the Lady Romana now. Your passage will be unimpeded. We look forward to meeting you again.

VANSELL: *(DISTRACTED)* What? Oh yes, yes, of course.

(FX: TWINKLING. BABBLE OF ANTI-VOICES)

ANTI-VOICE 1: You come with us now, lady —

ANTI-VOICE 2: — to the places underneath.

ANTI-VOICE 1: Join us —

ANTI-VOICE 2: — nourish us.

ROMANA: Oh, don't overdo it. I'm not frightened of yooooooooouuu——

(FX: ROMANA'S LAST WORD EXTENDED, WARPING WITH ANTI-TIME EFFECTS. REVERSING TWINKLE)

DOCTOR: *(WHISPERED, TO CHARLEY)* She's dissipating with them, being pulled through the crack in the ground ... Charley?

CHARLEY: *(WHISPERED, TO DOCTOR)* Mm?

DOCTOR: *(WHISPERED, TO CHARLEY)* While the Time Lords are distracted, do you suppose it's worth trying to leap the crevasse?

CHARLEY: *(WHISPERED, TO DOCTOR)* Oh, I'm game if you are, Doctor. After three? One ...

DOCTOR: *(WHISPERED, TO CHARLEY)* ... two ...

CHARLEY: *(ALOUD)* ... three!!! *(THEY BREAK FOR IT — BUT LEVITH GRABS CHARLEY)* Aooww!

LEVITH: Don't even think it, Charley.

CHARLEY: *(STRUGGLING)* Get off me, you cow!

DOCTOR: *(MID-SPRINT)* Charley ... ? *(THEN SLIPPING ON THE*

LIP OF THE CHASM, AND STEADYING HIMSELF) Whoa!
(FX: DIRT SLIPPING DOWN CHASM)
CHARLEY: Doctor!
DOCTOR: (BREATHLESS) It's alright. Nearly lost my footing on
the edge, that's all. Oh, put your stasers away, boys. I'll come quietleee-
(SLIPS AGAIN; GRABS RIM) — unhh! (FX: MORE DIRT CASCADING)
VANSELL: Why, Doctor, I do believe you're losing your grip.
DOCTOR: Very ... funny, Vansell. Come on, help me up. (FX: MORE
DIRT) Waa!
VANSELL: Now why would I want to do that? After all, Doctor, 'it's
not worth living if you can't live dangerously' — is it?
DOCTOR: Please, Vansell! I can't ... hold on ... much — (FX: LOTS
OF DIRT) — longerrrrrrrrr — (HE FALLS)
CHARLEY: Doctor!!!
VANSELL: Sorry — who? (BEAT) Keep a tight hold of the girl. You
guards, take the casket. Gently! The Time Station isn't far. We're going
home. The great Lord Rassilon is going home.

37. INT. TUNNEL
(FX: ROMANA BEING MARCHED ALONG. TWINKLING EFFECTS OF
ANTI-PEOPLE. SOME DISTANCE AWAY, AT THE END OF THE TUNNEL,
THE NOISE OF A BAYING CROWD OF ANTI-PEOPLE)

ROMANA: (AGGRIEVED) You don't have to chivvy me along with
... ectoplasm, or whatever it is you're composed of. I am here of my
own accord.
ANTI-CHARLEY: You are here because we wanted you here, Madam
President. Everything which has transpired in this place has happened
because we wished it.
ROMANA: And what do you mean by that? (BEAT) I am President
of Gallifrey and so far as I am concerned I am an honoured guest!
(BEAT) What's that noise? Where are you taking me?
ANTI-CHARLEY: To meet the rest of our people, Madam President.
They have been so longing to meet you. Indeed, there is talk of nothing
else in our world. There are many questions they wish to put to you.
ROMANA: What, like a diplomatic address?
ANTI-CHARLEY: More in the sense of a trial. Continue ...

38. INT. TIME STATION (CONSOLE CHAMBER)
(FX: WHOOSHING OF DOORS. ECHOEY, QUIET)

CHARLEY: This is your Time Station, Vansell? You should get the
cleaners in.
VANSELL: The damage is only superficial ... and the power easily
restored. (FX: BLEEPS — AND THE FULL CONSOLE CHAMBER
AMBIENCE HUMS BACK INTO LIFE) See? (ALOUD) Escort — bring the
casket through! (FX: FOUR GUARDS CARRY CRACKLING CASKET IN
AND PLACE IT ON THE GROUND) That's right, just there. Careful!
CHARLEY: Why don't you just open the box, Vansell? Let's hear
what your precious Rassilon has got to say about your behaviour!
VANSELL: Quiet! The Lord Rassilon will be revived in controlled
conditions on Gallifrey. Till then, there's no sense in risking his well-

being.

CHARLEY: You've got no intention of making a treaty with the Anti-Time people, have you?

VANSELL: That will be for President Rassilon to decide. Me, personally — I'd gladly see the universe rid of their filthy scourge. *(BEAT)* Under-Cardinal! Power report!

UNDER-CARDINAL: *(FROM ABOVE, SOME WAY AWAY)* Time Rotor drained, but Artron fuel will have regenerated in mass in ... twenty microspans, Co-ordinator.

VANSELL: That's 'Acting President', if you please. *(BEAT)* Levith!

LEVITH: Yes, Co-ord— *(BITES TONGUE)* — I mean, Acting President, sir?

VANSELL: Order the proton accelerator delivered from the Engineering deck. Miss Pollard needs to be readied for her little ... transfiguration. *(ALOUD, TO WHOLE ROOM)* I want this Time Station ready to launch in thirty microspans!

39. INT. TUNNEL

(FX: DIRT FALLING. DOCTOR PICKING HIS WAY DOWN WALLS. CHINKING OF METAL)

DOCTOR: *(TO HIMSELF)* ... hup ... hup ... hup ... *(FX: FEET ON FLOOR)* ... Oof! *(BEAT)* And relax, Doctor. Now, what do we have in this pocket, hmm? Oh dear... *(FX: DISCARDS TWO SMALL METAL OBJECTS — CLANG ON FLOOR. AS BEFORE, MUFFLED ANTI-CROWD NOISES FROM END OF TUNNEL)* Other pocket... ah ha! Excellent. I think I shall make this my First Law of Intergalactic Travel: you never know when a pair of Antarean Sensory Pitons might come in useful. Now. More tunnels. Hey, what's that? Sounds like quite a gathering...

(FX: FOOTSTEPS AWAY — AND INTO:)

40. INT. GREAT CAVERN

(FX: HUGE SPACE. THIS IS WHERE THE ANTI-CROWD NOISES HAVE BEEN COMING FROM - MUCH COSMIC TWINKLING. FADE UP VOICES: SOUND STILL SLIGHTLY DISTANT — AS IF THE LISTENER IS THE DOCTOR, PEERING INTO THE CAVERN)

ANTI-CHARLEY: Brothers, sisters — we have a visitor. The President Romana, ruler of the planet Gallifrey!

(FX: SNEERING, ANGRY ANTI-VOICES. UNDERTOW OF VIOLENCE)

DOCTOR: *(TO HIMSELF, CLOSE TO MIC - AS IF THE LISTENER IS RIGHT NEXT TO HIM)* There's hundreds of them! Thousands!

(FX: NOW CONTINUE SCENE 'STRAIGHT')

ANTI-CHARLEY: Stand here, up on the basalt!

ROMANA: Thank you. So many of you. Am I honoured?

ANTI-CHARLEY: Two of our people are especially keen to meet you. *(TO TWO ANTI-PEOPLE)* Come on, come on!

ANTI-VOICE 1 & ANTI-VOICE 2: *(TOGETHER, AFFABLE, NEAR-JOVIAL)* Hello!

ROMANA: Er, hello. *(BEAT)* Sorry, I thought there was something you wanted to say to me ...

ANTI-VOICE 1: Do you not know us, Romanadvoratrelundar?

ANTI-VOICE 2: Surely you remember? Oh, Romana, you must!
ROMANA: Sorry, no. *(BEAT)* I've never been inside this universe before — well, no-one has.
ANTI-CHARLEY: *(MOCKING?)* — except for your hero Lord Rassilon, of course.
ROMANA: Of course. But he didn't send me a postcard.
(FX: RIPPLE OF RESTRAINED ANTI-PEOPLE LAUGHTER - CUT OFF)
ANTI-VOICE 2: Oh, no, no, no! You really don't remember me, Romana? Oh, they said you'd grown cold and heartless — but I didn't believe them. And now I know it's true. *(SHE BEGINS TO SOB)*
ROMANA: Well, I'm sorry. I'm usually good with faces, but yours —
ANTI-CHARLEY: Then let us put names to the faces. The girl's name is Laris; the boy is her brother, Korvan.
(BEAT)
ROMANA: No. Those names mean nothing to me.
ANTI-VOICE 2: *(WAILS PLAINTIVELY)* She doesn't remember, Korvan!
ANTI-VOICE 1: How could you be so beastly?
ROMANA: Oh, come on! This is getting ridiculous!
(FX: GROWLS OF UNREST AND ANGER FROM CROWD)
ANTI-CHARLEY: When you were a little girl, Lady Romana, no more than sixty years or so, your family would spend most summers in a rambling house on the shores of Lake Abydos. You used to go swimming with the singing fish; you collected zinc hawthorns from the molten rushes near the water's edge.
ROMANA: I did — yes. But how do you know — ? And just what has any of this got to do with you lot, anyway?
ANTI-CHARLEY: Quiet! *(BEAT)* Did you go alone, Lady Romana?
ROMANA: *(WITH HER LAST RESERVES OF PATIENCE)* Yes. I was an only child. I didn't have many friends. I was usually too worried about my tribiphysics marks.
ANTI-CHARLEY: Oh, but you did have friends, my lady.
ANTI-VOICE 2: You had us!
ROMANA: Well, now you're just being silly. I know my own memories.
ANTI-VOICE 1: Then you'll remember the day we found the flurry-birds nesting in the old pavilion ... the time the hermit at the far side of the Ravos-burn chased us away with fire-sigils?
ANTI-VOICE 2: Oh, say you do, Romana — please?
ROMANA: No... no I do not... how can I?
ANTI-VOICE 2: But... but we were your friends. For years...
ANTI-CHARLEY: Enough, Laris. Don't hurt yourself any more. *(BEAT)* Tell me, my lady — with your investiture into the highest office, were you not made privy to all of Gallifrey's most closely-guarded secrets?
ROMANA: Well, obviously.
ANTI-CHARLEY: The Jaskud Records? The War Perceptors? The Cavux Imperatives?
ROMANA: Yes, yes, yes ...
ANTI-CHARLEY: — plus, of course, the Oubliette of Eternity.
ROMANA: *(CAGEY)* Yes.
ANTI-CHARLEY: What is the Oubliette of Eternity, Madam President?
ROMANA: A disused chamber, deep in the heart of our largest off-world station —

ANTI-CHARLEY: The headquarters of the Celestial Intervention Agency. Could you tell me, Madam President, what this chamber was used for?

ROMANA: Dispersal — a barbaric punishment, long since abolished. Is this relevant?

ANTI-CHARLEY: Very. And what exactly did 'dispersal' entail?

ROMANA: It was reserved for those found guilty only of the highest treason against Gallifrey. Inside the chamber, offenders would be dissipated from history — their entire timeline erased, as if they had never ... *(REALISATION DAWNING)* ... existed.

ANTI-CHARLEY: And where, do you suppose, did these dispersed people go?

ROMANA: Nowhere ... I mean, they'd never existed! There was nowhere for them to go!

(FX: AN INTERRUPTION FROM THE BACK OF THE HALL. HUBBUB AMONG ANTI-PEOPLE)

DOCTOR: *(LOUD)* Oh, but there was, Romana. Here! - They came here! *(TO HIMSELF)* It all makes sense, don't you see? A barren subdimension beyond the planes of our reality where the usual rules don't apply!

ANTI-CHARLEY: Doctor! How good it is to see you! (TO ANTI-PEOPLE) Bring him here.

(FX: MENACING HUBBUB)

DOCTOR: It's alright, I'm coming, I'm coming. I've got no reason to hide.

ROMANA: *(UNPERTURBED)* You mean ... all of you ... all these thousands of you ... once, you were Gallifreyans? Time-Lords even?

ANTI-CHARLEY: Banished from existence at the behest of the CIA. *(BEAT)* Biddulf here was a Chancellery Guard who got drunk on Malian Head Juice and babbled details of President Pandak's retinue. Savos beside him was the barman whose only crime was to listen to Biddulf's slurred nonsense. Both were dispersed here, their lives deleted and forgotten. Korvan and Laris were caught accessing classified documents in a bid to discover how they where orphaned; they discovered that their parents, Majos and Tesla, were student rebels, dispersed for unlicensed and unsponsored researches into mutogenic breeding. Everyone here has a story to tell.

ANTI-VOICE 1: And you forgot all about us. If we'd never existed, what was there to remember? But we remember. We remember you, Romana.

DOCTOR: Can I ask a question? You — the one with Charley's form. Who are you? Where did you come from?

ANTI-CHARLEY: I wear the shape of the space-time breach as a badge, a symbol of our means of escape. On Gallifrey, my name was Sentris.

DOCTOR: And what was your crime? What did you do?

ANTI-CHARLEY: My offences were many and terrible, Doctor. I was a cold killer, a ruthless murderer of innocents.

DOCTOR: Forgive me, but by the sounds of it you, at least, got something of what you deserved.

ANTI-CHARLEY: Oh, I was never sentenced — or caught, even. I sent myself to the Oubliette of Infinity, dispersed myself into this screaming tumult. I was the two-hundred-and-seventeenth Co-ordinator of the CIA. *(BEAT)* It seemed very rare, to authorise a dispersal. But when you cannot remember that the last person you had destroyed was ever alive at all — you go along with it. One day, I checked the records we kept in a time-protected vault. In just one year as the head of the Agency, I found that I had approved the non-execution of over two hundred non-people. The shame was too much to bear. I destroyed myself. And came here, to find myself surrounded by my victims. They have despised me for an eternity, but I have promised to make amends — to give them their lives back. This I shall do.

(AWKWARD PAUSE THEN THE HUBBUB RISES AGAIN)

ROMANA: *(OVER THIS AS THEY GET FRACTIONALLY LOUDER)* On behalf of the High Council of Time Lords, I tell you that I am desperately sorry for what has happened to you: to you, Biddulf and Savos; to you, Korvan and Laris; to all of you. And you, Sentris, I pity you, and I hope one day you find peace. This was a terrible chapter in Gallifrey's history, and if there is some way to give you something back, then—

ANTI-CHARLEY: *(UTTER SILENCE BEHIND THIS)* 'Was'! This 'was' a terrible chapter in Gallifrey's history? I pity you, Time Lady — I pity the fact that our ranks swell by the day, that the number of us continues to grow — by the men who carry out their actions in your name, Madam President, in your sacred name!

DOCTOR: Are you saying that — that these 'dispersals' continue? Now?

ANTI-CHARLEY: Yes, Doctor. Yes, I am!

ROMANA: *(TO HERSELF, WITH UTTER FURY)* Vansell!

41. INT. TIME STATION (CONSOLE CHAMBER)
(FX: ENGINES BUILDING)

VANSELL: *(NEXT TO CRACKLING CASKET, A BIT DISTANT)* Is the Time Rotor fully charged, Under-Cardinal?

UNDER-CARDINAL: Temporal reactors fully fuelled, Acting President — sir!

VANSELL: Good, good … *(MURMURING TO CASKET)* Great Lord Rassilon. I am but your humblest servant. I live to carry out your every instruction. *(BEAT)* *(FX: CRACKLING 'RIPPLES')* What? What's that? Yes, yes — of course …

(FX: SNAP OF VELCRO AS CHARLEY IS STRAPPED DOWN BY LEVITH)

LEVITH: Don't fight the straps, Charley. Only one more transformation.

CHARLEY: *(STRUGGLING)* So you say. Levith, we can't just abandon Romana — or the Doctor, if he's still alive. What you're doing is treason!

(FX: BLEEPS OF TECHNOLOGY — SEE Sc. 12)

LEVITH: I'm carrying out my Acting President's instructions. And for what it's worth, I happen to think that what he's doing is right. Oh, you wouldn't understand.

CHARLEY: I understand that your Acting President has flipped his lid! He's talking to the casket now!

VANSELL: *(DISTANT)* Is everything alright, Levith?

LEVITH: Nearly ready, sir!

VANSELL: Excellent. *(FX: A SLIGHT CRACKLING EFFECT ON HIS VOICE, BREAKING HIS WORDS. ANTI-TIME MUSIC)* Dematerialisation in

thirteen microspans!
CHARLEY: Anti-Time! Did you hear that, Levith — did you? *(BEAT)* Vansell's been infected with Anti-Time!

42. INT. GREAT CAVERN

ANTI-CHARLEY: Korvan, Laris — you may leave now. You know what you have to do.
ANTI-VOICE 1: Yes, Sentris.
ANTI-VOICE 2: Goodbye, Romana. We miss you.
(FX: COSMIC TWINKLING; THEY DISAPPEAR)
ROMANA: Goodbye — and I'm sorr— *(BEAT)* They've gone.
DOCTOR: Hm. So tell me, Sentris — is there no way back to Gallifrey, back through this Oubliette?
ANTI-CHARLEY: It isn't a doorway, Doctor — just a crude, cruel device. But when you opened the breach, when you saved your friend Charley — oh, to swim in real time, Doctor! To exist! To be! That small, simple right — denied us by you, and all who follow Rassilon!
ROMANA: Rassilon? What do you have against Rassilon?
ANTI-CHARLEY: Rassilon! Ha! That paranoid despot, the architect of the Web of Time? The worm who denied free will to the people of the Universe, chained them to his Eye, bound them to one single reality? Who decreed that any threat to his great empire's sanctity should be dispersed from all time?
ROMANA: *(INCREDULOUS)* What, Rassilon built the Oubliette? Then that means —
DOCTOR: Oh yes! Rassilon created Anti-Time!
ROMANA: *(INSPIRED)* And he called it 'Zagreus'! He realised what he'd done, and transported himself here, to — to ... No, no. That can't be right, can it?
DOCTOR: No, it can't. Oh, Romana - don't you see? There's no such thing as 'Zagreus'! There never was!
ROMANA: No such th— *(BEAT; TO ANTI-CHARLEY, ANGRY)* Is this true?
ANTI-CHARLEY: Ah, the legend of Zagreus! What a fabulous invention, a marvellous conceit — whispered in the ears of the gullible on a hundred worlds, in a thousand different eras. An enticement — and you, Madam President, have been well and truly snared.
DOCTOR: See? I knew it was too good to be true. Let's think now: Gallifrey has been sealed off, ever since the time distortions began to warp the weft of reality — yes?
ROMANA: Yes, but —
DOCTOR: So how to persuade its masters to take a trip into Anti-Time? Why not invent a legend, a myth which no Time Lord could possibly ignore? The survival of Rassilon, say. All very clever — a story just obscure enough to be plausible, a murmur given to chroniclers on twelfth century Earth, on Xerxes, on Sparbarus and so many others; a folktale which we, ourselves, might have forgotten. And it spread, throughout the ages, being repeated, becoming distorted until finally it gets brought to Gallifrey as a children's nursery rhyme. Then everything is set for one small, judicious intervention, perhaps, to nudge the tale beneath the noses of the CIA. And what a temptation that

would have been — the possibility that Rassilon himself might be alive. Of course Vansell swallowed it — baited, hooked and reeled in. *(TO ANTI-PEOPLE)* Am I right, or am I right, Sentris?

ANTI-CHARLEY: Close enough, Doctor.

ROMANA: But to what end? Why?

DOCTOR: Well, surely that's obvious. If the legend of Zagreus is a myth, then Rassilon still sleeps the sleep of the just in his Dark Tower, back in the Death Zone on Gallifrey.

ROMANA: So who was that man we saw, in the hologram?

ANTI-CHARLEY: A trick of the light? A mere phantasm? *(FX: HER VOICE BEGINS TO WARP AND DISTORT, BECOMING THAT OF THE OLD MAN IN Sc. 33)* Or simply a projection of the thing you most desired —

OLD MAN: *(ANTI-CHARLEY) (MOCKING, COMPLETELY TRANSFORMED)* — a man with the wisdom of all the ages. A hero from the mistiest shores of our planet's history. 'Know, then, that I am Conqueror of Yssgaroth, Overpriest of Drornid, First Earl of Prydon, Patris of the Vortex...'

DOCTOR: Very good, very good. Who else do you do? I suppose the wrecked TARDIS was a false construction, too?

ANTI-CHARLEY: *(WARPED BACK — A LINGER OF THE OLD MAN ON HER FIRST FEW WORDS)* Oh, my people include several TARDIS engineers — dissolved from history for sharing secrets with alien mechanics, or striving to over-ride Rassilon's Great Protocols. This whole world was fashioned from the debris of unlicenced time vessels, blasted out of continuity by your agents.

DOCTOR: Hm. All of which begs one final question ...

ROMANA: If that's not Rassilon in the casket ...

DOCTOR: ... what does it contain?

43. INT. TIME STATION (CONSOLE CHAMBER)
(FX: ENGINES BUILDING IN PITCH. BLEEPS AS LEVITH READIES EQUIPMENT, AS PER Sc. 12.)
(OVER, CHARLEY STRUGGLING WITH HER STRAPS)

VANSELL: *(ALOUD, SLIGHT CRACKLE BREAKING UP HIS WORDS)* We dematerialise in six microspans! *(TO LEVITH, ODDLY DISTANT)* Is the girl nearly ready, Commander?

LEVITH: Yes, Acting President. Are you — are you quite sure you're alright?

CHARLEY: *(STRUGGLING)* Oh, listen to the sound of his voice, Levith — there's something wrong! Something in the casket's corrupted him!

LEVITH: Don't make this harder on yourself, Miss Polla— *(CORRECTING HERSELF)* — Charley. Don't make me pacify you.

CHARLEY: Levith, please!! *(FX: COSMIC TWINKLING. TWO ANTI-TIME PEOPLE ZAP INTO CHAMBER)* What— *(BEAT)* Never-people! They're here!

ANTI-VOICE 1: Acting President, may we witness the transfiguration?

ANTI-VOICE 2: Will you share you knowledge with us?

VANSELL: *(CRACKLE NOW VERY SEVERE, VOICE VERY DISTANT)* Yes, yes, of course. Of course. *(ALOUD, TO CREW)* There's no need for alarm. Everything's going according to plan.

CHARLEY: No...

44. INT. GREAT CAVERN

DOCTOR: What are you planning, Sentris — you and your people?
ANTI-CHARLEY: Anti-Time cannot pass the transduction barriers which separate Gallifrey's continuity from the remainder of space-time. Your temporal locks are too strong.
ROMANA: Not one single atom can arrive on Gallifrey without authorisation, that's true — but —
DOCTOR: — but a Presidential vessel, especially one carrying the head of the Celestial Intervention Agency —
ROMANA: — need give no warning of its arrival; its signature will guarantee its conveyance automatically. What is in that casket? *(BEAT)* Tell me!
DOCTOR: Oh, I think we can make a pretty good guess, don't you? How about — a critical mass of raw and ravenous Anti-Time?
ANTI-CHARLEY: The casket will detonate as the Time Station materialises inside the barriers. A vast flood of Anti-Time will wash over the Capitol, swamping it, infecting it...
DOCTOR: The Web of Time is already stretched at the seams. Gallifrey is the last bastion of positive time. All that maintains the constance of the Universe is the Eye of Harmony — and if that is contaminated ...
ROMANA: All things will flux, wither and change their state.
DOCTOR: It will be as if the Time Lords had never existed! History will be a blank canvas, a churning chaos of twisted, unregulated time — the Empire of Zagreus ...
ANTI-CHARLEY: Freedom for all!
ROMANA: *(FURIOUS)* This cannot be allowed!

45. INT. TIME STATION (CONSOLE CHAMBER)
(FX: RISING MECHANICAL THRUM)

ANTI-VOICE 1: You know what do do, Vansell —
ANTI-VOICE 2: Give the order!
ANTI-VOICE 1: Open the gateway!
VANSELL: *(CRACKLING FX)* Yes, yes ... we must ... open the gateway. Levith — begin proton acceleration!
CHARLEY: Don't listen to him, Levith! His mind's been corrupted!
LEVITH: I — I don't know ...
VANSELL: Levith ... Levith. I am your Acting President. These Never-people are our friends. In the name of Rassilon himself — do it!
LEVITH: *(SLIGHT CRACKLING EFFECT ON VOICE)* Yes — yes, of course. Of course I must —
CHARLEY: Not you, too! Levith, no!
VANSELL: Activate!
(FX: PULSING BEAM - FWUB, FWUB, FWUB ...)
CHARLEY: *(SCREAMS)*
AAAAAAAAIIIIIIIIIIIIEEEEEEEEEEEEEEEEEEEEEEEEEE-EEEEEEEEEE

46. INT. GREAT CAVERN

DOCTOR: *(PASSIONATE)* I accept your grievance, Sentris — but this terrible revenge on the living cannot be justified! Maybe a compromise can be reached — the treaty you spoke of...

ANTI-CHARLEY: *(BLAZING)* There will be no treaty! *(BEAT)* Life is wasted on the living.

DOCTOR: I have to stop you, you do know that.

ANTI-CHARLEY: The Time Station is ready to launch. It cannot be stopped. And you, Doctor — your life has been rich. Your stories are many; your history has been filled to bursting. Your have lived more life than we could ever dream possible. But now your time is up. The Lady Romana — her absorption will be satisfying only as an act of rightful vengeance. Yours will be an act of charity, a feast for our starving people. *(BEAT)* Brothers, sisters — consume them now!

(FX: A RISING SWELL OF CHARGED, TWINKLING EFFECTS. ANTI-TIME MUSIC REACHES A CRESCENDO)

ANTI-PEOPLE: We hunger
We need you
We want your time
Give us your time

ROMANA: Get back, all of you! Get back!

DOCTOR: Please — no — don't do this! *(SCREAMS)* NOOOOOOOOOOOOOOOOOOO!!!!!

(END OF PART THREE)

PART FOUR

(RECAP FROM:)

46. INT. GREAT CAVERN

DOCTOR: *(PASSIONATE)* I accept your grievance, Sentris — but this terrible revenge on the living cannot be justified! Maybe a compromise can be reached — the treaty you spoke of...
ANTI-CHARLEY: *(BLAZING)* There will be no treaty! *(BEAT)* Life is wasted on the living.
DOCTOR: I have to stop you, you do know that.
ANTI-CHARLEY: The Time Station is ready to launch. It cannot be stopped. And you, Doctor — your life has been rich. Your stories are many; your history has been filled to bursting. Your have lived more life than we could ever dream possible. But now your time is up. The Lady Romana — her absorption will be satisfying only as an act of rightful vengeance. Yours will be an act of charity, a feast for our starving people. *(BEAT)* Brothers, sisters — consume them now!
(FX: A RISING SWELL OF CHARGED, TWINKLING EFFECTS. ANTI-TIME MUSIC REACHES A CRESCENDO)
ANTI-PEOPLE: We hunger
We need you
We want your time
Give us your time
ROMANA: Get back, all of you! Get back!
DOCTOR: Please — no — don't do this! *(SCREAMS)* NOOOOOOOOOOOOOOOOOO!!!!

47. INT. TIME STATION (CONSOLE CHAMBER)
(FX: AS BEFORE. PULSING BEAM, RISING THRUM, CHARLEY SCREAMING)

LEVITH: *(CRACKLING FX)* It's happening. The girl is changing!
(FX: AND CUE CHARLEY'S TRANSMUTATION, AS IN Sc. 16)
ANTI-VOICE 1: The gateway is open.
ANTI-VOICE 2: Vansell - we proceed!
VANSELL: *(CRACKLING FX)* Under-Cardinal! Are the breach co-ordinates locked?
UNDER-CARDINAL: *(CRACKLING FX)* Downloading ... now, Acting President!
(FX: BURST OF CHITTERING DATA)
VANSELL: *(CRACKLING FX)* Then set course for Gallifrey!
ANTI-VOICE 1: At last.
ANTI-VOICE 2: At last!
UNDER-CARDINAL: *(CRACKLING FX)* Course set!
VANSELL: *(CRACKLING FX)* Begin dematerialisation! *(FX: VAST PONDEROUS TIME ROTOR BEGINS TO VWORP) (BEAT; TO HIMSELF)* And so —
ANTI-VOICE 1: — we return!
ANTI-VOICE 2: Return!

(FX: ... AND THE TIME ROTOR STALLS, SOUND DECAYING)
UNDER-CARDINAL: *(CRACKLING FX)* Power ... failing, Acting President!
VANSELL: *(CRACKLING FX)* What?!?
UNDER-CARDINAL: *(CRACKLING FX)* Station static! Temporal reactors disengaged!
ANTI-VOICE 1: *(ROARING)* What is the —
ANTI-VOICE 2: — meaning —
ANTI-VOICE 1: — of this?!?

48. INT. GREAT CAVERN

ANTI-VOICES: Time
Time
Sweet time
Give us your time
DOCTOR: *(GASPING)* Sentris — this is ... senseless! Please - ! You're hurting us!
ROMANA: *(GASPING)* They're killing us, Doctor!
ANTI-CHARLEY: *(TO ANTI-VOICES)* Stop!!! *(BEAT)* There is something ... wrong. *(EXHALES)*
ROMANA: *(WHISPERED, TO DOCTOR)* What's Sentris doing?
DOCTOR: *(WHISPERED, TO ROMANA)* Communing with Never-people elsewhere — we saw it earlier, remember? Hm. A problem with the Time Station, perhaps? Do you know, I think we've earned ourselves a last-minute reprieve!
ROMANA: *(WHISPERED, TO DOCTOR)* Let's hope so. It's us against the death of yesterday.
DOCTOR: *(WHISPERED, TO ROMANA)* Romana, that's beautiful! What a time to discover poetry. *(BEAT; ALOUD, TO ANTI-CHARLEY)* Ah! You're back! Everything alright, Sentris? Can we get along with being murdered now?
ANTI-CHARLEY: A fault has developed aboard the Time Stat—
DOCTOR: *(INTERRUPTING)* Oh, a fault has developed aboard the Time Station, has it? See, Romana — what did I tell you? And I suppose you want us to fix it for you, hm? Your luck's in. Sentris — the lady Romana and I just happen to be fully qualified quantum mechanics! No call-out charge, very competitive rates, references on request—
ANTI-CHARLEY: Silence! We require the use of your TARDIS.
DOCTOR: My TARD— *(BEAT)* Oh, so you've been keeping my TARDIS, have you? Come on, come on — where is she?
(FX: RUMBLING OF EARTH. SCRAPING OF WOOD. CRACKLING FX. ANTI-TIME PEOPLE MURMURING)
DOCTOR: Ah, there she is! *(WALKING TOWARDS TARDIS, BRISKLY, CROSS. TO ANTI-PEOPLE)* Get off her, you lot! Do you mind? *(ALOUD)* I suppose you've had all a good suck on her Time Rotor by now? She's a time and space machine, not a lollipop!
ANTI-CHARLEY: Your vessel is undamaged.
DOCTOR: Saving her for pudding, I suppose. *(TO TARDIS, SOOTHING)* There, there, old girl. I won't let the nasty ghosts hurt you.
ANTI-CHARLEY: You will transport yourselves to the Time Station and use your machine to reinvigorate its Temporal Reactors.

279

DOCTOR: Well, I don't know. I might not have the jump leads. And if the fan belt's gone, pff — Romana, are you wearing tights?

ROMANA: *(REPROVINGLY)* That's enough banter, Doctor.

DOCTOR: *(DISAPPOINTED)* Is it? Oh. *(BEAT; TO ANTI-CHARLEY)* Well, Sentris? I suppose you'll be coming with us?

ANTI-CHARLEY: I will. There will be no deviation from the actions I have outlined.

DOCTOR: I could refuse ...

ANTI-CHARLEY: Your President is quite dispensable. She could die.

ROMANA: Then do it. *(BEAT; TO DOCTOR)* They're going to kill us anyway.

DOCTOR: *(REPROVINGLY)* That's as maybe, but no-one's dying on my account. Come on, Sentris. *(FX: TWINKLING SOUND - THEN WITH A 'FWISH', SENTRIS PASSES INTO TARDIS)* Will you please not dissipate like that? Kindly wait 'til I've opened the door and go through like a normal person!

ROMANA: Doctor, we're wasting time.

DOCTOR: I know. Good, isn't it? *(FX: TARDIS KEY IN LOCK, DOOR OPENS)* In you go, Romana. *(ALOUD, TO ANTI-PEOPLE)* Bye, all. *(FX: DOOR SLAMS. DEMATERIALISATION BEGINS)*

49. INT. TARDIS
(FX: TIME ROTOR IN MOTION. PRESSING BUTTONS)

DOCTOR: Hmm. This is tricky ...

ROMANA: What's the matter, Doctor?

DOCTOR: The TARDIS doesn't like this — hopping about in space with no temporal ties. *(FX: MORE SWITCH-FLICKING)* She's blundering about in the dark, and any second now ... *(FX: TIME ROTOR COMES TO A GRINDING HALT)* Told you!

ANTI-CHARLEY: If the machine malfunctions, then the President dies.

DOCTOR: Just a hiccup. And I'll need the President under the console with me, Sentris ... unless you can make yourself corporeal long enough to pass me that Astro-Rectifier? You can't? Well, then. *(DISAPPEARS UNDER CONSOLE; SLIGHTLY MUFFLED)* Romana! Toolbox is over beside the gramophone!

ROMANA: *(LOOKING ROUND)* Toolbox, toolbox — ah! *(FX: PICKS UP CLANKING TOOLBOX AND HOISTS IT OVER TO THE DOCTOR — BOTH NOW UNDER CONSOLE)* Call this proper equipment? Your Multi-Quantiscope's only got one head!

DOCTOR: It only ever had one head!

ROMANA: *(WHISPERED, TO DOCTOR)* Doctor, you stalled the TARDIS deliberately!

DOCTOR: *(PRETENDING TO FIDDLE ABOUT BENEATH THE CONSOLE FOR THE MEANTIME) (ALOUD, SO SENTRIS CAN HEAR)* I mean, how many heads does a Multi-Quantiscope need? *(WHISPERED, TO ROMANA)* I needed time to think. Think, think, think ...

ROMANA: *(ALOUD, SO SENTRIS CAN HEAR)* Well, one for uncoupling mergin nuts, obviously. *(WHISPERED, TO DOCTOR)* Don't worry, it's all in hand. Just get us up to the Time Station.

DOCTOR: *(ALOUD)* Mergin nuts? Oh, I use a Ganymede Driver on those. *(WHISPERED)* Am I to take it that you have a plan?

ROMANA:　　　*(ALOUD)* A Ganymede Driver? Oh no, a Multi-Quantiscope's what you need. Either that or a Demeter Uncoupler. *(WHISPERED)* Look, the Time Station can only pass Gallifrey's transduction barriers because it broadcasts my personal authorisation as its key — correct?

DOCTOR:　　　*(ALOUD)* Well, a Demeter Uncoupler will do fine for a two-gauge mergin nut, but anything above that, no. *(WHISPERED)* Of course! If we can change your authorisation code, the Time Station will be locked out of the Capitol! Romana, that's brilliant!

(FX: CLANKING OF MORE TOOLS. A COUPLE OF SPARKS)

ROMANA:　　　*(WHISPERED)* You don't get to be President of Gallifrey with a headful of turnips, you know. *(ALOUD)* Your Zeus Plugs are in a terrible state. And you've worn your Neutron Grips down to nothing! *(WHISPERED)* The signature's burned in, so I can't change the code from the Time Station — but if I can get to the Eighth Door, via the Matrix Chamber ...

DOCTOR:　　　*(ALOUD)* Well, you know what they say — a Neutron Grip is as a Neutron Grip does ... *(WHISPERED)* Yes, you can change the code from inside the Matrix!

ROMANA:　　　*(WHISPERED)* At least — in theory. *(ALOUD)* An Electron Crank? How quaint.

DOCTOR:　　　*(ALOUD)* You'd have me using one of those new-fangled Ion Grapples, I suppose? *(WHISPERED)* We just have to find a way to get you there. Hmm. I think an utterly transparent ploy is called for.

ANTI-CHARLEY: *(ABOVE THEM)* Quickly, quickly!

DOCTOR:　　　*(GETTING UP FROM BENEATH CONSOLE)* Keep your halo on, Sentris! A good workman never blames his tools — and you'll find no fault with mine. Now. *(FX: FLICKS SWITCHES; TIME ROTOR BEGINS TO RISE AND FALL)* Normal service has been resumed!

ROMANA:　　　*(HAVING GOT UP)* *(INSINCERELY)* Oh, well done, Doctor!

(FX: TIME ROTOR VWORPS ON)

50. INT. TIME STATION (CONSOLE CHAMBER)

(FX: THE WHIRLING BREACH EFFECT REVERSING IN ON ITSELF AS CHARLEY NORMALISES)

CHARLEY:　　　*(DEEP, SHUDDERING BREATHS; THEN, TO HERSELF)* I never want to go through that again as long as I live.

VANSELL:　　　*(CRACKLING FX)* But, Miss Pollard — you'll have to. After all, we have to go through you to get back into our universe.

CHARLEY:　　　What? We haven't ... ? We're not on ... ? Oh, no! Can't you just leave me alone?

ANTI-VOICE 1: You are a precious and fragile thing.

ANTI-VOICE 2: You will give us all our freedom back.

CHARLEY:　　　But what about my freedom? What about me?

(FX: TARDIS MATERIALISATION)

VANSELL:　　　*(CRACKLING FX)* Quiet, Miss Pollard. We have visitors.

CHARLEY:　　　The TARDIS! But—

(FX: MATERIALISATION COMPLETE. DOOR BANGS OPEN. DOCTOR, ROMANA AND ANTI-CHARLEY EMERGE)

DOCTOR:　　　Charley!

CHARLEY: I knew it! I knew you'd survive!

VANSELL: *(CRACKLING FX)* It's a very dreary habit, Doctor — cheating death. Someone will break that disposition, soon.

DOCTOR: Ah, Vansell! Enjoying your time as Despot-in-Waiting, are y— *(BEAT)* Vansell? What's wrong with your—

ROMANA: Levith, the Under-Cardinal, the whole crew — they're all the same!

CHARLEY: It's the casket, Doctor — something in there got to them!

DOCTOR: I imagine it did. Anti-Time infection doesn't suit your pasty face, Vansell. If you could only think straight, you'd see what you've enabled.

VANSELL: *(CRACKLING FX)* What I've —

DOCTOR: *(PERSUASIVELY)* That's not Rassilon in the casket, Vansell. Rassilon's dead. He was never there. Instead, you've brought into our universe a heaving mass of pure Anti-Time which is going to flood the whole of Gallifrey and disintegrate the Web of Time!

VANSELL: *(CRACKLING FX) (WEAKLY)* I — I'm not — *(ASSERTIVE)* You lie, Doctor. What we are doing is for the good of all Gallifrey.

CHARLEY: Is this true, Doctor? Is that what they're up to?

DOCTOR: It is, Charley — but I think Vansell's too far gone to care.

ANTI-CHARLEY: Enough! Doctor, you will attend to your duties.

DOCTOR: Yes, yes, yes. You megalomaniacs are all the same — rush, rush, rush. Never put off today what you can put off tomorrow, I say!

ROMANA: Doctor, you're talking nonsense.

DOCTOR: More often than not. *(FX: HI-TECH BLIPS AND BLEEPS)* Well, the control panel shows a power drain across the board — but like I told you before, these sensors aren't much use in this reality. Ah! Here, look — your flux curves are all out of synch.

ROMANA: Indubitably.

DOCTOR: *(SUCKING HIS LIPS AND CLICKING HIS TONGUE, LIKE A COWBOY PLUMBER)* Oh dear oh dear oh dear. Don't like this. *(BEAT)* Alright, Sentris — I can fix it. *(SLOWLY AND DELIBERATELY)* But I'm going to need a bit of help …

ROMANA: *(EQUALLY PONDEROUS AND OVERDONE)* Oh. What sort of help would that be, Doctor?

DOCTOR: You passed in Temporal Engineering, didn't you, Romana?

ROMANA: Oh, just a small Triple Alpha.

DOCTOR: I need a qualified person in the Reactors, to reset the flux pattern as I set the Time Station's pulses into phase with the TARDIS. Do you think you can do that?

ROMANA: It's a piece of cake, Doctor.

DOCTOR: No, it's a particularly fine display of lateral logic — but it'll get the Time Station moving again. Sentris — are we agreed? Romana can do my dirty work, down in the Reactors?

ANTI-CHARLEY: This is … acceptable.

VANSELL: *(CRACKLING FX)* Don't be so sure, my friend. The Doctor is a cunning retrograde, and the Lady Romana's no better. Send

Levith as her escort.

ANTI-CHARLEY: No. Commander Levith will stay here, keeping the Doctor at staser-point. You, Vansell, will go with Romana.

VANSELL: *(CRACKLING FX)* Me —? But I'm the Acting President! *(BEAT; SEMI-ASSERTIVE)* Yes, yes, I see that I must ... Of course, yes.

ANTI-CHARLEY: My comrades here will escort both you and the Lady Romana.

ANTI-VOICE 1: Oh, Romana — .

ANTI-VOICE 2: We're going on a little trip!

ROMANA: *(DRY)* Korvan and Laris. Splendid. Come along then. You too, Vansell.
(MOVING OFF)

DOCTOR: One moment, Madam President? *(BEAT)* I want you to have this.

ROMANA: Your sonic screwdriver? But—

DOCTOR: Oh, you may need it down there. Handy to have about, this old thing.

ROMANA: Yes, I remember.

DOCTOR: You will take good care of it?

ROMANA: I promise.

DOCTOR: Weren't you the one who told me not to make promises?

ROMANA: Only ones that can't be kept. *(BEAT)* Goodbye, Doctor.
(LEAVES)
(FX: SWISHING OF DOORS)

DOCTOR: *(TO HIMSELF)* Goodbye, Romana. *(BREATHES IN DEEPLY; THEN, ALOUD)* Well, then. Best set our noses to the grindstone. And please don't wave that weapon in my face, Levith — you're blocking all my light!

51. INT. TIME STATION (CORRIDOR)

ROMANA: Oh, do hurry up, Vansell! We don't want to keep our unalive friends waiting!

VANSELL: *(CRACKLING FX) (SLOWLY)* Unalive —?

ROMANA: You don't know? These Never-people are your victims — Time Lords blasted out of history at the CIA's behest!

VANSELL: *(CRACKLING FX)* No, no ...

ANTI-VOICE 1: He cannot hear you. You waste time, Madam President.

ANTI-VOICE 2: And Time is too precious to squander.

ROMANA: That's strange, coming from people who have want to destroy Time itself.

ANTI-VOICE 1: Your Time is a prison —

ANTI-VOICE 2: You lock yourselves within it.

ROMANA: You don't believe that any more than I do, Laris. Your sense is so blunted by anger that you'd deprive the Universe of meaning. But you're right: if I've only got a few more microspans of purposeful existence remaining, I'm damned if I'm going to waste them trying to persuade you that bitterness has warped your reason. *(BEAT)* We're here. *(FX: BLEEPS. DOOR SLIDES OPEN.)* The Temporal Reactors. Are you coming, Vansell?

VANSELL: *(NO FX)* What? Yes, yes — Romana.

ROMANA: *(ENTERING REACTOR)* Good.

52. INT. TIME STATION (CONSOLE CHAMBER)
(FX: BLIPS AND BREEPS. RISING THRUM)

DOCTOR: There. The console chamber is now fully aligned to the TARDIS's power rhythms — there'll be no more difficulties this end. We just have to wait for Romana.

ANTI-CHARLEY: Excellent. You will now assist the Under-Cardinal. Hurry! Under-Cardinal — connect these Delta Leads to the Radial Socket on the Lord Rassilon's casket.

UNDER-CARDINAL: *(CRACKLING FX)* I will.

(FX: CLUNKING OF RADIAL SOCKET. UP CRACKLING)

ANTI-CHARLEY: Now, Doctor — take the other end of the Delta Leads and wire them into the third panel on the Control Array.

DOCTOR: You ought to hire a handyman, Sentris. *(FX: HOISTS LEADS TO PANEL. BLEEPS — AND:)* Oh no you don't. Count me out. I'm not doing this!

CHARLEY: What's she want you to do, Doctor? *(STRUGGLING AGAINST STRAPS)* I can't — see!

DOCTOR: *(TO ANTI-CHARLEY)* You want someone to connect the casket to the Time Station's self-destruct mechanism, then find another pair of hands.

ANTI-CHARLEY: Oh Doctor, don't be so ... prissy. Commander Levith! Is your staser charged?

LEVITH: *(CRACKLING FX)* It is.

ANTI-CHARLEY: I shall count to three. If the Doctor has not completed his task by the time I've finished, I want you to raise your staser —

LEVITH: *(CRACKLING FX)* — I understand —

ANTI-CHARLEY: — and blast yourself through the head. One. Two. Three-

DOCTOR: *(ANGRY)* Alright, Sentris, you've made your point! *(FX: CLUNKS. BEEPS)* Happy now?

CHARLEY: *(TO DOCTOR)* What's that done?

DOCTOR: That has ensured that as soon as the Time Station materialises in Gallifrey's internal ionosphere, the ship's self-destruct mechanism will begin a short countdown. It will be completed the very nanosecond the casket opens —

ANTI-CHARLEY: Spreading Anti-Time fallout over the maximum possible area, corrupting all of Gallifrey before the Time Lords can marshal any kind of response.

CHARLEY: What — the Time Station will explode?

ANTI-CHARLEY: Miss Pollard, when I first tracked your form across space/time, I found your naiveté engaging. Now, it begins to grate!

CHARLEY: That's charming, that is. Doctor, will you kindly tell this Sentris person to — *(BEAT)* Doctor?

DOCTOR: *(LOST TO HIMSELF)* Come on, Romana. What's going on?

53. INT. TIME STATION (TEMPORAL REACTORS)
(FX: ROARING, LIKE A COSMIC FURNACE)

ROMANA: You like to feast on Time, Korvan and Laris? Well, there you are — a cauldron of pure Chronoplasmic Energy.

ANTI-VOICE 1: It is ... awesome.

ANTI-VOICE 2: We hunger for it.

ROMANA: Mouthwatering, is it? I wouldn't get too close if I were you — one inch past that Zybanium Shield and even you will be atomised. Vansell — could I have your assistance? *(BEAT; THEN, WHISPERED)* Correct me if I'm wrong, 'Acting President' — but the casket's influence over you has waned, hasn't it?

VANSELL: I don't know — there's something wrong —

ROMANA: *(WHISPERED)* Careful! While Korvan and Laris are mesmerised by the Temporal Reactors — let's not give the game away. *(BEAT)* You've been infected by the Anti-Time in the casket. It's been influencing you, affecting your behaviour — maybe for even longer than you think. But its hold over you seems to decrease with distance. Are you listening to me?

VANSELL: *(WHISPERED)* Oh, my lady — I remember now! I think I have done some terrible things ...

ROMANA: *(WHISPERED)* You have — and the purges you colluded in back on Gallifrey were only the beginning. So I ask you just this once — are you loyal? Come on, quick — the whole of reality may hang on it!

(BEAT)

VANSELL: *(WHISPERED)* Madam, I will serve you until the stars decay and the cosmos is naught but a dying ember in eternity's fire.

ROMANA: *(DRILY)* Well, the next five minutes will do. *(WHISPERED)* I need a distraction — time to get to the Matrix Chamber, change the authorisation code of this ship before it materialises and destroys the Eye of Harmony. Now — *(FX: BLEEPS)* — if we can lower both these shutters simultaneously, our floaty friends there will be trapped between the shutters and the Reactors — and if I then raise the Zybanium Shields, they'll be exposed to the Reactors' cores. That should sort them out — at least, long enough for me to reach the next deck down. I need you to raise the other shutter, over there, exactly when I say — got it?

VANSELL: *(WHISPERED)* I understand. *(BEAT)* Will you ever forgive me? It's just —

ROMANA: *(HISSING, FRUSTRATED)* What?!?

VANSELL: *(WHISPERED)* You remember the Matrix Projection we saw? Of the possible future? We watched you — a different, strong, Imperial you — deciding the fate of the Daleks. You elected to collapse the time pocket they were trapped in, destroy them forever. Their Emperor was on the viewscreen. 'Have pity,' it croaked. *(FX: ON 'HAVE PITY', WE HEAR THE DALEK EMPEROR RUNNING OVER, IN TANDEM WITH VANSELL'S VOICE — DISTANCED, LIKE A FLASHBACK)* And then you pressed the button, wiped them out, turned and said —

ROMANA: 'Does anyone else care to disagree with me?' *(FX: ON 'DOES ANYONE ELSE ...', WE HEAR THE IMPERIATRIX ROMANA'S VOICE RUNNING OVER ROMANA'S LINE — DISTANCED, LIKE A FLASHBACK)* I remember.

VANSELL: *(WHISPERED)* You could have been so magnificent, so powerful — and yet —

ROMANA: *(WHISPERED)* I saw myself as a vile, twisted, hateful monster. And if you found that hideous distortion of everything that I am somehow admirable — well, I feel very sorry for you, Vansell. *(BEAT; THEN, IMPATIENT)* We'll deal with this later, shall we? For now — will you kindly go and lower the other shutter?

VANSELL: My lady. *(WALKS AWAY)*

ANTI-VOICE 2: Are you not finished?

ROMANA: Nearly, Laris, nearly. *(ACROSS ROOM, TO VANSELL)* Are you ready, Vansell? After three. One. Two. Three —

(FX: BLEEPS; HUGE CLANGING OF ONE VAST METAL SHUTTER)

ANTI-VOICE 1: What is this?!?

ANTI-VOICE 2: What is happening?

VANSELL: *(SLIGHTLY MUFFLED — BEHIND SHUTTER)* *(PANICKED)* My shutter — it's jammed! *(BEAT THEN QUITE CALM AND PROFESSIONAL)* I ... I am opening the Zybanium Shield, my lady.

ROMANA: Vansell, you can't! The shutter on your side's not down — you'll be exposed to the Reactor Cores!

VANSELL: I do this ... gladly. *(FX: BLEEPS)*

ANTI-VOICE 1: No, Vansell! Do not open the shield —!

(FX: A VAST ROARING OF EXPOSED ENERGY, HEARD FROM BEHIND THE SHUTTER ON ROMANA'S SIDE. SCREAMS FROM VANSELL AND BOTH THE ANTI-VOICES ARE DROWNED OUT)

ROMANA: *(TO HERSELF)* Vansell? Vansell? I — *(BEAT)* — I won't waste the time that you've bought me. Must get to the Matrix Chamber! *(FX: SHE RUNS)*

54. INT. TIME STATION (CONSOLE CHAMBER)

UNDER-CARDINAL: *(CRACKLING FX)* Power surge in the Temporal Reactors, Sentris! The Time Station is back on-line!

ANTI-CHARLEY: Good, Under-Cardinal! Prepare to — *(SUDDENLY STIFFENS)* Unnh! I sense that something is wrong. Korvan and Laris — they are gone from us!

DOCTOR: *(TO HIMSELF)* Well done, Romana!

ANTI-CHARLEY: — and the Co-ordinator, too.

DOCTOR: Vansell? *(TO HIMSELF)* Poor old Nosebung. Shame.

ANTI-CHARLEY: Quiet, Doctor! Under-Cardinal — can you follow the President's biorhythmic trace?

(FX: LOOPING, RADAR-LIKE ELECTRONIC TRACE)

UNDER-CARDINAL: *(CRACKLING FX)* The Lady Romana is currently ... in the lower decks, heading for —

ANTI-CHARLEY: — the Matrix Chamber! Seal the doors!

DOCTOR: Oh no you don't, Under-Cardinal! *(FX: PUNCH)*

UNDER-CARDINAL: *(CRACKLING FX)* Oof!

DOCTOR: Terribly sorry — don't know my own strength ...

ANTI-CHARLEY: Levith — kill him!

(FX: TWO STASER BLASTS)

DOCTOR: Waah! Waah! *(BEAT)* Missed!

LEVITH: *(CRACKLING FX)* Doctor, this is futile. You can't escape!

DOCTOR: Alright, alright, I'll come quietly. *(BEAT)* You can't shoot a man who's surrendered — it's against the Genares Convention!

ANTI-CHARLEY: Levith, seal the Matrix Chamber.

LEVITH: *(CRACKLING FX)* Confirmed.

(FX: BLEEP)
COMPUTER VOICE:Sealing Matrix Chamber. Closing all internal bulkheads ...
(AND INTO:)

55. INT. TIME STATION (MATRIX CHAMBER)
(FX: FROM THE CORRIDOR JUST OUTSIDE THE CHAMBER, WE HEAR ROMANA'S RUNNING FOOTSTEPS)

COMPUTER VOICE:*(IN CORRIDOR)* ... Repeat, sealing Matrix Chamber. Closing all internal bulkheads.
(FX: ENORMOUS METAL CLANG)
ROMANA: *(COMING TO A STOP)* Oh no! *(FX: SLAMS HANDS AGAINST METAL DOOR)* Too late! What am I going to do now? *(BEAT - THEN SHORT LAUGH)* Ha! The sonic screwdriver! Thank you, Doctor!
(FX: SONIC SCREWDRIVER ON DOOR. DOOR MECHANISM REVERSES OPEN)
ROMANA: Handy to have about, this old thing. *(STEPS THROUGH INTO MATRIX CHAMBER)* Now ... *(FX: COUPLE OF BLEEPS. ELECTRONIC WHOOSH! OF MATRIX AS HEARD IN Sc. 9)* I only hope this works. Into the Matrix. Here ... I ... go ...
(FX: HER VOICE ECHOES AS SHE DIVES INTO THE MATRIX, LIKE THE DOCTOR IN Sc. 9)

56. INT. THE MATRIX
(FX: STRANGE, ECHOING AMBIENCE, AS IN Sc. 1. A LOW MURMUR OF BEATEN VOICES — A BIT LIKE A GREGORIAN CHANT — RUMBLING DISTANTLY, LIKE THUNDER. A STRONG WIND, WHISTLING THROUGH THE SCENE)

MATRIX VOICES:There is no alternative
There is no alternative
There is no alternative *[ETC]*
(FX: WITH A WHOOSH!, ROMANA IS DUMPED ONTO THE 'GROUND')
ROMANA: *(TO HERSELF)* Aoow! *(BEAT)* You might think, with the infinite resources at their disposal, one of our engineers would find a way to make entering the Matrix less — disrupting. *(ALOUD, AROUND)* Hello? Hello? This is President Romana! Is there anyone there? Can anyone hear me?
(FX: UP VOICES, STILL CHANTING, GROWING CLOSER, MORE AUDIBLE)
MATRIX VOICES: There is no alternative
ROMANA: *(TO HERSELF)* Data recorders! *(TO VOICES)* Hello? Hello? You must listen to me — it's of the utmost importance. The Web of Time is endangered! You — yes, you! I have to get a message to the High Council ...
MATRIX VOICE: Zagreus comes. There is no alternative.
ROMANA: No, no! There's no such thing as Zagreus. I am your President — don't you remember me, any of you?
MATRIX VOICES: *(ECHOING AROUND AND AROUND)* Zagreus comes
No past
No present
No future

287

We cannot remember
Cannot remember
Cannot remember!!!

ROMANA: Somebody, please, just listen to me!!! *(BEAT; TO HERSELF)* This is hopeless. Oh, Doctor — this is hopeless!

57. INT. TIME STATION (CONSOLE CHAMBER)

DOCTOR: There you go, Sentris — the Time Station is all yours. No more silly attempts at sabotage — Solar Scout's honour!

ANTI-CHARLEY: And all to ensure the Lady Romana made it to the Matrix Chamber. I wonder why? Ah. Of course. She's going to try and change the Time Station's conveyance signature from inside the Matrix, isn't she?

DOCTOR: *(BASHFUL)* Well, er — could be ...

LEVITH: *(CRACKLING FX)* She cannot succeed, Doctor.

ANTI-CHARLEY: See? The Commander knows. Even if the President was able to find anyone sane to speak to within the Matrix ...

LEVITH: *(CRACKLING FX)* ... no amendments can be made to transduction permits during a state of emergency, with no exemptions. This rule was only recently ratified at the behest of Celestial Intervention Agency Co-ordinator Vansell.

ANTI-CHARLEY: Every possible contingency has been considered and planned for. *(BEAT)* Well, Doctor? Have you nothing to say?

DOCTOR: Well, at least Romana's safe in there. But otherwise ... *(BEAT)* Do you know, I suddenly feel terribly old.

ANTI-CHARLEY: You're beaten, Doctor, and you know it. *(BEAT)* Of course, there is one way you may yet thwart our ambitions ...

DOCTOR: You do like a good gloat, don't you, Sentris? Typical CIA.

ANTI-CHARLEY: Oh, Doctor — don't dismiss it out of hand. I can't believe you haven't thought of it yet!

CHARLEY: Don't give up, Doctor! There's still a chance. *(BEAT)* I do know what she's talking about. You see, I've been thinking too.

LEVITH: *(CRACKLING FX)* Sentris, the Time Station is ready for flight. Shall I begin proton acceleration on the girl?

ANTI-CHARLEY: Not just yet, Levith! This is too fascinating to miss!

CHARLEY: It's me, isn't it, Doctor? Everything depends on me. So long as I'm alive, the breach in space/time has co-ordinates — and that's how they're going to travel through. But if those co-ordinates weren't there — well, they'd all be stuck in this reality, wouldn't they?

DOCTOR: Charley, Charley, Charley — don't even think about it.

ANTI-CHARLEY: Well, why not, Doctor? Miss Pollard indeed has a point. Commander Levith — place your staser on the ground, at the Doctor's feet.

LEVITH: *(CRACKLING FX)* Sentris, are you —?

ANTI-CHARLEY: Oh, I am sure. (BEAT) Go on, Doctor. Pick it up.

DOCTOR: This isn't a game, Sentris!

ANTI-CHARLEY: No. It isn't. It's a matter of life and death. The girl's life — against the death of the Web of Time which your entire civilisation was constructed to protect. Pick it up. There. That didn't hurt, did it?

CHARLEY: It's alright, Doctor. I'm not afraid. It's like I said in the

TARDIS — my time is up! There is no alternative. *(BEAT)* Oh, Doctor — you rescued me from the R101; you gave me these last few wonderful months. The things that I've seen, the places I've been — I've lived more than I could ever have dreamed of, and all thanks to you! And you're the sweetest, the kindest, most wonderful man I've ever met — and I'm sorry it's come to this and I'm sorry it has to end like this but if the Web of Time is destroyed then all the time I've had, everywhere I've been, all these fabulous, fantastic things we've done — they won't ever have happened at all! Don't let those times be taken away; don't let it all go to waste. I know it's an awful and terrible thing, but I want you to do it! Oh, Doctor — please do it, before it's too late!

DOCTOR: Charley, I - I can't. You're my friend and I love you. I can't look you in the eye and shoot you, no matter what!

CHARLEY: Doctor, I love you too and this is no way to say goodbye but please, please — *(BEAT)* Oh, what's wrong with you?!? You've saved the universe before — so do it again, the only way how!

ANTI-CHARLEY: That's right, Doctor. It won't take much. A quick burst of staser-fire and all these troubles will be over. And if your conscience pricks a little — well, it'll all have been in the noblest possible cause.

CHARLEY: *(BLAZING)* Oh, shut up, Sentris! *(BEAT)* You think we're alike, don't you? That's why you took my form. But we're not. We both died before our time — whether we should or we shouldn't, it just doesn't matter. The difference is, I'm grateful for every second that I've had. Charlotte Pollard, Edwardian Adventuress! We measure our lives in love, and I've loved every minute. But you, and all the lost boys and girls in your Never-Never Land — you're so fixated on what you might have missed out on, you've forgotten what living was like. I could get angry, too. I'm so scared, you know. But we're born into love, not anger — and love never dies, however brief our lives might be. *(BEAT)* Now, Doctor. Do it now.

(BEAT)

DOCTOR: I — I can't, Charley. I can't. I'm sorry.

(FX: STASER CLATTERS TO FLOOR)

ANTI-CHARLEY: Pick up the staser, Levith.

CHARLEY: No!!! No, no, no, no, no! I don't want it to be like this!

ANTI-CHARLEY: And now, Levith — activate the breach. Open the gateway.

LEVITH: *(CRACKLING FX)* Yes, Sentris.

CHARLEY: *(SOBBING)* Goodbye, Doctor. I hope you know what you've doooooooooooon—

(FX: AND CHARLEY'S VOICE TRANSMUTES INTO THE HUGE, VIBRATING

WHIRL — AS PER Sc. 16)

ANTI-CHARLEY: Fix and download the breach co-ordinates, Under-Cardinal! *(BEAT)* Well, Doctor. We have very few hands — just Levith, the Under-Cardinal and a handful of guards. Perhaps if you were to shoot all of them, then maybe the final outcome could be averted? But you won't. All hail the Doctor — the hero so squeamish he stood by while all that he loved was condemned to extinction!

DOCTOR: Sentris, you're not just evil and vindictive — you're confused. Once, you were so sickened by killing that you blasted yourself into this state. I won't destroy my friend, and I won't be

289

ashamed of the fact! Can't you see what you're doing? You're going to unmake the lives of innumerable billions if you carry this out! Don't they matter? Don't innocents count?

ANTI-CHARLEY: The living? No. Don't judge me, Doctor. I'm just looking after my own — something you've proved yourself quite incapable of. You see, once in a while, you have to pick sides. And if you don't stand with your own kind, well — you're a traitor. So hang your head, Doctor — you've betrayed the whole Web of Time because you can't bear to bloody your hands. How does that feel? *(BEAT)* Under-Cardinal! Is our course set for Gallifrey?

UNDER-CARDINAL: *(CRACKLING FX)* Course computed, Sentris!

ANTI-CHARLEY: Then commence the final dematerialisation!

(FX: THE VAST, PONDEROUS TIME ROTOR VWORPING)

DOCTOR: *(TO HIMSELF)* 'The final dematerialisation' ... ? *(EXCITED)* Yes, yes — it'd work!

ANTI-CHARLEY: Three point six-six microspans til— *(BEAT)* Doctor, where do you think you're going?

DOCTOR: I, uh ... just thought I'd like to spend these last few minutes of reality alone in my TARDIS. Call it a last request?

ANTI-CHARLEY: I don't think so, Doctor. Levith — it's time to put the Doctor out of his misery. Raise your staser — and shoot him through both his bleeding hearts.

LEVITH: *(CRACKLING FX)* Yes, Sentris.

(FX: TWO STASER BLASTS — BUT SIMULTANEOUSLY, WE HEAR THE TARDIS DOORS BANGING SHUT. A SPLIT-SECOND LATER, IT DEMATERIALISES)

LEVITH: *(CRACKLING FX)* He's gone.

ANTI-CHARLEY: It doesn't matter. We materialise in just two point eight-five microspans — and the Doctor can do nothing to prevent it!

58. INT. TARDIS

(FX: TARDIS ATMOS. FURIOUS VWORPING. FRANTIC SWITCH-PULLING)

DOCTOR: *(TO THE TARDIS)* Come on, come on old girl! Nearly there — nearly at the breach, and then — that's it, yes! *(BEAT)* Now, I can't pretend this next bit isn't going to hurt. I have to reconfigure your superstructure, and I can't do it gently. Brace yourself —

(FX: LEVER. ROTOR SOUND EXTENDS, SHRIEKING — AND FREEZE)

DOCTOR: What? You pick your moments, old girl — but not now! Please don't jam on me now!

OLD MAN: *(SUDDENLY APPEARED)* My friend, the mechanism is not at fault.

DOCTOR: *(CAUGHT UNAWARES)* You?!? It is you. Really you. *(BEAT; HARD)* My Lord, I am truly humbled — but I beg of you: do not intervene.

OLD MAN: Oh, Doctor. You should know better than to even suggest it. I have simply frozen us here — perhaps in your TARDIS, perhaps in your mind. Time marches on.

DOCTOR: It might not, soon. What you showed me, in the Matrix — the past and the future sacrificed to one single present — it could happen, now, unless ... well, unless I'm allowed to do what I mean to do.

OLD MAN: Then this is surely a desperate hour. Tell me, Doctor. Tell me how all this has come to pass.

DOCTOR: My Lord — I don't have the time!

OLD MAN: You do now. You can humour an old, dead man, can you not?

DOCTOR: I — well, if you're sure. Where did it all begin? One night on Earth, I suppose, high above the English Channel. I was aboard a magnificent airship — a vessel they called the R101. There was a boy, a steward, running towards me, running from someone — or something. But it wasn't a boy at all. It was a girl — Charlotte. Charlotte Pollard. Friends called her Charley, she said. *(FX: BEGIN TO FADE)* She told me I was the oddest man she'd ever met ...

59. INT. TIME STATION (CONSOLE CHAMBER)
(FX: ALL NOISES REACHING A FEVER PITCH)

ANTI-CHARLEY: The breach! The breach! We ... are ... going ... through!
(FX: HOLD. ECHO. FADE)

60. INT. TARDIS
(FADE UP)

DOCTOR: I honestly believed that Grayle was behind the time disruption. That with his redemption, I need worry no longer. I meant every word I said to Charley. I should have known better.

OLD MAN: Indeed! And what else do you have to tell me?

DOCTOR: I think the rest of the story can speak for itself, my Lord. Let's just say, not long after we left Singapore, Charley and I discovered that our troubles were only just beginning, first with the Daleks and now ...*(BEAT)* now, it's come to this. I have to stop the Never-people from reaching Gallifrey, regardless of the consequences to myself.

OLD MAN: And you mean those words too?

DOCTOR: Absolutely.

OLD MAN: You have considered every alternative?

DOCTOR: I have.

(BEAT)

OLD MAN: Then I must let you continue.

DOCTOR: Thank you, my Lord. *(BEAT)* Before you go — might I just ask why you've — well, dropped in on me like this?

OLD MAN: Doctor. I told you. I wanted to know what led you here, to this — decision. But if your mind is made up, I cannot intervene. That causes me sorrow.

DOCTOR: Sorrow?

OLD MAN: I have watched you these many long years — I have seen you in all of your adventures, seen the many things you have done in the service of your beliefs. Some I can hardly be seen to approve of ...

DOCTOR: *(COY, BASHFUL)* Oh. Well. You know. Sometimes things don't work out quite the way you planned them.

OLD MAN: Indeed. But for the most part — Doctor, you have made me proud. You have enriched the lives of more people in more worlds than I suspect you will ever know. You have made a difference. And I come here simply to tell you that. Before everything is ended. Before it's too late.

DOCTOR: My Lord — you honour me.

OLD MAN: No, Doctor. You have honoured me. Farewell.

(FX: SNAPS FINGERS —

(FX: — AND BACK TO THE SHRIEKING TIME ROTOR, AS BEFORE)

DOCTOR: *(TO HIMSELF)* Eh? Is it just me, or did something very odd just — *(BEAT)* Doesn't matter. Now, where was I? Ohhh yes …

61. INT. TIME STATION (CONSOLE CHAMBER)

(FX: VWORPING OF TIME ROTOR CALMS, STEADIES — CRUISING ATMOS ON ENGINES)

UNDER-CARDINAL: *(CRACKLING FX)* We have transgressed the breach, Sentris!

ANTI-CHARLEY: Then we have succeeded! Raise the observation ports!

(FX: THRUMMING AS SHUTTERS ARE RAISED, AS IN Sc. 21)

ANTI-CHARLEY: At last. At last, we have returned. *(BEAT)* Gallifrey, glittering beneath us, shining like a jewel … and about to be shattered. Begin the sequence, Levith!

(FX: BLEEPS)

LEVITH: *(CRACKLING FX)* Commencing countdown, Sentris!

COMPUTER VOICE:Time Station self-destruct sequence initiated. Sequence complete in point four-five microspans.

ANTI-CHARLEY: Oh, my lord Rassilon — your yesterdays are over. Tomorrow belongs to me!

(FX: CUE A VAST-SOUNDING MATERIALISATION, DISTENDED AND STRANGELY ECHOED — THE DOCTOR'S TARDIS VWORPING AROUND THE WHOLE OF THE TIME STATION)

ANTI-CHARLEY: What is this?!?

COMPUTER VOICE:Sequence complete in point four-zero microspans.

UNDER-CARDINAL: *(CRACKLING FX)* There's something around us, Sentris!

ANTI-CHARLEY: *(DAZED)* Where — where's Gallifrey gone?

(FX: INTERCOM VREEPS INTO LIFE)

DOCTOR: *(FUZZY, THROUGH INTERCOM)* TARDIS calling Time Station. TARDIS calling Time Station. Sentris, can you hear me?

ANTI-CHARLEY: Doctor?!?

DOCTOR: *(THROUGH INTERCOM)* It's that man again, Sentris! As you'll have observed, I've materialised my TARDIS around the Time Station. Yes, it's terribly tricky, and no, it's really not a good idea, and yes, she's bursting at the seams — but you didn't leave me any choice.

COMPUTER VOICE:Sequence complete in point three-zero microspans.

DOCTOR: *(THROUGH INTERCOM)* Point three-zero microspans? Oh dear. It'll take longer than that to abort the self-destruct.

ANTI-CHARLEY: Doctor, if the Time Station detonates inside your TARDIS both you and it will be utterly annihilated!

DOCTOR: *(THROUGH INTERCOM)* Oh, Sentris — this TARDIS is as

292

tough as old boots. She'll contain the material inside your casket — at least, long enough for the Time Lords to deal with it. And Charley — well, when she restabilises, she should be safe too. So you see, there's only me to consider — and if dying's the price I pay, to save all of history, to save my friend ... Well, I've had fun all my lives. I can't complain.

COMPUTER VOICE:Sequence complete in point one microspans. Point zero-nine. Point zero-eight. *(FX: COUNTDOWN CONTINUES OVER DIALOGUE. DUB VOICE TO FIT BACKWARDS FROM ZERO)* Point zero-seven *[ETC - TO 'POINT ZERO-ONE']*

ANTI-CHARLEY: Disconnect the casket! Disconnect the casket!!!

DOCTOR: *(THROUGH INTERCOM)* Too late, Sentris! This is how it ends. And I'm sorry. But you know what they say ...

(BEAT)

DOCTOR: *(THROUGH INTERCOM)* There is no alternative.

COMPUTER VOICE: — Zero. Sequence complete.

(FX: A BLEEP. CLICK. WHIRR. A VAST INRUSHING, BUILDING AND BUILDING IN SCALE AND PITCH AND TENOR, BUILDING AND BUILDING AND BUILDING —)

ANTI-CHARLEY: No! No! Noooooooooooooooooooooooooooooooooo

(FX: BANG — ECHO OVER AND OVER AND OVER — AND FADE TO NOTHING)

62. INT. THE MATRIX

(FX: AS Sc. 1. FADE UP INCOMPREHENSIBLE BABBLE OF HUNDREDS OF VOICES. BRING UP ROMANA)

ROMANA: *(TO HERSELF)* Everything's — normal. What's happening? What's going on?

VOICE 1:   *(CUTTING IN, AS Sc. 1)* Humanian Era. Earth. October the fifth, 1930. Airship R101 crashes in France. Charlotte Pollard escapes the flames.

ROMANA: *(TO HERSELF)* They're recording these events in the Matrix! *(TO VOICES)* No, no! There must be some mistake —

VOICE 2:   The Vortex. Indeterminate vectors. Charlotte Pollard's survival causes a transdimensional breach. Anti-Time forces flood through.

ROMANA: This isn't right! This isn't how it was supposed to be!

VOICE 3:   Rassilon Era. Gallifrey. 6978 point three. Manipulated by Anti-Time incursions, President Romana authorises a mission beyond the limits of the Vortex, through the space/time breach.

ROMANA: These things should never have happened!

VOICE 2:   Indeterminate vectors. Anti-Time forces plot to destroy the Eye of Harmony.

ROMANA: Unless — *(BEAT; MOURNFUL)* Oh no.

VOICE 3:   Rassilon Era. Gallifrey. 6798 point five. Their efforts are foiled when the Time Lord known only as the Doctor materialises his TARDIS around the casket of Anti-Time intended to destroy the Eye.

VOICES 1, 2 & 3:*(TOGETHER)* We remember this history. We remember it well.

ROMANA: Then all that's happened ... all that's occurred ... it's all part of the Web of Time now? Oh, brilliant. Just brilliant! The very fact of history's unravelling becomes part of its continuation. *(BEAT)* Oh, Doctor. You did it. You finally did it. It took you nine hundred years, but sooner or later you had to make one last, glorious gesture too many. And you saved Time itself by beating history at its own game. But history will remember you. The Time Lords will remember you. And I will never, ever forget you — objectionable, irrational, block-headed, impetuous ... *(BEAT)* ... magnificent you. *(DEEP, SHUDDERING INTAKE OF BREATH)* So. What happened next?

OLD MAN: *(FROM NOWHERE)* Daughter of Time, you should know better than to ask.

ROMANA: Sorry, wha— *(BEAT)* You! 'An old man — eternally sad and infinitely wise.' The Doctor said he'd seen you in the Matrix... my Lord.

OLD MAN: Ah, the Doctor. A favourite son. He saved his friend, whatever the cost — but the price he paid was terrible indeed.

ROMANA: Then Miss Pollard — Charley — lived?

OLD MAN: She did. When the breach was sealed for the last time, she was reconstituted in the Doctor's TARDIS — the paradox of her survival resolved forever. Because if history's web was saved by the very fact of her existence, then the very fact of her existence cannot have imperilled it at all.

ROMANA: A paradox!

OLD MAN: Which we can surely all live with. This will be but the first of the many challenges which face you, Madam President, throughout the fullness of your reign.

ROMANA: My reign —? Then I can return to Gallifrey? *(SUSPICIOUS)* This is cheating, surely?

OLD MAN: Were you to attempt to return through the Matrix door you entered, you would most certainly be destroyed. But there is more than one way out of the dreamscape ... to those whom the Matrix favours. The choice is yours, Madam President. *(BEAT)*

ROMANA: I think ... I hope I still have much to offer the people of Gallifrey, especially after today.

OLD MAN: Then it is our wish you should continue in her stewardship.

(FX: A 'WHOOSH!' TINKLING SOUND)

ROMANA: A doorway!

OLD MAN: Go with our blessing, Daughter of Time.

ROMANA: I — thank you, my Lord. The first thing I will do is rescue Miss Pollard, find a space for her in history's pages.

OLD MAN: Miss Pollard? Oh, her story is not quite finished. In fact, it's only just beginning. As the next chapter unfolds — and a dark and terrible chapter it is — I trust you to play your part, Romana, with all the wisdom and passion you have displayed today.

ROMANA: The next chapter? What do you mean? What's going to — *(BEAT)* Sorry, my Lord. I didn't mean to—

OLD MAN: *(LAUGHING)* If you do not wish to remain, I cannot grant you that knowledge.

ROMANA: Of course. I'll just have to take it — well, one day at a time.

OLD MAN: Go, Madam President. Go into the future.

ROMANA: I will. *(BEAT)* My Lord.
(FX: A FEW OF ROMANA'S FOOTSTEPS — AND, WITH A 'WHOOSH!', SHE IS GONE)
OLD MAN: Farewell, daughter. We wish you well ... *(WALKING AWAY, QUOTING TO HIMSELF)* '... for Zagreus waits at the end of the world/And Zagreus is the end of the world/His time is the end of Time/And his moment, Time's undoing ...'

63. INT. TARDIS
(FX: VAST, BARREN, STONE-WALLED ATMOS. FAINT CRACKLES AND HISSES OF EXPENDED ANTI-TIME ENERGY — LIKE ON RASSILON'S CASKET)

CHARLEY: Hello? Hello? Is anyone there? Oh, Doctor — are you there?
(DISTANT SHUFFLING, COUGHING: THE DOCTOR)
CHARLEY: Doctor? Doctor, is that you? It's so dark and cold in here, I can hardly—
DOCTOR: *(HISSING)* Keep away!
CHARLEY: Doctor! Doctor — it is you! Is this the TARDIS? I mean, what's happened? It's all been like a dream — I found myself here, when I was last in the Time Station with those awful Never-people and—
(THE DOCTOR HAS A SMALL, RACKING COUGHING FIT)
CHARLEY: Oh Doctor — come on, let me help you—
DOCTOR: *(ANGRY)* I said — keep away!
CHARLEY: Oh! *(BEAT)* Doctor — what's wrong? Have you been injured, or something?
DOCTOR: Injured? No, I have not been injured. This TARDIS contained all of the Time Station when it exploded. This ship was filled to bursting with a great mass of the fiercest, fizzing, energy —
CHARLEY: What, Anti-Time?
DOCTOR: A crude term for such matter of life ... and death. But now that the breach is resolved — now that the problem of you is resolved — well, all that remains of that stuff in this whole reality is held ... in here.
CHARLEY: What, in the TARDIS?
DOCTOR: *(CHUCKLING EVILLY — HINT OF CRACKLING FX ON HIS VOICE)* No. In ... here.
CHARLEY: Y— you're scaring me now. Stop it, Doctor, please—
DOCTOR: *(RISING CRACKLING FX)* 'Doctor'? 'Doctor'? I hold the last vestiges of the most awesome power ever imagined. Imagined — yes! How much better if I should take my title from a work of imagination — a creature willed to power by the undying anger of an unreal race!
CHARLEY: Doctor, I haven't got the faintest idea what you're on about but I really think you need help so if you'll just let me—
(FX: THE DOCTOR KNOCKS HER TO THE GROUND)
DOCTOR: Yaaaa!
CHARLEY: Aaaah! *(BEAT)* *(SHOCKED, FRIGHTENED)* Doctor — Doctor, what's wrong with you?
DOCTOR: *(CRACKLING FX)* I told you, girl — *(BELLOWED)* I ...

AM ... NOT ... THE DOCTOR!!! *(BEAT)* I am become he who sits inside your head ... he who lives among the dead ... he who sees you in your bed ... and eats you when you're sleeping. *(BEAT)* I ... am become ... ZAGREUS!!!

(FX: HOLD. ECHO)

(END)

APPENDIX:

THE FIRES OF VULCAN: PART ONE
ALTERNATIVE VERSION

By Steve Lyons

1. POMPEII, 1980
*WE HEAR THE OCCASIONAL CRIES OF SEAGULLS, THROUGHOUT THIS
AND ALL DAYTIME EXTERIOR SCENES UNTIL NOTED. THERE ARE
FOOTSTEPS ON RUBBLE, AS TWO PEOPLE APPROACH IN MID-
CONVERSATION.*

ARCHAEOLOGIST: ...walls and columns came tumbling down.
Tumbling down, I tell you! Some buildings lost whole storeys. Our people
are working to prop up what's left of Pompeii, but the damage, the
damage!
UNIT OFFICER: *(BORED)* I can see it must be frustrating for
you, Professor.
ARCHAEOLOGIST: Frustrating? It's disastrous! An archaeological
disaster! Pompeii is our window on the Roman world, you know. A
window! Thanks to the eruption of Vesuvius, this city was preserved like
no other, just waiting for us to revive it and learn its secrets. It has
survived looters, tourists, vandals... and now, for nature itself to do this...
UNIT OFFICER: I'm sure you're doing everything you can,
Professor.
THEY COME TO A HALT.
                      But this, I assume, is what we're here for.
ARCHAEOLOGIST: Yes, yes, this is the artefact. We haven't
completed our excavations of this region, you see. The artefact was
uncovered by the earthquake. It...
UNIT OFFICER: Could somebody have put it here? As some sort
of a prank?
ARCHAEOLOGIST: Oh, goodness, no. As you can see, it is still
partially buried under volcanic ash. No, the only way it could have
arrived in its present position is if it was placed there before Mount
Vesuvius erupted.
UNIT OFFICER: Which was when, exactly?
ARCHAEOLOGIST: AD 79. Almost two thousand years ago – which,
as you can see, is impossible. Quite impossible.
UNIT OFFICER: Indeed. *(BRUSQUELY)* OK, Professor, I'm taking
custody of this artefact. I'll have men down here within the hour.
ARCHAEOLOGIST: You want to dig it out? But...
UNIT OFFICER: I have to ask you not to speak to anyone about
this. You will be required to sign a declaration to that effect. A
representative of your government will be in touch shortly.
ARCHAEOLOGIST: I don't understand. Is the artefact dangerous?

297

UNIT OFFICER: I'm sorry, Professor, this is UNIT business now. If I were you, I'd forget that I ever saw anything here.
THE OFFICER MARCHES AWAY.
ARCHAEOLOGIST: But... but...
UNIT OFFICER: *(CALLS BACK TO HIM)* Thank you, Professor!
ARCHAEOLOGIST: *(FORLORNLY, TO SELF)* But what's so special about an English police telephone box?
THEME

2. THE TARDIS CONSOLE ROOM
THE USUAL BACKGROUND HUM. OCCASIONAL CLICKS AND ELECTRONIC SOUNDS, AS THE DOCTOR OPERATES THE CONSOLE.

ACE: Professor, I'm bored!
DOCTOR: Patience, Ace.
ACE: You've been messing about in here for ages. What do we need the scanner for, anyway? We could just look outside.
DOCTOR: It isn't only the scanner, Ace. The external sensors are completely inoperable. I can't get a fix on where – or when – we've landed.
ACE: I bet the door control still works, though.
DOCTOR: We also don't know what the atmosphere is like. There could be a vacuum out there, or noxious gases. *(MUTTERS)* Come on, old girl, what aren't you telling me?
ACE: *(AMUSED)* What, you think the TARDIS is keeping secrets now?
DOCTOR: I think there's something very wrong here.
ACE: I bet it's sent you to Coventry. Have you done something to upset it?
DOCTOR: No, no, Ace, she'd only do something like this if she thought she was protecting me.
HE STOPS PLAYING WITH THE CONSOLE.
(A THOUGHT STRIKES HIM; MUTTERS)
Protecting me...
ACE: I know what's happening. The TARDIS wants us to walk out there to our deaths. Then she'll be free to take over the universe.
DOCTOR: *(IGNORES HER)* So, I wonder if she'll let me...?
THE TARDIS DOORS OPEN.
You were right, Ace. The door control <u>does</u> still work.
ACE: At last!

3. A POMPEIAN BACK STREET, DAY
THE SPLASH OF A BOOTED FOOT STEPPING HEAVILY INTO A PUDDLE.

ACE: Eeww! Doctor!
DOCTOR: Our first clue, Ace. Wherever we've landed, the drainage system isn't as advanced as you're used to. I think we should keep to the pavements.
ACE: It smells, an' all.
DOCTOR: You'll get used to it. Earth, I think.
ACE: Yeah. Those buildings are Roman, aren't they?
DOCTOR: Or Greek.

ACE: Thought so. We must be a few years into the past, then.
DOCTOR: Millennia, from your point of view. *(THOUGHTFULLY)*
This could be one of the older, residential parts of the city, I suppose.
ACE: What city? *(PAUSE)* Professor, <u>what</u> city?
DOCTOR: Ssh.
SILENCE FOR A FEW SECONDS.
ACE: *(IMPATIENTLY)* What is it, professor?
DOCTOR: *(IN A LOW VOICE)* I don't think we're alone.
*A SCRAPING SOUND, AS SOMEBODY TRIES TO SLIP AWAY QUIETLY
BUT FAILS.*
ACE: Oi! Who's there?
DOCTOR: It's all right, don't worry, we aren't going to hurt you.
SLAVE: *(TERRIFIED)* My lord, my lady, I beg your forgiveness,
I... I did not mean to intrude upon your conference.
ACE: Hey, what's all this grovelling in aid of?
DOCTOR: He's a slave, Ace. Do you see that belt he's wearing? It's
inscribed with his owner's name.
ACE: *(READING UNCERTAINLY)* Eu-mach-ia.
DOCTOR: You, ah, you saw us arriving?
SLAVE: Take my unworthy eyes if you wish, lord, but I
witnessed your chariot as it descended from the heavens. I was fetching
material for my mistress and... and a sound, like a hundred elephants...
ACE: You mean somebody "owns" you? That's garbage!
DOCTOR: *(A WARNING GROWL)* Ace.
ACE: You don't have to bow and scrape to us, mate – or anyone else,
for that matter. You tell him, professor.
DOCTOR: What my companion is trying to say is that we aren't
going to punish you. We are simply, ah, messengers.
SLAVE: Is Isis then displeased with our offerings?
DOCTOR: Oh, no, no, nothing like that. However, we would like to
keep our presence here a secret – if you could perhaps...?
SLAVE: I swear, lord, I will speak of this to no one.
DOCTOR: Splendid. Well, run along now. No, wait! One more thing.
We've been travelling for some time, and we seem to have lost track of
the date. It's silly, I know, but I wonder if you could enlighten us?
SLAVE: Why, it is the day of the Vulcanalia, my lord. The tenth
day before the Calends of September.
DOCTOR: *(SUDDENLY DISTRACTED)* Ah. Thank you.
THE SLAVE SCURRIES AWAY.
ACE: What was he talking about, professor?
DOCTOR: He said it's the twenty-third of August.
ACE: What year? *(CALLS)* Hey, mate, hang on a minute! What
year is it?
DOCTOR: *(BRUSQUELY)* Come along, Ace.
*THE DOCTOR WALKS AWAY QUICKLY. ACE HURRIES TO KEEP UP
WITH HIM.*
ACE: But he didn't tell us what year it is!
DOCTOR: We can cross the road on these stepping stones. Be
careful.
ACE: Where are we going?
DOCTOR: Do you want to explore or don't you?
ACE: What's <u>with</u> you all of a sudden, professor? Where are

we? *(CALLS AFTER HIM)* Professor!

4. A POMPEIAN STREET
THE DOCTOR WALKS ON, ACE A LITTLE WAY BEHIND HIM. THERE
ARE A FEW OTHER PEOPLE HERE; WE HEAR THEM WALKING AND
SOMETIMES TALKING. AT SOME POINT, AN IRON-WHEELED CART
MIGHT TRUNDLE PAST, DRAWN BY TWO HORSES.

DOCTOR: *(MUTTERS SADLY)* So, this is it. The final journey. I had
hoped for a while longer. Time to prepare. Time, slipping away from me.
ACE: *(CALLS)* This is wicked, professor! An actual Roman
city. All this stuff looked dead boring when we did it in school, but close
up...
DOCTOR: Time marching on. Only just arriving, but we've already
stayed a lifetime. Too many lifetimes. Withering like roses...
SHE CATCHES UP TO HIM.
ACE: So, do you tell me where we are now, or is this another
of your big mysteries?
DOCTOR: I'm sorry, Ace.
ACE: What for?
THEY STOP WALKING.
DOCTOR: *(SIGHS HEAVILY, COMPOSES HIMSELF)* The year is AD
79. The Roman Empire is under the short-lived rule of Titus. We are in
the city of Pompeii, a prosperous trading centre on the Bay of Naples.
If you look between the buildings there, you can see a certain mountain
by the name of Vesuvius.
ACE: Vesuvius! That's a volcano, isn't it? Wicked! I've never
seen a real live volcano before.
DOCTOR: You may wish you never had.
ACE: It's gonna go up, isn't it? I remember that bit all right.
We made a big model of it in primary school, from papier mache, with
all this red stuff gushing out of it. When will it happen? Can we see it,
professor? Can we?
DOCTOR: I think it might be better if we just leave.
ACE: Eh?
DOCTOR: Leave. Go back to the TARDIS.
ACE: Why?
DOCTOR: Because you aren't dressed for this time and place.
Because, beneath their sophisticated veneer, the Romans are a quite
barbarous people. Because we have an unfortunate habit of attracting
trouble. Because this is your history, and no good can come of our
meddling in it.
ACE: *(SULLENLY)* You want to go, then.
DOCTOR: No. It's your decision, Ace. It has to be your choice.
ACE: Well... we can look round first, can't we? I mean, there's
no need for us to rush off, is there?
DOCTOR: None whatsoever.
ACE: *(IRRITABLY)* I wish you'd tell me what's wrong.
DOCTOR: Nothing's wrong, Ace. Quite the opposite. Events are
proceeding precisely as I expect they should.
ACE: That's all right then... I think.
THE DOCTOR WALKS OFF. ACE FOLLOWS. WE STAY WITH THEM.

ACE: So, when <u>does</u> the volcano blow its top?
DOCTOR: *(DOURLY)* Vesuvius will erupt, destroying Pompeii and killing thousands of people, at approximately midday tomorrow.

5. THE STREET OF PLENTY
NOW THEY ARE WALKING THROUGH A BUSY SHOPPING CENTRE. THERE'S A FESTIVAL ON. WE HEAR LOTS OF VOICES AND LOTS OF LAUGHTER. SOMEONE PLAYS A SIMPLE TUNE ON A REED PIPE, ACCOMPANIED BY CYMBALS OR A RATTLE.

DOCTOR: The Via dell'Abbondanza. The Street of Plenty.
ACE: Well, there's plenty of people about.
DOCTOR: That's because they're celebrating, Ace. If I remember my history – or rather, your history – correctly, we've arrived in the middle of the Festival of the Divine Augustus.
ACE: I see they've invented graffiti by now. It's all over the place. What does that say? Celadus the Thracian is... sus-pir-ium puell-ar-um?
DOCTOR: The girls' heat-throb.
ACE: Yeah? How about that one?
DOCTOR: 'Polycarbus ran from his opponent in shameful fashion.'
ACE: *(SARCASTICALLY)* Well witty!
DOCTOR: It refers to a gladiator, I presume. You can learn a great deal about a culture from its writings.
ACE: You said it was wrong to write on walls.
DOCTOR: There's a time and a place for everything.
ACE: Great! So, can I have a go?
DOCTOR: Certainly not.
ACE: Well, how about we go and <u>see</u> this Polly What's-his-name?
DOCTOR: The Amphitheatre will be closed for the festival. Thankfully. If you're looking for entertainment, I'd suggest the theatre or the Odeon.
ACE: *(TONGUE-IN-CHEEK)* The Odeon? Ace! What films are they showing?
DOCTOR: No films – but you might enjoy a recital of poetry.
ACE: I'll give it a miss, thanks. *(PAUSE)* Professor? You see that young guy back there? I think he's following us. He keeps looking over here and...
HER VOICE TRAILS OFF, AND THE SOUND OF THE CROWD GROWS LOUDER. SHE HAS LOST HIM.
     (WORRIED) Doctor?
BEGGAR WOMAN: Spare some asses, dear?
ACE: *(STARTLED)* Eh?
BEGGAR WOMAN: Some coins for a homeless old woman?
ACE: Oh. Oh, I see. I'm sorry, I don't have any money.
BEGGAR WOMAN: *(ANGRILY)* What? You claim poverty? You, with your clean face and your neat hair and your clothing of strange fabrics?
ACE: I don't. Really, I just...
BEGGAR WOMAN: You think yourself superior to me, but you are no more than a base dissembler! Why, you are fair laden down with metal

301

trinkets!
ACE:　　　　I only just got here, honest! I... I'm... *(SUDDENLY REMEMBERS)* a messenger from Isis. I'm only here...
DOCTOR:　　　...to honour Augustus with a quiet drink.
ACE:　　　　*(RELIEVED)* Doctor!
DOCTOR:　　　Come along, Ace.
ACE:　　　　Where <u>were</u> you?
THE DOCTOR HURRIES ACE AWAY. THE BEGGAR WOMAN'S VOICE RECEDES AS SHE SHOUTS AFTER THEM.
BEGGAR WOMAN: You have not even the decency to cover your head. You are shameless, woman. Shameless!
DOCTOR:　　　I don't think it's a good idea to encourage that particular rumour.
ACE:　　　　You started it! It's what you told that slave.
DOCTOR:　　　He saw the TARDIS materialising. I had no choice. Believe me, Ace, making claims of that nature can be very unwise indeed. I think you should leave the talking to me in future.
ACE:　　　　I'm not a kid, you know.
DOCTOR:　　　No. But you <u>are</u> drawing attention.
ACE:　　　　<u>She</u> picked on <u>me</u>!
DOCTOR:　　　Your clothing is anachronistic. Women should keep their heads covered, and badges are definitely out of season.
ACE:　　　　Hey, I'm not the one dressed in question marks!
DOCTOR:　　　I think we should find somewhere a little more private.
THEY WALK AWAY FROM US.
ACE:　　　　*(AGGRIEVED)* It's not fair, professor. Why aren't people staring at <u>your</u> clothes?
WE HEAR JUST THE SOUNDS OF THE STREET, FOR A MOMENT.
CELSINUS:　　Well? What have you learned?
BEGGAR WOMAN: That you must like the aspect of this stranger a good deal, Popidius Celsinus, that you, *(WITH MOCKING GRANDEUR)* a member of the municipal council, would pay for the favour of such as I.
CELSINUS:　　You try my patience, woman. What did she tell you?
BEGGAR WOMAN: A more precious secret, perhaps, than can be bought with the few coins you have promised me.
CELSINUS:　　*(HOTLY)* I offer fair recompense for a simple deed, hag! Would you have me talk to the duoviri and have you run out of this city?
BEGGAR WOMAN: *(AMUSED, TAUNTINGLY)* I merely find it strange that you know not the answer to your question already.
CELSINUS:　　Why say you that?
BEGGAR WOMAN: The woman comes from Isis, decurione. She is a messenger of the goddess. Now, how can it be that you, of all in Pompeii, were not aware of that fact?

6. VALERIA HEDONE'S INN

A SMALL BAR, CROWDED WITH REVELLERS, SOME OF THEM DRUNK AND QUITE ROWDY. ITS FRONT IS OPEN TO THE STREET, SO THE SOUNDS FROM OUTSIDE CAN STILL BE HEARD.

VALERIA:　　*(CALLS INTO THE STREET)* Come, handsome stranger, feast here with your chambermaid. Valeria offers the lowest prices for hot food, and the finest garum in all Rome.

DOCTOR: Yes, yes, thank you, I think we will.

WE STAY WITH THE DOCTOR, ACE AND VALERIA AS THEY MOVE INTO THE BAR TOGETHER.

ACE: Sounds good to me. But I'm not his...

DOCTOR: You keep an interesting establishment here, er...?

VALERIA: Valeria Hedone at your service. You are a stranger to Pompeii – but a man of good standing, I can see. It will be Falernian wine for you, I'd wager. I ask only four asses for the drink of the emperors.

DOCTOR: Very reasonable... Ah. But not just yet, I'm afraid. I appear to have left all my coins at home.

ACE: *(MUTTERS)* This is embarrassing!

VALERIA: *(ICILY)* Then perhaps you should fetch them, stranger, before you waste any more of my time.

SHE WALKS OFF.

ACE: I don't think she's pleased with you, professor.

DOCTOR: *(BITTERLY)* Why are you humans so obsessed with money? *(MUTTERS, THOUGHTFULLY)* Money, money, money...

ACE: Eww! Those fish aren't even cooked. They're rotting!

DOCTOR: They're not for eating, Ace.

ACE: So, what are they for?

DOCTOR: Throwing back into the river.

ACE: It's a bit late for that, isn't it?

DOCTOR: It's a ritual, Ace. Remember what that slave told us? Today is the Vulcanalia. The fish are an offering to Vulcan, the Roman God of Fire and Furnaces. *(MUTTERS, THOUGHTFULLY)* I always did wonder how that particular custom originated. Perhaps somebody could enlighten me?

ACE: So, it's Vulcan's day as well as that Divine August bloke's? Crikey, how many holidays do they have here?

DOCTOR: The Romans treat their gods very seriously.

ACE: Yeah, as a serious excuse to stuff themselves... So, this Vulcan bloke's the 'God of Fire and Furnaces', eh? That's a bit ironic, isn't it? You know, what with *(LOWERS HER VOICE)* what's going on tomorrow, and all that.

DOCTOR: I doubt if the Pompeians will see the funny side.

HE APPROACHES A TABLE AT WHICH PEOPLE ARE PLAYING WITH DICE MADE OUT OF BONE.

(HAPPILY) Ah. I think this may be the answer to all our troubles.

ACE: *(LOWERS HER VOICE, WARILY)* Are you sure, professor? Those blokes look a bit hard to me.

DOCTOR: *(AT NORMAL SPEAKING VOLUME)* Gladiators, I expect. But don't worry, Ace, they're only wielding dice, not swords. Excuse me, gentlemen, I wonder if you might be able to accommodate one more player?

MURRANUS: You have coins to stake?

DOCTOR: Ah, no. But I thought you might have a use for... *(HE ELONGATES THE WORD 'FOR', AS HE RUMMAGES THROUGH POCKETS)* this silver, er... yo-yo. No, no, that won't do at all, will it?

MURRANUS: We play for coins or nought. Now, leave. You disturb us.

ACE: I think he means it.

DOCTOR: Yes, yes, but there must be <u>something</u> I can interest you in.

MURRANUS: *(LAUGHS)* I am Murranus, stranger, the greatest mirmillo ever to do battle in Pompeii's Amphitheatre. What could <u>you</u> offer to me?

DOCTOR: *(FEIGNING DELIGHT)* Ah, Murranus! Delighted to meet you. I've heard your name spoken, of course. They say you are the most courageous swordsman in the whole of the Empire.

ACE: Much braver than that Polycarbus bloke.

MURRANUS: You hear right. Why, in the latest games, I vanquished my opponents with ease. Even Crescens, the people's darling, could not withstand my might.

THE DOCTOR PULLS BACK A CHAIR AND SITS DOWN.

DOCTOR: Indeed. And it would be a great honour to dice with such a renowned warrior. I'm the Doctor, by the way.

MURRANUS: *(ANGRILY)* I did not give you leave to sit.

DOCTOR: *(HE'S SUDDENLY THOUGHT OF SOMETHING)* My maidservant!

MURRANUS: <u>Now</u> what madness afflicts you?

DOCTOR: My maidservant. She must be worth... oh, two thousand sesterces at least, wouldn't you say?

MURRANUS: The girl?

ACE: *(HALF-LAUGHING, NOT SURE IF HE'S JOKING OR NOT)* Professor!

DOCTOR: Yes, the girl. What's wrong, Murranus? My wager too rich for Pompeii's greatest warrior? I will stake the girl against just thirty sesterces.

MURRANUS: Then you are a fool, Doctor. You must know that the gods will favour he who fights and wins in their name.

DOCTOR: Then I take it you accept?

ACE: *(URGENT WHISPER)* Should I be getting ready to leg it here, or what?

MURRANUS: Aye, Doctor. I accept!

DOCTOR: Splendid, splendid. Well, then... perhaps you'd like to make the first roll?

7. THE HOUSE OF EUMACHIA

EUMACHIA: *(ANGRILY)* Speak, slave! I require an answer. I would know how it is that you should take so long about a simple errand.

SLAVE: *(AFRAID)* Forgive me, Mistress Eumachia, I am pledged not to say.

EUMACHIA: To whom? To whom would you show greater fealty than to your mistress; to she who feeds and clothes and houses you?

SLAVE: Only to the gods, I swear it.

EUMACHIA: *(SARCASTICALLY)* Ah! Then 'twas the <u>Gods</u> who obstructed your work. Were my husband still alive, he would flog you for such lies!

SLAVE: 'Twas their... *(MUMBLES, ALMOST INAUDIBLY)* their messengers.

EUMACHIA: Do not mumble so. I cannot hear you.

SLAVE: Their messengers, mistress. *(DESPERATELY)* It is the truth, I swear. I would scarce have believed it myself, yet I <u>saw</u> their temple as it fell from the heavens. If you would have me, I can show it to you.

EUMACHIA: What temple is this, that a priestess of the true religion knows not of it?

SLAVE: It was sent to us by Isis, mistress.

EUMACHIA: Isis! Ha – the foreign goddess! Then these *(CONTEMPTUOUSLY)* messengers be false prophets indeed.

SLAVE: My lady?

EUMACHIA: *(THOUGHTFULLY)* Their deceptions may fool one such as you – but they will not bear the light of the <u>true</u> faith.

8. VALERIA HEDONE'S INN

A CROWD OF ONLOOKERS HAS GATHERED, AND THE BAR IS QUIETER THAN BEFORE. TWO BONE DICE ROLL ACROSS A TABLE, AND A COLLECTIVE GASP IS RAISED.

DOCTOR: I believe we agreed on thirty sesterces?

MURRANUS: *(BITTERLY)* By Jupiter, Doctor, the Lares smile upon you today.

DOCTOR: Apparently so.

AS THE DOCTOR PULLS A NUMBER OF COINS ACROSS THE TABLE TO HIMSELF, THE ONLOOKERS RESUME THEIR CONVERSATIONS.

And now, if you'll excuse me...?

MURRANUS: What is this? Surely you will not take your gains and leave us so soon?

DOCTOR: Well, time is pressing...

MURRANUS: *(THREATENING)* I would test your fortune further, Doctor. I think you will agree, it is only sporting that I be given a chance to recover what I have lost.

DOCTOR: *(RESIGNED)* Oh, very well, just a little longer... Ah, Valeria. Valeria, perhaps you could do me a small favour? I'm sure you've noticed how my, ah, maidservant here is dressed. Most inappropriate. I wonder if you could...?

COINS CHANGE HANDS.

VALERIA: For this price, Doctor, I will clothe the girl in the finest robes.

WE FOLLOW VALERIA AS SHE MOVES THROUGH THE CROWD.

Aglae? I have another task for you. Take these coins to Vesonius and purchase a stola for the Doctor's companion. I would say she has your build.

AGLAE: But, my lady, it is the Festival. My mistress expects my return.

VALERIA: You will do as I say, girl! Asellina will not miss you for a few minutes more.

AGLAE: As you wish, my lady.

WE FOLLOW AGLAE AS SHE HEADS FOR THE DOOR.

ACE: Hey, wait up!

AGLAE: My lady?

ACE: We can do without that rubbish. My name's Ace. You're Aglae, aren't you? I'm coming with you.

AGLAE: But... have you sought permission to leave your master's side?

ACE: You're joking, aren't you? Anyway, he's still playing with his new mates, and I'm bored. Come on. Where are we going first?
ACE MOVES OFF, BUT AGLAE HESITATES.
(CALLING BACK TO AGLAE) Well, come on!

9. THE STREET OF PLENTY / THE LUPANAR

ACE AND AGLAE APPROACH US IN MID-CONVERSATION. THEY ARE LAUGHING.

ACE: I should have brought my nitro-nine with me. I could have shown you.

AGLAE: *(STILL LAUGHING)* Oh, Ace, I do not understand some of your strange words, but you tell your tales so wonderfully.

ACE: You haven't heard the half of it.
THEY COME TO A STOP.
So, this is where you live, is it?

AGLAE: This is the Lupanar.

ACE: Nice and central, I see. Right on the main road.

AGLAE: We do good trade.

ACE: Eh?

AGLAE: Come in, Ace. With luck, my lady Asellina will have no need of me for a time yet, and you may change in my room.

ACE: *(WITHOUT ENTHUSIASM)* Oh yeah, I can't wait to slip into this toga thing. Hey, hold up a minute! *(AMUSED)* Are those things what I think they are?

AGLAE: Of what do you speak, Ace?

ACE: Up there, on the sign. They look like... well, you know...

AGLAE: *(PUZZLED)* They bespeak the nature of this establishment.

ACE: A bit forward, isn't it? *(PAUSE)* Oh. Does that mean you're a...? Oh.

AGLAE: Do you not also serve your master in this manner?
WE FOLLOW THEM INTO THE LUPANAR, AND ACE SLAMS THE DOOR BEHIND THEM.

ACE: *(LAUGHS HOLLOWLY)* Oh, great!

AGLAE: Does something vex you?

ACE: Oh no, nothing at all. The local creep makes a beeline for me, so I show him I'm not 'that kind of girl' by running straight into the local brothel. Nice move or what!

10. VALERIA HEDONE'S INN

MURRANUS AND HIS THREE GLADIATOR FRIENDS LAUGH UNKINDLY.

MURRANUS: Again, Doctor, you throw the caniculae. Truly, the fates have deserted you.

DOCTOR: As you said, the gods favour those who honour them.
MURRANUS GATHERS UP HIS COINS. THE DOCTOR PUSHES BACK HIS CHAIR AND STANDS.
And now, if you'll excuse me, I really must bid you good day.

MURRANUS: Hold!

DOCTOR: You have won all my coins, Murranus.

MURRANUS: Thirty sesterces did you take from me. Only ten have you staked in return.

DOCTOR: Ah, yes. Well, I had to buy clothes for my companion, you see, and...

MURRANUS: *(ANGRILY)* You will find something to wager! If you have nought else, then I should like another chance at your maidservant.

DOCTOR: Ah. I'm afraid she seems to have left. *(MUTTERS)* You wouldn't like her, anyway. She's not noted for her obedience.

MURRANUS: Then the clothes from your back may fetch an as or two.

DOCTOR: Perhaps they would. But, as you said, my luck really isn't holding out. Your, ah, skill at rolling the dice is a little too much for me.

MURRANUS JUMPS TO HIS FEET AND UNSHEATHES HIS SWORD.

MURRANUS: *(LOUDLY AND ANGRILY)* Do you accuse Murranus of cheating? I will run you through where you stand!

SILENCE FALLS.

DOCTOR: *(HARDLY FLUSTERED)* It's all in the wrist action, of course. But don't worry, I shan't hold a grudge. I just wish to find my companion...

A VIOLENT CRASH, AS MURRANUS HURLS THE TABLE ASIDE TO GET TO THE DOCTOR. THE SILENCE IS BROKEN, AS ONLOOKERS REACT WITH FEAR AND ASTONISHMENT.

MURRANUS: You seem well versed in the ways of the cheat, Doctor. Could it be that 'tis _you_ who have won your coins unfairly?

VALERIA: *(FORCEFULLY, UNAFRAID)* Gentlemen, stop this!

MURRANUS: It will stop when I have satisfaction!

THE DOCTOR PUSHES A CHAIR ASIDE AND RUNS. WITH A SNARL, MURRANUS LEAPS ON HIM. GRUNTS AND GROANS FROM BOTH AS THERE IS A BRIEF SCUFFLE. A CHAIR IS UPTURNED.

VALERIA: I will not have this brawling in my inn, do you hear? *THE DOCTOR GASPS AS MURRANUS GETS AN ARM AROUND HIS NECK.*

MURRANUS: Worry not, Valeria. This imp will trouble us no more – not once I have crushed the life from his body!

A STRANGULATED CRY FROM THE DOCTOR.

11. THE LUPANAR/THE STREET OF PLENTY

ACE AND AGLAE CLATTER DOWN A FLIGHT OF STONE STEPS.

ACE: Am I wearing this the right way round? It's uncomfortable.

AGLAE: You should not wear your old garments beneath the stola.

ACE: There's a lot of my history pinned to this jacket. I'm not losing it!

AGLAE: At least you will not draw attention now. If fortune favours you, then Popidius Celsinus will not spy you again. *THEY REACH THE BOTTOM OF THE STEPS.*

ACE: (*MUTTERS*) I'm not bothered about <u>that</u> spotty little perv.

AGLAE OPENS A DOOR, AND THEY EMERGE ONTO THE STREET OF PLENTY, WHERE SOMETHING IS HAPPENING. THE CROWD ARE SILENT, BUT FOR AWE-STRUCK GASPS AND MURMURS.

What's going on out here, then?

AGLAE: I do not...(*EXCITEDLY*) Oh! Look, Ace! Look over there!

ACE: (*IN A HORRIFIED WHISPER*) Vesuvius!

AGLAE: Oh, is it not magnificent? Smoke rises from the mountain. It can only have come from the furnace of Vulcan himself.

ACE: (*WITHOUT ENTHUSIASM*) Vulcan. Yeah, right.

A DISTANT RUMBLING STARTS UP. IT GROWS LOUDER.

AGLAE: He acknowledges Pompeii's offerings to him. Perhaps we are not so out of favour with the gods as we have feared.

ACE: (*WORRIED*) Aglae... Aglae, what is it? What... (*CRIES OUT*) no!

THE CROWD REACTS AS THE RUMBLING GROWS LOUDER STILL AND THE EARTH BEGINS TO SHAKE.

No, it can't be happening yet. It can't!

12. VALERIA HEDONE'S INN

THE TREMOR CONTINUES. POTS SMASH ON THE FLOOR. PEOPLE REACT FEARFULLY, AS ON THE STREET. THE DOCTOR BREAKS FREE.

MURRANUS: (*A GRUNT OF PAIN AND SURPRISE*)

DOCTOR: (*A GASP OF RELIEF*)

MURRANUS FALLS ONTO A TABLE AND BREAKS IT.

(*A LITTLE SHAKILY*) Oh dear, you appear to have slipped.

VALERIA: Enough, I say! Is it not trial enough that the earth betrays us, without that you continue this behaviour?

MURRANUS: (*ANGRILY*) Confound you, cheat! The gods themselves keep me from snapping your neck – but they will not save you twice.

VALERIA: You! Get out of here, now!

DOCTOR: Delighted to.

VALERIA: Go on, run! (*WARNINGLY*) No, Murranus, I care not about your reputation. If you wish to settle your differences, then you will find a place other than mine in which to do it, or you will settle them with me!

MURRANUS: I shall do just that, once this infernal quake has ended. If this Doctor has any wit about him, he will leave Pompeii before I find him – for he shall not have the chance after.

13. THE STREET OF PLENTY

THE TREMOR CONTINUES. A FRIGHTENED HORSE HAS TO BE CALMED DOWN. ACE AND AGLAE SHOUT TO EACH OTHER IN STRAINED VOICES.

AGLAE: Be not afraid, Ace. Hold on to me. This earthquake is not such a bad one, I think. It will soon end.

ACE: You mean this sort of thing happens a lot?

AGLAE: 'Tis the gods' way of showing us their displeasure.

THE QUAKE SUBSIDES. PEOPLE PICK THEMSELVES UP, WITH A
GENERAL OUTPOURING OF RELIEF.

You see? There has been no real damage. This was but a
warning. We shall have to honour our gods more diligently.

ACE: You're not making sense. One minute, Vulcan's pleased
with you – the next, you've got his mates cheesed off!

AGLAE: 'Tis true, I fear, that the earth shakes more often and
more violently these past weeks. None can remember such ill omens
since the upheaval of seventeen years since.

ACE: Then why doesn't somebody <u>do</u> something? Doesn't
anyone realise what's happening?

AGLAE: We observe the rituals, we make offerings, we pray to be
forgiven. What else <u>can</u> we do?

ACE IS DUMBFOUNDED FOR A MOMENT. THEN THE DOCTOR BREEZES
PAST.

DOCTOR: Ah, there you are, Ace. Yes, very fetching. Thank you
for your help, Aglae. Come along, Ace.

ACE: Doctor...?

DOCTOR: *(HE HAS PASSED HER NOW; HE CALLS BACK TO HER)*
There are at least two good reasons why we ought to be somewhere
else.

ACE: *(CALLS)* Well, hold up then! *(TO AGLAE)* Er... thanks
for everything, Aglae. Nice meeting you, and, er... see you around.
Maybe.

14. A POMPEIAN STREET
IN A QUIETER AREA, ACE CATCHES UP WITH THE DOCTOR.

ACE: It's the volcano, isn't it, professor? Causing the
earthquakes?

DOCTOR: I take it you're not quite so excited now.

ACE: It's horrible! This city... these people... Aglae! Valeria!
They're all going to die, aren't they?

DOCTOR: Many of them, yes.

ACE: Can't we do something?

DOCTOR: Against Nature? No. Against Time? Certainly not. This
happened a long time ago, Ace. We can't change it.

ACE: It's not fair!

DOCTOR: It never is.

THEY COME TO A HALT.

(GENTLY) Do you want to leave now, Ace?

SHE THINKS ABOUT IT FOR A FEW SECONDS.

ACE: Yeah. Yeah, I think I do.

15. A POMPEIAN BACK STREET
A FEW PEOPLE ARE MILLING ABOUT, TALKING IN CONCERNED
TONES. HEAVY STONES ARE BEING SHIFTED. THE DOCTOR AND ACE
APPROACH.

ACE: ...so, you <u>did</u> cheat, then? Just on that first roll.

DOCTOR: I observed our gladiator friend's technique and used it
against him.

309

ACE: Sounds like cheating to me.

DOCTOR: It's only cheating if you get caught.

ACE: Oh yeah, whereas <u>you</u> got clean away with... *(WORRIED)* Doctor... Doctor, what's going on?

DOCTOR: *(MURMURS, UPSET)* No. No, this can't be how it ends.

THEY RUN FORWARDS TOGETHER.

ACE: This can't be the right place! It isn't, is it, professor?

DOCTOR: I should have known. We should have turned back as soon as I realised...

ACE: It was the earthquake, wasn't it? It brought that building down, and the TARDIS... the TARDIS was right underneath it!

DOCTOR: ...but how could I? Time marching on. The future laid out before me. We've already stayed a lifetime.

ACE: Doctor, tell me we can get the TARDIS back. I mean, it's just a few lumps of concrete, right? Look – those slaves are clearing the wreckage already. We can dig it out, can't we? We can get away before... before...

DOCTOR: I'm sorry, Ace.

HE WALKS AWAY SLOWLY. ACE HESITATES FOR A SECOND, STUNNED, THEN RUNS AFTER HIM.

ACE: Oi, hold on a minute! What do you mean, you're 'sorry'? Doctor!

DOCTOR: It's Time, don't you see? Time, working against us.

ACE: *(ANGRILY)* No. No, I don't see. You've been acting weird since we landed here. What haven't you told me this time?

DOCTOR: I'm sorry for dragging you into this. I should have known. I <u>did</u> know. I found out a long time ago.

ACE: Found out what? Doctor!

DOCTOR: I've seen the future, Ace. I know what will happen. What <u>must</u> happen. *(COLLECTS HIMSELF)* In the year 1980, the TARDIS will be discovered. Dug out of the ash that will rain upon this city tomorrow.

ACE: You mean...?

DOCTOR: We can't escape it, Ace. No matter what we do, Time already knows. We've already lost this time.

ACE: But...

DOCTOR: We won't see the TARDIS again. Nobody will see it. Not for another two thousand years.

<u>END PART ONE</u>